W9-BRG-606

24N04

WARP
SPEED

BAEN BOOKS by TRAVIS S. TAYLOR

Warp Speed
The Quantum Connection (forthcoming)

WARP SPEED

TRAVIS S. TAYLOR

WARP SPEED

A Baen Books Original

Baen Publishing Enterprises
P.O. Box 1403
Riverdale, NY 10471
www.baen.com

ISBN: 0-7434-8862-8

Cover art by David Mattingly

First printing, December 2004

Library of Congress Cataloging-in-Publication Data

Taylor, Travis S.
   Warp speed / by Travis S. Taylor.
        p. cm.
   "A Baen Books original."
   ISBN 0-7434-8862-8 (hc)
  1. Physicists--Fiction. 2. Space flight--Fiction. 3. Women astronauts--Fiction. 4. Technology transfer--Fiction. I. Title.

   PS3620.A98W37 2004
   813□.6--dc22

                                                        2004020199

Distributed by Simon & Schuster
1230 Avenue of the Americas
New York, NY 10020

Production by Windhaven Press, Auburn, NH (www.windhaven.com)
Printed in the United States of America

10   9   8   7   6   5   4   3   2   1

To my wife Karen who told me, "You've read so many of these science fictions books, you ought to try writing one."

Good idea, here it is.

MOON BASE 1

JULY 20, 2018

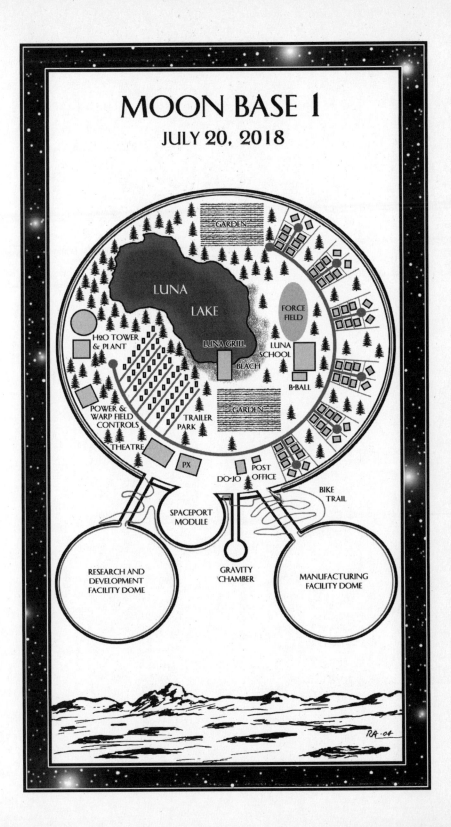

➤ CHAPTER 1

I was trying hard to breathe, but it wasn't coming easy. I tugged at my red team uniform top anxiously. Smacking my fists against my headgear was the only thing that seemed to focus me.

"All right! Bow to me!" the referee began. "Bow to each other. Touch gloves. Fight!"

Seeing that my opponent was dropping his back hand, I slipped to the right. I lunged like a sprinter out of a starting block and jumped. As I prepared to backfist the guy on the side of his headgear, I realized that I had let my elbows rise and I was not covering my ribs. I knew this because I presently spit my mouthpiece in my opponent's face while at the same time a searing pain ran through my ribs on the right side of my body. You see, I fight right side forward since my right leg is more flexible than my left. Not that it mattered this time, since I failed to lead with a kick.

I heard the shouts and cheers for the other guy increase in volume and enthusiasm while I fell to the floor clutching my ribs. That's just the way it is on the International Sport Karate Association (ISKA) tournament circuit. The referee was talking to my opponent.

"Turn and bow!" Then in my ear, "Do you want your

1

sensei or will you make it?" He handed me a slightly dirty mouthpiece.

"Nah, I'll make it okay." I blew dirt off the mouthpiece and noticed my instructor shouting at me as I made it to my feet.

"What's that rainbow jump crap! I never taught you that. Let's go Anson, one, two, three. White belt stuff! Stay tight!" He yelled and ticked off his fingers one, two, three at me.

I bounced back to the line with each breath burning like fire in my side. Two ribs were broken at the least. I was sure of it. But, if I had any intentions of staying in this fight, I knew that I had better not show a soft spot.

Mike and I have been friends for years and I'm sure he didn't mean to break my ribs. But he was here to win this tournament just like I was and we were tied in points for ISKA champion. This fight was going to be a tough one. The last fight of the season should be a tough one, I guess, especially if it's for the championship.

"Are you ready?" The ref asked.

I nodded and lined up left side forward this time, my right side being soft.

"Judges call, I got two points, blue uniform." With a look around the ring at the other two judges, it was obvious that I was behind two points.

"Okay touch gloves. Fight!"

Just like in class with the instructor yelling, I could hear in my mind, *skip side kick, backfist, reverse punch!* One. Two. Three! I got him!

"Break," yelled the center ref. "Judges call!" He held up two fingers in my direction and scanned the other two judges. "That is two red! Two blue! Touch gloves! Ready, fight!"

Skip side kick, backfist, reverse punch!

This time it didn't work as well. Mike sidestepped and down-blocked the skip kick. But that is why it goes one, two, three or *skip side kick, backfist, reverse punch!* The skip kick occupied his lead hand with a down-block leaving his head open for the backfist and his chest open for the reverse punch. Of course, I caught one to the body in there somewhere. But, I was first and that's what counts in sport karate.

"Break!"

"Judges call? Okay we have three red, two blue. Ready?"

"Time ref!" I called and motioned to my footgear as though it were loose.

"Time red."

I knelt and acted like I was fixing an equipment problem. My ribs ached and the second of extra breathing time helped.

"Let's go red!"

I bounced up like a rubber ball and nodded to the ref. I was thinking I couldn't take another second of this. A punch would mean one point. Not enough and I knew I wasn't going to make it much longer. I was starting to feel queasy but I lined up *right* side forward! Just a chance I would have to take.

"Ready? Fight!"

This time I was too slow. Mike rushed me with a barrage of hand movements. He is a Kenpo student after all, mostly hands. I slipped to the right and pulled my knee up and proceeded with a side kick. To my surprise, Mike did the same thing. Fortunately, or not so fortunately—I'm not sure—I'm more flexible. My foot got higher than his and as a result his foot slid down the inside of my leg and caught my cup with full force. I did the only thing I could do to defend against such an attack. I fell to the floor holding my crotch!

"Break! Blue, turn and bow!"

"Where did he get you?" The ref tapped my headgear to get my attention. I heaved twice and rolled over to my hands and knees. I heaved again. Lucky for me I hadn't eaten yet so nothing came up. I realized then, the heaving seemed to hurt my right side. My ribs. Funny how getting kicked in the Jimmy will make one forget how bad other things hurt.

I'm not sure how, but I made it to my feet again. I wiped the sweat from my forehead, which was pouring profusely out from under my headgear and down my face as I lined up, left side forward this time. I smiled at Mike and I put my mouthpiece back in. I had him right where he wanted me.

"Sorry man! You okay?" He seemed legitimately concerned.

The center ref called attention and then, "That is a warning blue for low kicks. Ready?"

We both nodded and touched gloves.

"We still have three red, two blue. Fight!" The ref dropped his hand and stepped back out of our way.

I was right, I did have Mike right where he wanted me. Like a freight train, all two hundred and thirty pounds of him came barreling right for me. I knew just what to do; I ran for my life. Without thinking, I turned my back and began to run, somehow I jumped while facing him and threw a right leg, spinning back kick. This was a survival technique only. I don't recommend it as a standard technique. My right foot caught him off guard right in the gut. Luck counts in horseshoes and hand grenades, in nuclear war, and sometimes at the ISKA championships.

"Break! Judges call? I got two red! That is five red!" I heard my instructor yelling something, but he seemed too far away and seemed to be getting further and further away. Then there was no longer any light at the end of the tunnel.

The next thing I knew I was back home in my study looking at my whiteboard. There were tensor equations scribbled all over it. In the middle was an equation written explaining that spacetime curvature is proportional to energy per volume, which is proportional to mass times the speed of light squared divided by volume, which is proportional to electricity and magnetism divided by volume.

I had been writing this equation in various ways since undergraduate school and never could figure out how to change the proportionality symbols to equal signs. Nobody could. Einstein died trying, as have many others. The equation is a very simple explanation of the Holy Grail of physics. Einstein's General Relativity (GR) states that space and time or spacetime is curved due to energy. Energy and mass are interchangeable just by multiplying by the speed of light squared, c^2. So, the curvature of spacetime is proportional to the speed of light in a way. Also, electricity and magnetism are forms of energy, somehow. Electromagnetic forces are most likely the cause of matter having form and in some way the cause of gravity where gravity is the curvature (sort of). The equation means that the spacetime is curved due to the amount of energy in a given volume or that a given curved spacetime causes a certain energy per volume. Each of these phenomena causes the other and this energy per volume can exist in many forms.

There was something else on the whiteboard that really caught my attention. On the bottom right hand corner of the board was the equation explaining that spacetime curvature is defined as the square root of stuff times electricity and magnetism divided by volume.

Of course, both of these equations were written in the Einstein tensor notation so they really didn't look like this. The actual equations take nothing short of years in graduate school sweating over tensor mathematics and things called *Ricci* tensors, *stress-energy* tensors, spacetime *metrics*, and the *Cosmological Constant* just to be able to read. Understanding them takes even longer. But, this is the general idea of what my lucidly dreamt whiteboard stated. Most importantly was that the proportionality symbol was changed not only to an equal sign but a "defined as sign," meaning that the equation was a fundamental equation describing the universe. After this equation was one that stated that *stuff* is "defined as" being equal to . . .

"Anson can you hear me?" Both of my instructors were yelling in my face and shaking me and I smelled something God-awful as I startled to consciousness.

"What happened!" I jumped up and felt a searing pain in my right side.

"Easy." Someone that I can only assume was the tournament paramedic started shining a light in my eyes. "Can you hear me?"

"Yeah, I'm fine, let me up."

"Hold still, Anson, and let him check you out," one of my instructors said. My instructors are a husband and wife team. She is usually more verbally sympathetic.

I didn't care what the medic did. My mind was still swimming with the tensor math on the whiteboard in my dream and I wanted to read it more closely. I smelled that awful smell again and startled completely to this time.

"Okay, okay. I'm awake!"

"Where are you hurt?" the medic asked.

"I have at least two broken ribs on my right side, maybe more. Did I win?"

The husband member of my instructor duo laughed. "You got him with the ugliest spinning back kick I have ever seen in my life. But you won!"

"Cool. Help me up." I rolled up very slowly. The crowd cheered. "I'm going to change. Could somebody pick up my award and then drive me to the nearest emergency room?"

I didn't expect that a doctor could do anything for me other than prescribe some good painkillers. Doctors, or as I prefer to call them, physicians, databases, quacks, etc., haven't cured anything, not one damn thing, since polio, which was way before I was born. Come to think of it, they didn't even come up with a cure for that; they simply committed something akin to genocide on the poliovirus.

I'm not completely sure why the quacks haven't gotten anywhere over the last sixty years, though it's probably because they don't have to take enough physics and math in school. A physician depends on the miracle of the human body's ability to heal and adapt. Any good physicist or engineer will tell you, if you have a broken support strut (a bone) you either weld that damn thing back together or you replace it. You sure don't sit around and wait for it to fix itself in six weeks or so. The way the quacks deal with a more serious illness is nothing short of magic or alchemy. Whatever it is, it sure isn't science! "My magic book says that if you look this way, smell that way, and have stuff coming out your nose then you should take two of these pills a day for ten days while standing on one foot and praying to Hypocrites. If you don't get better in two weeks then come see me again. That'll be a thousand dollars please." No way that's science. The guy who invented the pill may be a scientist, but not the guy administering it.

An example of the physician's incompetence is aging. Why we still grow old and die is beyond me. All of us are infected with a genetic disorder that causes our genes to break down and start producing "old" cells or cells that are mutated to create the symptoms of old age. This process is either caused by cosmic rays, ultraviolet rays, or other radiation exposure, or maybe some chemical mishap within our own bodies. Maybe it is a statistics problem. But whatever the cause, it is a disease we're all born with.

Physicians accept this as a natural thing because they simply won't do their homework and solve the problem. Fix the damn broken genes or replace them! The local university quit letting me teach the beginner level physics classes the pre-med and business students take. The student evaluations claimed I was "too hard" and assigned "too much homework." You get the idea. If the first American in space were still alive today (old age got him), you could ask him if he would've wanted to be on top of several tons of ignited explosives that guys who complained about "too much homework" designed. Maybe I'm cynical because I have had broken bones before.

Jim Daniels, one of my teammates and best friend and student and teacher, all in one, got my stuff together while I changed clothes. I still couldn't shake the weird "punch drunk" dream that I had. I mentioned it to Jim a time or two. I think. I was still a little shaky.

I had to have help getting my shirt over my head. I wished that I'd brought a button-up instead of the pullover. Next we went to the hospital, then back to the hotel though I still don't remember a major portion of the transition.

I do remember one part of the hospital visit that reaffirmed my position on physicians. When it was all over the wizard at the emergency room said, "There isn't really anything we can do for broken ribs. You just have to keep them immobile and let them heal on their own. It should take about six weeks. I'll write you a scrip for the pain." What a surprise. Fortunately, my insurance covers emergency room visits.

"Hell man, I knew all of that. Why'd I need you? Oh yeah I remember now. You bastards have it lobbied so that you think you are the only people in this country smart enough to administer pain medication. I wish you were in my physics class you . . ." I get irate when I'm in serious pain and dealing with quacks.

"Anson, calm down!" Jim grabbed me and put a nerve hold on me that hurt worse than my ribs. That was his way of telling me to either shut up or he would shut me up. Did I mention that Jim was my friend?

Unfortunately, my insurance only covered about twenty bucks of the prescription painkillers that cost two hundred. I have some vague memories of speaking very harshly to a short Pakistani pharmacist at an all-night drugstore. Jim has since assured me that the poor pharmacist didn't deserve any of the tongue-lashing. Like I said, I get irate with the whole medical industry in this country. It is an industry, not an art, or a merciful charity, or a scientific profession. Hell, it's not even magic for that matter.

By the time I got back to the hotel, the painkillers were working great. I was so loopy, I would never have made it into the room by myself. It seemed like the next thing I knew my alarm was buzzing at me. I hit it and it stopped. Then the phone rang. It was my wakeup call. I forced myself up and took a shower. Jim must have helped me pack, although I have no recollection of that. I got dressed very slowly, trying to withstand the pain. After a short while, I became more awake and less under the influence of the painkillers that I had taken the night before. My mind was clearing, but there was still a dull ache in my side and any sudden movement nearly killed me. Once, I sneezed, and I thought I was going to die it hurt so badly.

I got a cab to the airport but unfortunately I wasn't going home. I had a conference on "The Progress of the Breakthrough Physics Propulsion Program" to attend at NASA Goddard Space Flight Center the next day. I was looking forward to the conference before I broke my ribs. Thank goodness I had enough air miles built up to upgrade to first class. Coach seats would not have been fun.

➤ CHAPTER 2

Normally I don't drink on airplanes. It dehydrates me, and the air in commercial aircraft is dry enough as it is. But this was an exceptional circumstance. My ribs hurt and I was in first class where drinks are free. I figured a couple drinks couldn't hurt and might even help dull the ache in my side. I was on my second domestic beer before the coach section was boarding. I watched the sky marshal eye the coach passengers as they filtered past him at the entrance of the plane. I think he realized that I figured out what he was doing and he quit making eye contact with me.

After a few minutes of that, boredom set in so I began flipping through my slideshow on my laptop for my talk the next day. I just couldn't get in the mood so instead, I pulled up a game of chess I'd been playing the computer for about a week. I'd lost the game about fifty times, so I kept undoing the game back to when I was in the lead and starting over from there. Needless to say, I'm not that good at chess. I was on about my third beer when it looked like the plane was going to be closed up and I would have an empty seat next to me. Then, at the absolute last second, a woman in a U.S. Air Force uniform came through the hatch, made her way to the seat beside me, put her bag away, and sat down next to me. Her rank appeared to me to be light colonel. She looked very familiar also.

Once she was settled in her seat she finally gave me the cordial "hello" that you give the person sitting next to you in an airplane. I returned the "hello" and went back to my beer and chess game. The flight attendant wandered by and asked if I needed anything and told me that I had to turn off my computer for departure. I closed the laptop and replied that I could use another drink. Like I said, I never drink while flying.

By the time we leveled off at twenty-eight thousand feet out of Louisville, it was time to find the lavatory. The captain didn't turn off the seatbelt light a second too soon. I slowly made it up and by the "colonel" and found the restroom. If you ever try to use a bathroom on a commercial aircraft I suggest that you don't do it with two broken and three separated ribs. Each tiny pocket of turbulence I could feel travel up through my leg bones into my torso and finally my ribs. The four beers didn't help either.

I finally gathered my wits and felt my way back to my seat. This time I noticed the wings on the colonel's shoulder and realized where I had seen her before. She looked different with her red hair in a ponytail rather than floating around her on the International Space Station (ISS). She was an astronaut and I had seen her on television. In fact, according to the show I'd seen she had more space hours than any other female astronaut in history.

I said, "Excuse me," to her as I sat down. I got myself settled and then pressed the service button. When the flight attendant returned I asked for my fifth beer. Just as she turned to leave I sneezed. If you have ever had broken ribs you know this is not a good thing to do. I think I already mentioned that.

"Oh shit!" I clutched my side and swallowed back tears.

"Are you okay?" the colonel asked.

"Uh, yeah. I've got a couple of busted ribs and that sneeze suck . . . uh, hurt." The pain began to dissipate and hopefully, so did the grimace on my face.

"I see," she said. "This may seem a little strange but you look familiar to me."

I laughed and clutched my side. "That's funny. I was thinking the same thing. You are Colonel Ames, right? The female astronaut with the most hours in space?"

She smiled and presented her right hand. "Tabitha Ames. It's nice to meet you."

I reciprocated with, "Neil Anson Clemons. Friends call me Anson."

"I thought I recognized you," she said. "Didn't you give the talk on the modified Alcubierre warp drive at the Advanced Propulsion Workshop at NASA Marshall Space Flight Center last summer?"

"Well," I replied. "There were about four or five talks on warp theory last year, but I did give one of them. Are you going to the Breakthrough Physics thing?"

"Yes. In fact I'll probably be a lot more involved with that program in the future," she said and looked at me speculatively. I had no idea what she meant by that. I didn't really care since the attendant finally returned with my beer. Colonel Ames surprised me and asked for one too.

"Can you drink on duty?" I asked.

"Who says I'm on duty?" she retorted in a mind-your-own-business way.

"Oh," I said as if I'd been scolded. I'm not sure what it was but Colonel Ames has this air about her that she's the boss no matter who's in the room. The simple inflections in her voice are enough to make you feel good or bad, it just depends how she means it. Some people have this talent. Myself, I just trip and fumble over my heavy north Alabama accent and hope people at least understand what I'm trying to say. Then I usually throw in a "Well, Haiyul far! I just made all that sheyut up. It's probably all wrong" just to cover my ass. For some reason people believe if you talk with a Southern accent you're an idiot. Let 'em keep thinkin' that.

With both feet in my mouth, I asked, "Don't you astronauts usually fly trainers wherever you are going?"

"I have too many hours this week so it was either second seat or commercial," she replied.

"I see. You know I have put in an astronaut application each open time since 1999 and never once even got an interview. What's the trick?" I asked jokingly.

"Well, for a mission specialist I guess the trick is to come up with an experiment that has to be done in space that only you can do." She pursed her lips as if in thought, then replied, "You've only been trying for ten years?"

I nodded yes.

"Don't give up." She smiled at me and I felt like I could do anything. Some people just have the ability to inspire confidence. Colonel Ames definitely inspired something in me.

"If I may ask, why and for how long have you been so interested in space flight anyway?" She smiled and shrugged at me.

"Don't mind you askin' at all. I don't really know a date exactly but it is all I've ever wanted to do. My mom tells me it is because I'm destined to it," I replied.

"Destined to it?" Colonel Ames asked.

"Oh, yeah that's a neat story. You see I was born at the exact instant that the Lunar Excursion Module of Apollo 11 touched down on the moon. I'm certain thousands, heck maybe more, babies were born at that instant, but it must be destiny according to Mom. You know how mothers can be," I explained and kind of laughed.

She just nodded as if she understood. Then the plane rocked swiftly from turbulence and I grimaced in pain and held my side. She noticed.

"If you don't mind my asking, how'd you hurt yourself?" She seemed sincere and looked concerned. Then is when I realized her eyes were brown. I think that's common for redheads, or is it green?

"Well, I was in the International Sport Karate Association Championship yesterday. I left my right elbow up when it should've been down." I made a motion like a right backfist showing how it leaves your ribs open, and I placed my left hand on my right side. "I caught a side kick full-bore right here. I still won though!" I couldn't tell if she was impressed or not.

"So you do karate to stay fit?" she asked.

"Yeah, also a lot of mountain bike riding and some runnin', but my favorite is karate," I replied. "If I ever do get accepted into the astronaut program, I still have to meet the fitness requirements."

"Good, you have the right attitude," she said. "I do a lot of running and swimming and a little aerobic kickboxing. A lot of astronauts that I know are into karate and a lot are into cycling. Whatever works best for you."

The remainder of the flight consisted of small talk and my fascination with how things worked on the ISS. Of course, I had studied the spacecraft. I even worked on one of the modules as a subcontractor to one of the big aerospace firms in my late graduate school years. But there is no substitute for actually being there. I asked about the Space Shuttle ride and if she ever got sick. She said that she never did. I'm sure this was a lie. Doesn't everybody get sick the first time? I asked when she planned to go up again and her response was very political.

"I just want to do what is best for the program," she replied. I guess astronauts have to be good natured and careful about what they say around everyone. Things have definitely changed from the old "who's the best pilot you ever saw" Mercury astronaut days.

I did find out one thing about astronauts. They're not, or at least Colonel Ames is not, particularly good at chess. Mid-flight I beat her hands-down three games in a row and one of those with a fool's mate. Then again, all those hours I spent playing my laptop chess, she was practicing how to land the Space Shuttle and I sure wish I could trade!

The flight attendant was gently shaking my shoulder. I didn't even realize that I was asleep. God, we had already landed in Baltimore and were at the gate. When did Colonel Ames leave and when did I stop talking to her? Who turned off my laptop? Beer and painkillers, don't mix them.

The flight attendant helped me with my overhead bag and I headed for a very crowded rental car counter. Thank God for all the air miles I had that made me a gold medallion customer, which enabled me to go to the front of the line. Then I had to catch a shuttle from the rental car desk to the rental car parking lot.

The trip to the hotel was typical. I took Interstate Ninety-five down to Highway One. The "Parkway" was bumper-to-bumper and it took thirty minutes to get off One and onto the Greenbelt where my hotel was. By the time I got checked in to the hotel I was beat. I tried to rehearse my view graphs, but after about three of them I said, "screw it" and went to bed.

The alarm clock scared the living daylights out of me! I was so tired I don't even remember dreaming. I hate nights like that. Since I sleep on my back, I tried to raise myself sit-up style; nothing doing! My ribs still were causing me a lot of pain. I broke my hand once when I was a teenager. It seemed to take about a week before the really big pain subsided to a dull ache. I still get a dull ache in it just before it rains and it's been over twenty-three years. It must have something to do with the low-pressure systems usually accompanied by rain. I've asked physicians about that before. They always laugh and say it's in my head. There's enough crazy stuff in my head. Why would I put that in there too? Stupid alchemists.

Anyway, I had to tuck my left hand over my ribs and hold myself tightly. Then I rolled over counterclockwise and sort of fell out of bed. Getting shaved, showered, and dressed was just as tough, and I said many bad words that my great aunt Meg would've been proud of.

The "Breakthrough Physics Propulsion" Workshop or BPP Workshop was held in an auditorium-sized room. The start of the meeting was fairly standard for a technical conference. The director of the conference said a few words and corrected a few scheduling mistakes. One in particular caught my attention.

"Our guest speaker and new director of the BPP, Colonel Tabitha Ames has requested to be moved from first speaker this morning to last. So, make a note of that. Let's get started then. This change makes the first speaker this morning Dr. Anson Clemons from Metric Engineering Inc. Dr. Clemons is also a faculty member of the Physics Department at the University of Alabama in Huntsville, and he is a member of the National Space Science and Technology Center or NSSTC as it has come to be known. Dr. Clemons."

It was a damn good thing I wasn't late. I slowly moved up to the front of the auditorium and handed a CD with my slideshow to the audio/visual person. I fiddled around with the clip-on microphone for a minute or so, then got comfortable with the slideshow remote/laser pointer. Clearing my throat, I began.

"Hello, I'm Anson Clemons as you were just told, and I plan

to talk to you today about the status of spacetime metric engineering and how close we're to demonstrating faster-than-light space travel. Of course, everybody realizes that we can't go faster than the speed of light in the vacuum, but as Miguel Alcubierre showed us in 1994 it is possible to effectively create a region of spacetime that's 'warped' in such a way that the vacuum speed of light is increased tremendously. So, instead of the vacuum speed of light being one, assume it can be increased to one thousand. This means that a spacecraft could possibly travel at hundreds of times faster than the vacuum speed of light and never notice any Special Relativistic effects: no time dilation, spacetime contraction, nothing.

"Alcubierre himself stated up front in the abstract of that wonderful 1994 paper in *Classical and Quantum Gravity* that in order to accomplish this 'warp bubble' that a tremendous amount of exotic matter would be required. Of course, we all know that the exotic matter implies negative energy and the number of papers supporting, opposing, or correcting the Alcubierre warp theory absolutely snowballed over the next decade. I know that many of us here in this room are guilty of writing several of them." I gave a quick guilty smile and harrumphed in response to the chuckles coming from the audience, and then I added, "On a more personal note, it was one of these papers that inadvertently caused me to leave NASA and start my own company.

"This was the theoretical paper that showed up at the BPP Workshop in '07 on the possibility of using a very large static electric field on oppositely rotating conductor plates to cause a gravity-shielding effect. This paper was at first dismissed as the old Podkletnov spinning superconductor effect shown in the late nineties. It turned out to actually be a correction to the General Relativity. Where General Relativity must be gauged, using the Dirac type *zytterbewegung* oscillations as the reference frame thus yields an ungauged General Relativity! This was first reported by Maker in 2000. Then it was more precisely described in the '07 paper. Discovering this, I immediately gathered up as many grad students as I could find and started my own research effort to measure this effect.

"Thanks to funding from the BPP and almost three years of

hard work, we at Metric Engineering can say that the experiment not only works, but we have observed electrons moving at near the speed of light simply disappear after passing between the spinning plates. We have no idea where they went!"

I paused at this point to see what type of reaction I'd get. Claims have been so strange in the past BPP Workshops that most folks wait until all the data is displayed before they decide whether or not you're a nut. Well, I'm not a nut, and most of the people in the room knew that I was a careful scientist. I don't make cold fusion claims or yell that the sky is falling unless it really is. But nobody is perfect and I'd been wrong in the past. That is part of science; you can't be right all the time.

The talk continued for some time with a lot of graphs from data and some theoretical analysis in that crazy Einstein tensor notation I mentioned previously. I finished up to a resounding applause after stating that the problem still remains that there are sixteen equations, with four unknowns each, making it damn near impossible to get an analytical solution, which describes the experimental data. I also mentioned that if anybody ever does solve the Einstein equations for the warp field and if they win a Nobel Prize that he or she should share it with Miguel Alcubierre.

Then the questions started. Imagine a room where every person in that room believes that he or she is the smartest person in the world. Now imagine that you have somehow insulted every one of those people's intelligence. Forget that. Imagine that you have been dowsed in blood and fish guts, and then thrown into a shark tank during a feeding frenzy. That best describes what happened next.

There were questions like, "How do you know the electrons disappeared? Where did they go? Are you sure you didn't just make a sloppy measurement? They probably just got attracted by the conductor plates, moron!" Okay, that last one was not a question. These are the kinder comments. The only real question was, "Have you figured out a way to decrease the amount of energy required to sustain a warp bubble?"

That last question hit home. Even if we solve the Einstein equations and show that warp drive is possible, the latest and greatest calculations still suggest that over 1×10^{20} joules of energy are required constantly to maintain the warped spacetime bubble! That's more energy than the entire human race generates in one year. One problem at a time please!

At some point the frenzy subsided and the director introduced the next speaker while I gathered my stuff and headed back to my seat. About halfway back I noticed that the next speaker was tapping on my shoulder. I turned and he smiled at me, "I think I will need the microphone." He laughed.

"Hunh?" I was confused.

"The microphone," he said and pointed at my tie where the wireless clip-on microphone still remained.

"Oh sorry. I was hoping to keep it for myself." I laughed with the rest of the room, untangled the microphone from myself, and handed it over.

Once I got back to my seat I noticed that Colonel Ames had slipped into the back of the room. I gave her a nod and she smiled at me—sort of. Maybe it was just wishful thinking. Not that I was attracted to her that much, however she is a pretty woman. She is about five or so years younger than me and only about two inches shorter. Me, I'm five feet ten inches, in shoes. Her red hair was in some sort of military bun or something. What would you call it? I'm not a hairdresser. In fact, I've not even combed my hair with anything other than my fingers since 1987. At any rate, it wasn't a major attraction that I had for the colonel at that time; it was more a feeling of growing professional admiration and respect. After all, she is an astronaut. And if you believe that one, let me tell you about some swampland my grandmother is trying to sell.

After several more speakers and one coffee break, it was her turn to speak. Just before she began to speak something tickled my nose and I sneezed horribly. Twice! I also groaned once in agony and hugged myself tightly as I doubled over. Tabitha looked up realizing who had made all the noise. For a second she gave me a sort of motherly empathetic frown. One of those, *Oh sweetheart you have skinned your knee, haven't you?* kind of looks that your mom used to give you. *Let Momma kiss it and make it all better.* Had I not been in such pain I would've liked it. Oh, what the hell, I liked it anyway. Then she had to go and ruin it all with her talk.

"As many of you may already know, I have recently been appointed the directorship of the Breakthrough Physics Program. Since 1999 about sixty million dollars of the NASA budget has been spent on theoretical analyses and experiments with very—" then she hesitated for dramatic effect, I guess, "—questionable results. I by no means am making statements regarding the quality or heroism required for involvement with this program. On the other hand, for the past ten or more years very little has been accomplished." This time she paused due to the rumbling sound coursing throughout the room.

"The BPP hasn't been canceled but it is being reorganized and given a new focus. Instead of focusing on projects that are extremely high risk, the BPP will now be directed toward break-through physics that can be more readily applied to the space program in the near term. There is a lot of research needed on new launch vehicle propulsion, stronger materials for solar sails, safer fission reactors for nuclear electric propulsion concepts. Perhaps we should face it that the physics is just not quite ready for warp drive. I'm excited by the efforts made thus far in the warp field theory arena, but it isn't going to be the focus of this program any longer."

Her talk continued with budget charts, and a list of all the projects funded, and the errors in those projects. I can hardly continue describing her talk. How is a measly sixty million dollars over eleven years really going to affect the NASA budget? There were rumbles of "I will call my congressman you just wait" and "This isn't over yet!" I threw in a couple of much nastier comments myself: one particularly that I had heard my grandma use on a state trooper when I was twelve, but y'all don't need to hear that. Then it hit me.

"Hey! Quiet the hell down for a minute. What about the contracts already in place and the funding already promised to various organizations throughout the country?"

"I was expecting someone to ask that." Tabitha nodded. "This directive came from way above me and NASA HQ. Rumor is it comes from the Joint Chiefs, though I'm not sure why. So don't kill the messenger. The good news is that all contracts in place now will be continued throughout this fiscal year. As of FY 12 the funding will be reduced to half on currently funded projects and then phased out completely in FY 13."

"That's not very long," I muttered to myself. I was close. I could taste it. I only had ten months of full funding left and then a year at half that. Without other funding sources I would lose the company for certain. I said "Shit!" under my breath and hung my head. The only thing that I could think of at the time was, "Screw y'all. I'm going the hell home." I gathered up my toys and left.

It felt good to get home even if I did have bad news. Of course, Friday was the only one home and she didn't care. I opened the door and damn near stepped on her. She is a lazy and stubborn cat. I tried dogs when I was younger, but I could never figure out how to keep them from jumping on me with muddy paws just when I was wearing a white shirt. No matter how much pepper spray I would put on the flowers, they still dug them up and slept in the flowerbeds. Besides, I like cats: old man Farnham, Maureen Johnson, and Lazarus Long liked cats, 'nuff said!

I tapped the machine as I came in. *Beeeep! You have seven new messages. Message one.* "Hi Anson, this is Jim. I got something you ought to see as soon as you get back. You said something about the Casimir effect in your drunken stupor between the hospital and the hotel Sunday night. When I got back in Monday I went straight to the lab. I think I've got an answer to the energy problem! Call me when you get in. Oh yeah, hope you're feeling all right. Bye." *End of message one.*

Message two. "Neil Anson Clemons this is your mother! Where were you Saturday? I called and called and you never answered! You missed your brother. He came to town for a surprise visit. Oh well, call us when you get in. We love you, bye." *End of message two.*

Message three. "Yes Mr. Clemons, this is Angela Landry with the credit union. We noticed a lot of traffic on your debit card in St. Louis and then in Maryland over the past week and we just wanted to make sure it was authorized. Please contact us at your earliest convenience." *End of message three.*

Message four. "Hi, Dr. Clemons. This is Colonel Ames from the BPP Workshop. You left before we got to talk further. Could you please contact me? My contact info is on the BPP website and in the agenda for the meeting. It was nice meeting you. Okay, bye." *End of message four.*

Message five. "Hey Anson. Do you believe that crap about cutting the BPP? You bugged out of Goddard pretty quick man. I wanted to know what you thought. Didn't you tell me that you thought it would be good to get an astronaut as the BPP director? Boy, were you wrong. Oh well, call me. By the way, this is Matt Lake." *End of message five.*

Message six. "Son, this is your mother again. Where are you? Do you just not return your calls anymore? It wouldn't hurt you to come see us every now and then you know! Oh well bye for now. Call us when you get home." *End of message six.*

Message seven. "Anson, have you gotten home yet? This is Rebecca. Jim is about to die to show you what he thinks we've done. He told me about your ribs. Hope you're okay. Call us when you get in. B'bye." *End of message seven.*

Mom always did that when I was gone. I told her I would be out of town, but she still acts like I never told her about it. She does that every time. For a while I thought she might have Alzheimer's, but then I realized she just likes stirring things up.

Matt Lake is a colleague of mine from New Mexico State University. We had collaborated on some papers before and were presently working on one. I was supposed to meet Matt for dinner after the meeting at Goddard. "I should get in touch with him and explain why I left," I thought out loud. Friday looked up as if I were talking to her. I just smiled back at her and reassured her that she was the prettiest cat in the whole universe. You have to do that. Cats are pretentious and need constant ego stroking.

I didn't know which message to respond to first. So, I replayed the fourth one six times more. Just to be sure.

➤ CHAPTER 3

I picked up the phone. Then I put it back down. "Where is that damn agenda?" I said to myself. "Didn't she give me her business card on the plane?" After some scrambling through my bags and nearly knocking my copy of "MTW" (or *Gravitation* as it is so titled) off the coffee table and onto Friday, I found it. Friday looked at me like I was an idiot and then rolled over onto her other side. Once again, I reassured her that she was queen of all felines.

I started to pick up the phone again. It rang. I nearly jumped out of my skin. My ribs were getting better, but they still didn't like sudden moves. It rang again. Composing myself, I answered the phone.

"Uh, hello?"

"Anson, it's Jim."

"Yeah what's up? I just got yours and Rebecca's messages by the way."

"After you said something Sunday about having to suck the energy right out of spacetime itself for the warp field, I got to thinking. I went straight to the lab and haven't gone home since. I designed a couple of nanodevices that Rebecca is depositing in the vacuum chamber right now. It should be done and ready to test by the time you get here."

I wasn't sure what the hell Jim was talking about. I barely remember the hospital, much less a conversation about vacuum energy physics.

"Jim, slow down. What does this device do? And what conversation are you talking about?"

Jim gulped, or at least it sounded like he did over the phone.

"Anson, are you okay? It does just what you said it should do. Don't you remember talking about miniature pistons and such in the cab on the way from the hospital to the hotel?"

"No I do not!"

"Oh, well, you did and I paid close attention. Thank goodness. Anyway, it's a microscopic well to trap vacuum energy as an electric charge generated by a nanosized two-cycle piston system." I still wasn't sure what all this was about.

"Are you telling me that you have a design that will actually let you acquire energy from the vacuum using the Casimir effect?"

"Yes, uh, well, I think so. I calculate that it will capture about a microjoule per second."

I ran some numbers in my head real quick. "Let's see, a microwatt—and we need ten to the twentieth watts. That's ten to the twenty-sixth of these nano things. How small can you make them, Jim?"

"The prototype is about ten nanometers on a side."

"That's a cube one hundred meters per side!" I cried, excitedly. I calmed slightly and continued, "That's way too big! You couldn't get it in the Shuttle. It would have to be constructed in space. If it really works, we will have to either make them about twenty times smaller or figure out how to make them capture more energy. I will be there in about forty-five minutes. I want to take a shower first. I've been flying all day." I hung up the phone and turned toward the bedroom.

"Oh yeah, bye," I yelled over my shoulder at the already hung up receiver.

The twenty-minute drive to the lab gave me some time to think. The Casimir effect: an interesting phenomenon named after the guy who thought of it. The idea is that there is this vacuum energy all around us all the time at every possible wavelength.

It behaves like normal electromagnetic radiation except that we don't notice it. It is kind of like a fish in water. The fish probably never notices the water around him, but he sees the things in it. We never notice the spacetime around us, but we see planets and stars and people and fish all around us. We pay no attention to the spacetime just like the fish pays no attention to the water.

Anyway, this spacetime around us consists of all this electromagnetic energy at all different wavelengths. This bright guy Casimir suggested that if somehow we could get two conducting plates and put them very close together, say, less than some of these wavelengths, then the area between the two plates would shield out any energy that had wavelengths longer than the distance between the two plates. But, outside the plates, all of the energy at all of the bands would remain. In other words, there would be more energy outside the two plates than between them. Because of this, Casimir suggested that the two plates would be pushed together. The force pushing them would come straight out of the vacuum of spacetime itself! Cool, huh?

As micromachining became more developed over the past fifteen years or so, people started noticing that their machine parts (if they were made small enough) would stick together for some reason. Most of these guys attributed this "stiction" to static electricity; the same way a white sock sticks to your dress pants in a place that you don't notice until you see people pointing at you as you are walking down the street with a sock stuck to your butt or hanging out your pants leg. Jim and I had long thought that the "stiction" might be due to the Casimir effect instead of static electricity. So had a few of the other BPP scientists.

As I pulled into the parking lot of our lab at Research Park, I realized that I never returned Tabitha's call. "Oh well, wasn't sure what she wanted anyway," I muttered. When I got to the lab Rebecca was pacing outside the door to the lab. "Did you finish?" I asked.

"It's done. Did Jim tell you this is the fourth one I've sputtered today? No, he didn't, did he? Did he tell you neither one of us has been home in thirty-six hours? No, he didn't, did he?!"

"Uh, no, I, I don't know. Maybe he mentioned it. Look, if you are tired, just go home."

"Are you kidding? And miss seeing if this thing works or not? You gotta be nuts. What, are you trying to get rid of me? Do *you want* me to go home?"

I will never understand women. I guess Rebecca just needed to complain about something. She is like that. She shook her long black hair and rolled it back up under her paper hair hat. "*Well?*"

I replied, "Skip it. Let's just go have a look, shall we."

She led me through the rat maze to the clean room and vacuum chamber area. Jim came through the airlock with a blue paper outfit on. I never could get used to those damn things, but I began putting on a similar garment. As I was putting on my paper slippers I asked, "Jim, is it ready?"

"You're not going to believe what's in there. I think we've done it," he replied.

"If you two have, then we're going to stop and make sure you both graduate by May. That only gives us about two to three months to finish writing your dissertations and defend them and fill out all the paperwork."

"Neither Jim or I have enough credits yet. We're both two classes short. How could we?" Rebecca objected.

"Well let's worry about one thing at a time. Okay, Jim, let's have a look."

I could spend a while talking about what I saw here, but it would be technical and not real exciting to you. Or maybe it would if you are the techie geeky sort like me. Let's just say that the damn thing worked. There was a little box ten nanometers long on a side (one nanometer is one billionth of a meter by the way) and inside it were two moving pistons. One of them was attached to the other in such a way that the Casimir effect pushed on one and pulled on the other, then vice versa. This way the plates were never allowed to be pushed all the way together. Attached to the outer side of the box was probably the tiniest generator the human race had ever built. From the generator was a wire so small you could only see it with an electron microscope that was attached to a larger wire, which led to a microvolt meter. The resistance in the larger wire loaded the generator, allowing us to measure the power dissipated by it. We measured more than twenty times just to be sure. Each time we got one microwatt of power constantly coming from the generator. Energy for free right out of the spacetime! Now, mind you, this is in no way violating the law of conservation of energy. The nanodevices simply transfer from the vacuum energy via the Casimir effect to the nanogenerators. What an amazing concept. This could put OPEC right out of business. About time!

Of course, this was only one microwatt. The first step was to scale the thing up. Also, we had spent about two and half million dollars just to get this one little box. Of course, now that we knew how to build one, we could do it for say fifty bucks or so. A full up version would require 10^{26} of them. Yikes! Way too expensive. But Jim reassured me that it would cost no more to sputter a hundred thousand of these things than it would to sputter one. After some arguing and a lot of cursing, I agreed with him. Rebecca backed him up. So, with some tweaking, we had the energy for a warp drive.

All I need to do now is figure out how to actually do the warp! I thought. So close! So close.

➣ CHAPTER 4

We discussed the next step for at least two more hours. At one point I reached across the table to grab a pencil and something in my side moved too much, making a popping noise. I grimaced and winced and cursed as I decided the pencil could be damned and stay right where it was.

Rebecca looked at me. "Are you all right? Maybe you ought to go home."

"Don't worry about me," I said through clenched teeth.

"I think she's right, Anson." Jim looked concerned.

"Okay, who am I to argue with the likes of you two? Let's all go home. Sleep in tomorrow and we'll get together Friday night. I'll call tomorrow and have the two of you retroactively registered in two special topics classes. We will talk Friday about our next step. How's that?"

Rebecca looked over at Jim and frowned. "Could we just wait and talk about it at the grad student cookout Saturday, instead? I already have plans."

"Oh crap! I forgot about that. Can you two come over Saturday morning and help out with that?"

"You already asked us once," Jim and Rebecca simultaneously chimed in.

"Oh yeah, I forgot." I paused. "What did you say?"

They laughed. "Your mother was right about you. You *would* forget your head if it wasn't attached to you."

"Yeah," I said. "So, Saturday then?"

"Suits me." Jim shrugged.

"Hey, I'm just along for the ride. Whatever you say." Rebecca smiled cute as a button. That is the only way to describe her. Not that she is a supermodel, just cute—the kind of cute that makes the human race go round.

"Great. You two go home and get some sleep."

Ring. I rolled over and looked at the phone. *Ring.* "The machine can get it. I ain't movin'," I said. *Ring.* "*Hello, this is Anson. I can't come to the phone right now, but if you will leave a name a number and a message I will get back to you. Beeeep!*"

"Hello, Dr. Clemons this is Colonel Ames . . ."

You have never seen a man with busted ribs move so fast. I grabbed my side with my left hand, rolled hard to the right, sat up on the side of the bed, and grabbed the phone.

"Hello, uh, hang on a minute, let me turn this thing off." I slapped the machine hard. Composing myself, "Hello Tabitha, how are you?"

"Fine thanks."

"What can I do you for?" I said thinking I was being cool. I'm sure I wasn't and I'm sure she didn't think I was either.

"Uh, well. I wanted to talk to you about the meeting at Goddard. You left early. I hope you're okay?"

"What me, never better," I lied. Rolling over so fast really hurt.

"Well, good. I was hoping to come see you and talk for a while about what you can do with the funds we have left for your project. I'd also like to catch up on what you've been doing."

"Okay, sounds cool. When are you coming down?"

"What do you mean?"

"When will you be in Huntsville?"

"I'm sorry. I *am* in Huntsville. We talked about this on the plane, don't you remember?"

"Uh, no."

"Oh."

"How long are you here?"

"My plane leaves Tuesday next week. I have some things to do with Space Camp on Monday so I'm staying over the weekend. Could we meet sometime between now and Tuesday?"

"I'm open all day Friday."

"Are you okay?"

"I think so. Why?" She sounded confused.

"Today *is* Friday."

I looked at my watch. Sure enough it was Friday. I'd been asleep for nearly two days; no wonder I was so thirsty. I shook my head to clear it. "Maybe these painkillers are wearing me down."

"We could do this some other time. You can call me when you feel better."

"Hold on!" I pleaded. "Listen, do you like hamburgers and hot dogs?"

"I guess. Why?"

"Well, I'm hosting the spring semester graduate student cookout at my house Saturday evening. You're here anyway. Why don't you come over and join us? I'm sure the students would love to meet a big famous astronaut like you. We could talk then. What do you say?" It took a little more conniving and goading but I finally convinced her to come to the cookout—for the students, of course. I had a lot to do to get ready. I was now a whole day behind schedule.

First, I had to take care of Jim and Rebecca's classes. I called up Jan. She really runs the graduate school, not the dean. All he does is sign stuff when she tells him to. After a few minutes we decided that if both of them took *Physics 804: Topics in General Relativity* and *Physics 798: Special Topics in Vacuum Energy Physics* that they would be able to graduate. If they defended their dissertations on time, that is. By the way, there is no such class as *Physics 804* or *798*. Oops! Guess I will just have to teach it myself then and make up a curriculum for them. The *Graduate Handbook* allows for such things. The students then just have to write papers or take exams or something. I can do that no problem.

Jan and I also figured out all the final details for the cookout.

When I told her who would be the special guest there, she said that we had better buy more hamburgers and hot dogs. I guessed that meant more beer, too!

The cookout was going quite well I thought. My "Kiss the Physicist" apron and chef's hat went over pretty well. Thanks, Mom. That reminded me. Damn! Before I let everyone dig in, I had them join us in Alan Shepard's Prayer.

"Everyone, attention please." I banged on the grill top with the spatula until it reached a resonance just flat of a B.

Nothing happened until Jan yelled, "Shut up!" Everyone shut up.

I picked up my beer and held it high.

"Everyone please face the rocket, put your right hand over your heart, and raise your beverage with your left!" You can see the big Saturn V from my backyard. Hell, in just about any backyard in Huntsville you can see the big Saturn V.

I continued, "Please join in THE prayer. Dear Lord . . ." I began. The whole crew joined in, "PLEASE DON'T LET ME SCREW UP!" Of course some of the rather less refined students and faculty didn't say "screw," if you know what I mean. The way I have heard the story neither did Shepard.

"Amen, brother!"

"Amen!"

"Let's eat!" I yelled.

I noticed Tabitha laughed at the spectacle. She showed up about six-thirty in the evening, just as the grill was getting hot. Rebecca grabbed her and kept her away from me most of the night. She was a big hit. Tabitha didn't do too bad, either.

Jim came over to me and asked, "She's pretty cool, huh?"

"Who? Colonel Ames?" I asked. "I guess so."

Jim furrowed his brow at me.

"Not her! Oh . . ." He paused and looked back and forth between Tabitha and myself. Then did it again. "Ha! You like her!"

"Hey, shut up. How many of those have you had anyway?"

"Beers or burgers? Anson likes the astronaut!"

"Either. What, are we twelve now?"

"I know you are but what am I?" He laughed.

Then it dawned on me. "If you didn't mean Tabitha, who the heck were you talking about?"

"Never mind! And he's supposed to be the smart one," he muttered sarcastically, pointed his thumb at me, and walked away.

"Hey, you're not driving home are you?" I halfheartedly scolded to his back.

Most of the students had left by sometime around eleven, and I was beginning to feel my age and my ribs. So, I decided it would be best to sit in a lounger on the patio, watch the stars, nurse my ribs, and finish off another beer or three. Unfortunately, my bottle was getting low on beer and I was getting low on get-up-and-go. So, I sat there watching for satellites and falling stars. I laughed at the thought of that, a falling star. The cosmology of that being very silly, I corrected myself and started looking for meteors. I heard a whirring from the back part of the yard. My autodome had turned on and the telescope door began to open.

"Jim must be showing off the observatory," I said to no one in particular as I toasted the autodome with the backwash left in my bottle. It was a great night for it. Astronomy, not backwash.

Jupiter and Saturn were almost dead overhead. It was so clear. I would've sworn I could see one of Jupiter's moons with unaided eyes. I knew that wasn't what Jim would be looking for since nobody went out to aperture down the telescope. You see, Jim and I built a 3.5 meter Newtonian in a truss style Dobsonian Alt-Az mount. It is completely automated from my PC inside the house and is connected via an ultrawideband wireless local area network. The datalink is about four hundred gigabytes per second. The telescope has two optical paths. One runs to a charge coupled device (CCD) camera and the other to a microminiature spectrophotometer. I wanted one of these all my life but could never afford a glass mirror that large. When the small companies came out with composite very large optics in about '06 I knew it was time to start. The dome cost about two thousand bucks and the wireless LAN and computer system and other electronics were about that each. The primary mirror ran me back about six grand. After about four years of tinkering and adjusting and buying new gadgets one piece at a time, I had about fifteen thousand total in it. Hey, I know guys with golf clubs that cost as much. Heck, my dad has a bass boat that cost him more than twenty-five thousand bucks and it's a mid-range one! Then he built a new garage just for his boat; no telling how much that cost. But, my hobby can actually add real knowledge to mankind.

In fact, Jim and I found a planet around one of our local stellar neighbors about a year ago. We figured out a very subtle difference in the spatial coherence of the light from the star versus that of a large planet. It basically gave us a Michelson's stellar interferometer with much better resolution. There were some other tricks required, but once Jim and I calculated the right matched filter we could pull a Uranus-sized planet out of the background of its star. Provided that the planet was more than four astronomical units from its sun. So, we were lucky. Our hobby turned out to be of some importance—maybe? If we ever build a warp drive we should go where there are planets. Doesn't that make sense? At least it's fun in the meantime.

Anyway, I could tell that Jim was driving; the telescope went from one Messier object to another. Jim was putting on a grand tour for someone. He usually does that to show off even though the computer really does it. All a human has to do is hit the On button and run the Messier program.

I watched the sky and listened to the crickets and the whirring motors of the observatory. The three red flashing lights on the Saturn V rocket caught my eye off to the southeast. Come May the trees would fill out and the rocket would be obstructed from view.

I was in a peaceful mood—not really contemplative just peaceful. The vision of the whiteboard with the warp equations came to mind.

Somehow, I thought. We could build the power supply now, even if it does have to be a cube half the size of Alabama. Images of the Borg cubes from *Star Trek: The Next Generation* came to mind. I found that humorous for some reason. Then a very bright object popped into view traveling from the south to the northwest. I watched for a second or so making up my mind what it was. Just as I was about to decide I was interrupted.

"There is ISS right on time." Tabitha stretched her neck left then right, and sat down in the lounger beside me. "Here, I thought you might need this." She handed me a fresh beer.

What a woman! I hope I didn't say that out loud. Instead I hope what I said is, "You scared the living shit out of me!"

"Sorry. You're missing quite a show in there." She pointed in to the den.

"Yeah. Well, they are missing the real show out here. Besides, been there..."

"You have a cool place here, Anson." She took a draw from her own bottle. Not sure what it was. Some kind of lemonade thing, I think.

"Thanks, ma'am! We aim to please. You aim too, please!"

"I beg your pardon?"

"Sorry. Just a little men's room humor. Don't rightly know where I picked that up, but I've been saying that since I was twelve."

She smiled, "Oh, I get it. *Men!*" It was too dark to see it, but I know she shook her head and made that face all women make when discussing men.

"I can't believe you've actually been there." I half-heartedly pointed at the now fading International Space Station. "Hey, did you guys ever really call it Alpha?"

"I think the first Russians did," she explained. "But it just wouldn't stick. Not sure if it was political or just not as catchy as 'ISS.'" She laughed. Then with a slightly more commanding tone she began, "You know I never got to talk to you since Goddard."

"How about that," I said. "You cut the legs out from under a lot of people there. When BPP started, it was seriously peanuts—not even a million bucks a year. Not really even worth the effort, but this is going to set the human race back to stone tools." I like being dramatic. If I thought it would've helped, I would've pissed on a spark plug.

"Anson, I said it then and I'm saying it now. And I won't say it again! This decision came from far above me. The White House I think. I've actually been trying to determine where the directives came from and have gotten nowhere."

"Sounds like a conspiracy to me. Elvis and JFK probably did it from Roswell or the Bermuda Triangle!" I said sarcastically and then proudly tugged on my bottle.

"Look I'm bearing an olive branch here. If you are going to be a smartass, just forget it." I think she was genuinely hurt, or at least pissed.

"Okay. Sorry. I believe you. So what did you want to tell me?" I tried to smooth it out but I was firing a little early on cylinder number two and cylinder seven was about to seize up. I'm not sure I even had spark plugs in the rest of them. Maybe somebody'd pissed on them.

"That's just it. There really is nothing I can do other than apologize. Maybe if you had some real results we could go to the Space Science Subcommittee—"

"But we do have results! Didn't Rebecca *tell* you!"

"Tell me what?" She looked over at me just as the patio torch behind her ran out of oil and sputtered out.

I was distracted for about four seconds by the spectacular colors the thing produced in its dying upheaval. "We finally have developed a Casimir power source! It would have to be many . . . uh, many, tens of meters on a side, but it would produce a Global Annual Energy Expenditure per second—constantly!" She dropped her bottle.

"She said nothing about it."

"That's typical of those two. Hell, Jim and 'Becca did most of the work. You have to come see it! An absolute marvel! Oh yeah, I guess you *have* seen a few of those haven't you?" It's real easy to forget that you're talking to an astronaut, since they seem just like normal people when you meet them outside their day jobs.

We talked about the future of my research and how we might continue to finagle funding here and there. Neither of us had any bright ideas. I realized she really did believe in the BPP research and she had nothing to do with budget cuts. The last thing I remember talking about is my crazy lucid dreams and how I knew that we were close to something. I could taste it, I told her. I think she thought I was a little nuts.

The next thing I knew I was waking up with the sun in my face and Friday licking my left middle finger. Somehow, I had been covered with an afghan from the screened porch sofa.

I passed out on her again! Damn it. I got up and crawled to the bed and passed out again.

Later in the day I finally got up and stirred around the house. I managed to wake Jim up as I shut the microwave for about the third time. Leftover cheeseburgers are great hangover medicine once heated up in the microwave. I looked around and noticed that someone had sort of cleaned up. My money was on 'Becca.

"Lazarus has arisen!" I said as Jim came through the breakfast nook.

"Arisen, hell!" He wasn't firing on all cylinders yet either or he would've had a snappier come back—he's usually pretty witty. "What time is it?" he asked.

"Not sure, uh, about twelve-thirty," I replied.

"We've gotta be at the studio at one!"

"Dang! I've been forgetting a lot of stuff lately. I think these painkillers are bad on my short-term memory. I'm gonna quit taking them, if I can stand it. We better get our stuff and go."

We had upper belt tests today at the karate studio. Jim and I, as black belts, had volunteered to help with the testing. The thing I regretted was that I wouldn't get to fight because of my ribs. I had entertained the idea of wearing the rib protector and fighting, but I just hadn't healed enough yet. Besides, it'd only been one week. The doctor said six, but what does that quack know?

We got there and bowed in just in time. Our school is one of the more fighting oriented and not very traditional. Oh sure, we do the traditional stuff like katas, traditional stances, and an occasional bow, but we don't do all of the "Yes Sensei, No Sensei" junk you see in the movies. In fact, the head instructor Bob is actually a year younger than me and much less disciplined (if that is possible). Bob cuts up worse than most of his students. His wife Alisa keeps him in check, sometimes. But, I have never seen anybody do pushups because they neglected to say, "yes sir" or "no sir" or because they forgot to bow.

I got my score sheet and began watching and scoring the students. Alisa came over to me.

"How are you? The ribs?" she whispered and pointed at my side.

"I'm okay; there's still a lot of pain, but nothing serious. I'll be out for a couple more weeks. I'm gonna try to do pushups by the end of the week. I figure it'll be another couple of weeks before I can do crunches. Might be able to do some katas next week." I was probably lying about any or all of that.

"I'm sorry." She smiled and went about her business.

Rebecca finally made it. She bowed and frantically tied her belt. "Why didn't she just stay and come in with us?" I nudged Jim.

"She didn't have her gi or her pads with her," he replied.

"'Becca you are late! Stretch real quick and get in line!"

Bob seemed a little perturbed. I'm surprised she didn't have to do pushups, but test days are a little rushed and frantic. Bob is really just an old softy.

Finally, after about three physically grueling hours they got to fight. The main goal of our tests is to get you to a point where you feel there's nothing left to do but give up. Then we ask even more of you. This would be the case if someone or some group of people were mugging, raping, or trying to kill you. You never quit. Never!

Each student had burned at least eleven hundred calories. That is how grueling the test is. Now we were asking them to fight ninety-second rounds. One one-on-one round for each belt earned every three months (up to brown, that's five rounds, then) and one two-on-one fight for each brown belt stripe (three stripes required for a black belt with a test each six months). To test for a black belt there is a three-on-one also. But this was brown belt tests; black belts test separately.

Now you might think that ninety-second rounds aren't that long. Try running twenty-meter sprints while forgetting to breathe and while people are hitting and kicking the living hell out of you for a minute and a half and then talk to me about it. No, wait a second. First do one hour of aerobics, thirty minutes or so of isometric-type exercises, then do another hour and half of aerobics. Then do six or seven minute and a half rounds as I just described with just one minute in between each. *Then we will talk about it!* Why do it you ask? Simple, it is fun as the dickens! (Not sure I know what "the dickens" are but to hear my grandma tell it they must have been real fun.)

Jim geared up and got in the mix. I wanted to get in and play so bad it hurt. But had I gotten in the mix, I'm sure it would have hurt. It was like when you were a kid and your mom wouldn't let you go in swimming for thirty minutes after you ate lunch. All the other kids were out there having a ball and you had to set there twiddling your thumbs. That is how it felt. So, I ref'ed and ran the clock. Bob wanted to fight, too.

"Bow to your partners, touch gloves, fight." This wasn't the sport karate point stuff. This was a continuous fight for ninety seconds. The only rules are no hitting below the belt and no grabbing. If somebody grabs you, you can throw them. While you are on the ground you are liable to be kicked in the head and if you don't get up you fail the test and have to wait six more months to be promoted to a higher belt.

Rebecca got set up against Jim and Alisa for her first one. She did pretty good. At one point she did a spinning backfist that caught Jim on side of the head. His mouthpiece flew halfway across the ring. We all laughed appropriately. Alisa didn't let her get away with it though. Although it looks good in the movies, spinning isn't really a good idea when you are fighting two people. It gave Alisa time to slip to her back side and bully up on her.

Rebecca finally "turtled up" and covered very well and let them hit her for a second or two. Once she got her breath she shoved, kicked, and punched Alisa into Jim, who was punching her in the headgear from behind and around Alisa with big slow looping hook punches. She ran to the other side of the room being chased and punched the whole way. This time she didn't stop running. She turned a long arc and threw a few kicks and punches and ran back the way she had come, fitness really becoming a factor now. The timer beeped.

"Stop!" I yelled.

She collapsed on the floor gasping for air.

Bob smiled as he looked around the room, "'Becca, die over there so we can start the next fight."

She crawled to the side of the colored-tape marked rings and sat with her back to the wall, gasping for air and sweating profusely.

"Don't sit still 'Becca! Keep breathing and keep moving. Get you a quick drink of water while you are at it," I told her.

Jim said something to her inaudible to me. She responded by kicking at his shin. Jim did a quick hopping two-step and decided he had better go get a drink of water and leave well enough alone.

A minute or so later it was Rebecca's time again. This time Bob and Keri (a one stripe brown belt that just wanted to fight another round) fought her. It looked pretty much the same except, Bob is much taller and can hold his ax kick up over his head and drop it at the most inopportune times. 'Becca found this out, the hard way. Defending Keri's attack of multiple kicks, she's kind of limber, 'Becca dropped her guard a little too much for Bob. He drove her to her knees with an ax kick on top of her head. Everyone gasped and paused for a split second to see if Rebecca was okay. She responded from her knees by reverse punching Bob just above the belt as hard as she could.

I think she was a bit mad. As she scrambled to her feet, Keri decided to give it to her with both barrels. Roundhouse kick to the midsection, hookkick to the head, another roundhouse to the head, she did all this balancing on her right leg and never sat her left foot down. Keri then followed up with a jab, cross, and a ridgehand. 'Becca took all this in stride and never stopped moving. With an amazing display of balance she bobbed and weaved into a spinning side kick and followed with an outer block to stop the ridgehand. By this time Bob had given her enough of a break and poured it on even harder. He raised his ax kick again. This time 'Becca was having none of it.

She ducked under his leg to avoid the kick and slipped to his back side and reverse punched Bob in the ribs following it with a left hook to the solar plexus and one to the side of the headgear. Of course, Bob wasn't there for the second punch and Keri had slipped to the side of Rebecca. Rebecca must have realized this and threw a real ugly half side kick half front kick. At the same time Bob was throwing a backfist to her headgear, Keri caught Rebecca's foot and pushed her backwards (our rules are that you are allowed to grab on blocks for one second or so). Rebecca was now falling backward with a backfist moving toward her head. Using the momentum of her fall she did a backwards handspring as Bob's backfist passed right through the air where her head had been a fraction of a second before. I'm sure she could see his fist go by her face. 'Becca rolled through the handspring and onto her feet into a traditional back stance with a knife hand outer block (I think by accident, but it looked amazingly cool). She side kicked Bob to hold him off as the timer beeped.

"Stop!" I yelled.

Every person present looked on in awe. I said, "Hell yes! That was awesome." Jim applauded and whistled. Rebecca fell to the floor gasping for air, her mouthpiece falling to the floor as she threw her headgear off.

"That was impressive! You rock!" Alisa cheered and clapped.

I had never seen anything like that outside of a movie. I seriously doubted that I ever would again. I guess that I should mention that Rebecca did her undergraduate schooling on a cheerleading and gymnastics scholarship at Auburn University. She still tumbles every now and then at the karate studio, just to show off I think. Keri helped drag a gasping 'Becca to the side of the rings and Bob organized another fight. After about three more rounds it was all over. Everyone had passed.

An hour later we were sitting around a table at one of our favorite sports bars just off of University Drive. We were on our second pitcher of beer, waiting for our food. Bob and I talked about when I would be back in class and if I thought I could compete next month. I wasn't quite sure about either, so I lied about both. Eventually the conversation turned to the various topics that are covered after three pitchers of beer.

"Who sang that song?"

"Just how tall is the Empire State Building and what would happen if you dropped a penny off of it?" I actually make my freshman physics students work that one out every semester.

"Don't be silly," I say to them. "A raindrop weighs about the same as a penny and they fall from as much as forty thousand feet high during thunderstorms. You ever see a raindrop crack the sidewalk?" Terminal velocity is tough for some people to grasp.

And so the conversations continued. "If you were driving along at the speed of light and you turned your headlights on, what would you see?"

"Could Jackie Chan whup Bruce Lee?"

"Which Heinlein book was the best?"

"Was Kirk, Picard, Sisco, Janeway, or Archer the coolest captain?"

I always voted for "Q" myself, but didn't he always make himself an admiral?

"Who was the best guitarist of all times?" No contest there. Hendrix, period, exclamation point.

"Second best?" Stevie Ray Vaughn. Of course you can't discount Robert Johnson, George Thorogood, Jimmy Page, Joe Perry, Slash, Jeff Beck, Eric Clapton, B.B. King, Ron Wood, Kirk Hammett, and that new kid, what's his name, and of course our local great, Microwave Dave. But there is an order of magnitude problem between second and third best that I'm sure the other guitarists would point out.

A pitcher later and Tabitha came through the door. Rebecca waved at her and she joined us.

"Did you call her or something?" I asked.

"None of your business," she replied.

'Becca introduced her while I tried to figure out just how I was supposed to react. The group accepted her willingly and didn't quiz her too hard about being an astronaut. Alisa asked her a question that I never really thought about.

"Did you have to take some sort of self-defense stuff in the Air Force?"

"We had some training, yes. I'm sure it wasn't as involved as what I hear all of you do."

I responded to that, "Well, none of us have ever flown a Space Shuttle, either." She seemed to like that remark. I seemed to recall having used it the first time I met her. Maybe I just thought I did. That day is still pretty fuzzy.

Our food finally got to the table. Well, mine almost did. Some crazy drunk guy in the middle of a story made a big hand gesture and knocked my plate right out of our waitress's hand. I laughed at first, until I realized it was my food. It all went downhill from there.

I slept in a little Monday morning and got to the lab about eleven. Tabitha was coming by after her Space Camp thing later that evening to see our experiments. I spent some time explaining it to her, but without seeing it, it's hard to explain. Rebecca and Jim were already in the warp bubble experiment lab setting it up. We had never figured out why the electrons had completely disappeared on us, although, the experiment is actually kind of simple. There's a one-and-a-half-meter-long glass tube with an electron gun attached at one end. The tube has huge electromagnets situated along it to steer, accelerate, and focus the electrons. The other end of the tube is a larger vacuum chamber in the shape of a cube about a half meter on a side. In the middle of the chamber is a misshapen toroidial superconductor with coils around the upper and lower half—the device looked kind of like a squished and twisted donut with thousands of wires wrapped around it in random looking fashion. A few centimeters away is a second misshapen toroidial superconductor with similar coils around it. A high current is set up moving counterclockwise in the first toroid and clockwise in the other and a rather complex alternating current function is set up in the coils. It's in the region between the two toroids that the spacetime metric should change to allow for the warp bubble—if the field strength is large enough, and if the theory is correct, that is. We based the field shapes on approximations to the Einstein equations and numerical solutions, but there still hasn't been any real closed solution discovered. If I could only have that dream again, maybe I'd figure it out.

All the apparatus is inside a clear plastic sphere that has electron detectors deposited on the inner surface of the sphere. This way electrons scattered at any angle could be detected. The problem is that you can't see the experiment because of the detectors—there are so many of them and they're all in the way from an outside viewer's standpoint. So, we modified the sphere by drilling a few holes here and there between the electron detectors and placed tiny CCD cameras in them. We sealed the holes around the camera connections with epoxy and vacuum sealant—that was an ordeal within itself. Now we could rerun the experiment and actually see what was happening inside the sphere. Some of the cameras are for ultraviolet, some for infrared, and some for visible wavelengths. We hoped that would shed some, ahem, light on the problem.

Jim and 'Becca had completed the modifications early and now had the chamber pulling down to a vacuum. That would take several hours. In the meantime we decided to have a bull session about the next step for the energy collectors.

"There has to be a way to make them more efficient or smaller."

"Well, smaller is really out, Anson. We're at state-of-the-art and then some right now!" Rebecca said.

"Maybe there's a way to increase the surface area of the Casimir effect regions," was Jim's input.

"That would increase the efficiency all right. Any ideas, 'Becca?" I asked.

"I dunno?" She shrugged. "The most efficient use of surface area is a sphere, but how the heck can we use that?"

"That's it! Why didn't I think of that?" I went to the whiteboard and started drawing.

"What's *it*?" Jim asked.

"Well, instead of plates for pistons we use hollow spheres. One inside the other. Like this." I drew a large circle, which is a two-dimensional sphere, then a smaller circle inside it. Then I erased a portion of the larger circle and drew a rod from the smaller circle through the hole in the larger one and extended the rod a little. I drew the same thing on the other end of the rod.

"The question is, how do we support the rod and keep the inner spheres from touching the outer ones." I tugged at my lip for a second and realized that I was chewing on the end of the marker cap.

"Maybe we can do it this way." Rebecca took another marker and drew squiggly lines to represent springs from the rod. She drew two springs on top and two on bottom of the rod at equal distances from its center.

"But what about collecting the energy. How do we do that?" I asked.

This time Jim figured it out. "Easy. Just make the rod a magnet and we put a coil around the rod. *Voila*, we have a generator!"

"Could this work?" I thought aloud. I did some quick math on the board and showed that the surface area was an order of magnitude greater, hence making the energy collection that much greater. "The efficiency of this coil idea might even be better than the plates configuration. This might be win-win. Can you guys make it?" I looked at them hopefully.

"We'll figure it out! I don't think it's more complicated than that guitar we made you for Christmas," Rebecca said with excitement and confidence in her voice.

They had made me a guitar that was about one micron long for Christmas the previous year. The darn thing actually played, but you had to have a microwave receiver to "hear" it. Of course, we could never figure out how to chord the thing. It was one of the neatest Christmas presents I had gotten since Sadie Jo Livingston kissed me at the fifth grade Christmas party at Priceville Elementary.

Jim and 'Becca went off to the nanotech lab to work on the energy collector. I went to my office to catch up on some emails. My colleague Matt had sent me a note wanting to know why I hadn't called him since Goddard. I wrote a quick response back telling him that I was overwhelmed with work and that I would get with him in a week or so. After finishing up about a million emails, I decide to catch up with Mom. After all, I owed her a call or two.

Nothing new had happened. Dad had caught a nine-pound bass down by "the pump house" and my twelve-year-old nephew who was with him netted the thing. It was the highlight of their summer. They put up a picture at the local country store of my nephew holding the fish. Grandma was still claiming to be deathly ill. Oh and by the way her eighty-second birthday was coming up. My brother was probably going to be reactivated and sent back to the Middle East. He was in the Air Force Reserve. My first cousin's twin girls turn five next week. Don't forget to call them. And when am I going to come visit them again?

Anybody who has parents has had that conversation, as Carl Sagan might have said, "billions upon billions" of times. I guess I had rather have the conversations than not have the parents. Small price to pay, don't you think?

I hung the phone up finally after, "Yeah, uh huh, no I have to get back. No. Yep, uh, I don't know. Okay then, I will see you soon. Yeah. No. Maybe, soon. All right. We will see y'all later. Naw. I don't know. Yes. Okay then. All right then. Nope. Okay I gotta go. Yep. Uh, maybe. Uh huh. All right, we'll talk to you later. Okay I gotta go. Bye. Unh huh, love y'all too. Okay bye now."

"Now back to work," I muttered to myself. I got my notes out and started looking over the tensors for the metric we were using in the current configuration. There are just too many equations so I ran the tensor math package on my computer. There were nearly too many for that thing, even at six hundred gigahertz. I tweaked a few equations here and there and set the calculations in motion. It would be an hour or so before they were through, so I decided to see how the kids were doing.

I put my paper tux on and headed for the airlock. Jim was running some mechanical arms from the computer and 'Becca was looking through the eyepiece of a microscope giving Jim orders. This was funny because Jim could see everything she could from the computer monitor.

"Damnit!" he said. "Do you want to drive?"

"If you can't drive any better, I might need to."

"Children, children, please be calm." I said. "Don't make me separate you two."

"Boss," Rebecca began, "do you remember that thing you told me about too many chefs making the soup taste like crap?"

"Point taken, 'Becca. I will just set over here and watch like a good televangelist." I sat down next to Jim and kept my mouth shut. Well, except when I was sniggering my ass off at the show.

"Okay, 'Becca say when." What they were doing was loading various materials that would be vaporized and then deposited on a dielectric substrate. Jim could indeed see the objects as the materials began to deposit and adhere to the substrate but the contrast wasn't as good as through the phase contrast microscope 'Becca was using. He was waiting for her to tell him when the center portion of the wafer they were looking at had enough silicon—or germanium or gold or whatever they were depositing at the time—on it. Of course, 'Becca could probably eyeball it and get it right since she had done this so many times. But she also had a nanogram balance readout right in front of her to tell her when. The computer would do most of the etching and depositing once the design was drawn in the special CAD system they were using.

"That's good Jim. When already!" She raised her voice to make the point.

I sniggered again. Realizing the sensitive part was over; I figured that I could speak now.

"Have you guys already drawn up the blueprints?"

"Nah, we just thought we would load up the machine and get that out of the way. Here is what we have so far." Jim punched a few keys and a drawing not unlike the one on the whiteboard in the conference room popped up.

Rebecca finished for him, "We still have to put in all the materials, thicknesses, and so forth, and so on, and so on."

"And scooby dooby dooby," I sang. They just looked at me funny. I'm getting old. But I am still everyday people, by God!

"Anybody ever told you just how weird you really are, Doc?" Rebecca asked.

"My mom told me about thirty minutes ago." Of course I was lying. Mom may think it but she would never say it.

"We're going to have to start having some sort of comic relief around here. Maybe like 'Punday' in those Spider Robinson stories. You guys are getting a little stiff," I said.

"Stiff as that little super tool gadget," 'Becca said as she picked up a *spider wrench* sitting on the table. It was a cross-shaped tool like a miniature tire tool with a different size socket on each end of the cross. I'm sure she asked for it on purpose. She wielded it like a real cross. "Be gone, evil demon!" she said to me.

Jim followed suit by singing just in time, "Here's to you, Mr. Robinson Anson thinks he's cool but he don't know. Woah, woah, woah."

"Huh," I grunted.

We were quiet for a few minutes as Jim spun up the centrifuge for a test. Then 'Becca asked, "Hey did you guys see the news last night? There was the strangest thing on about this murder."

"No. I missed it. What about it," I asked.

"Well, apparently some local materials engineer guy was working on this new fiberglasslike alloy that would be used for aircraft and spacecraft. He was working on it in his basement lab. The material was supposed to be like Kevlar but more modern, stronger and lighter. So anyway, this guy was mixing some of this stuff up in a big tub in his basement when he was attacked. There must have been a scuffle and the police said that at one point it looked like the engineer pushed his attacker's head into the tub of the not-yet-dry resin and fiber material. Unfortunately for the engineer, the attacker did get free of his hold and shot him. His wife came home from work and found him dead in the basement floor." She paused for a breath.

Jim chimed in on cue, "Did they have any leads?"

'Becca continued, "Well, the sketch artist and the forensic specialists examined the material in the tub once it hardened."

"Hey, that is pretty cool and lucky." I was awed by our local police.

"Yeah." 'Becca laughed. "They were able to make a really good *composite* drawing!"

Jim added, "Yeah, he had made quite an *impression!*" She and Jim guffawed.

"Okay, okay." I shook my head. "You got me. And I'm sure they will find out that the attacker was an out-of-work impressionist, and that forensics got all the evidence they needed from *fibers* found at the crime scene. And the analysis from the material stuck to the dead guy's hands led the coroner to believe that he had 'resin' from the dead." They simultaneously rolled their eyes and groaned in pain.

"I'll let you guys get back to work." I laughed smugly. I left before they could top me. As I closed the airlock I thought about how proud I was for finding those two.

My computer had finished its calculation by the time I had gotten back to my office. Three of the equations in the stress-energy tensor didn't converge to a solution.

"Dangnabit! @$$%%&?!" Oh, well. I changed a few other things here and there and started it up again. It was about four-thirty in the afternoon—Tabitha would be here soon. I checked on the vacuum chamber and it was ready to go. I brought the warp experiment online and so I was ready whenever she was.

She arrived at the lab about an hour later. By that time Jim and 'Becca were about finished with the new energy collector.

They left the computer running the manufacture of the prototype and joined us in the warp experiment lab.

"Nice of you two to join us. How is the collector coming?" I asked.

"It should be done in an hour or so," Rebecca guessed.

"Good. Let's get to work here shall we? I already brought the system up. The electron gun is ready to go. All of the detectors are ready and the cameras are online," I assured everyone.

Jim sat down at a computer and started firing up the warp field generators. In other words, he started increasing the current in the toroids and he turned the function generators on that are connected to the field coils.

"Everything is ready. The fields are on," he said.

"Rebecca, fire the electron beam."

We all watched the detector monitors and the camera monitors with anticipation. A very bright blue light flashed on all of the camera monitors and nothing happened on the electron detectors.

"What the heck was that?" Jim exclaimed.

"Blue photons," 'Becca said smartly.

"Why were there blue photons?" I rubbed my chin and thought out loud. "There's nothing in there for the electrons to react with. If they ablated some of the toroids away, the particle detectors would've measured that. What the heck is going on?" I scratched my head.

Tabitha looked concerned.

"It couldn't be Cerenkov radiation could it?" she asked.

My brain did a double backflip. *Of course!* Cerenkov radiation!

"'Becca hit the e-beam again!" I almost shouted. She flipped a couple of interlock switches and pressed the fire button. Again the blue flash! "Oh my God!" I grabbed Tabitha and kissed her right on the mouth. I turned and ran to the whiteboard and never looked back.

It was so obvious! How could I not have thought of it before? Jim, Rebecca, and a slightly red astronaut filtered into the room. I hoped she was just blushing and not mad.

"What gives, Anson?" Rebecca asked.

Jim followed with, "You gonna let us in on the secret?"

"Shhh! Give me a second—us old people think slower than you youngsters," I scolded. They sat patiently while I worked out tensors in my head, on the board, on pieces of notes on the table, and back on the board. It was like an avalanche. It took one tiny snowflake to trigger a flow of ideas that were so powerful I couldn't control the rate they came or where they were going. I just had to follow along for the ride. When the smoke and dust settled I had a group of equations on the board circled and a diagram drawn.

"Jim, get the digital camera and record this now!" I looked over and noticed that he had already been doing so. Good kid.

"So, what gives?" Rebecca posed with her hands on her hips.

"Okay, here it is. We just broke the speed of light barrier in a vacuum!" I let that sink in for a second. "Tabitha was absolutely right. The blue light was Cerenkov radiation." I paused and turned to Rebecca, "Let's hear it, Rebecca." She frowned at me and flipped her laptop open. After typing in a few things a website came up. She began to read.

"Cerenkov radiation was discovered in 1926 by Mallet. Mallet observed that the light had a continuous spectrum instead of having 'dark lines' which are characteristic of emission spectrum. The unusual electromagnetic phenomenon was extensively studied between the years of 1934–1938 by Pavel Cerenkov (1904–1990). Cerenkov discovered fluorescence wasn't the cause of this effect and he measured speeds of particles over 230,000,000 meters per second. In other words, the particles traveled faster than light in that medium. However, Cerenkov never demonstrated faster than light motion with any particle in the vacuum." She looked around the room, "So what are you saying Doc?"

"First, you should have known that without having to look it up. Get the math down on that before your defense," I scolded her a little. "I know you'll remember it now. Just in case . . ." I winked at her to ease the tension so as not to embarrass her too much in front of company and to let her know that it damn well would be a question on her oral defense.

I turned back to the board. "Here's what happened," I started. "The electron beam hits the outer edge of the Alcubierre warped spacetime here where space is expanded and so the speed of light in this region is maybe thirty times ten to the eight meters per second—ten times the vacuum speed of light. We don't know how to measure that accurately yet. Then it passes through a region just beyond the expanded spacetime to the center between the two toroids. Here spacetime should be flat, so the speed of light is smaller, roughly three times ten to the eight meters per second—or normal vacuum speed. But the electrons didn't slow down and they are now traveling faster than light speed in normal flat space. Boom! Cerenkov radiation and they decelerate. Then they pass through the bubble edge near the second torus and were decelerated again because space is contracted in there and the speed of light is less than in flat space. Maybe three times ten to the seven meters per second. Boom, more Cerenkov radiation as they decelerated." I paused for air. "If we had fast photo-detectors instead of cameras, I'll bet you we would see two quick flashes overlapping each other. I'm guessing about one to ten nanoseconds pulsewidth each. Oh, one more thing, the Cerenkov radiation had to occur at the edge of each spacetime region in order to prevent any violations of causality. In other words, the electrons were never traveling faster-than-light for that region for more than the smallest possible time increment as they passed from one region to the next. Otherwise, there would have been time travel things goin' on and Gawd I'm glad that didn't happen."

"That doesn't explain why we couldn't detect the electrons though," Jim pointed out.

"That's right," Tabitha added, no longer blushing.

"Give me a second and I'll get there. Sheesh!" I overdramatized and kept talking.

"Remember that in order to keep the Alcubierre type field stable we had to use the Van Den Broeck idea of placing a second bubble around the main Alcubierre bubble once we got the matter inside. Ha!" I laughed at the pun. Nobody else got it. So, I continued to press onward, "And in order for us to control that bubble it is electrically charged on the outside. I went back through my notes here on the table. Once decelerated the electrons aren't fast enough to penetrate the negative charge on the outside of the Van Den Broeck bubble. So, they just get bounced around inside until they decelerate to a point where they aren't energetic enough to trigger the detectors once we turn off the field. They just scatter off at low energies. Remember the Alcubierre field only lasts like a nanosecond so the electrons don't get re-accelerated." I looked around the room. My heart was pounding a million beats per second.

"Do you realize what this means, Anson?" Tabitha asked.

"You're damn right I do. We just built the first warp drive and accelerated the first matter to warp speed! YES! And the crowd goes wild." I shouted. "Goal!"

I ran to my office with both arms still in the air and shouting, "Goal!" I stopped the calculation, and reentered the new data. We might have been warping for weeks and didn't know it! Kind of like Yeager and the sound barrier—he said in his book that he believes they broke the sound barrier a few days earlier than they realized. History repeats itself I guess.

➤ CHAPTER 5

"Looking back on the experiment, I realize that we were lucky the motive force caused by the warp bubble wasn't stronger than the Coulomb forces which we used to hold the bubble in place between the toroids. Also, if the warp field forces had been strong enough to overcome the mechanical strength of the mounts holding the toroids in place . . . whew-*wee* that could have been messy!"

I explained to Jim and 'Becca how we might have punched a hole through the lab wall and most of the buildings in its path half way across the state. Hopefully, hypersonic pressures would've disintegrated the thing before it went too far. But, who knows how strong a Van Den Broeck warp bubble is?

"Messy to say the least. Why didn't we think of that before?" Rebecca scolded me. I smiled at her charisma.

"I don't know. Hey give me a break will you. We just invented the warp drive!" I said.

"Yeah, yeah. That was thirty minutes ago. What have you done for me lately?" Tabitha said, laughing.

"There are some possible military applications here." I rubbed my head in contemplation. "Maybe we can squeeze some cash out of DARPA. What do you think Tabitha?" I asked.

"I'll ask," she said.

Jim looked around the room. "Nobody move. I'll be right back!" He was gone for about seven minutes. We had just about given up on him when he finally came back in with a bottle of cheap champagne and some plastic cups.

"This is all they had across the street at the gas station but it'll have to do." He began pouring and distributing. "I don't know about you guys," he began, "but this deserves a drink!"

'Becca flipped through her notebook and found a passage. She held up her glass and said, "I found this in your library a few months back and I thought it would be cool for this occasion. It comes from your *Star Trek: The Next Generation Technical Manual* in the section on Warp Field Theory and Application." She started reading from her notes about how the fictional Zephram Cochrane had gone through this crusade of developing new complex math and procedures required to invent the warp drive. It was interesting how the writers of that book closely paralleled the work that we'd done in Breakthrough Physics.

"Cheers!" she exclaimed as she finished reading the passage.

Like I said, I'm proud of myself for finding these two. "Cheers," I said as I raised my cup. I had to cover the tears of joy so the others didn't see them.

"Cheers!" cried Tabitha.

"I know we have to verify all of this better and do some optimization. But, seriously, what next?" Jim shrugged his shoulders.

I started to respond. To my surprise, Tabitha jumped in before I could get the first word out.

"First thing we have to do is get you guys more funds! And I'm going to see about getting moved down here, if that's okay. You'll need some help if we're gonna do a flight experiment."

"Whoa there, Tex!" I interrupted her. "First things first. The chocolate starfish is my man Fred Durst!"

"Limp Bizkit?" Tabitha asked.

"Yeah, good." I nodded at her approvingly. Then I realized how old I was. Who would've ever thought I would be listening to Limp Bizkit on classic rock radio?

"Anyway," I got back to my original thought, "we go about our job and you go about yours. We would love to have you here, of course. But before you do that, somebody is going to do some lobbying and maybe even make a visit to the White House. However, let's keep this completely under wraps until we're damned sure we got it right. Okay?" If my calculations turned out to be wrong and we didn't warp space, this could be a much bigger fiasco than cold fusion ever was.

We had gone through several months of rigorous experimentation and simulation. Everything turned out to be repeatable. We even found a way to quantify the strength, stresses, and projected speed of the warp bubble, provided we turned off the electric field holding it in place and let go of it. Jim and Rebecca finished the design on the Casimir type energy collection system and they were in the process of building a tenth scale of that required to power a manned-size, warp-capable spacecraft. The largest problem proved to be funding.

On top of all that, Jim was able to complete his dissertation and graduated. I guess that is Dr. Jim Daniels now. I think I'll still call him Jim. 'Becca wasn't quite so lucky. She had trouble getting her dissertation finished before the deadline and although she finished, it wasn't in time to walk in this year's ceremony. She is supposed to pick up her diploma sometime in August at the records office. She can walk next year if she wants, but by then the new will be worn off of her diploma—it just won't be the same. What if she took a job out of town? Would it be worth it to fly back in town just for the ceremony? Graduation ought to be every semester even if there are only two students walking. I've complained about this problem at the local university for more than a decade. It always falls on deaf ears. Bureaucrats never understand human needs. I started introducing her to people as Dr. Rebecca Jean Townes.

Tabitha finally came through for us in early June. She found about a million dollars in DARPA (Defense Advanced Research Projects Agency) money, a few hundred thousand from DOE (Department of Energy), and we squeezed NASA BPP for the following half-funded year now. NASA In Space Transportation Program threw in about a million and a half and NASA Office of Space Science claimed if we could prove the energy collection system they'd throw in ten million dollars for a prototype.

I found a few private investors locally and it looked like we had just enough to put together a warp drive flight demonstrator experiment. Provided that the Casimir energy collector scaled prototype worked, we would then be in the business of building a faster-than-light spacecraft.

We hired two cooperative education students, one graduate and one undergraduate. The plan was that the two students would work full-time one semester while attending classes part-time and vice versa the next semester. They were set up on opposite semesters so one of them would always be there full time. Al Rayburn was working on a Ph.D. in Aerospace engineering and was on part-time for the summer. Sara Tibbs was an undergraduate in physics with hopes of continuing on to a Ph.D. in cosmology or astrophysics.

As you can tell, the activity around the lab really picked up. I was e-signing time cards now for the pay period including July the fourth. We needed to have the scaled prototype done by mid July to meet schedules we sold to our benefactors and we hadn't even successfully tested the new design yet.

We also hired a clerical slash secretary slash everything else person. Johnny Cache (I'm serious—that's his name) came in and offered to do some maintenance on the front door after a thunderstorm blew a tree limb through it. The weird part is that there aren't any trees around the lab. Thunderstorms in the southeast are screwy that way.

Johnny never left—and he has proven to be priceless. Apparently he worked as a general contractor for the last eight or nine years and was laid off a few months ago. He went around the area doing odd jobs to pay the bills while he was looking for something more permanent. Once I found out that he was fluent in Spanish, Linux, HTML II, C++, could type about eighty words a minute, and was a licensed subcontractor and a travel agent I grabbed him up.

It is hard to find a resume like that. He explained it easily though. His mom was first generation American. His grandmother brought her here from Mexico. I didn't ask if she was legal or not. Johnny said that he grew up on the Internet and computers were a hobby. His dad was a carpenter until he retired. Johnny learned the contractor profession from him. He and his wife became travel agents to earn extra money on the side. It all sounded logical enough to me.

Johnny was putting the finishing touches on the drywall of two new office areas that was previously useless storage space when Tabitha finally joined us. One of these offices was to be hers. She had convinced NASA that she needed to be here until it was time for mission training. We weren't quite sure anyway how we were going to get the spacecraft to orbit. Cart before the horse.

"Colonel, give me one more day and I'll be through painting your office," he assured Tabitha. It turns out that Johnny also spent four years in the Air Force. From the time they met Tabitha was never able to break him from using her rank.

"That'll be fine." She didn't have a lot of stuff to unpack anyway. Most of her things were still in boxes in her apartment living room floor.

Tabitha stuck her head in my office. "How are you?"

"Hey, when did you get here?" I was pleasantly surprised.

"I just got in. The new guy, Johnny? He said that my office won't be ready until tomorrow." She smiled and sat down on my couch. Offices really need a couch. I've spent many all-nighters working and catching catnaps every now and then on it. I've caught Jim and 'Becca on it a time or two also. Uh, I mean I caught them one at a time—not together—although I have recently noticed some chemistry going on there.

"How did it go in D.C.?" I asked.

"Not sure. But let's keep on plugging and figure out how to do the experiment. We'll get it flown somehow."

All of a sudden a crash—no, more like an explosion—came from the clean room. Then I heard Jim.

"Call 911!" he was screaming.

Tabitha and I bolted to the airlock door where we found Jim walking Rebecca to the kitchen. Her left arm from the elbow down was covered in blood and her hand was mangled severely and coated with glass fragments. She was shaking but not making a sound. When the cold water hit her hand she collapsed to the floor.

Johnny came around the corner, "What the hell was tha—" He

fainted when he saw Rebecca's hand. Obviously, medic isn't one of the things on his resume. Tabitha put a cushion from one of the chairs under 'Becca's head. I immediately propped her feet up and held her arm over her head as well.

"We gotta stop this bleeding now!" Jim screamed.

"Calm down Jim!" Tabitha barked. "Get the first-aid kit!"

"Doc, we never replaced it after we lost it in Tsali when we went mountain biking up there, remember!" Jim looked frantic.

"Then get me a couple of towels. Fast!"

Johnny came to. "What can I do to help?"

"Go get the car and pull it around front." I told him. Looking back at 'Becca's hand once the blood flow had slowed some, I realized that her ring finger was missing and there were hundreds of shards of glass sticking out of her arm. The missing finger wasn't bleeding that badly, but the ugly gouges that the glass had made were bleeding profusely. I looked at Tabitha. She saw and only nodded back at me. Jim returned with the towels.

"Jim hold her arm up like this! I'll be right back." I grabbed a sandwich bag out of the cabinet and headed for the clean room.

There was nothing left of the vacuum chamber and there were glass fragments all around where it used to be.

"What the hell happened in here?!" After a minute or so I found her finger inside the remains of the vacuum chamber glove. It had been severed cleanly, most likely by a large piece of glass. I held the bottom of the sandwich bag and turned it inside out so my hand was on the inside (or outside rather) of the bag. I picked up the finger and turned the bag right side out and zipped it.

By the time I returned Tabitha had 'Becca's arm wrapped in the towels and 'Becca had regained consciousness. She was calm, everthing considered—she was probably in shock. Jim on the other hand, was nuts. They were getting her upright and on her way to the car.

"We're close enough to the hospital that we can have her there in ten minutes or less," I told them. Johnny was apparently out in the car waiting. I found the twelve-pack cooler under the sink and ran to the refrigerator. Once I was sure there was enough ice in the cooler I placed the sandwich bag in it and closed it up. I also grabbed my laptop on the way out.

"Johnny get us to the hospital safely. You understand me?"

"No problem, I just don't want to see the blood," Johnny replied.

I sat in the front and Tabitha, Jim, and 'Becca were in the back seat. We made 'Becca lie down with her head in Tabitha's lap and her feet in Jim's. Jim continued to hold her arm up. 'Becca was fairly catatonic.

I popped open my laptop, pulled up my duckbill antenna, and logged onto the Internet. I punched in the Huntsville Emergency Room online service. I adjusted the camera lens of my laptop to see me. A person wearing scrubs appeared on the other end and asked how they could help. After explaining the situation and putting 'Becca in the camera's field of view they took us a little more seriously. I told him our ETA was about fifteen minutes tops.

"What is her heart-rate?"

Tabitha was way ahead of me. "It is about sixty-nine beats per minute."

"How much blood loss has there been?" He seemed concerned. I realized part of the problem.

"I forgot to mention that she is very athletic and her resting heart-rate is probably much lower than that." I often get double-takes in the doctor's office when they take my pulse. Why are Americans so out of shape that when somebody isn't it's a surprise? The doctor/nurse whatever he is on the other end seemed to relax slightly.

"She's lost a considerable amount of blood. And there are glass fragments imbedded throughout her arm." Jim shouted over my shoulder.

The doctor, as it turns out, stayed online with us all the way to the door of the emergency room. When I told him we were pulling into the hospital he signed off and met us at the door. It must have been a slow day. He and an orderly helped us get 'Becca out of the car. By this time the towels were dripping wet with blood and 'Becca was getting very weak. We got 'Becca and the cooler with her appendage in it on a stretcher and they rolled her off. Jim tried to explain the accident but he had no idea why the nanotech chamber exploded. Most likely it imploded first. Tabitha had gotten Rebecca's purse and we rummaged through her wallet until we found her insurance card. Once the clerk had swiped 'Becca's card through the machine, there was nothing we could do but wait.

"Should we call her parents or anything?" Johnny asked.

"Well, she never knew who her dad was and her mom died when she was in high school. We're really all she has as far as family goes." *And don't worry we're damn sure gonna take care of her, I thought.*

"What did her mom die of?" Johnny asked.

"Bad crack," is all Jim said.

After Rebecca's mom had died she worked her butt off in school and at life to make sure she wasn't going to end up another tragic story. At least now she could say she had friends and that she was part of something—something big for the entire human race. Well, if it worked.

We waited while Jim paced the floor. I read everything I could on the Internet about lacerations and puncture wounds and amputations.

"God I hope they can save her finger." I cried.

Tabitha was the only one of us who stayed completely calm. It was from years of being in very dangerous situations, I'm sure.

At some point Johnny disappeared for a while and he returned with soft drinks for everyone and a box of chicken fingers. There's a little place about three or four blocks from the hospital that makes the best chicken fingers. We ate quietly. Johnny looked at his watch and told me that he had to go pick up his kids from baseball camp and his wife from work. Since he had been laid-off, they only had the one car. We were in my SUV, so someone had to take him back to the office. Jim was in no shape to drive and Tabitha didn't know the town well enough. So I had to leave. The thought of that killed me. Johnny didn't want to leave either, but we understood it had to be done.

So I took him back to the office and his car. "I'll get to work cleaning that lab up tomorrow boss," he said.

"No! Do *not* touch anything in there until I figure out what happened. Okay?"

He nodded and rolled up his driver's side window as he departed.

I woke up sometime around midnight with Tabitha nudging me. Sleeping sitting up in a hospital waiting room chair is no good for a person's neck—I'll testify to that in any court.

"What is it?" I stretched and yawned.

"Here comes the doctor." Tabitha pointed down the hall. Jim was already on his feet and Sara had joined us at some point.

"The surgery went well and she's resting now," I could hear him telling Jim as we approached. "We reattached the finger and there doesn't appear to be any complications. It will take some physical therapy but she should regain full use of her arm and hand."

"That's great, Doc!" I cried. No, I mean it. I cried.

"Anything else, Doc?" Jim asked.

"I've never seen that much glass in an injury before. Were it not for the new MRI we got a few months back we might not have found it all. There may still be microscopic fragments in there that will surface over time. I don't think she will need other surgeries, though. If we can keep the skin from coagulating and keep good blood flow to her hand, we might not even need cosmetic work. It's much too early to tell about that yet."

"Can we see her?" Tabitha asked.

"Go home and get some sleep folks. She'll be out until tomorrow."

Jim looked at me, "You go home. I'm staying. Just bring me some clothes tomorrow."

The doctor looked up at that. "No. She is in the intensive care ward tonight and cannot have overnight visitors. All of you go home."

"Doc, there ain't no way in hell that we're leaving her here alone tonight!" I looked him square in the eyes so he could tell I was dead serious.

He sighed. "I figured as much. I'll get the nurse to show you to the ICU waiting area." He left shaking his head but with a smile on his face.

"Okay Jim, Sara is going to take you home while I wait here

for a while. You can drop Tabitha off at the office to get her car. Get some things and come back. Then I'll go home and take a nap. I'll be back here bright and early. How is that for a plan?"

Tabitha looked at me with fire in her eyes. "Well, first off, I'm staying for now. I'll leave with you later."

I left it at that. Jim went home. Tabitha and I found the ICU waiting room and got checked in as her "Parents." Once we finally got into 'Becca's room I nearly lost it. Tears welled up and I choked them back.

"I'm so sorry 'Becca." I touched her good hand and rubbed her cheek. Tabitha looked at me with puppy-dog eyes. I didn't know she had those. Death-ray eyes, sure. Fire-and-brimstone eyes, sure. But not puppy-dog eyes.

"She'll be fine, Anson."

"I should have known whatever happened was going to happen. Have you ever heard of a nanomachine construction accident?"

"Maybe it was something you couldn't have known about. What if there was a flaw in the chamber materials or seals?"

"Not likely. We paid a lot of money to make sure it didn't have any flaws."

"It isn't your fault. Accidents happen." This time she touched 'Becca's face. The two of them had bonded considerably in the short few months they had known each other.

"Maybe it's because I don't have kids of my own or I'm not married, but she and Jim are like kids to me. Like my kids. Sure, I would've had to have them when I was fourteen but that's possible. That's about how old people were when they had kids around here a hundred years ago. Hell, it still happens." I was blabbering. I'm not sure if it was because it was late or because I was so upset. Tabitha seemed to think it was cute. She said as much.

"What about you? Why don't you have kids?" I asked her.

"I do. I have a daughter, Anne Marie Ames. She will be starting college this fall on an Air Force scholarship." She smiled at me as she laid this on me. I was absolutely stunned.

"Are you married or were you?"

"No, I've never been married, Anson. I was planning on getting married but her father was killed in a car accident before I ever knew I was pregnant. He was such a good man, a Marine jump jet pilot. He taught me everything I know about flying Harriers." She paused for a brief second. "My parents helped me raise her when it got tough on me. She made it easy though. She's a great kid."

"I'm sorry. I didn't mean to pry so much." I felt even sadder than before.

"No, really, it's okay. I came to terms with that grief twenty years ago. Besides it always cheers me up to think about Annie."

"Well, okay then, how did you manage the Air Force as a single mom?" I had never heard of such.

"That part was simple. I wasn't in the Air Force yet. I was on scholarship, so they had to honor it provided I kept my grades up. I made a point to be on the dean's list every semester." Tabitha's pride shone through the grief for a moment and she smiled.

"You *are* an amazing woman Tabitha. I barely made good enough grades to keep from getting kicked out of school." I laughed at that.

"Yeah, you and Einstein and Edison and countless others," she goaded.

"No comparison. They had cultural and physical things to deal with. Me, I just like to drink beer," I replied.

"And how has that worked out for you?" she laughed.

"Not too bad!" I guffawed, snorted, and hee-hawed as only a real Southern nerd can.

"Hey, will you guys hold it down—I have a headache!" Rebecca whispered lightly.

"'Becca, honey how do you feel?" Tabitha grabbed her right hand, careful of the I.V. needle in her wrist.

"My arm hurts bad," she said quietly.

"I'll take care of it." I kissed her on the forehead and went to the nurse's station for help. The nurse showed her how to use the painkiller button and then told us to let her sleep or "get out!"

As soon as the nurse left, 'Becca opened her eyes. "Thanks." She began crying.

"What is it? Are you still hurting?" Tabitha asked.

"My finger?" she asked, tears streaking her cheeks.

"Don't worry. They got all the parts back in the right places.

The doctors don't even think you'll have any scars. They may do some laser treatment stuff in a few months or so," I told her.

The nurse and Jim returned. The nurse told us that only two visitors at a time could stay. Since Jim was her "husband" he should get to stay. I winked at Jim and kissed 'Becca goodbye.

"We'll see you tomorrow. Get better." We waved on our way out.

We left the hospital feeling a little better that 'Becca had come around. I still felt responsible for whatever it was that had happened. I was so zoned out I drove right past the turn for the office, reflexively driving home. Tabitha tapped me on the arm.

"Anson?"

"I know. I missed the turn," I looked over at her.

"Not that. I don't want to go back to that apartment and all of those boxes right now."

"Do you want to come over to my place? I've got plenty of room."

"Yes."

➤ CHAPTER 6

It had taken months for us to figure out what had happened. Rebecca had nearly completely healed by September. She had a laser treatment to do in another month and her ring finger was still in a splint, but other than that she was nearly back to normal. She had even started light karate workouts with kicks and some aerobics and been on her road bike some. There had been setbacks though. Her allergies had started acting up on her while she was recovering. The congestion led to sinusitis, which then led to bronchitis. She has continued to have a nagging cough and a bit of a wheeze, but she is getting there.

She recollected that she had been standing at the computer watching the seven hundredth Clemons Dumbbell (as she and Jim had started calling them) being constructed. Her left hand was in the vacuum chamber glove and she was adding materials to the new process. She recalled a flash of light and then everything exploded in front of her. That is all she could remember.

Jim, 'Becca, and I had tried and tried to piece the accident together, but were getting nowhere. No one could remember enough for the accident to make any sense at all. We decided to take a mental break and put in some physical playtime that Saturday. Jim and I were discussing her recollection of the accident on our way up to the mountain bike trailhead at Monte Sano State

Park. Mountain biking is one of the coolest things. It requires endurance, strength, balance, and lots of nerve. Jim had turned me onto it a few years back and I was hooked. 'Becca usually goes with us and wears us out, but she was still on the "injured reserve" list. As I was putting on my shoes he asked me about the flash of light.

"I can't understand what the flash of light was. Could we have tapped into some fundamental force of the fabric of spacetime?" he asked.

"Before we get all hocus-pocus let's rule out standard stuff first," I warned. "There were some big pieces of plexiglass and one piece of aluminum that slammed into her body pretty hard. It's not unbelievable that one of them hit her in the head. You've had your noodle knocked around before. You know that flashes of light aren't uncommon with that." I was still grasping for straws. You know what they say about drowning men.

"You ready?" He hopped on his bike as he asked.

Click! Click! I popped my cleats into the pedals and stood up on the bike hopping it slightly off the ground three or four times.

"Last one to the switchback buys the first pitcher!" I started hammering up to the trailhead in about gear two-three (eleventh gear) getting the jump on Jim. He pedaled up beside me not even breathing hard yet.

"You cheat, old man!"

"I'll show you old!" I cranked my right shifter down changing to about seven so I was in fifteenth gear. Then I moved my posterior further back on the saddle so I could push the pedals through and over the top of the stroke. Once I got rolling good, I cranked up to three on the left shifter and up to two on the right one. Now I was in eighteenth gear and in my hill-climbing stroke. My legs are stronger than Jim's, so I knew I could take him on the hill. The trek up the mountain to the switchback trailhead is a good couple of miles at a grade of at least forty-five degrees. A good warm-up.

By the time I got to the switchback at the top of the mountain I was at least fifty yards ahead of Jim. I dropped back down a couple of gears and stood up and dropped my center of gravity back as far behind the saddle as I could and dove straight down the switchback trail. The switchbacks are about every forty yards or so on that particular trail and they're very steep. The worst part is that there are trees and stair steps all across and down the trail. I don't recommend it for beginners. The first time I tried it I had my center of gravity too far forward and did an "endo" right over the handlebars. Had I not known how to fall from years of being thrown in karate, I would've been seriously injured.

The trail was much too technical and tricky for me to look back and see where Jim was. I turned a switchback and then I caught a glimpse of him. To make up time he'd decided to forgo the switchback, bunny hopped his bike off the trail, and turned head first down the mountain at ninety degrees to the switchback. His body was way behind the saddle and he was screaming.

"Let's go, you old fart!" he yelled as he tore down the mountain, blazing his own trail.

"Now who's cheatin'?" I yelled just as I did a left foot plant and locked the back break, swinging my bike around counterclockwise at the last switchback. I entered the main trail crossroads by the big marker boulder just behind Jim.

Jim hopped his bike up on the boulder and held it up on just the back tire. Then he dropped down and hopped up on the front tire. He did a three-sixty off the rock and landed pointing in the right direction and never missed a pedal stroke.

"Show-off!" I said. Jim used to do bike trial tournaments where they would hop over cars and waterfalls and you name it. He has a picture of himself hopping his bike on its front tire in the scoop of a bulldozer while he's giving a peace sign with his right hand. Like I said, he's a show-off.

We raced down the logging road for a while and cut to the left, and down the "screamin' downhill-between-the-benches" we had to have hit thirty miles per hour. An "endo" here at that speed wouldn't be fun. We leapfrogged each other back and forth through the rocky "whoops" and I took him on the "crazy-uphill-by-the-tree." When the trail opened back up to the logging road we were dead even. Jim bunny hopped the big oak tree across the road by nearly a foot! I had to pop my front tire up and dig my big front chain ring (that's a sprocket to you hairy-legged non-bikers) into the tree and then grind up and over the tree until my back tire caught it. I almost went over the handlebars from not keeping the front tire up high enough when I hit the ground on the other side of the tree. Somehow, I managed to stay upright.

"Thank God for gyroscopic motion. Amen, brother!" I muttered to myself and the squirrel that ran across the trail in front of me.

Finally, after about six miles we were up the last hill and back to the boulder.

Jim cried out, "One more lap!" and kept on going.

I plowed in behind him holding my own. I looked at my heart rate monitor readout on my handlebars: *one hundred eighty three beats per minute!* That is about ninety percent my max and I had kept it there for about thirty minutes so far. Not bad for an old man. This time around he dropped me on the big oak. I didn't have enough left even to do a chain ring grind over it. I had to hop off my bike and climb over it dragging my bike along with me. Jim was waiting on me back at the boulder.

"What happened, old man?" he laughed.

"Whew!" I panted. "I got hung up on the tree again. One of these days you have to show me how to get over that thing. By the way, you know you're not but about fourteen years younger than me."

I laid my bike off the trail with the deraileur side up, which is proper bike etiquette. My legs felt like lead. I sat down on the boulder sucking on the tube in front of my face, which came up out of my jersey around to my back and into the water bag in my back jersey pocket. I felt my rear middle jersey pocket to make sure there was still plenty of water. I'd finished about a fourth of a liter, not enough.

"I was thinking," I said still breathing hard, "about the light 'Becca saw."

"Yeah?" Jim took his helmet off and handed me an energy bar.

"What if it was like sonoluminescence?"

"How, there was nothing in that vacuum chamber but vacuum?" Jim asked.

"When we get back to the lab Monday remind me to make you work out on the board how many different molecules are actually in that vacuum chamber, at least fifty times. Where did you get your Ph.D. anyway?" I scolded him.

"Okay, sure it's not a *perfect* vacuum, but how could there have been enough molecules in there to luminesce?" he asked.

"Just like sonoluminescence. With that you have a bunch of sound waves pressing a tiny amount of water and other additives into such a small ball that it gets it as hot as the sun for a microsecond or so. Hence, the little flashes of light. What if the dumbbells set up some kind of crazy electromagnetic field configuration that trapped enough of the particles from the vacuum chamber into a small enough ball that the same type of thing happened? Maybe the flash of light didn't cause the explosion but was a symptom of a bigger problem."

"You thought of all that while we were racing? No wonder you couldn't get over the tree. And those chain ring grinds are hell on your big chain ring by the way. I wish you would quit doing that, because I'm always the one who has to put the new one on." He paused for a second and shook his head. "You *are* focused, just not on riding," Jim said.

"I can't help it Jim. It was my fault that 'Becca got hurt. I can't put it out of my mind that I could've done something to prevent it."

"It was all our faults, Anson, not yours alone. You want to get it out of your mind for another hour? I know what'll do it." He looked down the trail and put the energy bar wrapper in his pocket. "Two laps the other way before it gets dark." He buckled his helmet and put his sunglasses back on.

"Fine with me. Double or nothing on the beer?"

He nodded and took off. He needed it this time. The other way means going up the "screaming downhill" at the end of each lap. Hills are my specialty. Going up them I mean. Going down them scares the living hell out of me.

We called it a draw. On the last lap we were dead even on the last "whoop" before the big uphill climb. Jim hit a rock just right and went over the handlebars. We were moving fast so I was worried that he was hurt. Jim rolled up on his feet laughing hard as he dusted himself off and wiped the blood from the big scrape on his left elbow.

"Cool!" he said.

"Kids!" I said.

We surveyed the damage to his bike and realized that his front rim was a wavy curve shape like a potato chip.

"Well, you really potato-chipped that one!" I told him. He popped the quick release skewer and took the wheel off the bike. Jim grabbed the wheel at the four and seven o'clock position and commenced to beating the thing against the ground. He rolled it around in his hands about ninety degrees and repeated the process. Finally, he held up a perfectly good wheel and then put it back on his bike.

The first time I saw that trick I thought, *Now ain't that the damnedest thing!* Since then, I've done it myself a million times. The problem is that the wheel, although back in round, is structurally very weak afterwards. Any good knock would potato-chip it again for sure. So we rode out two-up (again, for you civilians, that's side-by-side) talking about our next step for finding out what happened to 'Becca.

Monday I decided to go about reconstructing 'Becca's accident. That would be the only way to really see what happened. Nevertheless, it had to be done in a controlled manner this time. After a week or so of planning, we rented the huge vacuum chamber over at NASA MSFC. We hired a local alphabet soup contracting firm to help us set up the experiment. Finally, after weeks of trying to recreate the disaster, we did!

Apparently, some sort of chaotic resonance set up between all of the generators. This resonance field shielded the energy coupling system from allowing the energy to bleed off from the Casimir effect spheres. An analogy would be that we were filling up seven hundred little air tanks with a constant inflow of air at infinite pressure with no release valve. Once these tanks reached their stress limit, they exploded. From the sheer nature of the vacuum energy physics, these tanks had quite a large stress limit. I hadn't expected that.

In other words, the Clemons Dumbbells had a constant inflow

of energy into them, but they couldn't dissipate that energy fast enough. Final result: they exploded. I calculated that a piece of material smaller than could be seen by the human eye exploded with as much force as an eighth of a stick of dynamite. DARPA gave us more money.

The only slight problem with the new DARPA money is that the program all of the sudden became deeply classified. Security was tightened up and we had to hire security guards to sit at the office around the clock. There were a lot of retroactive security *issues* that had to be dealt with. I had worked security programs before and had a Secret clearance. God knows how high Tabitha's clearance went. And Jim and 'Becca were cleared from previous programs as well. The others were put on temporary "need to know" company clearances, but they still were only privy to proprietary information. It didn't take but about two months for Al and Sara to be cleared at the Secret level also. Johnny presented documents as proof of his clearance that were passed on to the Defense Security Service. He was cleared at Secret.

For some reason Tabitha put me in for a Top Secret clearance and some other clearance that I had never heard of. She had explained that if things worked out we could find much, much more money in the "black projects." It all sounded cool with me.

After a bit of experimentation and analyses, we figured out just how lucky Rebecca had been. 'Becca was lucky that the thick vacuum glass, the plexiglass shield, a metal enclosure at head level, and the computer at body level were between her and the explosion.

Once we figured out how to recreate the accident we went about figuring out how to prevent it. That was hard. We determined that it was very easy to set up the chaotic resonant field and very hard to dampen it. One of the subcontractors had the idea of designing each individual collector in an orientation that would cancel out the effect of the next one. Then we could construct them in stable pairs. This worked. I put Sara to working with 'Becca on this. 'Becca still needed another hand. Her bronchitis was acting up and you could tell it was wearing her down.

Finally, we were back on track for building the warp drive

experiment flight demonstrator. We left the setup in the NASA MSFC facility with hopes that we would soon be building a very big Casimir effect energy collector.

All of this time I had been giving Tabitha and Al the possible spacecraft requirements and general dimensions. The two of them began solid model simulations and finite element analysis of the concept vehicle. They also contracted out a lot of the work to some local shops.

The architecture of the spacecraft started out as empty boxes on the whiteboard with names of spacecraft components written in them. Then we expanded each box and filled it with larger boxes. It turns out that Tabitha is a super genius with systems integration and solid modeling for spacecraft design. Al is pretty sharp, himself. The two of them together were amazing and accomplished some of the best spacecraft engineering I had ever seen.

The problem wasn't the design or complexity, but the sheer size. The size of the damn thing kept growing. Sometime in November we decided that the only way to get the thing in orbit would be to either build it there or take it up on the Shuttle. Expendable Launch Vehicles (ELVs) were just not big enough. Tabitha called me after they figured this out.

"How much do you weigh?" she asked.

"Why?"

"So I can account for it in the mass budget for the mission."

"Hunh?" was the wittiest thing I could think of.

"Well, somebody has to deploy this damn thing. It ought to be the guy that invented it? Besides, there is budget now for a payload specialist." I could hear her smiling through the phone.

I tried and tried, I really came close, but in the end, I failed to shit a gold brick, which I said I would do if I ever made it to be an astronaut. It had never dawned on me that somebody might have to deploy this thing from the Space Shuttle. I always had envisioned some sort of ELV. To tell the truth, I expected to be about ninety by the time we ever figured out how to do the experiment, for sure not going on forty-two.

"What about you?" I asked Tabitha.

"Nope. I plan to be flying the Shuttle on NASA's dime," she said. You see, payload specialists aren't NASA employees and a company pays for their training and their ride. Taking me was a smart idea on Tabitha's behalf. Now both Tabitha and I could be there for the test.

"I love you!" I told her.

"I know." She laughed. Solo and Leia thoughts popped in my head. I'm sure she'd planned it that way.

We ended up hiring another subcontractor firm to help us with the spacecraft bus and the systems engineering and integration for the demonstrator. You would absolutely not believe the amount of paperwork required just to get something on board the Space Shuttle. It almost seemed like we would invent a better access to space vehicle before we had the dang thing qualified to fly in the Shuttle. It might have been easier to wait for the second generation reusable launch vehicle (2nd Gen RLV) being constructed via the Shuttle Replacement Initiative. However, that thing was falling behind schedule and over budget. After all, Congress changes its mind on funding for that program on a daily basis. In addition, it would have to be tested for a few years before payloads were put on it. It just wouldn't be ready in time. So, Space Shuttle it had to be.

First, we had to demonstrate that we could completely control the warp field and the energy systems working as one system in the environment chamber at NASA MSFC. That was a scaled experiment. The fact that all of this was now classified slowed down some of the progress due to security, but it sped up the process due to processes that could be sidestepped. Then we constructed the full-scale experiment: not actually warping just powering up to the available power level in the chamber, then down. Even though the power level for the warp field was at fractions of that required to actually drive the warp for an object the size of a spacecraft, the stress on the field coils were still tremendous. We couldn't figure out how with modern materials to support such huge stresses as would be caused by a full-scale warp bubble. A full-up test on the ground was out of the question. Besides, the power supply wasn't complete yet.

Once as much of the full-up tests as possible were complete, we had to start integrating all of these components into a spacecraft.

This part was complicated. Everything we used on the spacecraft had to have been spaceflight proven in some fashion or the other down to the last nut, washer, and bolt. This is where I relied on the experience of Huntsville, Alabama. There were a couple of local firms that could do this integration properly and at the right security levels. We ended up choosing the same company that built the lunar rovers forty years ago. The sheer size of this development project had grown to hundreds of people and millions of dollars. My program management skills were being pushed to their limits. I relied heavily on Tabitha.

By the time Thanksgiving rolled around, the scaled tests were almost complete. Rebecca was basically back to her old self again, although she was now four months behind on her black belt quest. The only scar that remained, after the laser treatments, was a hair-thin ring around her left ring finger. The engagement ring that Jim gave her on her birthday (October second), covered that up nicely.

Finally, Rebecca and Sara had started on the actual flight hardware pieces for the energy collector. This was going to take a while. It took them about a day to grow the prototype element, which was a ten-centimeter by ten-centimeter wafer with four hundred layers in it. Each layer is four thousandths of a centimeter thick. The final system will have to be a rectangular solid about three meters by three meters by nine meters. We chose these dimensions so it would fit in the Space Shuttle payload bay, which is about four meters by four meters by eighteen meters. Effectively we're building three cubes three meters on a side and connecting them linearly. At the rate it took us to actually build the microscopic prototype it would have taken about twenty-two thousand years to make the three cubes.

'Becca and Sara hooked up with one of Sara's friends who works at a local printed circuit board company. They make tens of thousands of computer motherboards a day. By Christmas they had set up the first automated assembly line process to construct Clemons Dumbbell etched boards. The first few weeks were dismal failures and the assembly line was constantly shutting down or failing in some manner. Worst of all, 'Becca found that the quality of the products they had made didn't meet specs. She had to explain to them the severe catastrophic possibilities of Clemons Dumbbells not built to spec. She told then the horror story of having her finger blown off and embellished it very well. Years of being around a lying scoundrel like me paid off.

Sara worked that company over pretty good until they produced a line of to-spec products. They managed to get a final line output of about eighteen thousand boards a day with about five and a half of a percent quality control. This meant that we had to throw away about a thousand boards a day. That leaves us with seventeen thousand boards in a day. This meant that nearly a half a million boards are just thrown in the recycle bin. We all considered the problem, but just didn't have the manpower or the resources to worry with that little amount of quality control. Each board cost about a dollar to make. So the final cost of the cube would be about eight million dollars plus the half million plus that we have to throw away. It would've taken at least a half million dollars in man-hours to figure out how to reduce the quality error.

'Becca was about to make the wrong decision and spend some money to fix the problem. I would like to say that I caught the mistake. But it was Johnny that figured out that it would be better just to bite the bullet on this one. It was a good call. Johnny had spent all those years on construction jobs learning how best to use resources. It's easier for a contractor to throw away a half of a two-by-four that cost three dollars than it is to spend an hour of labor at ten dollars an hour trying to find a use for it.

Our biggest issue with the energy collection cubes, or ECCs, was safety. All of the bad boards had the potential of building up explosives energies. Sara figured out that a very high electric discharge through a board would basically weld the concentric spheres to each other and short out the circuit. This rendered the Clemons Dumbbells into a smoking pile. 'Becca pointed out to her the following very important information.

"Electrical Technicians Corollary Number One: Electronics runs on smoke. Once the smoke is removed from them, they will no longer function properly." Using this corollary, Sara could then conclude that the boards would no longer operate as an ECC subcomponent.

We thought there was an error in this corollary once when a recycle bin exploded and blew a hole in the storage room wall into the adjacent ladies room. The niece of the company president happened to be in there at the time. She was okay, but messy, wet, and scared and . . . no, wait a minute, she was *really* messy.

After investigating the accident (ha! pardon the pun) Sara and 'Becca found that that board hadn't been shorted out (Sara likes to say "electrocuted").

'Becca started in on the vice president of the company.

"You may be able to get away with a half million bad boards a year." She stopped and took a hit off of her albuterol inhaler. She caught her breath and continued, "But you can absolutely not get away with one single board not being shorted out! Ever!"

Had OSHA ever gotten wind of what we were doing, there would've been hell to pay. Fortunately, all of this effort operated under the DARPA money and everyone working on it was under at least a Secret clearance. The person who had made the mistake of not shorting out the board was fired, probably because of the company president's niece.

'Becca and Sara kept the ECC effort running smoothly from then on. We expected to have the ECCs delivered in a little less than a year and a half. Jim, Al, and I were working the spacecraft design while Tabitha and I were working the mission plan. The spacecraft was coming along pretty good. The problem was that we couldn't figure out how to put the warp field generator or WFG on top of the ECCs and have it fit in the Space Shuttle payload bay.

"Then there is the problem with the bus, the C and DH systems, the ACS, and the comm systems. Where do they go?" Al was fairly frantic by now.

"What if we distribute all of that around the ECCs?" Jim said.

I put in my two cents. "I don't know about you guys but I think that would create a whole new research program for distributed spacecraft systems." I decided we needed an expert's opinion. "Tabitha! Hey, Tabitha, you got a sec?" I yelled down the hall.

She put her head in the door. "What's up!"

"We still can't figure out where to put all of the systems. I mean, we finished the WFG a month ago but have no idea how to attach it to the ECCs and get it in the Shuttle," Jim told her.

"Much less the other systems." Al added.

"So don't attach them," she replied and turned back toward her office. "Haven't you guys ever heard of EVAs? Sheesh. What do y'all do in here all day anyway? Anson, you didn't think you were just going along for the ride did you?" She said this very sarcastically as she went back down the hall. We just looked at each other with our chins on the table.

"Okay, is it just me, or does everybody else feel really stupid about now?" Jim asked.

"Don't beat yourselves up. She practically built the last few modules of the ISS on extravehicular activities herself. It *was* very obvious to her what to do." I laughed. "Amazing," I added as I shook my head back and forth.

The main design problems were finally worked out. We would build the thing on orbit from three subsections. The subsections consisted of the warp field generator, the energy collection cubes, and the spacecraft bus. We bought a bus from one of the commercial spacecraft bus manufacturers and then tailored it to our specific needs. We decided to separate the three ECCs by one hundred twenty degrees and place the WFG in the center. The WFG would be encased in a cylindrical composite container about one meter in diameter and about three meters long. We then decided to suspend the ECCs from the WFG cylinder by support booms. Attached to one end of the WFG cylinder will be the spacecraft bus. The communications antenna attached to the outside of the bus will deploy to one meter in diameter once the spacecraft is powered up. The attitude control system (ACS) and the other science instruments all will be packaged in a cube-shaped container at the base of the rectangular-shaped bus. Two small spherical pressure tanks were added on each side of the science box to house the fuel and oxidizer for the ACS. Small arcjet thrusters were then placed all around the spacecraft. The final design was in three easy to snap together chunks.

That is what I thought, anyway. Then, six months later I tried to put a full-scale mockup together in the full EVA gear in the neutral buoyancy tank at NASA Johnson Space Center. Tabitha ended up having to help me. It was a two-man, uh two-person, job for certain. She would be the only other astronaut on board not already tasked to the max for other jobs and who was "read onto the DOD/NASA program need to know list." Unless you consider flying the Space Shuttle a job. I hadn't known it, but Tabitha had continued to fly more than fifteen hours a month all this time to maintain her currency. I had to start flying with her at least four hours a month. I say that like it was a chore. I love to fly. I got my instrument rating by the time I finished undergraduate school and had been to more fly-ins than you could shake a stick at. But this was *really* flying!

We would get our hours by flying back and forth between Houston, Texas or Cape Kennedy, Florida and Huntsville, Alabama. Fly out to Houston to do some more training. Fly back to Huntsville to keep the construction, testing, and integration of the spacecraft components in order. Then back to Houston. Then back to Huntsville. Then to Kennedy for payload integration meetings and training. Every now and then there would be a flight out to Pasadena, California to JPL or to Baltimore-Washington International to Goddard, HQ, or other government entity buildings. We were burning the candle from both ends, the middle, and from several other places.

Things were rather chaotic during that time. Tabitha and I tried to run or do Kardio Kickboxing type workouts together as often as we could. I got on the road bike and went to karate every chance I got, which wasn't often. Mountain biking and fighting were completely out of the question now though. No way I was going to risk an injury that would scrub me off the spaceflight mission.

Between Jim, Rebecca, and myself we were able to cover my classes at the university, but we did have to schedule quite a few make-up sessions. The chairman of the physics department saw what was happening and suggested that I take a leave from teaching until after the mission. That was a load off my mind. He assured me that my job would be there as long as I wanted it. Why not? What university wouldn't want to boast having an astronaut on the faculty?

The first ECC was completed by June. To celebrate, Jim and

Rebecca got married! They had asked Tabitha and me about it beforehand.

"We don't have a lot of money for it and neither of us has any family to speak of," Jim was saying. "Think we ought to do a small church thing or just elope or what?" 'Becca wasn't too keen on the elope idea for some reason.

"I don't know. Its y'all's wedding," I responded, helpfully.

"'Becca, what do you want?" Tabitha asked.

"I just want something to remember," she said.

"If you had a formal kind of thing, who would you really want to invite?" Tabitha asked. We had some ideas of our own. But we hadn't spoken a word of it to the kids.

"Really, just Sara, Al, Johnny, Jim's folks—but they won't come—a handful of people from the dojo, you would be a bridesmaid, and I was hoping Anson would give me away." 'Becca looked sheepishly at me.

Jim chimed in, "He can't give you away and be the best man, too!"

"Sure he can," 'Becca said giving Jim a look that he better start getting used to.

"I would be honored," I said to both of them. Then I asked them, "Are you sure that is all you wanted to invite? Can you give me a number?"

She counted on her hands for a second and said, "I don't know—fifteen or so?" She shrugged her shoulders and looked at Jim.

"Tim. Don't forget Tim," Jim replied.

"Okay," I said, "Let's assume twenty." I looked at Tabitha. "Colonel, you have any bright ideas?"

"Don't colonel me!" she started. "Look at this." She handed them brochures from a cruise line. "The big dolt there and I did some checking. If we have a party of fifteen to twenty-five go on one of these three-night, four-day things it would only run us about two hundred seventy-nine dollars per person. Then you two would swap boats when it returned to port and then do another four-night, five-day cruise for your honeymoon."

"Yeah and they have wedding services either on the boat or on one of the islands. They take care of everything." I added.

'Becca was almost in tears. She grabbed her inhaler and took a puff. She had hardly used that thing in months.

She wiped her eyes and said, "That's beautiful but we can't afford that." Jim said the same.

"I'm sorry, did I forget to mention that it's on us? We already talked it over and we want to do this for you. Bob and Alisa said they would pay their own way and so did some of the other karate folks. And I have some money just lying around collecting dust anyway," I joked.

Tabitha smiled, "Goofball! I do have one request. I would like to bring my daughter along."

'Becca was crying full flow now. "I would love to meet her. In fact she can be a bridesmaid, too!"

Jim punched me on the shoulder. "When you get back from outer space, I'm kicking your ass!" He laughed.

That's pretty much how the wedding went. Almost everybody but Sara paid his or her own way and we got a good deal on the price of the cruise. Tabitha and I covered all the other stuff. We ended up splitting about seven grand between the two of us and most of that was the open bar! Jim and 'Becca seemed happier than I had ever seen them. As a second wedding gift, I gave them each a bonus and a new pay scale. After all, the company was doing a lot more business now, mostly because of them. I had planned on giving them raises earlier for graduation presents, but we had been so busy that administrative details were falling behind. The bonuses were the retroactive raises plus a little. We were all very emotional and 'Becca had to take a hit of albuterol. The ocean air seemed to help 'Becca's respiratory condition and she didn't use her inhaler but that once during the whole cruise.

We all had a great time. When we stopped at Key West, I made a point to visit a certain restaurant and tip the bartenders well. We all needed the short break, anyway. My mind was fried from the round-the-clock hours we had been putting in. I could tell Tabitha's was also and she looked even more beautiful in a bathing suit and smile, although I'm not upset with the way she looks in her colonel's outfit or her astronaut gear.

I didn't mention her daughter, did I? If you can imagine Tabitha twenty years younger, there you go. Same bright red hair, same big brown anime eyes, and the temper and spunk to match. Instead of the Texas accent that her mother sports, Anne Marie grew up in Florida where Tabitha's parents had moved for retirement and to be close to Tabitha when she launched. I fell in love with her from the moment I laid eyes on her. Although Tabitha and her parents had done a bang-up job raising her, you could tell that she didn't have a father or big brother figure in her life. Maybe that's why we got along so well.

At one point I showed her how to get out of a chokehold; she wanted to see more. So, I gave her a plastic butter knife and told her to stab me in the stomach with it. After she said, "Uncle!" I helped her up off the deck of the promenade and asked her if she wanted the knife back. Jim told me to quit showing off. Anne Marie stuck her tongue out at him and held onto my arm.

She kept asking me, "Could you whup that guy? What about that guy? Him?" I told her that that wasn't why I learned karate. Then she pointed at Bob and asked if I could beat him. "He don't look that tough," she said. I laughed and so did 'Becca, who was eavesdropping in on our conversation.

I reassured her that I and three or four other guys couldn't "whup" Bob in a million years. Jim and I have tried several times. We always went home rubbing our knots, bruises, and bumps wondering just what in the hell were we thinking.

"You ever heard the expression, I'll put knots on your head faster than you can rub 'em?" I asked Anne Marie. "Well, believe me, he can."

After kissing the bride "so long" and shaking the groom's hand, Tabitha, Anne Marie, and I left the Port of Miami and I drove up to Titusville near the Cape to see Tabitha's parents. We stayed at her parents' for another two days, Tabitha took care of some business at NASA, and then we flew from the Cape back to Huntsville. A few times Tabitha let me fly the trainer. Pretty cool! It wouldn't be long before I would have enough hours in the trainers to be rated to fly it since Tabitha is a certified instructor.

We altered our flight plan a little and flew to an unrestricted airspace where I practiced maneuvers. Tabitha took me through some stalls and slow flight. Then she had me do some S turns and some three-sixties and seven-twenties. After a while she showed me how to do a simple barrel roll and a few other neat tricks that you can't do in a Cessna. Then it was back homeward.

Tabitha took over coming into Huntsville International. It was socked in with rain and we had to land under ILS (instrument landing system). I have an instrument rating and I know how to do that in a Cessna 172 prop job but not in a T-38 jet. I was glad to have her at the controls.

When we got back to my house we were exhausted. Friday *meowed* at me for being gone so long. Tabitha stroked her on the head.

"Hello kitty. That's a pretty kitty," she told Friday.

We watched the idiot box a bit and got real friendly with each other on the couch. Finally, Tabitha and I went to bed and didn't budge until near lunch the next day. Why is it that you're usually more tired after vacation than you were before you went? Isn't the point of the vacation to rest and relax? Oh well, we had to get back to work tomorrow and from herein there would be no more resting. There was only ten months left before our scheduled launch date.

The line in *Aliens* where Sergeant Apone grunts, "Okay, Marines, you know the drill. Assholes and elbows let's move it!" rang in my head as I drifted off, a big smile on my face.

➤ CHAPTER 7

They came and woke us up about four thirty. I was dreaming about my whiteboard again. Somewhere in the dream, Jim came in the study and began erasing the board.

"You just don't get it. There are other things that are more important," he said.

Then good old Albert Einstein looked at us both and said, "Mathematics sucks!" He finished the beer he was drinking and threw it at the fireplace. Then he morphed into a large purple emu and ran off trying to fly the whole time.

Jim looked at me and said, "Hey man, it's your dream." Then he shrugged his shoulders and finished cleaning the whiteboard.

Of course, I was thoroughly sore at him for erasing my life's work from the slate of my life. But then, Tabitha's voice came through the haze of the dream and I saw not the clean whiteboard that Jim had left me, rather it was a different one. One that contained many solutions, which were underlined.

I woke up.

"Anson! Wake up! You're having a nightmare again," she said as she shook me.

"Yeah, uh, I guess so." I blinked furiously and woke up a little shaky. She helped pull me out of bed.

"Did you sleep much at all?" She looked concerned.

"I slept enough to get me through today," I assured her. There was a knock on the door and a voice telling us that we were running a little late. We quickly showered and were down the hall for our final flight checkups. This took about twenty minutes.

For breakfast I had insisted that I would have steak and eggs just like the Mercury guys did.

"We don't do that anymore," Tabitha ribbed me, but that didn't matter to me. I was having steak and eggs, just like I had planned it since I was eight years old.

At about T-minus five hours and fifty minutes, out on the pad, the Space Shuttle OMS propellant tank had been repressurized and the solid rocket booster nozzle flex bearing and nozzle-to-case seals joint temperature requirements were checked off by the prep crew, while I was trying hard not to fall back to sleep in my eggs. Once, Tabitha gave me a swift elbow in the ribs to bolster my alertness.

For the past three weeks I had probably slept about forty-five hours. Something had gotten my old graduate school insomnia back full fling. Tabitha promised to help me keep it a secret, although I could tell it gave her serious ethical issues, her being the mission commander and all.

The trigger for the insomnia must have been all of the intense studying that I'd been doing. The past six months was nothing but study, study, study, then practice, practice, practice, and then study, study, study, some more. A lot like graduate school in many ways, but mostly in that there is no time for sleeping. It was probably like riding a bike; my body just remembered how to stay awake for long periods of time.

I tried every trick I knew to combat the problem. Two nights previously Tabitha wore me out on the basketball court, then on the track, and then in (ahem) bed, and she gave me twice the normal dosage of diphenhydramine hydrochloride, which usually knocks me right out. While she dozed off I reread Feynman's *QED* and then L. Sprague De Camp's *The Ancient Engineers*.

When that didn't work, I turned to one of the more credible alien conspiracy investigative books I've found. It's good for entertainment. All of those cattle mutilation pictures in that book confused me. Why is it that alien conspiracy folks believe that extraterrestrials would travel billions of miles just to kill cows, make neat patterns in fields, and leave pink bismuth stains on people? I've never really fallen for the whole UFO conspiracy thing myself. However, the thing that has always bothered me most is, who, what, and how is all of this stuff getting done? Are there that many nuts who need attention out there or is there more to this thing? I don't know.

And how did all the UFO stuff impact religious beliefs? I mean, aliens or gods? I had asked Tabitha what she thought about it the next morning. She looked at me with a sour look on her face.

"Anson, don't you have flight hardware manuals that you should be studying?" she said.

"Really, I need to know," I asked her.

"You're asking about what I believe. Well, I'll tell you." She paused and placed her hands on her hips.

"I believe that nobody has a clue what really happens after you die. Not the pope, not the preacher at my folks' church, not some Tibetan monk who has meditated and pondered all his life—no one! I believe that religion is personal and is for every individual to decide for his or herself. Mostly it's none of anybody's business what I believe. I believe that public prayer is for show. It should be done in private and kept between you and your supreme deity, whoever or whatever it may be. I believe that maybe one day we might find some of these answers through scientific experimentation and observation." She paused for air.

"But, most importantly, and as your mission commander, you better hear me now. I believe that you have spent most of your life trying to get an experiment flown in space and to ride along with that experiment. And finally, I believe that you had better get back to studying your preflight, flight, and postflight checklists before you get the biggest chance of your life to really, and I mean really, screw the pooch!"

That was the last we talked about religion for a long time.

That was two nights ago. The following night I had taken her advice and studied my spaceflight hardware parameters. By the time the sun rose, I was going over the mission plans, chronology, and EVA requirements. I had pretty much memorized them in the past few weeks. Studying never hurts. At six-thirty I got back in bed and was able to get about an hour of sleep while Tabitha was getting ready.

This was pretty much my routine for last night as well. Except last night, after studying the mission, I did a little recreational reading again. Mission commander be damned. This time I started with the King James version of the Holy Bible. Actually, I only read my favorite part. You know the part where the space fighter craft powered by four rocket-based combined cycle engines comes down to Earth and the pilot sitting in the cockpit uses the spacecraft's loudspeakers to tell the primitive Earthling that he must go enlist the devotion of all these various countries. When the poor primitive admits that he cannot speak all of the languages in those countries, the alien inside the spacecraft solves this problem real easy.

"No problem eat this," the alien tells him.

A little robot hand comes out of the spacecraft and gives the guy a scroll with a nanotechnology spread. Once he eats the scroll and the nanotechnology reworks the primitive's brain, "lo and behold" he could speak the various tongues of these nations. Then the alien pilot spins up the turbojets in the engines making the great rushing sound and then flies off on a pillar of flame from the rocket engines. Cool!

I never studied the literary history of the theological texts, but those guys could sure give Heinlein a run for his money. I finally got bored with reading and found myself at the desk in our quarters scribbling notes.

By the time I had solved the entropy equations for a spinning neutron star and got to the part where there is some mass/energy missing due to gravity shielding by the degenerate matter of its interior, a ray of light peaked through the curtains. I realized that I had better go to bed. Then an hour and fifty minutes later Tabitha was waking me up from my Einstein/whiteboard nightmare.

At about T-minus three hours the complete crew complement, including yours truly, was having a weather briefing inflicted upon us, while a whole bunch of smart guys were busy outside making sure that the SRB tracking systems were being powered up. It had taken me forty-four years to get here. I figured I could wait an hour or two more. On the other hand, I wasn't quite sure I could make it through this boring weather briefing without falling to sleep again.

Finally, the countdown was resumed and we left the O and C building for the launch pad. I still don't know what O and C stands for—I assumed it was operations and checkout, but I wasn't sure. I know it was in the tons of material I was supposed to have memorized, but I didn't think it would matter what they call that damn building once I was in space.

The six of us astronauts began the ingress into the flight crew seats. Tabitha took her place in the front right seat beside Major Rayford Donald, the pilot. After that were Carla Yeats and Roald Sveld. She is a Canadian and he is a Norse astronaut both headed for the ISS for a few months. Lieutenant Terence Fines and I sat in the very back. He was a payload specialist also. He had plans of doing some microgravity experiment involving radar pointing and tracking state-of-the-art for the next generation national missile defense system. Most of his stuff was classified like mine.

Just why was my mission classified? Wouldn't the whole world want to know that humans had learned how to breach the speed of light barrier, thus, enabling a whole new era of space travel? It was my guess that it was a political move on NASA's behalf. If this experiment turned out to be a big blunder, nobody would be the wiser. If it worked, then we could do a better demonstration in a few months or years and make a big promotion of it. There was also the turmoil of the energy system and the possible weapons capabilities that these entailed. And would we want FTL travel in the hands of just anybody in the world right now? What if some nut decided to fly a spacecraft at ten times light speed into the Earth? What would happen? Of course, there was always the fact that DARPA had some say so in this matter, since they funded the lion's share of the effort. But really, what would happen if some nut did fly an FTL missile into the Earth?

Well, actually the spaceship would never interact with the Earth because of the physics involved. A couple of guys wrote a paper back in the early part of the decade called something like "The

View from the Bridge" or something similar. The paper showed that no data (which would include matter) could be transmitted to the interior of the warp bubble while it was active due to causality violations. Of course, the authors of that paper had no idea how to create a warp bubble. Just like our electron experiment, we had to set up the electrons to flow just inside where the bubble would be and then turn on the warped field. If we hadn't done this, the electrons would never have made it inside the bubble. The paper does allow for data or matter to escape the bubble at right angles to the travel direction. We had hoped to see some electrons deflecting off the inside of the bubble and out of its side to the electron detectors. As you recall we had no such luck for other reasons.

I digress. So, assume this nut flies the FTL craft into the Earth. What would happen? The warp field would push *anything*, and I mean anything, in its path right out of its way. The warped field would be stressed by the impact and eventually collapse the spacecraft inside the bubble. Most likely, it wouldn't poke a hole all the way through the planet before it destroyed itself either. The stresses on the warp device would be tremendous—it would become a self-eating watermelon. At any rate, I wouldn't want to be either the nut in the FTL craft or an innocent unsuspecting bystander on Earth who was walking down the street of some city a hundred miles away from impact. The damage could be catastrophic. Maybe that is why my mission is classified. That led me to wondering what if it wasn't a meteorite that killed the dinosaurs. What if it was a spacecraft that ran on iridium? The science fiction story possibilities here were outrageous.

My mind was spinning with these possibilities. Once they got me strapped in after ingress I had nothing to do really but lie there on my back anyway. During the Orbiter close-out procedure a light came on, back at the O and C building I assumed, that said there was a pressure leak in the crew module. The engineers and technicians outside the spacecraft on the tower attempted several times to verify if the light was correct or not. This took about three extra hours.

Apparently, the entire payload bay had to be brought to a particular pressure and temperature before they could make an accurate measurement. Boy, it sure will be nice when we develop spaceships like in the movies, where we just hop in and fly off to Dagobah or Naboo, or to pick up our date, the green animal woman slave from Orion. Until then, space travel will be damned complicated, risky, expensive, inconvenient, time consuming, difficult, and a hell of a lot more uncomfortable. Outside the spacecraft there were smart folks running around completing complicated tasks that took three Master's degrees in engineering just to qualify to watch. I didn't really know about all of this because by then my mind had stopped spinning. The adrenaline rush of being on the launch pad had worn off and I had fallen sound asleep. In fact, all but the flight surgeon cut my mic because I was snoring so loudly.

T-minus nine minutes and holding. I woke up to, "Dr. Clemons . . . Anson!"

"Um hem . . . Payload Specialist Clemons is go, Flight!" I snapped. Tabitha held back a giggle.

"Glad to hear it, Anson. I was beginning to think you were going to sleep through the whole mission." I could just imagine the smile on her face. I didn't respond further. The next eight or so minutes were exciting. The vocal traffic picked up between launch control and the commander and pilot seats.

To me it was mostly a great big blur. At T-minus four minutes I recall hearing something about "Verify SSME valve movement in the close direction."

"Verify SSME valve movement in the close direction. Check!" Major Donald replied.

Then at T-minus two minutes and fifty seconds there was something about terminating the GOX vent hood purge. And transfer the PRSD to internal reactants. Tabitha ordered all of us to close our visors and then rechecked the LH2 replenish. Then a lot of things on the checklist began zooming by, very fast.

```
RETRACT GOX VENT HOOD GLS CGLS (Auto)
T-MINUS 02 MINUTES AND 35 SECONDS PRSD TRANS-
    FER TO INTERNAL REACTANTS GLS CGLS (Auto)
T-MINUS 02 MINUTES AND 00 SECONDS CLOSE
    VISORS
```

T-MINUS 01 MINUTES AND 57 SECONDS TERMINATE
   LH2 REPLENISH GLS CGLS (Auto)
CLOSE LH2 TOPPING VALVE GLS CGLS (Auto)
CLOSE LH2 VENT VALVE GLS CGLS (Auto)
T-MINUS 01 MINUTES AND 46 SECONDS INITIATE LH2
   PREPRESS GLS CGLS (Auto)
T-MINUS 00 MINUTES AND 55 SECONDS PERFORM
   SRB FWD MDM LOCKOUT GLS CGLS (Auto)
T-MINUS 00 MINUTES AND 50 SECONDS GROUND
   POWER REMOVAL
T-MINUS 00 MINUTES AND 48 SECONDS CLOSE LOX
   & LH2 OUTBOARD FILL & DRAIN VALVES GLS CGLS
   (Auto)
DEACTIVATE SRB JOINT HEATERS
GLS CGLS (Auto)
T-MINUS 00 MINUTES AND 31 SECONDS GLS GO FOR
   AUTO SEQUENCE GLS CGLS (Auto)
ARM CUT OFF GLS CGLS (Manual)
INITIATE RSLS GLS CGLS (Auto)
ORB VENT DOOR SE9 START GPC CGLS (Auto)

You get the idea.

Finally, at twenty seconds things started to happen that I could feel, physically through small vibrations or large jolts. Down below us the launch pad exhaust reflection pool was being flooded with water to suppress the sound waves from the lift-off. Just ten seconds later the SRB safety inhibits were removed. Three point four seconds after that main engine three was given the start command. My teeth started chattering as I was lunged forward then backward violently. The ship had jumped about a meter. I had been warned that the Shuttle would sway a meter or two at main engine firing. We affectionately refer to this as the "twang" because the initial reaction of the spacecraft structure is to "twang" like a tuning fork when it is struck. To an outside observer, the shuttle seems to sway a bit. But to an inside observer . . .

"Sway hell," I mumbled to myself. It was more like being thrown in a car wreck.

Nine seconds later I couldn't hear a thing and I felt like I weighed five hundred and seventy pounds or more. What a ride! I tried to raise my arms once just to test how heavy they were. It wasn't easy. I was even more impressed by the space jockeys in the front two seats. I could barely blink. How the heck were they flying this thing? A few seconds later we went through throttle up and then to SRB separation and I couldn't remember a happier day in my life. This is what I had always wanted to do since I was a kid.

A moment of calm came over me. I was in a daze and things around me seemed like they weren't real but more of a dream. When the final jolt from the External Tank being dropped hit me, I was sure this was real. As the Orbiter made its way to a stable orbit in low earth orbit (LEO) I really had nothing to do, for the next few minutes anyway. So, I went back to sleep.

When Fines finally woke me up we were at stable LEO and were given the okay to get out of our flight gear. We helped each other with our suits as we played with the microgravity effects on things. Like my stomach for instance. I lost my steak and eggs almost immediately. Fines wasn't amused. So, I threw up on him again.

This time he was amused to the point where he lost his break-fast. We had a lot of fun repeating this procedure for the next hour or two. Finally, the nausea subsided to drunken spins. I wished that I had some of my grandmother's "dizzy pills." I hadn't spun like that since playing quarters with tequila that night in undergraduate school after we won the Iron Bowl.

After several hours of the spins followed by nausea followed by a severe pain in my ego, all of the symptoms disappeared and I felt wonderful. I even offered to help clean up but the flight surgeon had ordered both Fines and myself to take a shot of motion sickness medication and try to take a nap. I slept like a baby. In other words, I pissed and moaned the whole time.

A few hours later Tabitha wandered, or drifted rather, back to see me. I was absolutely fine at this point, showing no symptoms other than feeling like a kid on his birthday. In fact, I was near the aft viewport looking down at the Earth in awe. She actually startled me when she came up behind me.

"Feeling better?"

"Yeah, lots!" I assured her. She put her hand on my shoulder and steadied herself. I still hadn't been able to do that. What a pro this Colonel Ames was.

"Beautiful, isn't it? I'll never get tired of seeing that." She looked at me with her puppy-dog eyes then kissed me on the cheek. She whispered in my ear, "Feel better." Tabitha kicked of the wall and did a backward flip into a Superman style flight in the other direction. She looked back over her shoulder at me. "Since you seem to be feeling up to it, why don't you contact your ground support console and go through a postlaunch and preflight check of your experiment hardware as per the mission schedule? You're about four hours behind. And do me a favor."

"Yeah, sure. What do you need?" I asked.

"Stop looking out the window until you're caught up and back on the mission timeline," she scolded me with the Colonel voice. I was tempted to say, "Yes, Colonel!" but thought better of it.

I found my way to my laptop and brought it online for checklists. Velcroing in and donning my headset, I punched up the frequency for my ground support console operator. We were somewhere over the Indian Ocean at the time but either ground relay or TDRS would patch the signal back home. Jim was riding the console back at the Huntsville Operations Support Center or HOSC as it is affectionately referred to.

"Hi Jim! I guess I need to make up some lost time here and get the postlaunch and preflight started," I told him.

"I hear you are bulimic these days, trying to fit in a new prom dress," Jim kidded me.

"Just trying to watch my girlish figure. You know how it is. Actually, I think the colonel slipped some ipecac into my steak and eggs. How's everyone dirtside?"

"For the most part better than you. Let's get started."

"Roger that, Jim. Okay, I've got no outside tolerance range parameters from my sensor suite here. Does your telemetry agree?"

The postlaunch and preflight took the next three or so hours to assure each of us that the components of the warp drive demonstrator, we had been calling Zephram, had indeed survived the launch and the exposure to the space environment at LEO. No powered tests other than the motherboard of the spacecraft bus and the sensor suite could be made because the fields created by the ECC devices would be so large that the internal instruments of the Orbiter would be affected. That would be bad. Also, the device was in five separate pieces in the Payload Bay and wasn't an integrated spacecraft at this point. Jim and I wished Zephram a good night and I said I would chat with Jim in two sleep cycles.

We had to make a pit stop at the ISS before construction of Zephram could begin. I had completed my checklists and I was now a fifth wheel. I located Colonel Ames in the middeck eating area.

"Payload Specialist Clemons on schedule Colonel," I saluted her and laughed. She didn't seem amused.

"Can it, Anson. Have you eaten anything?"

"Uh, not sure that's a good idea." I hesitated at the thought of nausea and spins coming back.

"We don't need you passing out from low blood sugar. Eat!" she more or less ordered me. I wondered if she was giving the other astronauts as much of her attention or if I was just being a big baby—the word *rookie* came to mind.

"Okay, I'll eat. Just stop pampering me, okay."

"Anson." She clenched her jaw and I could tell she was changing her mind about what she was going to say. She started over.

"Listen. Just do your job, okay? No ego. If you feel the least bit funny, I don't want you on an EVA barfing all in your suit. Just do your job. I *am* doing mine by telling you this."

"We have nearly two days. I have acclimated almost completely now. I'll be fine," I told her. To prove it I squeezed out a bite of a peanut butter and jelly sandwich and watched it float in front of me at over eighteen thousand miles per hour. Since I was moving along at the same speed and Newton's First Law—or in General Relativity speak, we were on the same geodesic—was working as expected, I leaned forward and then gulped it down. No problem. I finished my first meal in microgravity and prepared for a sleep cycle. Tabitha didn't say two more words to me that day.

Fines, on the other hand, must have been feeling better, too.

He must also have been bored. He talked endlessly about his super polymer that when super cooled allowed for state-of-the-art piezoelectric micromotion control. His work would enable a whole new era of pointing accuracy. Not only would it be beneficial to military applications but to any space based platform. A modification of the Next Generation Space Telescope with his device would increase the camera long-term exposure times by a factor of ten to a hundred. This in turn would increase the number of objects that deep sky astronomy would be able to image by orders of magnitude.

It was all very interesting and exciting. But, thank God he finally shut up! I presently dozed off for my first real sleep cycle in space. The nap I had previously didn't count because I'd been sick out of my mind. This time I had no trouble getting comfortable and dozing off. What a relief from the past few weeks. *Tomorrow the ISS*, I thought calmly.

➢ CHAPTER 8

I was looking out the window whether Colonel Ames liked it or not. The International Space Station loomed over as we approached the Universal Docking Module. Television just doesn't give you a feel for how immense the ISS really is. As you get closer you can tell that parts of it were made by different countries. The Russian components are either black or shiny. ESA and NASDA modules are shiny. The majority of the space station is white, these sections being made by the United States of America. Although the space station looks like a jumbled mish mash made by several different manufacturers, it does look like it was designed with some sort of madness to its designer's method.

I held on to a computer terminal stand as we docked, expecting a jolt. I never felt a thing. Ray and Tabitha knew what they were doing up front. A period of protocol passed (I assumed pressure equalization) and we were all allowed access to the station. I roamed wherever I could go. I bumped into a fellow from Japan and I realized that I was in the Japanese Experiment Module. I asked if there were any experiments going on outside mounted to the "back-porch."

Wang Che, as I gathered was his name, told me that, "We had a marfunction on the Lemote Manipuratol system yestelday.

It damaged the terescope plimaly millol and seized the tlacking motols togethel."

"You don't say," I responded. "What caused it?"

"Not sule. But, we are wolking on it," he replied.

My trek through Russian territory was about the same, so I returned to American soil, uh aluminum and composites, and just hung out. Tabitha finally relaxed a little. She introduced me to one of the astronauts who would be going home with us, since Carla and Roald were staying behind.

"Anson Clemons, this is Tracy Edmunds. Tracy has been up here for going on three months," Tabitha informed me.

"Wow! Are you ready to go home yet?"

"Yeah, I miss my husband and kids," she told me with a smile. Tabitha giggled a bit.

"Anson, this is Malcom Edmunds, Tracy's husband." Tabitha laughed. Getting the joke, I shook Malcom's hand.

"Nice to meet you. You better hurry home. I think your wife is looking for you. Are your kids here, too?"

"The eight-year-old really wanted to come, believe me."

Tracy shrugged, winked at Malcom and said, "I don't know why they wouldn't let me bring her."

I could tell that Tabitha must have known the infamous eight-year-old, since she responded with an outburst of laughter and then, "ISS ain't ready for that type of malfunction yet."

We talked for a while longer and then Malcom and Tracy began to ingress to the Space Shuttle.

Tabitha held my arm. "Wait a second, Anson."

"What's up?"

"I want to know what you think about something." She looked at me seriously. I couldn't tell if these were her Colonel eyes or her Tabitha eyes. She'd make one hell of a card player. Actually, I had heard she *was* one.

"Well, *something* is a rather broad topic. Not sure what I think about it. Could you narrow it down a little?"

"Okay smart guy. The Japanese wrecked the telescope on the 'back-porch' yesterday." Colonel Ames (not Tabitha) said. That solved that.

"I know. Wang told me. Or is it Che? Do Japanese use their

first name as their first name or their last name as their first name?" I asked, and then repeated it to myself to make sure I said it correctly.

"Wangche is his surname. And he's not Japanese, he's Chinese— it's a political thing. And Wangche was supposed to use that telescope tomorrow to image a planned rendezvous of two satellites. They're meeting up for the first in-space robotic satellite repair." Tabitha spoke as if she were giving a debriefing.

"Hold on a minute. Does it have to happen tomorrow? I mean, why can't they wait?" I was perplexed by the dilemma.

"The microspacecraft has used up most of its fuel supply to achieve a matching orbit with the satellite. More than a few more days of attitude corrections would use all of its fuel and not leave enough for the orbit raising to the GEO disposal or junkyard orbit."

She continued with the main problem. "There are a few smaller telescopes here on the station that could be used but they would require an EVA to locate them in line of sight of the rendezvous."

"I don't think that would work anyway." I interrupted her again. "The pointing and tracking system required for that type of rendezvous would be high-tech stuff. I don't think you could just move a telescope over here to watch it. There are a couple of commercial scopes and software packages that might could do it. You reckon Meade delivers up here?"

"I was afraid of that. Any other suggestions? You're the astronomer after all." She held onto a rail and righted herself a little closer with respect to me.

"Pointing and tracking is the big bugaboo here. Let's see . . ." Something dinged in my mind. "Let's go find Fines."

We found Terrence in the Russian Zarya Control Module poking around.

"Terrence, my man, I have a puzzle for you." I filled him in on the problem. The two of us started talking and drawing on pads. Tabitha interrupted with an occasional comment. After about an hour of deliberation we still hadn't come up with any brilliant ideas.

"Well Tabitha, I guess it is an EVA after all," I admitted. She seemed disappointed. While we were talking, one of the Russian crewmen drifted by with a piece of equipment in his hand and a roll of duct tape in the other. I watched out of the corner of my eye as the cosmonaut delicately taped the instrument he was carrying to a telescopic extension rod he was supporting against a control panel.

"What's that?" I asked him, interrupting Terrence mid-sentence.

"This is a star tracker camera. It needs to be extended further from the airlock door for the experiment we're performing."

"You mean that the duct tape will survive in space?" I was flabbergasted.

"You Americans always think things must cost billions before you can use them." He scowled and drifted back out of the module with his star tracker on a makeshift extension pole.

He was right. NASA would have done a study for six months on extension poles and then released a Request For Quote to several different contractors to bid on the pole. After Peer Review Services paid, fed, and boarded a small army to grade them and Legal okayed the decision, an award would be given to one of the contractors. The contractor would have to build three or four of these things and destroy them in shake tests, vacuum tests, and the like. Then a fancy new space-qualified extension pole would be manufactured. Of course it would fail somehow and need a modification. All of this to the tune of about three million dollars. How much does a roll of duct tape cost? Heck NASCAR has been using it for years. But I digress again. I went back to the conversation with Terrence and Tabitha.

"Terrence, how much mass is the dish on your mini radar system?" I thought aloud.

"No way, Anson. If we use that system for pointing and tracking, it would give away the accuracy of it to the Japanese. No more secret." Terrence tugged at his lower lip.

"Can't we just not use it at optimum capacity? Besides, If we duct tape a telescope to it, there would sure be a heck of a lot of jitter in that connection."

Tabitha interjected, "No matter anyway. Terrence's system is in the payload bay of the Shuttle. I just don't see a way to do this without an EVA."

"How much time do we have before the rendezvous?" I asked.

Tabitha looked at her watch, "About twenty-two hours."

"Even if we do an EVA, what do we do?" I wasn't sure if this problem *had* a good solution.

"The Japanese do an EVA and bring in their broken telescope. Wangche has been depressurizing for a while now. Then we go from there."

"Yes ma'am, Colonel." Terrence saluted and departed. I hadn't seen anybody salute Tabitha before. It must have been an instinct for Terrence.

Wangche Lynn brought the Japanese Low Noise Optical Instrument Package in through the airlock a couple of hours later. While waiting, Tabitha and I had dinner in the Habitation Module. We played around for about ten minutes in the microgravity. I spun her around a few times and she had me do some flying spin kicks. I soon realized that spin kicks are virtually impossible without gravity. Tabitha did a few dazzling spins and tucks and flips that affected me in just the right way. I really wished there were some hidey-hole that we could find and get friendly. That just wasn't going to happen. This was the longest period of time we'd been in space that Tabitha was just Tabitha and not Colonel Ames—and it was very short-lived, too short-lived. I had had something on my mind that I wanted to talk to her about at the right moment, and this one didn't last long enough. Or I chickened out.

Upon further inspection of the JLNOIP, Wangche decided that the optic was damaged but salvageable, but the pointing system was completely destroyed. Tabitha and I knew that there would be only one way to fix it and accomplish the tasks that the Japanese/ Chinese crew had been preparing for the past month. We also knew that they couldn't have access to the classified equipment in the payload bay either.

"Here's the plan," I said to Tabitha, not giving her time to interrupt once I had her attention. "You sneak the telescope and the focal plane instruments away from the Japanese module. I'll give the optics and detectors a once over. Then Terrence and I will go out into the Shuttle and attach the thing to the radar assembly of his experiment. We feed the telemetry, point and track data, and the focal plane images through the modem on Terrence's experiment. Tomorrow, during the rendezvous, we send Wangche and company the feedback control sequences and let them point the telescope for the experiment. When it's over we cut the circuit and fly off in the Shuttle." I paused for air.

"We have to get approval first!" I knew she would say that.

Believe it or not, we got approval for the EVA and for the process we planned. The biggest hurdle was getting Terrence's bosses to okay the project but we assured them no damage or exfiltration of the equipment technology would take place.

Typical of NASA, some group of engineers dirtside were put to work developing a schedule for us. After the bright boys figured out about how long it would take us to do the job, they added a twenty percent contingency to that, then added another time delay according to some formula for designing EVAs. Tabitha was told to schedule a four-hour later departure from ISS than in the original flight plan. I really didn't believe that it would take us four extra hours to complete the tasks, but I kept my mouth shut. Besides, Terrence and I had to start preparing for the EVA. The Shuttle environment would have to be brought back down to lower than atmospheric pressure immediately. Lowering the pressure in the environment would help prevent getting the bends in the very low pressure environment of the spacesuits.

Since this was a NASA-sanctioned plan, Tabitha didn't have to sneak the telescope away from Wangche after all. She just explained that we had a fix and the foreign astronauts couldn't be involved with it. Then she asked them plainly if they wanted to get the data for the rendezvous or not.

The JLNOIP focal plane detectors were all in good and operational condition. The primary optic on the other hand, had a scratch about an inch wide across it from one side to the other. Even worse, the scratch had been caused when the support for the secondary mirror, called a spider, collapsed into the larger primary mirror due to the force on it from the "Lemote Manipuratol Alm" or Remote Manipulator Arm. So, a new spider had to be rigged somehow or other. I was able to repair the structural pieces from parts on the Shuttle and the ISS. However, the large primary mirror couldn't be made as good as new without serious repolishing and recoating. I did some quick calculations on a scratchpad and discovered that the total aperture of the telescope wouldn't be required in order to gather enough light to image the satellite rendezvous only twenty-eight thousand miles away. This meant that the efficiency of the primary optic could be a little worse than its original specifications. I did comment that the inch wide scratch across the optics diameter wasn't to factory specs. I also did some image calculations and decided that the error in the image that the scratch would cause would be negligible. Some slight spatial filtering would take place, but that just couldn't be helped. Maybe the Japanese team had an optical wavefront guru working for them who could clean that part out of the images later.

I managed to bang the telescope and the rest of the JLNOIP back in working order and Terrence and I completed the EVA to mount it on his radar pointing and tracking experiment hardware in the Shuttle bay. We used some bungee cord, a few hose clamps, a lot of duct tape, and some ISS camera-mounting hardware we "McGuyvered" into a mount for the JLNOIP. Terrence and I played with the point-and-track algorithms until we had the telescope pointing to classified parameters. Duct tape is amazing. Then Terrence wrote a random noise function into the code that would cause the JLNOIP to demonstrate a pointing jitter just short of state-of-the-art. I was impressed by Lieutenant Fine's engineering prowess.

We handed the datalink over to Wangche and the Japanese team about thirty minutes before the rendezvous. From the oohs and ahs and the machine gun Japanese banter we could hear over the UHF, they must have been impressed. I high-fived Terrence and reminded him that we weren't getting paid for this work since we were payload specialists.

"Hey! Perhaps we should bill NASA when we get back," he joked.

"I'll have my lawyer look into it," I agreed only a little more seriously. "I'm certain there would be a way to call this misuse of private resources or some other legalese term. Maybe since you're Air Force, we could get the Inspector General involved."

We left ISS about three hours and fifty-eight minutes later than the original flight plan. Those bright boys at NASA are good at schedules I guess. As we departed from the Docking Module I muttered to myself, "Glad I kept my mouth shut about the schedule thing."

"What's that?" Terrence overheard me.

"Nothing. I'm just glad to be here."

"Me too!" he said.

➢ CHAPTER 9

Two sleep cycles later I was on the line with Jim doing my preflight fire-up sequences. Zephram, the warp flight demonstrator, was itching to be put together and fired off—or at least I was ready for it to be put together and fired off. The computer bus for the three ECCs was placed on standby mode. The star trackers and the attitude control system (ACS) was brought online and the onboard command and data handling or C&DH was powered up.

"Jim, does the plumbing check for the ACS thrusters?"

"Roger that, Anson. Lox and Hydrazine tankage is nominal. My numbers show the same as yours."

"Okay, I'm going to run the sequence to bring the data stream off the hardwire direct connection with the Shuttle to the temporary wireless UHF link."

"Have you cut the circuit breakers to the probe main communications bus? We don't want to fry the TWeeTA system." Jim reminded me.

"Roger, Jim. Per the checklist the TWeeTa bus circuit breakers are open. Here we go. I'm cutting the hardline." I waited to see if data still flowed through my laptop from the wireless digital UHF modem connection. "Jim, I read a strong radio signal with eight-seven percent signal quality. Copy?"

"Roger, Anson. My numbers concur. It looks like we're done until you go out there and start snapping some parts together."

"Yeah. Jim, I'll start suiting up and will be back online in about fifty-six minutes or so. Anson out."

I made my way through the forward cabin to the flight deck. The air in the Shuttle was a little thinner today since an EVA was planned. I was trying to acclimate myself to it again. It was easier this time than before the EVA at the ISS. On the way to the forward section of the flight deck I bumped, and I mean that literally, into Tracy and Malcom Edmunds. They seemed busy. I'm not sure doing what. How could they have been training for a Shuttle mission while stationed on ISS for the past two or three months?

"What're you guys doing?" I asked.

"Malcom and I are working on the video equipment. We thought we would help document your EVA." Tracy smiled, then turned back to her work.

"Have you guys seen the boss?"

"She's up front," Malcom responded.

Tabitha was reading some flight data from a monitor and marking checks on a pad. I watched her for a second before I considered interrupting. I had a lot on my mind. An EVA, the first ever warp drive, and the woman I love—quite a bit to process while navigating close quarters in microgravity.

"Just a sec, Anson," she said without looking up. How she knew it was me I will never know. I didn't even get to interrupt her. She finished flipping a switch or two and checking boxes on her pad. She stuck the pad to a Velcro patch on the side of her seat and turned to me, "Ready to go outside?" She had a big girly grin and looked less business-as-usual.

"That's what I was coming to tell you. We have about forty minutes of sucking pure O2 to do," I said.

"Yeah, don't want to get the bends."

"But before we get to that . . ." I looked around and made sure we were alone. "Can we talk for a second?" I asked. I felt in my pocket to make sure the reason for this conversation was still there.

"Sure, what's on your mind? We're about eight and half minutes ahead of schedule. We've got time to burn." She looked at her wristwatch.

I floated up close to her. "Well, uh. You see, uh. It is like this—"

"Spit it out, Anson. We only have a few minutes." Colonel Ames said.

"Boy! You can sure spoil a mood. Anyway, I was just thinking that we have been seeing a lot of each other over the last couple of years and all. And that I have really enjoyed it." She seemed to soften slightly.

"I have also," is all Tabitha said.

"Uh, I mean, I like your daughter a lot. And your parents," I stalled.

"They like you too," she added.

"Well . . ." I began again, "Uh . . ." Major Donald stuck his head through the hatch into the flight deck.

"You guys ready for your EVA? You ought to be on oxygen by now." Tabitha snapped to attention as if she had been caught with her hand in the cookie jar. I had to wait. The time would come. Maybe later. Maybe later! Damnit-all-to-hell!

"Yeah Ray. Take over the checklists here. Anson and I are going to suit up." We left for the aft section of the Shuttle.

"So, what were you saying, Anson?" she asked.

"Never mind. I'll tell you later. Besides, we have stuff to do."

Twenty minutes later we were in our Liquid Cooling-and-Ventilation Garments (LCVG) and had been on the oxygen masks for a while. The LCVGs are basically just white Spandex long johns with tubing running throughout them. Water flows through the tubes to keep the body cool. The water is handled by the Primary Life-Support System or PLSS. The PLSS pumps the coolant around the body and also accomplishes any air handling. The PLSS can handle up to a million joules of heat per hour. You have to be working really hard to generate that kind of heat. As an example, I like to tell students that if a postage stamp is burned only about 200 joules of heat is released. So, the PLSS is fairly robust. The major portion of the PLSS is housed in the backpack unit and interfaces to the LCVG through ductwork and ventilation tubes in the suit. Tabitha and I helped each other with the various parts of our suits.

The Hard Upper Torso (HUT) and the Space Suit Assembly portions of the suits were snapped in place and we began running diagnostics. Finally, we managed to completely suit ourselves into the Extravehicular Mobility Units (EMUs). I still prefer to call them spacesuits or environment suits. But when in Rome!

We did our final checklists for the EMU communications systems and then made our way into the airlock. The airlock of the Shuttle is just big enough for two fully suited astronauts to fit inside. The two D-shaped doors were closed and the pressure hatches were ready to be cycled. Tabitha and I did one last visual check of our suits. This being my second EVA, it was all old hat to me. The hatch for the outer exit has six interconnected latches with a gearbox and an actuator system. I looked through the polycarbonate plastic window in the hatch as Tabitha checked the actuators and then the pressure gauges on each side of the two pressure-equalization valves. Both the inner and outer hatches were sealed.

"Okay, Ray, I'm going to cycle the pressure." Tabitha announced.

Depressurization of the airlock started. I could hear a slight hissing at first and then nothing. I checked my suit pressure one last time. Everything was A-okay at about four pounds per square inch.

"The pressure gauge shows zero. I'm going to open the hatch." Tabitha called out each step by the book. She grabbed the latch mechanism and the dual pressure seals let loose without a sound. I didn't even feel it through my EMU. I could see the payload bay through the hatchway.

"Entering the payload bay."

"Roger that," someone from Houston responded.

"Houston, this is Clemons. I am following the colonel into the bay."

"Go for EVA, Anson! HOSC online here!" Jim had just come back online down in Huntsville. The warp probe components, soon to be call sign Zephram, was more than ready out in the payload bay.

Several minutes of preparation and disconnecting and connecting things followed next. Rayford piloted the Remote Manipulator Arm from inside the Shuttle so that the end of the Arm seemed to hover ever present above—or was that below?—us. Final disconnect process had been checked through for the cylindrical warp field system and for one of the ECCs.

"Houston, we're ready to detach the containment system for the probe and ECC number one." Tabitha started to work with her powered ratchet and removed a set of bolts. Once, just for fun, I held the ratchet on a bolt and turned it on while my feet weren't planted to anything. I slowly began to spin about the bolt axis in a clockwise fashion. Tabitha wasn't amused.

"Quit clowning around, Anson!"

"Hey, I paid for this ride. I'm going to get some fun out of it!" I joked.

She still wasn't amused. Getting back to business I tethered both of us to the ECC as Rayford powered the Remote Manipulator Arm over to us. I worried with catching the Arm and attaching it to the ECC while Tabitha danced around like a busy bee in prime honey season connecting this, undoing that, and fiddling with the other thing.

"That's good there, Ray. Houston, I have the Remote Manipulator Arm Platform connected and Tabitha and I are go for an egress from the payload bay." I waited for a reply from Tabitha, Rayford, Houston and Huntsville, in any order.

"Roger that, Anson," Rayford said.

"Houston here. Go for ECC egress," Houston confirmed.

"Hunstville here. Roger that. Go for ECC egress," Jim replied.

"Tabitha, are all the ECC egress connectors locked?" Jim's voice came over the UHF.

"Roger that. Connector cables linked and we are go."

Both of us were extremely busy. I really would've liked to have been able to stop and take in the incredible view, but we had to make sure that each of the three ECCs went through the same egress process and then were connected, via special thin-walled telescopic titanium connector tubes about ten centimeters in diameter each and ultra-strong polymer support cables about five millimeters in diameter each, before letting them float out into space away from the shuttle. Also, the main fuselage and spacecraft bus housing, the central cylinder, would then have to be guided by the Arm, Tabitha on one side, and me on the other making minor course corrections. We had to thread the central cylinder through the three ECCs like a needle and thread. Once the ECCs were in place, they looked like large ice cubes supported by toothpicks. The toothpicks were in turn stuck into a large cylinder (an analogously scaled object would be a toilet paper roll) about its circumference at one-hundred-twenty-degree intervals. They were also closer to one end of the cylinder than the other.

Being an astronaut nowadays is more like construction work than the glory of flying high-tech spacecraft. Tabitha and I had been turning bolts and making electrical connections for the better part of three hours. It was time for a scheduled break.

Tethered to the probe, Tabitha and I watched as the Arm disconnected from us and folded back toward the payload bay. An incomplete Zephram, Tabitha, and myself simply floated there above the shuttle, Newton's Laws still being in effect.

"Rayford, you drive that thing like a pro," I teased as he locked onto the final component of the probe, the ACS Fuel Supply and Science Instrument Suite Sphere. Tabitha and I watched and panted trying to catch our breath in the thin atmosphere of our EVA suits. Rayford manipulated the Arm right into the sweet spot of the universal connector on the probe component. The tank grabbed back at the arm and was connected. The internal circuitry kicked in and blew the circuit breakers for the other connectors around the tank. In a matter of seconds the tank was free from the Shuttle other than at the connection with the Arm.

About fifteen minutes had passed and Tabitha and I had caught as much of our breath as you can at about a third of atmospheric pressure. Although the PLSS pumps an oxygen rich environment into the suit, it's still like snow skiing, wrestling a bear, running a marathon, and attacking Mount Everest all at the same time. EVA astronauts had better be in shape. All that cardio kickboxing had paid off for me. All the extracurricular activities with Tabitha didn't hurt either.

"Until you've done it, you can't imagine it." Tabitha had told me that a thousand times about astronaut stuff. It turns out that she was right about this one. Actually, she was right about it all, but I didn't tell her that. She's cocky enough as it is.

I connected a cable to the major portion of Zephram and then thrusted my way over to the upcoming final component. The Arm had halted about two meters from us. I slowed my descent to the Tank and lightly touched down on it. I had lined up on the hook perfectly. I grabbed the handhold with one hand and snapped the carabineer on the hook with the other. This was a lot easier than working in the neutral buoyancy tank in Houston—you can move quicker. Some astronauts had told me that the difference would be hard to get used to. I couldn't understand why. It seemed more natural to me not to have the resistance from the water.

"Probe tank is secure. Release the Arm," I said over the UHF.

"That was good work, Doc!" Jim said over the comm.

"Thanks, Jim. Preparing cable engage and final component attach!" The motor on the other end of the cable started spinning. Tabitha ran the motor as she pulled the two parts of the spacecraft together, slowly pulling us together.

As Tabitha and I slowly maneuvered the two spacecraft parts together, the Shuttle began slowly pulling away from us. Neither of us were concerned since this was part of yet another NASA scheduled event. As we began connecting the components of the probe, we would need to power them up. The immense electromagnetic fields created by the probe would wreak havoc on the Shuttle's systems so it had to be backed off to at least a hundred or so meters from the probe. Once Zephram was completely constructed and brought online, Tabitha and I would use our SAFER MMUs (Simplified Aid for Extravehicular activity Rescue Manned Maneuvering Units) to fly back to a safe distance where the Shuttle could catch us. No problem!

I could see the Shuttle in my peripheral vision (what little of it you have in a spacesuit) drifting farther and farther away.

"Hey, that's my ride home," I joked.

"Well, you guys finish all your chores and then we'll think about giving you a lift," Rayford announced. At least he had a sense of humor.

I guided the Tank the last couple of feet with my SAFER MMU. The two components came together with a *clank* that I could feel through my suit. Tabitha quickly snapped some of the connection clamps that were closest to her. I began feeling around the tank, doing the same.

"This is Huntsville. We read that all components of the probe are connected," Jim reported.

Tabitha and I completed closing the clamps around the circumference of the connection between the cylinder and the tank. We finished face-to-face with each other. She raised her visor and winked at me.

"It's your show," she said quietly over the UHF.

"Roger that Jim!" I said into the mic. "Call sign Zephram is complete. We just need to give a few bolts up here a couple extra turns and then kickstart it off." I raised my visor and winked back at Tabitha. I could tell Jim was excited from the sound of his voice. I was equally thrilled. What am I saying? I was tickled shitless! If you're from the South, tickled shitless is about as good as it gets.

"Can't wait down here Ans—" the communication blacked out.

I could see a bright light glare off Tabitha's visor and she winced as in reflex and tried to turn her head. Instinctively, I tried to turn and look over my shoulder. Then I realized that I was wearing a spacesuit and that isn't a move you can do very easily in a spacesuit. I started to request that Jim copy me on the last transmission, but instead Tabitha snapped her cable onto my belt and hit her thrusters full reverse, pulling me with her.

"What are you doing?!"

"Move, Anson!" she said as she dragged me with her. She said *move* so I hit my forward thrusters to go with her. Just after I kicked my thrusters toward her, Tabitha reversed thrusters and I flew into her, hard! We were now chest-to-chest. Our facemasks smacked together with a *THWACK!* I hugged her whether I meant to or not. Knowing that Tabitha knew what she was doing, whatever it was, I killed my thrusters, hoping not to counteract something she did. I also kept my mouth shut and just hung on for dear life hoping that she wouldn't kill us. She fired her thrusters again. This time we moved toward the probe. The probe was only a half a meter away and it didn't take long for her to sandwich me between her and one of the ECCs. Tabitha locked a safety cable onto the ECC and grabbed a handhold. I figured what's good for the goose is good for the gander and started to follow suit. In order to lock onto the ECC I would need to fire my thrusters and turn around. Tabitha realized what I was doing and bearhugged me, sandwiching me again.

"Don't move!" she cried.

"What the hell is going on?" I had to know! How could I help if I had no idea what was going on?

"The Shuttle exploded!" she screamed.

"What!?" I wasn't sure that I heard her right. Ignorance is bliss, I have always heard. It would've been nice in this case had I remained ignorant.

"Hold on!" Then Zephram started vibrating and I could feel through my suit millions of small impacts dinging into it. I just prayed that nothing came through the ECC and into my suit from behind! A large section of one of the payload bay doors flew by us about fifty meters to my left—Tabitha's right. There were like pieces passing below, above, and to the other side as well. A hard *thud* hit the warp spacecraft somewhere. I could feel it. Zephram was given a slight rotation by the impact of whatever it was that caused the *thud*.

Tabitha and I held on for the ride of a lifetime. I don't know about her, but I was scared to death. Earth rolled by underneath us. Then it was gone and then back again. We were spinning pretty fast. I prayed that no debris hit while we were facing the direction of the explosion. A cloud of tiny shiny debris zipped past us and made our rotation worse and more unstable. Then we were inside the blast wave and it was over—I thought. Whatever hit the probe must have hit the propellant or oxidizer tanks enough to cause a rupture, which let go just then. All at once the pressure vessel gave way, spewing pressurized gas out of the tank. This increased the rotation of the probe we were holding to an all-out random three-dimensional uncontrolled spin. The centrifugal force slung us away from the probe too fast for me to hold on. Fortunately, Tabitha had the foresight to snap a carabineer and a cable onto her handhold. But the force was too great for her to keep her hold while the fuel was still spewing and accelerating the spin.

"Hang on, Anson!"

"Hang on to what?" I cried, not knowing if I should try to keep holding her, hold the cable, or try to grab at the vacuum. None of which seemed to help.

"Just keep breathing as normal as you can!"

My handhold on her slipped and I was flung away from her. The meter-long tether connecting us jerked taught. It felt like it cut me in half. The tether hung on my left leg somehow and caused me to be slung outward headfirst. I tried to unhook it, but the g-forces were too much for me to overcome. My head was on the outer end of the centrifugal force—my head felt like it would explode.

"My head is going to pop!" I couldn't stand the build up of pressure in my head much longer. The gees were approaching my limit.

"You can take it, Anson! Just hold on. The tanks will empty soon."

"They better! I'm starting to tunnel out." All I could see was a small white circle way off in front of me. Everything else was tunneling in around me. I tried to blink my eyes, shake my head, anything. Nothing helped.

Finally, the angular acceleration stopped. The rotation didn't. I was getting very dizzy and very nauseated. Tabitha fired her thrusters until she slammed into the ECC. She grabbed the handhold tight. This pulled me upright and into her back. I was still fairly useless, nearly unconscious. Tabitha expelled all of her thruster fuel over the next few minutes trying to stop the spin of the probe. She succeeded only in slowing the induced spin to a tolerable rotation. I was able to upright myself with her. I grabbed a handhold very tightly and panted near hyperventilation.

"Anson! Anson, look at me! Focus on your breathing. You have to slow down your breathing!" she ordered me over the UHF.

I closed my eyes and tried to relax and breathe normally.

"Focus!" she yelled.

"Okay," I puffed. "I . . . am . . . okay." Just talking was tough.

For a while I thought I was seeing red, but that faded within a few moments.

Earth rolled by underneath us about every ten seconds or so. That was still considerable rotation, or so I thought.

"Anson. My thrusters are out. You have to stop the probe's rotation or at least slow it some more." I was too confused and disoriented to ask questions right away. I followed orders and fired my thrusters a few times. That stopped the probe's spin the rest of the way. We were now facing Earth constantly.

"What happened?" I asked her.

"Don't know. How much air do you have?"

I checked my Display and Controls Module (DCM). I ran through a few diagnostics on my suit. Tabitha was doing the same.

"I have three hours fifty-seven minutes. How about you?"

"Same," she said.

"What do we do? We're in space with no way to get home!"

"I ain't sure. First I think we should try communicating with someone. Although they'll be out of range." She was right. We both tried and failed to hail anybody. The UHF circuits on the suits only reach about ten kilometers or so. The Shuttle that relayed our signal to ground stations was gone. Earth was about three hundred kilometers below us and the ISS was about twelve thousand kilometers on the other side of the Earth.

"We're so screwed. Oh man, we are so *screwed*!"

"Anson, don't ever say that again! you hear me?" she scolded. "Think! There's a way out of this. We just have to find it."

"You're right. I hope." I was still trying to shake off the massive headache and the feeling of having been on that nasty roller coaster from a few minutes before.

"I don't hope. I know. That is the only way to see it in your mind. You know we will make it. Got it!" That last was more of an order than a question so I didn't answer.

I could imagine Bob's face while he was yelling at 'Becca, "Never give up!" That look of determination on his face was the same that I was seeing on Tabitha now. I realized that by God they were right! I wasn't giving up no matter how bad things got. Ever! I looked at Tabitha and realized that I knew we were going to make it somehow. I had a whole new fire burning in me. There was a way home. I just had to find it.

Now you might think, *what about those poor folks on the Shuttle that just got destroyed? Where's the compassion for them? Weren't they your friends?* I remember a decade or so ago how I felt horrible and cried while watching all those folks die when the World Trade Center towers were destroyed and I didn't even know any of them. Well that was different—I wasn't about to die myself then. At this point my main concern was survival—not compassion, anger, remorse, or any other emotion. Tabitha and I had all the time in the world to cry later—if we survived. My guess is that this is how soldiers must feel when they see their buddy beside them get blown away. They must know that they have to complete their mission or die, too. Then, later when they are safe, they cry. Tabitha is a soldier—I was certain that she was operating in pure survival mode. So, that was the only way that I could think—that I would think—until this was over and we were safe at home drinking a beer. Then I would cry for hours or days.

I touched the ring I'd tucked in my EMU in anticipation of popping the question during the EVA. "Tabitha, will you marry me?" I asked her.

"What!"

"Marry me! I said. "Marry me, Neil Anson Clemons."

"You are asking me *now*? We don't have time for this." She was frantic and looking furious.

"Tabitha," I began calmly and slowly. "I know that we're going to make it. And I want you to spend the rest of your life with me and I want to spend the rest of my life with you. If we don't make it, and we will, I would rather make it with my fiancée than my commander. Marry me!" I pleaded.

Tabitha took a long pause and a deep breath, if you can do that in an EMU. Then she nodded.

"Are you sure you aren't just asking me this because you're hysterical?"

"No! I was going to ask you earlier. I just never got the time. I have a ring right here in my pocket! I haven't let it out of my sight since we launched."

"Are you serious?" she asked.

"Hell, yes, I'm serious!" I was hurt a little.

"I will," she said quietly.

"Yes! I wish I could kiss you." I laughed. I'm not sure if I was hysterical, but I probably appeared to be.

After a few moments of silence, we set to work thinking about a plan to get us home. Communicating with those bright boys dirtside at NASA was our first priority.

We spent the next thirty minutes reconfiguring the datalink system for the probe to accept the UHF signals from the EMUs and then relay them over the digital data dump back to the HOSC in Huntsville. Had Al Rayburn and I not redesigned the spacecraft bus as a graphical interface this wouldn't have been possible. Any off-the-shelf spacecraft bus would've required actual rewiring that couldn't be done in an EMU. The dexterity in the gloves just wouldn't allow that. However, Al and I had the idea of making the entire spacecraft modular. Each wire connects to the generic connection point on the spacecraft bus. Then that connection can be allocated by the central computer system and some solid-state and mechanical relays. All the wires are the same but each has a different job as assigned by the computer. Al and I had taken the commercial bus we bought and spent a good deal of effort reverse engineering and reen-gineering it.

Tabitha and I finally reconfigured the data comm system to accept our UHF signal as data in. Then we retransmitted that signal through the Traveling Wave Tube Amplifier or "TWeeTA" system. The TWeeTA was designed to handle more data than had ever been attempted with a spacecraft. The warp field data would be vast when operational. Standard communications systems just wouldn't have been able to handle the data rates needed. So, Al, Jim, 'Becca, and I spent a good bit of time and money designing a newer more updated system. This communications system works a lot more like the Internet than a radio. That amount of data required a lot of power amplification. A TWeeTA is the only way to go about that. Tabitha and I used this to our advantage. Since the communications dish hadn't been deployed yet, we planned to use the omnidirectional antenna. We pumped plenty of power through the dipole so that the relay satellites could receive it with no problem.

But there was a problem: the datalink was just that, a datalink. Nobody would be expecting a voice signal over it. Jim would have to realize that the data he was receiving was a frequency modulated signal, then decode it to an audio circuit. Who knew how long that would take? The plus side is that with the Shuttle now destroyed, the folks dirtside wouldn't expect anybody to turn on the warp probe, either. The fact that it came on should surprise them, if they were watching their consoles properly. Also, while in orbit the probe was designed to communicate directly with the HOSC through the Tracking and Data Relay Satellite System or TDRSS (pronounced "tea-dress") network. And we were in line-of-sight with one of those constantly. This meant that as soon as we turned on the transmitter, the HOSC would be receiving the data. We weren't worried about choking the bus of the relay satellites because an audio data file doesn't require much bandwidth.

"HOSC operations come in please. Is anybody there?" I began repeating.

Tabitha followed. "Come in Jim. Are you there?"

We kept talking so a constant audio file would be sent through Zephram, over TDRSS, to the HOSC, and hopefully to Jim.

"Tabitha, I'm going to survey the probe while we wait. There might be something on it we could use. Use for what I don't know."

I powered up the forward thrusters and moved slowly around the spacecraft. Where the large *thud* had taken place was on the ACS Fuel Tankage and Science Instrument section. We wouldn't be measuring the electromagnetic field strength and the gravimetric effects of the warp field today. We sure wouldn't be firing the attitude control thrusters either. The rest of the probe looked okay. I made my way back to the GUI panel and did a system diagnostic using its graphical user interface. The probe checked out, although the warp field coils hadn't been completely connected and the ECCs hadn't been brought online yet.

"HOSC, do you copy?" Tabitha repeated.

"Come on, Jim, where are you?" I looked at Tabitha's DCM.

"Give me the bad news, Anson."

"We still have about three hours of air left. That is plenty of time." I assured her. Plenty of time for what neither of us would admit. It takes days at best, usually weeks, to get a Shuttle ready for launch and about the same time for a Russian rocket. It takes even longer for a Chinese rocket. We discussed the possibility of the Crew Return Vehicle on the ISS.

"HOSC, are you there?" I said. "The CRV could never get to us in time. At full thrust I don't think it could make it to us in three hours."

"Maybe, Anson. Don't give up."

"Who's giving up? Jim, are you there?" I turned to her and approached. I hugged her suit as best I could and touched my faceplate to hers.

"I love you, Tabitha."

"Well, you may not live to regret that." She smiled.

Twenty or so minutes had passed and still no response from the HOSC. We were beginning to think nobody would find the signal.

"Jim, are you there? Huntsville, is anybody there? This is Anson Clemons—come in, Earth!" I was ready to try something else.

"Roger that, Dr. Clemons. This is Mission Control being patched through the HOSC. Is Colonel Ames with you? And what has happened?" It wasn't Jim's voice, but we didn't care. Tabitha took command.

"Mission Control, this is Shuttle Commander Tabitha Ames. The Shuttle Orbiter has been completely destroyed by some type of internal explosion. I repeat. The Shuttle Orbiter has been completely destroyed. The cause is unknown. Dr. Anson Clemons and I are the only survivors. We each have," she looked at her DCM readout, "roughly two hours and thirty-nine minutes of air left. Please advise on possible rescue scenario. The probe ACS thrusters are off-line and out of fuel and O2."

"Roger that, Commander. Understand that we are working on escape possibilities. We will advise you momentarily," Control replied.

"Roger, Houston."

The response came five minutes later—it seemed like forever.

"Colonel Ames, Tabitha, uh, we haven't got a working scenario that will save both of you. If you two have any suggestions, we're open for it down here." Hal Thompson was talking now. He was the boss down at Mission Control. I had met him a few times. He was shooting straight with us.

"Houston, this is Clemons. What do you mean by you can't save us *both*?" I had an idea what he meant, but I had to hear it.

"We don't have another Shuttle anywhere near ready for launch. We have called the Russians and the Chinese. The Chinese have one on the launch pad but they won't be ready for launch for at least another seven hours or so. The Crew Return Vehicle is your only hope. It's already enroute to your location. The Hohmann Transfer required will take about four hours to reach you and another couple of minutes to match velocities with you. That's all we have right now. Sorry." Hal truly sounded sorry. I knew he was right. I had been running rough order of magnitude calculations in my head. One of us would have to survive long enough for the CRV to make it to us. Only one of us could with the combination of air from both suits—it would be Tabitha. At least she would make it. I told her it had to be her.

"No way! Anson, there's a better solution," Tabitha cried.

"Tabitha. It is the only way. You have a daughter back home. There's no choice to be made here." Heinlein always said (through his character Lazarus Long) that he wasn't afraid of death and that he knew it was part of the deal. I can't say that I'm that philosophical about it. Maybe I'm just not the superman he was. Death scares the living hell out of me. But I had to make sure Tabitha made it home alive. If I didn't do that, what kind of husband would I be?

"Stuff that, Anson. No way, period. End of that. You're the smart one—figure it out!"

"Houston, how long until I have to stop using my oxygen in order to give Tabitha time to wait for the CRV plus a few minutes of extra air?"

"Just a second on that, Anson," Hal replied solemnly.

"We'll see how long we have to work other solutions," I told Tabitha.

"Guys, this is Hal. Flight surgeon says that one of you would have to stop breathing in sixty-one minutes for the other to make it long enough for the CRV to get there."

"Okay, Hal. We have an hour to work this out. Get Jim at the HOSC on the circuit now. He might can help."

"Roger, Anson. It's already done." Hal replied.

"Jim, here, buddy. I heard it all so far. This bites. What do you need from me?" Jim asked.

"I don't know yet, Jim. I do have one question for you though."

"Yeah, what is it?"

"Will you be my best man at my wedding? Tabitha said yes!"

"You got it, Anson! Congratulations. Let's get you home first." Jim said.

No brilliant ideas hit any of us. The one idea I had was to use the large electromagnets in the warp coil to generate a magnetic sail from the material in the upper atmosphere at LEO. The sail would then surf along the Earth's magnetic field. The idea would be to set up a mini-magnetospheric plasma propulsion (M2P2) system. The probe was far too massive and the coils would have to be reconfigured. Another task that couldn't be accomplished from an EMU. I decided then that if I survived this I was going to invent a better damn spacesuit or better yet some sort of magical warp bubble that would wrap around you like Spandex. But, first things first!

"There is no way to adjust the coils to set up the magnetic sail at all? We can't get any thrust that way?" I asked Jim after we'd been through the math a few times. I looked at my DCM. I only had about ten minutes left before the big decision. Tabitha remained quiet most of the time.

"Sorry, Anson. I don't see how you could get in there and redirect the field. Zephram was designed to warp space not build plasma balls. Too bad you can't just warp to the station. Damnit! What are we going to do?"

"What did you say!?"

"I said too bad—" Jim began again.

"Skip it, Jim. I know what you said. That's the answer. *We'll warp home!*" I cried over the UHF. It could work! I would save Tabitha *and* myself!

"Anson, you know as well as I do that you can't warp around the Earth. The rotation causes to much frame dragging for you to know where you would end up. You can't warp around the Earth to the ISS or the CRV. Our calculations just aren't sophisticated enough for that," Jim concluded sadly.

"Jim, who said anything about the ISS. I said *home*. Earth!"

"What?" Jim exclaimed.

"The warp can be radially outward from the Earth so why can't it be radially inward to the Earth? We just never thought of that. Start running the numbers. Tabitha and I will start preflight on the probe."

"Anson, are you serious? This could be risky. You might miscalculate and come out of warp too high or too low and *smack*!"

"Jim don't forget that the warp position errors will be along the Earth's surface due to its rotation; the frame dragging problem will cause angular errors in our calculations by maybe as much as a kilometer or two. The radial position errors should only be a few meters or so. Theoretically at least," I responded.

I adjusted my visor and looked at Tabitha. "Tabitha, I can't make this decision by myself. You can still make it to the CRV. My way is very risky. We could come out of warp too high above the ground and fall to our deaths or we could warp into the ground and who knows what that would cause?"

"Then why not warp out over the ocean?" Jim interrupted.

"Warping out over the ocean would have pretty much the same effect. Falling more than fifty feet into the ocean might not kill us, but we have no flotation gear so we will sink right to the bottom in these SAFER MMUs attached and the spacesuits at such a low inflation pressure we would be boat anchors. Also, if we ended up too deep we would be crushed by the pressure or just plain drown. Don't forget, we're out of air and these suits are heavy; the boat anchor thing is still the main problem! This spacecraft was only designed to fly in space so there aren't any flotation devices, landing gears, lifelines, or you name it; we're just going to have to do a controlled fall close enough to the ground. And one more thing, I would much rather try to walk home with a broken leg or something similar than swim home with one. Face it, anyway you look at it we're screwed, but it is the only way I can think of to get us both home. Tabitha, what do you think?"

Tabitha pulled her visor up and looked me deep in the eyes. She didn't take her eyes off me as she spoke. "Jim, this is Tabitha. Not only that, I'm not sure the Navy could deploy to rescue us in time, we can't wait here without air and we can't wait in the water in these suits and no air to inflate them, Anson's right, we'll sink! I agree with Anson, I had rather take my chance walking home than swimming home. Get to work on those numbers Anson asked for. Houston you might as well call back the CRV. We won't be here when it arrives." Tabitha looked at me and said, "What the hell. Lets get this preflight started. You aren't getting out of marrying me that easy."

➤ CHAPTER 10

It took almost all of the time we had left to prep the probe for warp since Tabitha was out of propellant and had to use the crawl, grab, and tether method. Tabitha looked at her DCM and whistled.

"Cutting it close, Anson. I have about sixty minutes of air left. How are you doing?"

"Not much less. I have about fifty-nine. My body weight is more than yours. No matter, we're about ready to fire this thing. Jim you got those last calculations completed?" I broadcast over the makeshift communications network.

"Here comes, Anson. Gee zero one is zero point zero zero zero one seven. Copy that?"

"Roger Jim. Gee zero one is zero point zero zero zero one seven. Go next sequence."

"Gee zero three is zero point zero zero zero zero zero zero zero six zero one two five."

"Got it. Gee zero three is zero point zero zero zero zero zero zero zero six zero one two five. Next sequence." This continued for about seven more sequences. We were rewriting our gravitational metric for an inward travel vector. Jim had—in just a few minutes—completed calculations that had taken mankind millions of years to achieve. He should have gotten accepted to

MIT, Princeton, Harvard, or Yale. He didn't get a scholarship' and he sure couldn't afford it. Neither could I. We were both products of the state university system. That's okay. We went to the Harvard Karate Open two years ago and put a couple of those Ivy League geeks in the emergency room. Yeah I know, karate is for self-defense and self-defense only. We both had axes to grind. We felt both better and worse afterwards. We never acted like that again and we sent cards to the guys we had fought. I think we both matured some because of that tournament. Besides none of those guys were even close to warping space. *We* were damn sure going to give it the old state college try.

"Okay, Anson. That's it. All that's left is hitting the little red button," Jim said.

"I hope our numbers are right, Jim."

"Well, you were right about the frame dragging due to Earth's rotation causing position errors mostly along the surface. My calculations suggest maximum x and y position uncertainty of more than five kilometers, but errors in the z direction are only about two meters. And if you come out of warp just a couple of meters low you won't have that deep of a hole to crawl out of. And if you're high, that won't be too far to fall."

"You guys better be waiting on us in New Mexico when we get there," I told him.

We had decided to try and warp to the desert in case something went wrong we would probably be the only ones killed. Jim, of course, was kidding. There really is no red button on the probe. The sequence is automated and initiated either from the GUI interface or the uplink from Earth. Tabitha and I decide to do the initiation sequence ourselves. The only thing to do now was wait for New Mexico to roll up underneath us. According to Houston that would be in about fifteen minutes.

"Tabitha, are you ready for this?" I asked her. I touched her helmet and looked at her.

"Just as soon as New Mexico rears its ugly head." She laughed. "We'll punch a hole in it."

"Jeeze! I hope not. The plan is to land gently," I told her.

"Anson. What about the atmosphere? What happens when we

slam into it at the speed of light or however fast it will be?" She looked concerned.

"We've talked about this a little before remember. General Relativity and Causality won't allow anything to penetrate the forward and rearward portions of the warp bubble. We should be completely shielded."

"What about Earth?"

"Well that's why we're aiming for the desert. The air is a little less dense and nobody lives there. Mostly, nobody lives there."

"Hal, this is Anson. Jim, Tabitha and I are go for the firing sequence. I can see the coast of Lower California," I claimed.

"Roger Anson. Good luck you guys. God speed. Hal out."

Jim piped up. "Good luck, you guys. See you soon. Anson, thanks for everything, you know?" He sounded sad.

"I know, Jim. Don't worry. It's going to work." I held Tabitha's hand and depressed the warp sequence start command.

"Warp sequence is go," I said.

"Jim, if we don't make it tell my daughter and my parents that I love them!" Tabitha cried. Tears were slowly running down her cheeks. *Tears were running down her cheeks!*

Then the communications went blank. I could see New Mexico rolling up beneath us, then Tabitha and I were in total darkness other than the GUI panel illumination.

"It'll be just a few more seconds before the ECCs are powered up completely. The bubble must be forming nicely," I said as I surveyed the GUI panel. Then we were surrounded by a sphere of blue flashes of light.

"When will we know if it worked—aheeey!" Tabitha screamed.

The world got very bright all of the sudden and I could tell that I was falling. We were falling at one gee. We were at Earth, but where? Then something hit my back hard and rolled me over. Now I was facing downward and I could see that I was falling through a canopy of very thick pine trees. We were at least thirty feet from the ground. Another pine tree limb smacked my face-plate and cracked it, whiplashing me. The fall seemed as though it took hours. It really only took a few seconds for me to crash into the sand at the base of a very large tree. I had landed on my back staring upward. I heard Tabitha *thud* against the sand a few meters to my left.

The probe had become entangled in the limbs of the tree and was hanging twenty feet or so above us. I did a quick survey of my body and could feel no breaks or puncture wounds, but I felt like one large bruise. My muscles were still slightly traumatized and I couldn't move yet. The EMU made moving even more difficult. My PLSS was buried no telling how deep in the sand.

"Tabitha, are you okay? Tabitha?" I yelled. I was able to move my arm enough to open my sun visor, then I twisted and lifted the helmet free. Hot moist and very thick air rushed into my face and nearly choked me. It felt great to be home.

"Anson, I'm okay, but I think I bruised or broke some ribs. I can't really move. I need help getting up."

"Me too. I'm kind of stuck in the sand."

Then the trees above us bent nearly over to the ground and swayed back upright several times. The wind had picked up so strong that several of the smaller pines in my peripheral vision snapped in half. One of the tops of the trees was airborne and collided with the probe in the trees above Tabitha and me. The collision was just enough to jar the probe loose. The wind whipped the trees around and the probe began a gravity-assisted plunge toward us. I screamed like a little girl, but the adrenaline rush from my fight or flight reflexes gave me the strength to roll over and bear-crawl out from under the crashing six-ton spacecraft. I hoped that Tabitha could move. Although I didn't count on it since the spacesuits weigh about three hundred pounds each in one gee of gravity.

The probe crashed only inches behind me. I was able to stand to my feet with the strength from the adrenaline. I lost the PLSS, HUT, SSA, and helmet as quickly as possible. As quickly as possible was several minutes. I began removing my LCVG gloves and footies and a serious gust of wind caught me and threw me over the probe. My suit partially inflated from the hellacious wind but remained weighed down where I removed it. I grabbed at a tree as I flew by it and stabilized my fall.

"This wind makes no sense at all," I said to myself. I thought possibly it might be some sort of wind vortices anomaly due to the warp bubble appearing then disappearing in the atmosphere. Whatever it was, the air was chaotic as hell now. The wind pushed me over again and I landed about two meters from Tabitha who hadn't moved when the probe fell. An ECC support tube was across her left leg. Fortunately she was lying in sand and the tube merely forced her deeper into the soft ground. I dug her out and dragged her from beneath the tube.

"How are you?" I asked.

"I'm okay. What is happening?"

The bottom fell from the sky as torrential rainfall pounded us. The winds grew even stronger. The air was getting colder.

"I ain't sure, Tabitha. Let's get you out of the suit and try to figure out where the hell we are." Pine trees don't grow in the desert, and it was way too humid for New Mexico. As we were getting Tabitha down to her LCVGs the weather turned for the worse. It began hailing golfball-to-baseball size chunks of ice. Tabitha and I crawled under one of the ECCs for protection. Then lightning struck a tree about ten feet away from us. The tree burst about five feet from the ground and fell over. It landed on one of the other ECCs with a loud crash and pieces of the device were scattered about. We huddled together under the protection of ECC two.

I could hear even stronger winds and the lightning increased. The hail continued to pummel the ECC. Tabitha pointed out several treetops flying off into the sky.

"Look! I've seen that before!" she cried.

Tabitha grew up in Austin, Texas. I grew up in Huntsville, Alabama. Both places are right smack dab in the middle of tornado alley. We both knew a tornado when we saw it. And holy shit we were seeing one now. A big one!

"How the hell did we happen to land right in the middle of a twister?" she yelled over the clanking of hailstones.

"Let's worry about that later. We've got to get out of the path of that thing," I said and I began looking around. There didn't seem to be any place to go that would offer shelter. A pine tree zipped past us at fifty miles per hour.

"That way!" Tabitha pointed in a direction that appeared to be orthogonal or at a ninety-degree angle to the direction of the tornado's path. The hope was to not be in front of the tornado when it passed by. The tornado was maybe a quarter mile away from us and was cruising at probably forty miles per hour. No way we could outrun it. Maybe we had time to get out of its way. We started running. Fast! Tabitha clutched her side as she ran.

Lightning struck to my right about ten meters away.

"Shit! That was close!" I said.

"Shut up and run!" Tabitha was holding her left side. She had said she thought her ribs were cracked. It had to hurt but worry or talking about it couldn't help the pain and staying here in front of that tornado was not an option either of us liked.

We ran hard through an endless pine thicket just ahead of the sound of breaking trees and limbs. I soon realized that this was no natural thicket. The trees were all about the same age and they were all growing in lines. We were in a timber company's pine grove—and fortunate for our bare feet that there was a nice sandy path between each row of pines.

I looked over my shoulder and noticed that the large tornado had spun off three smaller ones that were in a merry-go-round circling it. The large central storm had to be a four on the Fujita scale at least. Maybe even an F-five.

We came to a small creek that cut through the pine grove. We were running too fast to stop easily so Tabitha and I jumped and landed right in the middle of it. Fortunately the creek bed was sandy or we could've twisted or broken feet and ankles. The creek wasn't more than knee deep in water, but the banks were five or six feet high.

"Let's dig in right here," I yelled. The wind was still so loud we could barely hear one another.

"Good. I can't run much more." She gasped holding her side.

We crawled up as close to the bank of the creek as we could and grabbed onto anything we could hold. The lightning was getting closer and the sound of the storm was getting louder. I thought of rising up and looking over the embankment, but then a tree trunk whooshed by inches above the ground. It would have taken my head off. I hunkered down and stayed put. Those tornadoes were only a quarter of a mile or so away and I never once heard the sounds of a damn freight train. All I could hear was an intense wind and the sound of trees breaking. There was thunder, but no freight train.

The storm turned away from the crash site and away from us. As the tornado sounds got further and further away I decided to brave a peek over the edge of the creek bank. I could see the tornadoes ripping through the trees in the distance.

"I think we're out of the woods for now." I stood and offered Tabitha a hand. I looked around and remembered that we were actually in the woods and laughed at the pun.

"What a day." She grabbed and kissed me hard. "That's for marrying me." She kissed me again. "That's for getting us back to Earth alive." She kissed me once more and said, "That, is just for the hell of it."

I gazed into her eyes and commented on how beautiful she looked.

"Phew! You're blind." She shrugged.

I started to respond to her when the world suddenly started spinning. I tried to keep focused on Tabitha's face, but I couldn't. Everything spun around and around as if I was on a merry-go-round moving at fifty miles per hour. Then I lost my balance and fell sideways into the creek. I struggled to keep my head above the water level, but I had no connection to what up or down was. My sense of direction had completely vanished. Tabitha pulled my head above the water and grunted from the painful effort.

"Anson, what's wrong?"

I was able to make it onto all fours with my face slightly above the water. Then I vomited violently. Tabitha didn't move. She made sure my head stayed above the water. Several dry heaves later the nausea subsided somewhat and I was able to get to my feet with Tabitha's help.

"Your inner ear isn't used to the gravity yet," Tabitha told me. "That happened to me the first couple of times." She tried not to laugh. "Can you stand on your own?"

"Sure I can." She let go of my shoulders and I fell flat on my face. This time I was able to pull myself from the water without her help. I rested on all fours for a couple of minutes. "Just give me a minute or two. How long does this take to pass?"

I cupped creek water in my hands and splashed it in my face several times.

"It took me a good couple of hours before I felt okay the first time. But some people it never bothers. Motion sickness is weird that way. Take your time. What else have we got to do?"

We sat at the edge of the creek for another ten or fifteen minutes while I regained my equilibrium. I should have realized that I would be affected. I had such a hard time adjusting from gravity to microgravity that it just makes sense that I would have some difficulty with the reverse process as well.

"This is about like getting the drunk spins. Did you ever get so blasted that all you could do is just lie on the bed with one foot hanging off and stare at the ceiling? You know that if you move you'll throw up."

"I did a few times in undergraduate school and when I was accepted into the astronaut program," she replied. "I had an inner ear infection once in high school that made me just as sick. I remember sleeping in the bathroom because I was afraid I wouldn't be able to make it there if need be."

"Yeah. I had an ear infection like that once. That's exactly how this feels. It is slowly subsiding though." I shook my head hard a few times hoping to reset my inner ear. The first time I did it I thought I was going to heave again. The second time the spins stopped. I saw stars for a split second and then I was better. "That is much better," I told Tabitha.

"What are you doing?" she laughed.

"Trying to reset my inner ear gyroscope system. Friday does it whenever she falls a long distance or gets tumbled. I figured if it works for cats, why not humans?"

Tabitha laughed at me and said, "I've heard flight surgeons suggest that to folks before, but I've never seen anybody do it." She laughed again, "You're weird."

"Well, it seems to have helped." I stood up with no help.

I reached to my EMU pockets and realized that I wasn't wearing my EMU.

"Tabitha. We have to go check out the probe." We helped each other out of the creek bed. I will always remember thinking that we must have been quite the sight, two people wearing white

Spandex long underwear, covered with mud, soaking wet, and traipsing practically barefoot through the woods. We basically had no survival tools other than ourselves, a wrecked spacecraft, a few multi-million dollar hand tools that would only fit the million-dollar bolts on that spacecraft, and two highly damaged spacesuits at our disposal.

We made our way through the debris, backtracking the hundred or so meters we had covered while running from the storm. Tabitha picked up a hailstone that must have been the size of a softball. It was beginning to melt in the heat.

"Have you ever seen a hailstone this large?"

"Nope. I've also never seen a tornado that size."

"Yeah," she replied. "It was an F-five I'll bet."

"Uh huh! How are your ribs?"

"I don't think they're broken. But I guarantee they're bruised badly."

As we approached the probe I noticed a very very low pitched humming sound. I found my EMU and dug out the engagement ring. I took Tabitha's left hand and put it on her ring finger. I got down on one knee.

"Marry me," I said.

"Get up idiot. I already said yes." She pulled me up. "Besides, we need to figure out where we are."

The sun poked out from behind the clouds and rays of sunlight filtered through the pine trees. It was good old Sol all right—I could tell by the color. Any fantasies about having warped off to some other planet had been parlayed.

"Earth," I said.

"What?"

"We're on Earth. That is where we are." I held up my hands as if to encompass the world.

"Smartass. I know this is Earth. But where on Earth? I never saw a pine thicket like this in New Mexico." Tabitha rested her right hand on her hip and cocked her head sideways like she always does when she is being a smartass in return.

There was a path a half of a mile wide south of us that had been cleared away by the tornadoes. I knew which direction it was now that the sun was out.

"You're right. This ain't New Mexico. Reminds me of southern Alabama," I replied.

The humming sound got louder.

Tabitha and I poked around the probe trying to determine where it was coming from. First we tried the comm system. It had been crushed completely by debris or landing—it was difficult to determine which. Tabitha pulled a limb out of ECC number three, the one that was damaged the most. The humming got louder and turned to a buzzing.

"Holy crap! The sound is coming from the ECC!" I looked at Tabitha. She looked back at me with a horrified expression on her face.

➤ CHAPTER 11

"How long, Anson?"

I plowed through the wreckage looking for the precise origin point of the sound. "Dig the batteries out of the science suite if they are still intact," I told her.

I found the general area where I thought the sound was coming from and tried to isolate a subset of circuit boards. The horrified looks we had had on our faces were warranted. The Casimir effect energy devices were oscillating asymmetrically. In other words, the Clemons Dumbbells were going chaotic. Not just a few of them like the ones that destroyed the bathroom at the manufacturing facility or the handful that injured 'Becca. The amplitude of the buzzing sound implied hundreds of thousands of these things could go. I started doing the math in my head. If all of them went at one time, the explosion would be bigger than Hiroshima or if I slipped a zero or two, which I often do without paper and pencil, much bigger than Hiroshima. Of course, it had occurred to all of us working the project from day one, that we were dealing with much larger than nuclear-explosion levels of power. That is why the ECCs were to never be activated until we were in space. The conventional propulsion system on the probe was to take it up to about a thousand kilometer orbit and there we would turn them on.

131

"Only one of the batteries is still operational, Anson. How long till it blows? Answer me!" Tabitha implored.

"Bring it over here. And I'm working on it." I ripped some cabling from the probe. I fumbled through my EMU and found the Swiss Army knife that all astronauts are issued. I stripped off the ends of two wires and tied them to the battery poles. Then I stripped the other ends and shunted across a section of the Clemons Dumbbells. The buzzing returned back to a humming. The battery was drained completely.

"Shit! That battery wasn't enough. This thing is going to blow, in like, an hour or so. If we can't find a power source to overload the Clemons Dumbbells in the ECCs, they get stuck in that positive feedback loop and will eventually go big bang!" I said.

"There's nothing else we can do? Is there no other spacecraft power system?"

"Sure. The ECCs delivered all the power we needed, but they're fried and this one is about to go kablooie!" I shrugged my shoulders and did an explosion gesture with my hands.

"What about that one?" Tabitha pointed at good old ECC number two. The one we had used as a shield from the hail.

I ran to the diagnostic panel on the side of it and tore off the plate. Tabitha grabbed her electric ratchet and started in on the bolts. In a few short seconds we were peering at a perfectly good cube of Clemons Dumbbells. I shorted the breaker, which in turn kicked the dumbbells loose. The ECC started producing power. Then an arc jumped out of it and tossed me about four meters away from it. Smoke and sparks poured out of the cube. Tabitha ran to my side and helped me to my feet.

"Are you okay?"

"Yeah," I shook the numbness out of my hands. "Oh well. That's that, I guess. I can't stop the cube from blowing now."

"How big will it be?" Tabitha was scared. She looked even more scared than she had when the Shuttle exploded.

"Judging from the size of the area that's humming, I would guess that in about two hours or so everything within a radius of about ten miles from where we're standing will be totally destroyed. That is only a guess mind you. About two times as big as Hiroshima comes to mind however." I looked south at the pathway the tornadoes had cleared for us.

"Anson, are you sure we can't stop it?"

"Yes. Hell I wish we could just hit the damn thing with a rock and get it over with, but that might trigger more of the dumbbells to go chaotic and make the thing blow up sooner and bigger!"

"Then I guess we have no choice but to run! Let's go." She started to take off.

"Hold on," I grabbed her by the wrist. "Get your water bag out of your EMU first."

"Good thinking." She nodded.

I was thirsty and borderline dehydrated and needed to drink—being sick earlier hadn't helped either. We tore the PLSS backpacks apart and dug out our water supplies. They were about a third full each. Better than nothing. I fashioned some straps from the backpack material and we tied the bags on to our backs. The plastic tubes from the bags we threw over our shoulder so we could grab it and drink from it whenever we pleased.

"Just like my water pack for my mountain bike gear," I told Tabitha.

Tabitha also grabbed the Velcro NASA mission patches off our suits. "We should have some sort of visible identification other than just my dog tags," she said.

"Ready. Now, can you run with your ribs?" I asked.

"Yeah, I'm just a little sore. Are you going to make it? Any more dizziness?"

"I'm fine. Let's get out of here," I responded.

"Which way?" she asked as she scanned the area.

"Path of least resistance," I said pointing to the tornado's track.

We started running at a slow pace and watching our footing. At least we were on sand. The Spandex footies in the LCVGs helped some. I wish we would've had shoes.

"Tabitha," I started, "if we have ten miles to run, and to be safe say, we have an hour and forty-five minutes to do it, then we better run nine minute miles. No problem with shoes on and no bruised ribs. Can you make it?"

"The ribs aren't hurting so bad right now. The sand is okay

to run in. Let's hope that we stay in the sand. How are you doing?"

"Good. Nausea is completely gone now and my nappy old karate feet will take a lot more damage than this. Besides, I invented the warp drive!" I mentally patted myself on the back.

"I was thinking about that. Are you sure?" Tabitha asked.

"Sure about what?"

"How do you know that you broke the speed of light? We didn't have any of the science instrumentation operational to measure our velocity."

"Couldn't you just have kept that to yourself!" I joked. "Okay let's do the math for worst case. We were about three hundred kilometers from Earth. The Earth blinked out and then we were here. The time inside the bubble seemed to me to be about a second or two. Do you agree?" I took a sip of water from the tube hanging over my right shoulder.

"Yes, I agree with that. Even if you consider the start time when we saw the blue light flashes around us, there was still a second of delay." Tabitha saw me drinking water and decided to do the same.

"All right, then we'll call that three hundred kilometers per second or three times ten to the five meters per second. Light speed is three times ten to the eight meters per second. We were three orders of magnitude short. Hey that's still faster than any human has ever traveled."

"Maybe the transit time really only took a millisecond but we have no way of ever knowing that do we?" She asked.

"None that I can see. The blue light probably was Cerenkov radiation but who knows. Whether we broke the speed of light or not, our propulsion came from warping space. We were still the first humans to travel with warp drive." I looked at my watch. We had been running for about twelve minutes. We still had a long way to go.

An hour or so had passed when I noticed a break in the trees at the edge of the *Finger of God* path that the tornadoes had made. "Let's veer toward that opening in the trees."

The opening turned out to be a logging road. This was most definitely a planned timber grove. It could possibly be a state forest. Sometimes when fires, tornadoes, hurricanes, etc. tear through a park pine trees are planted to fill the holes and protect from erosion.

"I need to breathe for just a second Anson. My side is hurting."

"Only for a minute or two Tabitha. We have to keep moving."

"Okay. We'll keep walking, just slowly for a minute or so." She held her side. We stopped for a second. Then started walking.

"So, any ideas where we are?" I asked her.

"Not really. The air feels like the southeastern United States to me though. It has to be ninety-five degrees and at least eighty percent humidity. It is almost like Titusville. Every now and then I even think that I can smell the ocean." She continued to hold her side.

"Yeah, I thought I could smell salt earlier also. Are you sure you're okay?"

"I have to be, don't I." She made the last statement as more of an order to herself. It was definitely not a question.

"Hey stop!" I yelled. "Don't step any further." Tabitha obeyed but she looked at me very confused.

"What is it?" She took a defensive posture.

"Tabitha, without moving look down about two feet in front of you." She did and if it were possible to sweat more than we already were, she did so.

"Anson, *I hate snakes!*"

A small colorful snake was sunning itself in the sand on Tabitha's side of the logging road. I slipped way around so as not to startle the snake and found a tree limb that was about four feet long. I broke it off a sapling that was overhanging the road.

"Come here, fella! You're all right, mate!" I did my best Steve Irwin impression. I made a slight disturbance behind the snake with the stick and it turned away from Tabitha. "Okay, Tabitha, slowly back up, then come around to me mate. Whoa, you're okay, mate." The snake struck at the twig a few times.

"Would you quit talking like that!" She did just as I had told her although she was obviously annoyed by my sense of humor.

"Red touching black you can pet him on the back. Red touching yellow will kill a fellow." I recited the poem that my dad had told me when I was a kid.

"You mean that thing is poisonous, right?" Tabitha held my shoulder, keeping me between her and the snake.

"Well, at least I know where we are now. With this vegetation, the sand, and this little coral snake, which by the way is more poisonous than a rattlesnake—or at least as poisonous. Though it is kind of like comparing apples and oranges since they carry different types of toxins. I digress. Anyway," I continued, "I would guess that we're in south Alabama, Georgia, or northern Florida. I'm not quite sure why we missed our mark so far. Probably a miscalculation of the frame dragging effect or something. Maybe somebody is fiddling with the laws of physics and not telling us." I laughed at the thought of that. Then I remembered that Tabitha's parents lived in Florida and began to wonder just how much damage our return home had caused, would cause. I hoped that the tornadoes had blown themselves out before they reached population centers. I started to bring it up but Tabitha had enough on her mind with the physical pain and all—not to mention the mental pain of losing several of her long time friends in the Shuttle explosion. We didn't dare think about that. *Keep moving soldiers; we'll mourn our brothers later.*

"We better get back to moving," Tabitha nudged me away from the little snake.

"G'day mate." I said, tossed the stick away, and we began running again.

We ran quietly for the next four or five minutes. I let Tabitha set the pace. She must have been feeling better because we were cranking out probably seven-and-a-half-minute miles. The terrain was rather flat. It was easy running except that we had no shoes and were both wearing Spandex long johns. The sandy roadbed became slightly more compacted and there were fresh tire tracks on it.

"Tire tracks," I said.

"That means people might live close by. Anson we are going to be responsible for killing them." Tabitha seemed to up the pace but maybe it was my imagination.

"I know. Maybe we can get somewhere in time to warn people

or to go back and stop the explosion. We still have at least twenty-five minutes, maybe thirty or more."

"Listen!" Tabitha said. "I hear a vehicle! It sounds like it's coming from around the curve ahead."

"You're right! I hear it too!" We pushed a little harder hoping to catch whoever was ahead of us. We turned the curve and three other roads joined into a slightly larger one. The noise was a HUMV about thirty yards ahead of us on the main southbound road. As we approached it became clear that the HUMV was stopped at the gate of a fence. The fence was about eight feet tall with barbed wire at the top. At the edge of the road was a guard shack and a sign that told us that we were at one of the gates to Eglin Airforce Base. We were in Florida.

➤ CHAPTER 12

"Anson, let me do the talking," Tabitha warned as we approached the guard shack. I nodded to her.

"You got it, Colonel!"

The guard looked to be between twenty and twenty and a half somewhere. That is, if he was a day over eighteen. Tabitha postured herself with her best voice of command that she had learned in officer's school. Looking back on the scene, I realize that we must have been quite a sight to see. Both of us were sweaty, wet, muddy, and in our white Spandex long johns—but none of that fazed Tabitha a bit.

"Airman! I am Colonel Tabitha Ames and this is Dr. Anson Clemons." Tabitha showed off our astronaut wings and her dog tags. "We are survivors of a Shuttle crash and it *is* important that we see your commanding officer immediately."

The airman must have recognized her. He snapped to and saluted her. Tabitha returned the salute. "It is an honor to meet you, Colonel ma'am. I've been a long-time fan of yours. I always wanted to be an astronaut. That is why I am in the Air Force so I can pay my way through school and—"

"That's great soldier and I would love to hear it some other time, but we're in an extreme hurry. Where is your C.O.?"

"Well Colonel, other than that truck that just came through

I've been the only person on this side of the base all day. We'll have to use the radio. Follow me." He led us to the small truck parked behind the guard shack. He made a call to his superiors and handed Tabitha the radio.

"Who am I speaking with?" Tabitha asked.

"This is Sergeant James of base military police—who is this?"

"Sergeant, my name is Colonel Tabitha Ames. It is very important that you listen to me carefully. I and one other occupant of the Space Shuttle are the only survivors of a crash that took place about three miles from this gate. There are security-sensitive elements in the crash site. More importantly, one of the classified components at the crash site has gone critical. That device will, I repeat, will explode in about twenty minutes or so unless we return and stop it. The explosion will have a total destruct radius larger than the atomic explosion at Hiroshima. Do you understand?"

There was a pause on the other end of the radio for a moment. The airman looked at me as though what Tabitha had just said scared him out of his mind. It well should have. I was scared shitless!

"Uh, ma'am is this for real? Jason is this some sort of gag?"

"Sergeant, I assure you that this is no gag. If we don't take action right now, there will be serious consequences!" She pretty much screamed that last bit at the microphone.

The airman took the microphone from Tabitha.

"Excuse me, Colonel," he said. "Sergeant, this is Airman Jason. This is real, Sarge! It really is Colonel Ames—I recognize her from television. Her and this other fellow just walked up out of the woods still in their astronaut gear. They both look like they've had a really bad day."

"All right, Jason. Put the colonel back on." Airman Jason handed Tabitha the mic.

"What do you need, Colonel?"

"First you need to start a civil defense evacuation of the area. A ten-mile radius from here at least. Do that now. Second, get us a helicopter or something that can land in a tight spot here five seconds ago. Also, hold a second . . ." She turned to me. "What do we need Anson?"

"Uh, a set of jumper cables and about five car batteries. How about some clothes and shoes. I wear a size ten and a half. Oh, and some duct tape. You can never have too much duct tape."

"Good idea. I wear a women's nine. Did you copy that Sergeant?"

"Copy that, Colonel. It will be there in five minutes or less."

I had expected him to ask about the car batteries and stuff but he didn't. He just followed orders and didn't waste time. Good soldier.

"Colonel, you guys look thirsty. I have some sodas in a cooler in the shack there if you want them and there's a water cooler back there, too." Airman Jason said. I could tell Airman Jason wasn't from the South. The thing about there being "sodas" instead of "cocolas" in the cooler was a dead giveaway.

"Airman, I want you to get in your truck and drive south at least ten miles before you stop," Tabitha ordered him.

"Sorry, ma'am. From the sound of it you two will need some help carrying all those car batteries. I'm going with you. Besides, my Aunt Rosie lives about five miles from where you are talking about. If I can help, I plan to. "

"Airman!—" Tabitha started in on him. I interrupted her.

"Tabitha, he's right. We need the help. I don't want anybody else involved either, but he signed on to help protect the country. This is his job."

Tabitha scowled at me and stormed over to the truck. She didn't say a word. She rummaged through the cooler for a soft drink. I followed her.

"What?" I asked her. I did something wrong. I could tell.

"Anson, I love you, but never, and I mean never, contradict me when I'm giving orders to subordinate soldiers."

"Tabitha I love you too—more than anything in the world. But, I'm not a soldier and I don't have to follow orders here. We aren't on the Shuttle anymore. And although I will admit that you are better suited to be in charge here, if you do something wrong or if I disagree with you I should be able to tell you. Shouldn't I?"

"Next time do it in private!"

"Yes ma'am, Colonel."

"Don't Colonel me, civilian," she tossed right back at me. She was still obviously sore at me, but not as much. After all, I had invented the warp drive.

"Listen," I began. "You're right and I'm right. I don't want to involve anyone else either. Hell, if there was a way that I could do this myself and put you in that truck with Airman Jason I would do it." Tabitha halted me there.

"The hell you would!"

"Well, I'd try. Maybe between Airman Jason and me we could hogtie you and throw you in the back of that truck."

"There would be a helluva fight," she said. Then she smiled. That was good. I didn't want Tabitha mad at me. We had enough on our minds.

We grabbed a Coke each and started drinking them. I managed to get out of Airman Jason that he was from Ohio somewhere and his Aunt Rosie was retired and living here in Florida.

Tabitha and I both needed the caffeine and sugar rush. Of course, neither of us needed to be dehydrated and that is just what the caffeine will do to you. We chased the Cokes by filling the bottles with water from the water cooler in the guard shack.

About three minutes had passed since the radio conversation. I looked at my watch. There were only about seventeen minutes left. Whoever was coming had better hurry.

"If they don't show within ten minutes, all three of us are getting in that truck and heading south," I told Tabitha and Jason.

Then a jet silently passed into view from behind a small hill. A few seconds later we could hear it. It came straight for the clearing at the guard shack.

"That's a Harrier Jump Jet," Tabitha exclaimed.

"Doesn't look like any helicopter I have ever seen," I replied.

"Yeah, I like Harriers. The VTOL capability makes them very useful like a helicopter, but still as effective as a fighter jet. Just check out how it lands in as small a space as a chopper can." Tabitha watched in approval of the pilot's skill.

The jet landed in a small clearing and two men crawled down from it. One of them was carrying a small duffle bag. The pilot confronted Tabitha.

"You Colonel Ames?"

"That's right, Captain. I thought I asked for a helicopter."

"Sorry ma'am. All the helicopters were ordered out when the tornadoes came through. There are none within twenty minutes of here. This Jump Jet came in just after the storms. We were fortunate to get it. It is a real mess out there." He pointed to the southeast.

The other man handed me a flight suit, a pair of socks, and a pair of combat boots. Then he handed the duffle bag to Tabitha, after he saluted her of course. Tabitha looked around and then stepped behind the truck.

"Gentlemen, please look the other way. Anson, get dressed quick."

I was still trying to tie my boots when Tabitha stepped out from behind the truck.

"Captain, I'll take your gear. Dr. Clemons will take the lieutenant's. Move it!" The two of them moved it.

"Sorry, Airman. I guess you won't get to go with us after all." I shook his hand.

"Good luck sir and ma'am," he said.

"You three men get in that truck and drive south. That is an order! Where are the batteries?" Tabitha asked.

"Sorry, ma'am. No time to find them. But, we did get a small generator fully fueled and the jumper cables. They are in the back seat," the lieutenant said.

"Anson, will that work?"

"Yeah, it should. We will probably have to reset the circuit breaker on it every time we fry a board though. Hope we have enough time." At least I thought it should work. There were no physical reasons why it shouldn't.

Tabitha saluted the three men and we were off. I climbed into the backseat and Tabitha climbed into the pilot's seat. She cycled the canopy as she brought the engines on line.

"Have you ever flown one of these things before?" I prayed that the answer was yes.

"Never. How hard can it be?" She laughed. "Relax, I have over a thousand hours in these things," she informed me as we lifted vertically and then started horizontally. "Oh and hold on," she said as we cleared the treetops and then she slammed me back into my seat with maximum forward thrust. Then we were on our way back to the crash site or should I say ground zero. Tabitha flew due east until she hit the tornado's track. Then she banked and followed the track north until it turned ninety degrees back west.

"The crash was right at the bend in the track," I told her over the headsets.

"I know." She brought the plane in facing west up the track and descended.

I saw something flicker in my peripheral vision. To the north, just beyond the creek there was something shiny. It looked like a small clearing. Maybe there was a house with a tin roof there. It could have been a fire watchtower. Once we were below the treeline I could no longer see it.

Tabitha brought us down quickly with a bit of a *thump!*

"Come on, we have about thirteen minutes," she announced. The canopy cycled up. Tabitha was on the ground looking back up at me. I worked the small generator out from between my legs and handed it over to her. I grabbed the cables and jumped to the ground. It was a longer drop than I had expected. I nearly did a faceplant in the sand. I caught myself and rolled. I stood up brushing myself off. Tabitha just giggled a little but said nothing.

We both threw our gear down by the plane and each took a side of the generator. Tabitha set a fast pace up the slight hill to the edge of the clearing where the probe was. I could hear no humming or buzzing. That worried me. The calculations we did for the DARPA program showed that the dumbbells go critical just as the frequency or the sound shifts too high for human ears to detect.

We popped into the clearing and there were already four men hard at work dismantling the probe. All of them wearing military gear and clothing and were armed to the gills. The ECC had stopped buzzing because there were large Van der Graaf generators sitting all around it. They were plugged into a battery supply. The strong static electric field must have frozen the Clemons Dumbbells' motion keeping them from going further critical. They still weren't drained or destroyed I assumed. Tabitha and I assumed that help had arrived that we were unaware of. We stepped closer to the probe and the leader of the four men turned toward us with his pistol in his hand.

Johnny Cache (my handyman and secretary not the singer) was there by the probe pointing a handgun at Tabitha and me. I looked at Tabitha. She looked back at me with the same confused look.

"Hello, Dr. Clemons," he said. "I didn't expect that you would come back. You have bigger balls than I thought." Two of the men finished disconnecting the warp field coil housing and lifted the subsection of the cylinder. They rolled it over a network of cabling and cargo straps that they had laid out on the ground. The shiny object I had seen in the clearing just north of the creek must have been a helicopter because it was now hovering over us. A set of cables lowered and the three men other than Johnny Cache connected it to the lowering cables. Johnny talked into his left wrist telling the helicopter to take it up.

"Johnny, what the hell are you doing here?" I asked him.

"I'm earning a living. I wish you hadn't come back, because I kind of like you. But now you will have to die here." He seemed sincerely apologetic.

"What are you doing with the probe components?" asked Tabitha.

"Well, Colonel, I'm selling them to the Chinese. They were going to pick up the whole thing in orbit once the Shuttle was destroyed, but somehow you two managed to bring it back to Earth. Now I'll have to figure out a way to deliver it to them. Of course, it will cost them more. The talk of a meteor crashing in Florida—buzzing all over the news—gave me the idea that this could be the probe. My hunch paid off. Fortunately, I was only an hour or so away by fast helicopter."

"Hunh?" I shook my head. "I don't get it." I also wondered where the good guys were. If Johnny could figure it out, why didn't Space Command?

"He blew up the shuttle." Tabitha pointed at Johnny.

"How could he have done that?" I asked nobody in particular. I was trying to decide how I was going to get that gun away from him. *Keep him talking,* I thought. Somewhere in the conversation, we could find a distraction. Bob had never taught me how to dodge bullets. I always hoped he would someday. I guess I would just have to wing it, if I got the chance.

Johnny's buddies, employees, or whatever the other three guys were didn't seem to be paying us any attention. They had moved on to removing parts of ECC number two.

"She's right, Dr. Clemons. Security at the Vehicle Assembly Building isn't so tight these days. I placed the explosives in the Shuttle over two weeks ago using your security badge. It wasn't easy to get that from you. You should sleep more. Of course the plan was for the shuttle to explode once you two had assembled the probe and gone back onboard the Shuttle."

"How did the bomb know when to explode? That's impossible," I said, still trying to keep him talking. Tabitha tried to edge slowly sideways toward him.

"Hold still, Colonel or I'll shoot you now," he said calmly. "Planting the explosive and setting it to start the timer after a seven-minute gee loading was easy. Just a simple accelerometer and some simple timing circuitry, nothing fancy required. Your unplanned EVA delayed the flight plan by nearly four hours, hence you were still in the middle of the EVA when the timer set off the explosives."

"Johnny, why are you doing this? The Chinese could shift the balance of global power using this technology. What about your family? Do you want them to grow up communists?" Tabitha said. Johnny laughed at her.

"Screw 'em all! I'm going to live the rest of my life on a beach surrounded by naked women. I've been waiting for one more big score, and this is it, baby! Who cares about the politics of the rest of the world? Let 'em get their own island." He touched his ear as if someone was talking to him. He held up his left wrist and said, "Okay, move out!" The three men left for the north clearing, each of them carrying probe components. Johnny shot the battery pack powering the Van der Graaf generators. It spewed acid on the ground as the generators wound down. The Clemons Dumbbells started whining loudly and at about the pitch of a referee's whistle. I could see occasional flashes of light coming from the interior of the damaged, ECC number one. I guessed that we had about six minutes, maybe less.

Johnny looked at the generator that we had brought up the hill. He fired a couple rounds into it. Fuel drained from the tank. I guess we should have been glad that it didn't explode. I looked to my left at Tabitha. She seemed calm. I shifted my weight so that my right leg was slightly in back. I knew if I made a move it would have to be like a sprinter out of the starting blocks and I wanted my strongest leg in back to push off with.

"I can't have you flying off and telling anybody about this, can I? It was nice meeting you two." He turned and raised the pistol toward Tabitha. I rushed him. I was one step further away from him than I needed to be. He fired a shot just as my right hand slammed into his right wrist. I gripped his wrist tightly and yanked his arm forward under my left armpit. Then I completed the move with a Jackie Chan style arm crawl. I quickly grabbed his arm with my left hand just above the elbow on the nerve center and pressure point there, and pulled him further toward me. I held his hand tightly under my left armpit as I let go of his wrist with my right hand, and then proceeded to karate chop (knife hand strike) Johnny Cache on the right side of his neck. His hand went limp from the blow to the neck and the gun fell to the ground. With my right hand, I pushed up on his chin and tried to sweep his feet with my right leg. The intent was to throw him to the ground, but Johnny Cache was obviously a pro and was having none of that.

Johnny grabbed my flight suit by the right shoulder and rolled his weight backward. He threw his legs out from under him as he twisted to his left. We both hit the ground hard staring each other eye to eye and on our sides. The next few seconds were a flurry of grabs, counter grabs, attempted leg wraps, and punches. Each of us was trying to get an advantage over the other as we grappled and rolled on the sand. I was able to get his left hand barred for a split second, which allowed me to get a punch into the side of his head and roll on top. Johnny rolled his head minimizing the damage. He must have allowed me to bar his left hand as a ruse, because I felt a searing pain on my right side. Then I saw a shiny glint from the corner of my eye—Johnny Cache had a knife!

I lunged as hard as I could forward and over his head. Judo-rolling to my feet, I faced Johnny, ready for his attack. He got to his feet a little slower and more cautiously. He smiled insanely as if he were enjoying this.

"Not bad, Doc. At least I'll have some fun out of killing you, after all!" he said.

I felt my right side with my left hand. I was bleeding but not bad. The wound was a slice not a puncture. It was nothing fifty or so stitches, some antibiotic ointment, and a few bandages wouldn't fix. I readied myself for a knife attack. Although Bob had never taught me how to dodge bullets, he had taught me seventeen different ways to defend against a knife. Ten of them are very painful to the attacker. The other seven are passive. I planned to use one of the painful techniques.

Johnny and I circled each other cautiously. This allowed me to survey the area. Tabitha was on the ground motionless. I thought she was still breathing, but it was hard to tell. Johnny's crew had already disappeared from the clearing and were on the way to their helicopter. It was just Johnny Cache and me.

Johnny held the knife hilt forward in his right hand. The blade pointed back toward his elbow. Obviously, Johnny had some military self-defense training in his life. I was guessing Special Forces. He shifted to a left side forward fighting stance with his fists high and his elbows out Muay Thai kickboxing style. I always loved to fight people using this style's fighting stance. The high elbows leaves the ribs wide open for a roundhouse kick. Of course, real Muay Thai fighters train from childhood getting kicked in the ribs. Their ribs are broken many times throughout their lives. As they are repeatedly broken, they get calcified and harder. Johnny looked American. I didn't believe he was a *real* Muay Thai fighter.

Johnny and I made several feints at each other attempting to bait the other into a bad move. Like I said, Johnny was a real pro. I decided that it was now or never. I kicked him low at the knee with my right leg. He picked up his knee and let his calf take the blow. Without setting my kick down I rechambered it and side kicked him just below the belly button. He moved backwards from the force of the kick so I kept coming at him. I sat down the side kick into a spin side kick followed by an inner crescent kick that was aimed for the hand with the knife in it.

I missed the knife! As I sat the kick down I knew that I had better get out of the way. Johnny lunged toward me with a left jab then a spin backfist, which was really a spin knife jab. I backed up as best I could. The knife blade whizzed by my face two inches in front of my eyes. Had I been two or three inches closer, the knife would've buried hilt deep into my temple and that would've been that.

The reality of the knife strike shook me slightly. I backed off a bit more and composed myself. I tested the waters with a couple of very quick jabs and knee high front kicks. Johnny slapped them away with ease and sliced at me a time or two. I picked up my left foot to feint a kick. Johnny didn't buy it. But when I faked a punch with my right I could have sold him swampland in the Everglades to go with it. He stepped in to slice at me thinking that I was going to commit to the right punch. I was trying an old tournament trick—called a dash punch—that I had used successfully a thousand times. I pulled back the punch and slipped to the left. Then, I hammer fisted his right wrist with my left hand as hard as I could and the knife fell free. I followed by rotating my body into a front stance to get the full force of my body weight into a right palm heel strike to the bridge of his nose. Grabbing the back of his hair with both hands, I yanked him forward, slamming his chest into my right knee and then threw him past me to the right as I stepped through and turned back to a right side fighting stance. I kicked the knife as far away from us as I could.

Johnny rolled to his feet. I could see he was pulling something from his left boot so I didn't give him time to finish standing. I tackled him, expecting a full fifteen-yard penalty for clipping. The only whistle that blew was the constant screeching of the soon to explode ECC.

The thing was getting so close to exploding now that the randomly collapsing electromagnetic fields were creating shock waves in the air around the device. The shockwaves in turn were causing luminescence all around the ECC. Micro supernova explosions were taking place every second.

Johnny and I rolled into the ECC as I was grabbing for his hand. We had all four hands on the small handgun and were kneeing each other and I attempted to head butt him twice with very little success. His nose was bleeding profusely where I had just broken it with the palm heel strike; I didn't care for getting his blood all over me, but, it couldn't be helped. We rolled back and forth and the gun went off twice. I managed somehow to roll on top of him and force his hand against the ECC into the region where the sonoluminescence was occurring.

I was lucky. One of the microscopic supernova explosions sparked just inside his hand. It looked as if someone had set off a firecracker underneath his skin and the gun fell into the gaping hole in the ECC. We rolled up staring each other down. Johnny shook his bloody hand and snarled at me.

"That's gotta hurt, Johnny," I taunted him. Then I saw motion out of the corner of my left eye. Johnny made a dash for the motion and I followed.

Tabitha had been playing 'possum. She bear crawled as fast as I had ever seen her move for the first gun that Johnny had dropped. Unfortunately, she didn't make it. Johnny stomped on her hand with his left foot and kicked her hard in the chest with his right. Tabitha's ribs were bruised already and were probably broken now from Johnny's kick. I was on top of Johnny before he could kick at her twice. *He would pay for that!*

He turned to me as he swept the gun away from Tabitha with his right foot and turned the momentum of the sweeping motion into a left-leg spinning side kick. I blocked the kick with my stomach. Had I been wearing a mouthpiece I could have spat it on him. I heaved out twice as I backed up, blocking at his follow-up punches. He got me good on the side of the head with one of them and I saw stars for a second.

"Turtle up!" Bob would have yelled at me. Therefore, I did. If you are ever being attacked too quickly to defend against, cover up as best you can and take it. Try to get inside to cut off the full force of the attack. Bruce Lee was always fond of saying that there are three regions of fighting. One is within a few inches where you're grappling with your opponent. The second is at kicking and boxing range from your opponent. Everybody trains for these two distances. The third distance is in between one and

two where most people don't know how to attack. This is why
Bruce Lee developed the famous Six-Inch Punch.

I realized that I had to get inside region three if I was going to
survive. So, I turtled up and crowded him. This cut off his kicks.
He countered by throwing hook punches to my ribs and head. I
bobbed and weaved, and ducked and covered until I could catch
my breath. The spin sidekick to the stomach had taken some of
my wind. With all of the astronaut training over the past six
months, I hadn't done as many abdominal exercises as I usually
do, so my stomach wasn't as hard as it should have been.

Most fights don't last long because they are typically
asymmetric—the better fighter usually whups the lesser one
quickly—but Johnny and I were very evenly matched, except
that I had already had a pretty rough day. I was getting tired
and something had to give. So, I shoved Johnny back and pushed
him harder by following with a thrust front kick, stomping him
in the bladder thus pushing him as far away from me as I could
manage. His knees buckled for an instant but I needed to recover
for that instant and couldn't continue to press.

"This has been fun, Doc," he said, as he wiped blood from his
nose with his sleeve. He held up his wrist. "Will one of you guys
get over here and shoot this bastard for me!" he yelled into it.

"What's the matter, Johnny? Can't beat an old man by yourself?" I taunted him while trying not to give away that I was
very tired.

Johnny moved around to keep himself between the handgun
and Tabitha who was trying to stand, obviously in serious pain.
I saw a flicker of motion through the trees at the edge of the
clearing and knew I didn't have much time before Johnny's backup
would be drawing a bead on me. I circled counterclockwise toward
Tabitha, trying to keep Johnny between me and his crew.

"Enough of this!" I screamed at Johnny as I rushed him with a
left leg jump bicycle roundhouse kick that caught Johnny square
on the jaw turning his head.

"You are going down, Johnny fucking Cache!" I was enraged.
Left leg outer crescent kick, right leg round house, spin left outer
crescent kick, right leg tornado roundhouse kick, backfist, reverse
punch, "Kia!" I yelled.

Johnny dodged and parried, and slipped and blocked. He was on the defensive. I had to keep pressing while the adrenaline was flowing because I knew that when I came down from this rush I would be physically wasted.

I had to use the adrenaline. I had to get angry! *He blew up the Shuttle and killed all those people! Our friends! He shot Tabitha!* I blocked every punch Johnny attempted and I managed to slip by each kick.

Forget that "Luke never succumb to the Dark Side crap," if someone is trying to kill you, get angry, get pissed, get evil. Do whatever you have to do in order to stay alive. You can get philosophical about it afterwards, if you survive that is. The Dark Side was coursing through me like water through a sieve. *Son of a bitch, HE WAS GOING DOWN!*

I followed an uppercut with a jab. Johnny ducked the jab so I turned it over into a hook punch and caught him right on the jaw. His eyes rolled white for a split second, which was all I needed. I jumped and switched feet in the air bringing my back leg into a roundhouse kick that landed in his left ribcage solid enough to break bricks. He heaved. I heard a *crack*! Then I heard several *whizzing* sounds whip past me followed by *cracks*. I realized the *cracks* were from a rifle.

Johnny punched at me with his right, so I slipped left and caught his wrist with my right hand and pushed through his elbow with my left palm heel. His elbow snapped into two pieces like a stick. Skin, pulled muscles, and torn cartilage were all that held his ulna and radius forearm bones to his upper arm bone. Johnny let out a scream.

Then a searing hot pain ripped through my right shoulder. I had been shot. I grabbed Johnny by the hair and pulled his body to mine, his back to my chest. Bullets slammed into Johnny forcing us to the ground. One of the bullets pierced his neck and entered my chest just below and to the left of my right nipple and we fell to the ground, Johnny twitching slightly and bleeding profusely on top of me.

I could hear return fire and some scrambling around me, but the firefight lasted only a few seconds. I wheezed and coughed a few times as if I had to clear my throat of mucous drainage from a bad sinus infection. I turned my head toward the probe and could see the pulses of light getting much more frequent and the screeching sound was so high it was almost inaudible and the flashes of light were ranging in color from white hot to near blue. It was actually quite beautiful, in a deadly kind of way.

We had to get out of there soon I knew, but at the moment nothing mattered. I was simply observing everything around me. I was dazed. Seconds passed and a helicopter shadowed the sun briefly. I could see sparks flying from the tail and the fixed wing portion of it. As each shot was fired I could hear Tabitha cursing violently. Then Johnny rolled off me to my left.

Tabitha's silhouette was above me. She helped me up. It was all I could do to rise to my feet. I coughed several violent coughs. I covered my mouth and when I looked back down at my hand it was covered with blood. Johnny jerked twice and rolled over. Tabitha reacted instantly and emptied the rest of the clip into his head.

"That's for Ray." She pulled the trigger. "That's for Terrence." She fired the weapon again. "And that's for Tracy and Malcom you piece of shit!" She fired the last four rounds into his face, or what was left of it. She screamed curses at him and then kicked him in the side and then screamed at him again. Then she turned her attention to me as she nonchalantly tossed the empty pistol to the ground.

Tabitha unzipped my flight suit and pulled it down to my waist. I was still dazed, nearly catatonic, and my chest was a wet blood-soaked deep red. Tabitha looked at both my chest and my back, then she unzipped her flight suit.

I noticed that in the clothes that Tabitha had been given there must have been a T-shirt. Why didn't I get a T-shirt, I thought? My mind could only seem to focus on unimportant and trivial things. Then she took off her T-shirt and was standing topless in front of me and I tried to focus on that. She ripped the shirt into two halves and rolled one of the halves into a tight wad. She poked her finger into the half of the T-shirt she had rolled up and then into the hole in my chest. The pain snapped me out of my catatonia for just a second or two.

"Ouch! Shit, that hurts," I cursed.

"Hold still, damnit. You're bleeding like a stuck pig and I think one of your lungs is punctured." She placed my hand on the bandage, causing a squishing sound, and my hand began to feel even wetter than when I coughed. "Hold this and press down hard."

She scrambled over to the now defunct generator and rummaged around for the duct tape. She wiggled and pulled her flight suit back over her shoulders, her breasts jiggling lightly in the sunlight as she zipped it most of the way up. I'll always remember that sight for the rest of my life, but at the time in my weakened state I was nearly numb to it, nearly.

Tabitha made a cross of duct tape over the makeshift bandage, then stepped behind me.

"Eyow shit! That hurts," I cursed in a loud gurgling whisper and cursed again as she repeated the process to the exit wound on my back, the pain bringing me a little closer to normal consciousness.

"Hold your arms up."

I did. She wrapped the duct tape over the bandages and around my torso several times. Then she wrapped my right shoulder with it. When she was done with my shoulder she taped the knife wound across my right oblique abdominal muscles together. Then she wrapped several times around her right thigh where Johnny had shot her earlier.

"Sorry I couldn't stop him earlier, Tabitha. But aren't you glad I asked for the duct tape? I told you that you could never have too much of it." I gurgled again and looked at her leg.

"Stow it! We have to get out of here now!" Colonel Ames ordered.

We helped each other down the hill and to the Jump Jet. Once we fell flat on our faces and I was thrown into some sort of wheezing frenzy. I gurgled a few times and felt like I was going to drown. Tabitha dragged me to my feet and forced me to keep moving.

"You better not die on me you son of a bitch! You still owe me a wedding." She was trying to keep my adrenaline flowing.

"Yeah, well you . . . *cough cough wheeze* . . . owe me a honeymoon!"

"You make it out of this alive and you'll get it. Whatever you want, hot shot!" She laughed. I tried to.

"Well maybe I have something to live for after all!" I said faintly.

After what seemed like fifty miles and three years, we finally covered the hundred yards or so to the airplane. We scrambled in it as best we could, which wasn't very good. Tabitha fired up the engines and we were gone.

"We have to find that helicopter Tabitha!" I wheezed and coughed blood from my mouth and nose.

"I'm already on it. Radar shows nothing," she responded. "Maybe I hit it when I shot at it. I don't know? Look on the ground."

For the first time I paid attention to the area around the crash site. There were three other tornado tracks in the area. All of them stretched radially outward from the probe. One track about a quarter of a mile wide stretched southeastward, one was due east, and the third zig zagged to the north and a little northeast. Something flashed from the northeast track.

"There, northeast, Tabitha!"

Alarms sounded in the cockpit of the jet. I knew that couldn't be good. I was slammed into my seat hard.

"Hold on, Anson!" Tabitha banked the jet sideways and fired the jets full throttle, pushing us into a down and outward dive. "Aaarrrgghh!" she grunted as we pulled straight up. The g-forces were more than I could handle in my condition. I started to tunnel out. I tried squeezing my abs and thigh muscles. I even tried grunting. It didn't help.

The stinger missile that had been fired at us from the downed helicopter zipped by the canopy not twenty feet away. Tabitha pulled us over and straight back down hard toward the ground. The missile exploded behind us. My head slammed into the left wall of the canopy. The blow brought me to more than it dazed me.

"Forget them, Tabitha! They're stranded and will go with the probe! Get out of range before they can shoot at us again," I screamed.

"I'm trying, Anson!"

"We have to get away from the probe!" I reminded her.

"I'm trying, Anson!"

She pulled the jet nose up and climbed, then angled it over some. I was being pushed hard into my seat by the aircraft's acceleration. I could see the ground beneath us in the rearview mirror mounted in front and to the left of Tabitha. Then the mirror turned white with light.

We couldn't have been more than three miles along the surface from ground zero. Maybe we were five or six miles above it. One thing for certain is that we were too damn close.

"We're too close, Tabitha, move!"

"Hold on, Anson! If I tell you to eject, you eject!" She continued forcing the jet upward as hard as it would go.

At max velocity the Harrier pushes Mach one. The blast wave approached us hard at about Mach three. Tabitha pulled off some magical flying that allowed us to surf the edge of the shock wave for a split second. Then the aircraft tumbled tail over nose and was thrown into a spin that ripped the wings right off.

"Eject Anson! Eject, Eject, Eject!" she screamed as the canopy flew off the aircraft. I ejected. I felt something hit me. Hard!

➤ CHAPTER 13

"Anson, wake up!" Tabitha slapped me across the face. My head was pounding and I couldn't breathe. I heaved. Tabitha rolled me over onto all fours as I heaved again. I vomited mostly blood and very few other fluids. I held myself steady on all fours for a moment longer and heaved once more.

"Anson, are you okay?"

"I think so." I made it to my feet, shook my head lightly, and looked at Tabitha. Her face was scratched up badly and her left eye was swollen shut with a big bloody gash just above it. Her flight suit was torn and bloody across her chest and left side. A slight trickle of blood was noticeable on her left earlobe.

"Are you okay?" I asked.

"I'll live. It's superficial stuff. The worst part is that I think my left wrist is broken. Mostly, I just have a lot of pain. I can deal with that." She grimaced. "We have to get some help soon. You've lost a lot of blood. I'm getting concerned about you."

"Hell I can't believe we're still alive. How'd we survive that blast?"

"Simple shock wave aerodynamics," she replied. "I maxed our velocity to get us as high as fast as we could get. The air pressure is lower as you get higher of course. I managed to surf the wave as long as the aircraft would take it, which wasn't that

157

long. When the aircraft came apart, the blast wave overtook us. Then we were on the inside of the wave. What is the air pressure behind a shock wave?" she quizzed me.

"Of course. The pressure behind a shock is at stagnation pressure of that gas. In Earth's atmosphere, that is one atmospheric pressure of air, mostly harmless. Genius! You knew we weren't going to make it. That is why you told me to wait on ejecting until you ordered me to. And you didn't order us to eject until we were inside the shock wave letting the plane take the force of the blast wave." That was more than I felt like saying at the time, but it was so brilliant I had to say something.

"That's it. You win the prize."

"God I love you," I gurgled. "Let's find a way to civilization. What do you think?" I scanned the area. "Where the heck are we?"

"I think we're about three miles north of the crash site. Airman Jason said that his Aunt Rosie lives near here. There might be civilization there." Tabitha paused and gazed at the total destruction around us. "Or at least what is left of it. Can you walk?"

"I guess I'd better." I coughed up more blood and gurgled a little as I inhaled. I felt weaker and more tired than I ever had in my life. It had been a long day. Thanks to the ECC explosion the terrain was a one big pile of rubble and smashed pine trees after another—it wasn't easy going. Jesus, the destruction!

We had been walking for more than thirty minutes before we came to a paved road. I was feeling weak. I was so weak that each step took all of my will power and strength to accomplish. I felt like I was about to "bonk."

For you non-athletes out there "bonking" might mean something else—something, erh, sexual—but to the athletes you know what I'm getting at. I had bonked before once when 'Becca and Jim and I were mountain bike riding in Tsali, North Carolina. Tsali has some of the most beautiful single track in the country. Well, we had been riding for most of the day. I remember being on top of 'Becca's wheel, then we hit a hard climb. My muscles started aching halfway up. Then I had no more energy to turn the cranks. No matter how hard I tried to stroke the pedals, there was no strength in my legs. The next thing I knew Jim was standing over me squirting his water bottle in my face.

"What happened?" 'Becca asked. "You were right on my ass then you just died and fell over. I looked back and you were on the ground."

"I don't know?" I told her.

"Drink this, Doc." Jim handed me his bottle.

My hands were too shaky to hold on to it and I felt sick to my stomach. "I don't understand what is wrong with me," I stated.

"Have you eaten anything, Doc?" 'Becca asked.

"Well I ate lunch with you guys."

"Anson, she means have you eaten anything while you were on the bike. We have been riding for over three hours and your hydration system only has water in it." Jim pointed to my pack.

"You mean, I'm supposed to eat while on the bike?" That was the weirdest thing I had ever heard.

"Newbie!" 'Becca laughed and shook her head.

"You never read the magazines I give you, do you, Doc?" Jim asked. "Never you mind. Eat this." He handed me a sports bar. "If you're riding for more than a couple of hours, you need to restore your energy supplies here and there. You've used up all the glycogen in your muscles and your body is now trying to use your excess body fat for energy."

"Yeah, good. What is wrong with that?" I interrupted him.

"Newbie!" 'Becca laughed again.

"Well Doc, nothing is wrong with that. In fact that's where you do some really good fat burning. But, your body cannot convert stored fat to energy fast enough to keep up with the demands of a hard riding pace. Hence, the need to supplement with external calories." Jim took the sports bar wrapper from me and stuck it in his jersey pocket.

"Here Doc, drink some of my sports drink. It will get into your system faster. You basically had a low blood sugar crash like diabetics do. It is called bonking. Good news is that you'll live. Bad news is that Jim and I are going to leave you here for the bears to eat." She helped me up and winked at me.

We rode back to the parking lot at a much slower pace. I didn't fully recover for at least fifteen minutes or more. Even then

I was tired. I chilled in the air-conditioned car while Jim and 'Becca made a lap on another section of the single track. I had a completely new respect and sympathy for diabetics. Moreover, I felt very bad about missing some of that awesome single track due to my own ignorance.

This's how I was feeling now as Tabitha and I crawled onto the pavement. Then I started getting cold and my feet were falling to sleep. The tips of my fingers felt like ice and it was well over ninety degrees. It was getting harder to breathe.

"Tabitha, I don't think I'm gonna make it. I think I'm gonna pass out," I told her.

"Enough of that! You *will* make it do you hear me?" Colonel Ames ordered.

"Yes Colonel . . ." I fell flat on my face and didn't get up.

I don't think that I passed out either, because I can remember watching Tabitha, and I could hear her also.

"Anson! Anson, wake up," she cried. Then she slapped me on the face a few times. "Anson can you hear me?"

I continued to stare up at her. I tried hard to move or say something, anything. No motion or sound came from my lifeless body. I tried harder and harder to speak. I couldn't.

Tabitha held her right ear over my mouth and then my chest. Then she held her fingers to my neck as if she were checking my pulse. I remember watching all of this. Then she leaned over closer as if she were going to kiss me. I tried to ask her what she was doing. I still couldn't move. Then the sunlight faded out and Tabitha seemed to be far away from me looking at me through a long dark tube. Then she was gone.

Bright lights hit me from all sides. A thumping sound filled my ears. I was hearing my own heart beat arhythmically, then it stopped. The lights went out again. Then I felt a serious pain throughout my body. For a second I thought that I was back at the ECC trying to short it out and getting electrocuted. Then the light came back and I could see that I was still on the side of the road with Tabitha and three other people I had never met before. I could hear again.

"Anson! Oh my God, Anson, wake up." Tabitha was crying now.

"Dr. Clemons, can you hear me?" one of the men asked. Then the second man held a breather over my face.

The lights went out again. Everything was dark. Then I realized that I was sitting in my study back in Huntsville, Alabama. For some reason that didn't seem strange to me. It felt right. Why, I cannot explain.

"So you finally did it, did you?" Albert asked.

I turned to Professor Einstein and responded, "What? I did what finally?"

"You fixed my blunder," he said and pointed to the whiteboard.

The whiteboard had the complete story spelled out in undergraduate math. From beginning to end in front of me was *The Grand Unification of All Forces of Nature.* Everything was described, gravity was a simple ungauging of the electromagnetic field, inertia was due to the vacuum energy fluctuations and something similar to Mach's principle, renormalization of the Standard Model wasn't required, and Einstein's Cosmological Constant when moved to the right rest frame turned out to be proportional to Hubble's constant for the expansion of spacetime. It was beautiful, absolutely magnificent!

"I didn't do that," I told him.

"But of course you did. In one experiment, you accomplished all of that. You just have yet to write it all down." He smiled and shook my hand approvingly. "I just wish," he began, "that such a large sacrifice didn't have to be made for such great achievements."

"Large sacrifice?" I shrugged.

"The death and destruction!" He pointed out. "The tornadoes caused by the experiment destroyed countless lives and property. The blast from the ECC must have killed any survivors. My guess is that the blast was larger than Nagasaki."

"Jesus! Al, I killed them all didn't I? I should have never attempted to warp the probe back to Earth. But, I didn't know what else to do. I couldn't let Tabitha die." I justified my actions.

"Ah, I see. But wasn't she going to be saved by the Crew Return Vehicle if you sacrificed yourself?"

"Well, uh . . ."

"Yes she was! You could have prevented the destruction couldn't you?"

"Oh my God! I could have. I should have. If only I would have known I—"

"No! You wouldn't have! You shouldn't have! And you couldn't have!" Einstein slammed his fists down against the arms of my reading chair where he always sits.

"But you just said that I could have saved her."

"Anson my dear fellow she might have been saved. But as we now know there was a Chinese spacecraft being fueled and prepared to rendezvous with the spacetime distortion device." He never would say *warp drive*.

"So?"

"The device would have been used for the gain of power, Anson. That type of power shouldn't fall into the wrong hands. This is why I signed the letter to President Roosevelt endorsing atom bomb research. I feared a madman might gain that knowledge first. Although I will never forgive myself for the evil device that I took part in creating, I wouldn't have been able to forgive myself for letting it fall into the wrong hands either."

"What is this? Is this some kind of sermon? I know good and well that this technology shouldn't fall into the wrong hands—*Hell, that's why most of it was classified.* But I also know that I do want the United States to have this technology and I don't feel bad about being able to ensure the safety of Americans from tyrants by inventing a better and more destructive mousetrap. I only feel bad about the way I was forced to test it and about the horrible loss of life of my own countrymen that I caused. I'm not a warmonger. I was merely trying to develop a way to go to the stars so that the human race might have a chance at growing up. And anyway, Al, you helped get *the bomb* built that saved us all from World War Three."

"Very good, Anson—" Einstein started.

"Stop interrupting me," I shouted. "I didn't ask to be put into that life-or-death situation. Johnny Cache and his employers put us there. They killed my countrymen not me! I was a pawn! But, Tabitha and I stopped the bastards! So there! I think I'm done with you and your philosophical and utopian views." I paused for air. I noticed Einstein was smiling back at me. I was getting angry and my adrenaline was starting to flow—If I were Bruce Banner, I'd have turned green and started smashing shit about then.

"Very good, Anson. I don't believe that you need me anymore either. You will do just fine." Instead of turning into a purple emu and flying away this time, he slid down the helmet of his EMU and locked it into place; EMU not emu this time. "Just fine," he said as he opened my closet door. "Perhaps you will be able to sleep now."

Funny that the whole time he was sitting there talking to me, I didn't notice that he was wearing a spacesuit. Somehow, it just seemed right. He was wearing an EMU, not becoming an emu. My mind was trying to tell me something but I wasn't sure what.

"Hey wait!" I shouted to him. "You aren't here and this ain't real is it?"

"Of course I'm real, Anson." He paused at the closet door. "I'm as real as your subconscious and I'm as real as your need to be humble. You did all of this amazing science and engineering and will not admit that to yourself. Perhaps you created me in your dreams to tell you what you wouldn't tell yourself. But you will not be needing me any longer, I think."

Then he stepped into the airlock in my closet and exited out into space. A gush of air hit me in the face as the airlock cycled. He was gone.

Then the lights blinked off, then on, and then off and on again. I cold hear a loud repetitive noise and then something hit me hard in the chest. It felt like a truck.

"Dr. Clemons, can you hear me?" A fourth man that I had never met was looking down at me.

"I have a pulse!" I could hear in the background.

"The epinephrine is working. How much farther to the hospital?" he asked.

"Pilot says four minutes."

"It'd better be two!" the man replied. Then he turned from me to Tabitha, "What's his blood type?"

"O-positive," she said.

I tried to say thanks to them but I still couldn't move or speak for some reason. The head medic turned back to me.

"Dr. Clemons if you can hear me I want you to blink your eyes," he said.

I blinked at him twice.

"Oh Anson!" Tabitha continued to cry.

Then I started feeling slightly better. Probably the adrenaline or whatever this was in my arm. I noticed an I.V. hanging from the roof of the helicopter and I felt like I would be able to speak so I tried. Nothing happened.

"Don't try to speak, Anson!" Tabitha shouted.

"Dr. Clemons you have a tube in your throat. Don't try to speak. Do you understand? If so blink twice."

I blinked twice. Then I started feeling weak again. The adrenaline probably wouldn't hold me for long. I was here though and I was damned sure going to stay, no matter how much it hurt or how hard it was to stay awake. Besides, there were a lot of things left for me to do. Tabitha squeezed my hand. The feeling had returned to my fingers. It wasn't very long before I could tell that the helicopter was descending. Tabitha continued to lock eyes with me. Or rather, eye with me. Her one eye was still swollen shut.

Tabitha held my hand all the way from the helipad to the elevator. While in the elevator she leaned down and kissed my cheek. The elevator doors opened and she followed beside me until we hit the operating room. A gentleman wearing scrubs told her that she needed to come with him.

"I want to know how—" Tabitha was saying as the doors closed. Once they closed, I could no longer hear her voice.

"Okay ready to move him on three," one of the men in scrubs said. "One, two, three!" They heaved me onto a table. I saw a lady inject something into my I.V.

"Don't worry sir, you are going to be fine. . . ." Everything went black again.

➤ CHAPTER 14

"Sorry about that, General," Tabitha said as she leaned her cane against my bed and saluted him.

"At ease, Colonel Ames." The general approached my bed and looked down at me with a stern smile. He offered me his right hand. "It is good to meet you, Dr. Clemons. I'm General Bracken."

"Hell . . . unh . . . *cough, grunt* . . . oh," I tried to talk. My throat was very sore for some reason. Tabitha handed me a cup of water with a straw in it. I took a sip.

"He's still having trouble speaking, sir. He had a tube down his throat and into his lungs for more than a day now. He just got it removed about an hour ago." Tabitha explained my situation to him. It was the first time I was conscious enough to understand what anybody said, so I listened carefully. The general gist (ha, pardon the pun) of what Tabitha told General Bracken was that I had been stranded in low Earth orbit after my ride was destroyed by terrorists, ingeniously found a way back to Earth, was hailed on and chased by an extremely large and violent tornado, electrocuted, forced to run about eight miles barefoot, my ass was well kicked—although I had done a good bit of kicking myself—stabbed, shot twice, fired upon by surface-to-air missiles, ejected from an exploding aircraft during a hundred-kiloton explosion, walked about six miles while bleeding profusely, died, was brought back to life, died again, brought back to life again, died a third time, brought back to life again, operated on, remained unconscious for about a day, and finally slipped out of the hospital in a clandestine fashion. It sounded like a tall tale if I ever heard one.

If I wasn't in a hospital, I didn't understand where I was. This was all very confusing to me. I took another sip of water. I tried to clear my head and gain some recollection of the past day or so. No good.

"I see," the general acknowledged. "Dr. Clemons, Colonel Ames here has debriefed me on your adventure of the last few days. Not only is the story amazing, but nobody must ever hear a word of it. The implications alone of the high speeds that were achieved give a completely new meaning to intercontinental ballistic missile and to rapid force deployment. I needn't even discuss the ramifications of the energy collection devices." He turned to Tabitha. "Has he seen the news?"

"Not yet, General. Anson has only been awake for an hour or so. I'll bring him up to speed soon." Tabitha touched my shoulder and took the cup from me.

"What . . . is on the . . . news?" I whispered and cleared my throat.

"The news, my dear boy, is telling the world what really happened in Florida the day before yesterday. I will let the colonel debrief you. In the meantime, get better. You did well from what I hear. You would've made a good soldier." He nodded to Tabitha and moved toward the door. The general stumbled slightly and caught his balance on the slightly smaller than usual doorframe.

"We'll talk further when we get on the ground," he said as he departed.

I looked at Tabitha and then around the room. For the first time since I'd been awake, I realized that we were in an aircraft. Tabitha saw the confusion on my face and stopped me from talking by holding her hand on my lips.

"We're on a jet to Edwards. We left about two hours ago. Just sit still and I'll explain." Tabitha stroked my hand. "I thought I'd lost you for a while there. You really scared me." She paused and dried her eyes. Her wounded eye was open now, only slightly bruised and swollen. Her face was still a little scratched and there was a large Band-Aid on her forehead.

"You were getting delirious for the last twenty minutes or so that you were awake, Anson. You were going on and on about having killed thousands of people. Actually, about four hundred were killed and another twelve hundred wounded. The damage was in the billions of dollars. Nevertheless, we had no way of knowing any of that. Finally, you told me that you didn't feel good and you didn't think you would make it. It was about then when you fell flat on your face taking me down with you.

"For a while, I tried to revive you. You were just unconscious at first. Then you quit breathing and I couldn't find a pulse. I . . ." She paused again and squeezed my hand harder. "I tried everything to keep you alive. To get your heart beating. You can't imagine how hard emergency medical techniques are with a fractured wrist. I'd been doing my best at giving you CPR and mouth-to-mouth for two or three minutes when a convoy of National Guard and Federal Emergency Management Agency teams drove by. Actually, I learned later that there was also a National Security Agency and a Central Intelligence Agency contingent with them. Lucky for you there were two doctors in that convoy! They were part of the disaster relief teams headed to one of the local towns totally destroyed by the explosion and tornadoes.

"They took over and brought you back. They got you going with the first jolt from the crash cart. Then they hit you with enough adrenaline to jump-start a horse."

Tabitha continued to explain the events of the day but she got very emotional at parts. Apparently, I died three different times. But, the emergency medical professionals working on me managed to save me each time. The first time was on the roadside. The second time was in an ambulance on the way to the helivac location. The third was in the helicopter on the way to the hospital. Somehow, I managed to stay awake after the third resuscitation. The doctors say it's because of the I.V. I had in me and from the three adrenaline shots. Most importantly, Tabitha never once left my side or gave up on me, even though she had a broken wrist, a shot-up leg, cracked ribs, and a bruised and lacerated face. What a woman!

I was in surgery for several hours during which one of my lungs had to be repaired. The major problem was my loss of blood. One can't bleed internally that badly for an hour or more and expect to keep walking. Most of the pain I felt was from the broken bones caused by the bullet as it zipped through my chest. The knife wound was superficial and the bullet wound in the shoulder was muscle damage only, though, I'm sure I'll feel a good bit of pain there for a long time to come. The doctors said I could walk to the bathroom in a couple of days or so if there are no infections. Phooey! I ain't laying in bed that long. And, I sure as Hell ain't using a bedpan!

"I plan on walking off of this airplane on my own two feet," I told Tabitha. "Where are my clothes?" I rose from the bed. My chest felt like a ton of bricks, but at least I was no longer breathing through water and coughing up blood.

"Anson, lie back down for now. We're still a couple of hours from Edwards," she informed me. "Rest now, hard head!"

Tabitha continued to explain that the news reports were saying that several meteorites hit the area in northern Florida, and, that two of them were rather large. The first one spawned the tornadoes and the second exploded on impact. The large tornado that Tabitha and I had run from turned south and tracked all the way to Fort Walton Beach. It left a path of destruction more than a mile wide in places from ground zero to the Gulf of Mexico. It dissipated miles out to sea but only after sinking four fishing boats and damaging one cruise liner. The National Weather Service did classify the big one as the *Finger of God*. It took large chunks of Santa Rosa Boulevard out to sea with it.

The northbound tornado tore a path clean up to Dothan, Alabama before it spun down. It was classified as a four on the Fujita scale. It tracked up Highway Two Thirty-one. There were large miles-long sections where the highway no longer existed. The westbound tornado destroyed a lot of forestland on the Air Force base and then crossed over to Pensacola. The damn thing tore a path of destruction through to Gulf Shores. The nightclub at the Florida and Alabama line was totally destroyed. Fortunately, this occurred in the middle of the day. The eastbound tornado was classified as a three on the Fujita scale. That one turned southeast and made it all the way to Panama City before it died out. It tried to spin up again further south near Tampa, but it had run out of energy. The devastation from the tornadoes alone caused several billions of dollars worth of damage. Miraculously only twelve people were killed as a result of them. Doppler radar coverage gave ample warning for people to take cover. Way to go National Weather Service!

The ECC explosion on the other hand, caused tremendously more damage and a serious loss of life. The final death toll was still being determined but it was over four hundred. And I thought I was going to win a Nobel Prize! Hopefully, I won't be tarred and feathered, drawn and quartered, stoned, imprisoned, bludgeoned, and twenty other horrible things. Perhaps I will at least be allowed a burial in an undisclosed location so that my remains won't be desecrated.

Oh yeah, what happened to the Space Shuttle? Well, that is an interesting story. Apparently, the same meteorites that tore through the atmosphere destroyed the Shuttle. Colonel Ames and Dr. Anson Clemons were conducting an EVA when the meteor shower destroyed the Shuttle. They miraculously survived and were rescued by the International Space Station's CRV. The CRV landed at NASA Dryden yesterday. Dryden is across the runway from Edwards. Unfortunately, they were the only survivors. The two of them were injured during the disaster and are recuperating at the hospital near Edwards. No press has been able to see the two astronauts as of yet, but the NASA press release states that the two of them are in good condition. Also, doctors say that they may be able to hold a press conference later today. That explains that.

"Tabitha, why were we the only good guys able to make it to ground zero? I would've thought that the Strategic Air Command or the Space Command would have been all over an incoming projectile as destructive as the probe was. And Jim had to have told somebody that the phenomena in Florida was us," I asked Tabitha rhetorically. I didn't realize she had an answer.

"Of course, SAC and Space Command and NASA knew that

we caused the ruckus, Anson. Jim didn't have to say a word. Although we traveled way too fast for a telescope or radar to track us, it was obvious when one second we tell Mission Control that we're going to press a button, then the next second all hell breaks lose. Crisis teams and security protocol teams were dispatched immediately in three helicopters total-ing seventeen courageous men and women. All of them were killed by the violent weather and extreme wind shear patterns created by the probe."

"That doesn't explain what happened after the storms settled. I mean, I feel horrible that all those people died," I coughed a couple of times. Tabitha looked concerned until I showed her my hands, "See no blood. My throat is still just a little scratchy from whatever they had stuck down it. Quacks!"

"Anson, those quacks saved your life. Three times!"

"Maybe I'll have to rethink my opinion. Be patient please, it is hard to change years of bad behavior and beliefs over night. Believe me, I'm far from ungrateful. I like the scratchy throat much better than the alternative."

"Well, okay for now. But I don't want to hear you talking like that around the doctors. It would just be plain rude," Tabitha scolded me with her best Mama-said-don't-do-that voice.

I nodded and asked again, "Okay. So why was there no help from the good guys after the storms?"

"By the time the weather had settled down enough for aircraft to be sent in, we had managed to stumble along to the back gate at Eglin Air Force Base. Our communication filtered up the food chain much faster than you would believe. An order was sent out to stay out of the area until more was heard from us. Boy we sent a message in a big way didn't we?"

"Uh huh." No words could describe how badly I felt for the people involved in this whole ordeal.

"I know Anson. I had no brighter ideas of how to save us either. But, we're here and alive—and we kept the probe out of the hands of the communists, or terrorists or whoever."

"Johnny said the Communist Chinese, remember?" I corrected her.

"Sure he did. But why should we trust him? How do we know

that he wasn't sending us down a blind alley? It could have been Usama Bin Laden as far as we know."

"I thought he was dead?"

"Are you sure?"

"Good point."

"One problem is that Johnny must have known everything about our program. Hell, he was our secretary and he had somehow managed a clearance. I guarantee that his customers have all of our blueprints, drawings, data sets, and everything else. Do you think they could rebuild an ECC or a warp probe?"

"I never thought about it. I don't see why they couldn't, if they were smart enough. If it's terrorists who were his customers, I would be more worried that small ECC bombs would be created and used. They just wouldn't have the bankroll to fund anything as large as a Warp Probe."

"That sounds logical, maybe. Remember how bankrolled the terrorists back in '01 were. Uncle Usama was loaded." Tabitha reminded me.

"That's why I just can't rule out the terrorist theory. Johnny was too well financed for it to be anything less than a large cell structure or a government. He had superfast fixed wing helicopters, surface to air anti-aircraft missiles, and he did mention that the Chinese were going to steal the probe on orbit. Didn't Mission Control tell us that the Chinese had a rocket on the pad but it wasn't ready for launch yet? We need some more intel on that."

"That's right. And he must have had a top-notch crew to get into the Vehicle Assembly Building to plant the bomb on the Shuttle. I think you're right. It must have been a government or at least an organization as big."

"We need to tell somebody this. These people or government could change the balance of power in the world!"

I was terrified. Much like I had been as a kid in the seventies and eighties during the Cold War. Now I was far more terrified by a warp missile than any intercontinental ballistic missile. The worst part is that I had invented the terror. Now I know how Einstein and Oppenheimer must have felt after the Rosenbergs. Or was Einstein already dead by then? For that matter, was Oppie?

"Relax Anson. After the press conference with the Vice President in New Mexico, we're flying back with him to D.C. to debrief the Joint Chiefs and the President."

"Vice President?" I asked Tabitha. She told me to read the cup in my hand, the one that I had been sipping water from for more than thirty minutes. I did. The logo on the side explained that the cup was from the Office of the Vice President of the United States of America.

"Air Force Two?" I asked while studying the cup.

"Bright boy." Tabitha smiled at me and patted my arm with her good hand. "Buy 'em books and send 'em to college . . ." she hinted at the old joke. She kissed my cheek.

"Give me a break," I said. "I've been mostly dead all day!"

I only waved and smiled and said that I was fine as they rolled my stretcher by the press corps at Edwards. Then I shook the Vice President's hand as he thanked me for what I'd done for the country. I never got to discuss the state of world affairs with him. He must be a busy man. Tabitha and I did get about thirty minutes with the Joint Chiefs and with some guys from agencies that didn't exist. They basically told us that they had "top men" working on it. I was beginning to understand how Indiana Jones must've felt.

The general premise was that "black bag" guys and Special Ops could retrieve whatever was lost and discredit anything left behind. Tabitha and I weren't as confident in that assessment. I tried to make myself clear on that point, but arguing while lying in a gurney isn't a real power position.

So, we went home and Tabitha checked me into Huntsville Hospital for a few days of observation. The second morning—let's see that would be four days after the space-warp—Tabitha and I were eating breakfast in my room when Jim finally got around to seeing me.

"Jim! What took you so long?" I asked.

"Hi there slacker. How you doing? Tabitha is he really just goldbrickin'?" Jim replied.

"Oh absolutely, Jim. He is the laziest S.O.B. I ever met." Tabitha laughed and clutched her ribs.

"Forget him, how are you feeling?" Jim asked Tabitha.

"Side hurts when I laugh or sneeze, but I'll make it."

"Jim," I started, "it worked! Can you believe it? It worked." Tabitha gave me a dirty look, meaning that we weren't supposed to discuss the space warp outside of a secure area.

"Cool." Jim smiled and winked.

I noticed Jim was looking rather tired and that his clothes looked slept in, peaked around the gills as my dad might have said. So I asked, "Jim, you been out partying or something? You look kind of rough."

Jim looked at me with tears in his eyes, "No, Doc. I've been here all night. 'Becca's not doing so well."

"What do you mean?" I asked. Tabitha held my hand and I could tell that she was holding back tears as well.

"Anson, she's in the intensive care unit. About five days ago she took a turn for the worse with all of her asthma and allergy symptoms as well as some sort of flulike thing. She's been incoherent for the past two days and running very high fevers. Nobody knows what to do here and the doctors don't have much hope." Jim's head sunk and he cried.

"What!?" I rose from my bed and threw the covers off of me. "She is here?"

"Anson sit down!" Tabitha started.

"Tabitha, can it. No way I ain't going to see her." I stood up and dressed. About that time a nurse came to collect my tray and give me my dose of daily antibiotics and pain meds. She asked where I was going and I told her that I needed a drink and that the stuff they served in this bar was watered down. She "harrumphed" and exited. I pulled on my pants and a T-shirt that was in my overnight bag. Tabitha had even brought my toothbrush.

By the time I was dressed, the nurse had returned with a doctor and a much larger nurse—or maybe he was an orderly.

"Mr. Clemons I suggest that you stay in bed a while longer," the doctor told me.

"Sorry Doc, I'm going up to the ICU to see a friend. You can join me if you like." I told him. The orderly stepped between me and the door to my room.

"Perhaps you should listen to the doctor," the orderly said.

I looked at Jim and Tabitha as I stretched my arms slowly and yawned. I needed to see how strong I felt. I felt fine—just very sore. I rolled my head around to loosen my neck and then stepped toward the door. The orderly placed a hand on my chest.

"Sir, you should reconsider." He smiled.

"Doctor, I am paying for medical attention and this room, not for imprisonment." I said as I wrist-locked the orderly's hand and twisted his hand backward and showed him his own palm. He must not have like the way his palm looked because he collapsed to his knees in either disgust or pain. Probably, pain. I walked past him and let go of his wrist. Jim and Tabitha never said a word. They just followed me.

"Lead the way, Jim." I motioned him around me.

The three of us found the elevators, then up to the ICU. There was some slight resistance until I told a nurse that Tabitha and I were Rebecca's parents. She didn't seem to care if I was lying or not and let us through to see her.

'Becca had an I.V. in her and several other machines appeared to be connected to her. I touched her hand and nearly cried.

"Hang in there, girl," Tabitha said and hugged up behind me.

"Jim, what do the doctors say?" I asked.

"Well, her pathologist thinks she has some sort of weird virus. He asked where all we went on the cruise but nothing seems to add up. I still think she's never been fully well since the bronchitis after the accident."

Jim was right. Although she had been well at times, 'Becca had never been as sick as much as she had the last two years.

"Jim, did the doctors say anything about opportunistic infections?" Tabitha asked.

"That's exactly what we thought it was," a voice from behind me said. I nearly jumped out of my skin.

"Dr. Reese, this is Professor Clemons and Colonel Ames," Jim introduced us to 'Becca's physician.

"The astronauts?" Reese asked. Tabitha and I just nodded.

"It's a pleasure to meet you both." He shook our hands. "As I was saying, we thought it was just multiple opportunistic bacteria coupled with allergic reactions but not any longer." He looked at his pad. "We sent several blood samples to Atlanta. The CDC has isolated some new mutated flulike virus. It is the first time it has ever been reported. CDC is trying to develop a cure but it would help if we knew where she caught it. Its host might have antibodies."

"What exactly does flulike mean?" I asked.

"Well, it's a flu virus with something else attached to it. Here's a print out of the electron microscope image Atlanta emailed me." He held his pad where we could see it and began explaining what we were looking at.

"You see this filament shape here—that's a typical looking influenza filament. But there's something funny about these glycoprotein spikes that extrude from the filament. On this picture here," he flipped the page, "zooming in on the spike you can see that there's a shape instead of a single spike like would be expected. Instead of a spike it's more the shape of a . . . I dunno a . . ."

"A dumbbell," I said. I suddenly felt as if the weight of the world rested on my shoulders, again.

Tabitha, and Jim said in unison, "Holy shit!" Then neither of us said a word for a long moment. Dr. Reese paused to see why we were so amazed.

"I wish I would have never invented those damn things!" I bit my lower lip in anger.

"Anson, if they're really Casimir effect devices can't we just give them a good jolt?" Jim said hopefully.

Tabitha looked grim. "Jim, we can't risk it. What if one of them . . ." She couldn't bring herself to say what Jim was now thinking, what we all three were thinking.

"Exploded!" Jim finished it for her.

"Okay everybody, just calm down." I turned to the confused Dr. Reese, "Doc, can she be moved safely?"

"What? Are you serious? Invented what things?" He thought we were all nuts. "She is in ICU. You can't seriously think she could be moved?"

"Listen to me, Doctor, and listen very carefully. If the things in this picture you just showed me are what we believe they are, then 'Becca is contaminated with Top Secret nanoscopic explosives. Don't ask where they came from. One, and I mean *one*," I emphasized by holding up one finger, "of these tiny devices could blow her arm off." I told him.

"Whew!" Reese whistled, "There are most likely millions of them in her body!

"I was afraid of that," Tabitha said. "More than enough to destroy the whole city."

I was beginning to realize the awesome power of the dumbbells and how they might could be used as a weapon of terror. There would be no way to detect a dumbbell or millions of them. And they could be hidden inside the terrorist's own body until, *kablooie*!

"Why haven't they gone chaotic?" Jim mentioned.

"Good question, Jim, but first things first." I tried to think of a plan of action. "Doctor, she has to be moved to a safer location and we may be able to cure her with your help. Tabitha . . ." I turned to see if she could get us some help but she was already on her cell phone ordering a helicopter, security containment, and general support.

"No I don't care what your orders are! They just changed damnit!" she was ordering into her cell phone.

"Tabitha, we need to track who has seen these pictures." I reminded her. She just nodded. Tabitha knows how to do her job so I decided not to micromanage. I switched gears to something I could do to help. "Jim, are you parked here?"

"Yes. Why?" he replied.

"Let's get over to the lab and gather some diagnostic equipment, my laptop, and whatever else we can think of that might help. Doctor, please keep her healthy as long as possible." We left Tabitha to take care of business at the hospital. Jim waved his cell phone at her as we were leaving as if to say, "Call us if you need us. You have the number." Tabitha gave us the thumbs up and waved us out.

Down the elevator and out to the parking garage we went. We had to climb about fifteen steps to the level where Jim's car was. I realized on about the fourth step that one of my lungs was healing from a bullet wound. My chest was on fire, but I pushed on to the car.

"Are you okay, Doc? You look pretty bad."

"Fine," is all I could gasp out. After a few minutes sitting in the passenger side as we made it to the lab I began to feel better.

"Anson, how is it that you have stitches in your chest and back and Tabitha's face is all cut up? That is, I mean, if you two were in your spacesuits, how bad was the crash?" Jim was figuring things out even though he had been told by security not to even speculate.

"Let's not talk about it right now, Jim." I gave him the nod that now wasn't the time or place.

"Okay," Jim said. "Then what is your take on 'Becca's flu."

"The answer is obvious, I think. The only problem with that obvious answer is that it's too damn unbelievable."

"You mean that you think the dumbbells have been in her since the accident and somehow a flu virus mutated with them?"

"That's the only way I can see it. It's just amazing." It *was* amazing. How versatile viruses must be if they can mutate to capture physical objects. Or at that scale, is everything physical or biological the same? In other words, on the nanoscale is there no way to distinguish live from mechanical? If you think about a bacteriophage for example, some of them look just like a nanoscale Lunar Excursion Module (LEM). And what do they do? They land on a cell and inject the occupants of the LEM cabin into it. The occupants go and rewrite the code of that cell to reproduce more bacteriophages and the cycle continues. The cell is just redesigned to manufacture a different product. That's pretty damn amazing. Is it biological or mechanical? It's my view that everything in the universe is due to electromagnetic interactions. Just some interactions appear to have been animated.

"I don't know, Jim. Let's just hope we can figure out a way to get those things out of her and neutralized."

As we came to the guard shack of our laboratory parking lot, one of Tabitha's security requirements, we both noticed that there was no guard anywhere to be seen. "Jim, stop the car!"

"There should be a guard here." Jim did his best to rubberneck over the windowsill of the two-man shack.

"I don't like this." I began to feel edgy and thoughts of Johnny Cache flooded my mind. I opened Jim's glove box. "Jim, the Orbiter didn't just explode due to some accident," I began as I chambered a round in Jim's Glock. I grabbed his other clip and placed it in my pocket.

For you folks that don't live in the South, I guess I should mention that most everybody has at least one pistol in his or her glove compartment. Those who don't, well they are carrying theirs on them somewhere. That's why our crime rate is so much lower than the big "no-gun" cities. There, only the criminals are armed. If you recall history, the "shoot out at the O.K. Corral" was over a no-gun ordinance in the city of Tombstone. In the South we try to keep the playing field as even or better as we can. Therefore, criminals know that if they want to start something in the South that they *will* be shot back at. Deterrence is a very good crime prevention technique. Hell, it kept the Soviets at bay during the Cold War.

"Jim, you're right. The stitches are to fill up the bullet holes left by terrorists. Tabitha is limping on a shot up leg. Johnny Cache shot her. Long story. Do you have any other weapons in the car? I asked.

Jim smiled and popped the trunk. His karate gear and his tournament bag were in there. He rummaged through the gear and dug out two kamas, two escrima sticks, and one set of nun-chukas.

"Which do you prefer?" he grinned.

"This will do fine," I brandished the Glock 19 with the pre-Clinton-Reno era clip. "Sixteen shots ought to do. Besides, I ain't in any shape to be fighting. I'll have to keep you covered. Sorry."

The front door to the office had been opened effortlessly. Obviously, the guard's keys came in handy for somebody. We cautiously scoured the entire facility and found no signs of foul play, except that my laptop was missing from the safe, the lab was nearly destroyed, the contents of the offices were strewn about everywhere, and *my* whiteboard in *my* office was gone.

"They even ripped the whiteboard right out of the damn wall." Jim exclaimed. We grabbed what equipment we thought would still function and loaded the car.

"I guess they got what they came for," I told Jim and shrugged my shoulders.

"What do we do now?" he asked.

"Call Tabitha and ask her."

Jim tried twice and got Tabitha's voicemail message. "That's odd," he said.

"Well, let's head back to the hospital and keep trying to reach her on the way."

The terrorist effort or war effort, whatever it was, had reached into my everyday life more deeply now. While we were away Johnny's people must have ransacked the lab. It would have been a big operation. The safe had to weigh a ton. It must have taken a forklift to move it. And it happened fast. Something else was bugging me on a more subconscious level, but I couldn't wrap my mind around it just yet. Then I thought to look at the alarm system.

"Jim, check the silent alarm," I pointed to the hidden panel on the wall where the system's keypad was hidden.

Jim slipped back a wall plate and punched in a code on the keypad. The display read today's date about thirty minutes ago.

"We just missed 'em Anson!"

"What?"

"They triggered the alarm just thirty minutes ago!" Jim exclaimed.

Then my subconscious grabbed hold on whatever it was that was bugging me before. "That means it's still going on! What if they had come in when Sara or Al were here? Crap! They might go to their homes, Jim."

"We gotta help them, Doc!" Jim looked frantic.

"Jim, get Sara and Al on the phone and tell them to get out of their houses now. They can meet us at a public place or someplace safe," I told him. I couldn't think of where to send them.

"Tim's place?" Jim asked.

"Perfect."

Jim got Sara at her apartment. He told her to leave this second. Don't change clothes, don't put on makeup, just go. I hope she listened. We were only five miles from Al's house so we headed that way while Jim called. There was no answer on the phone. I also tried Tabitha at the hospital again, but had no luck reaching her either.

We reached Al's house; there were two vehicles in his driveway that we hadn't seen before. There was a truck and a van. Jim pulled up in the neighbor's driveway and we crawled over the fence into Al's backyard. I barely had the strength to get over the four-foot chain link.

Jim and I hugged the back wall of Al's house and eased around the chimney to the back door. The back door flung wide open and Al came flying out the door headfirst and he skidded across the patio into a large ceramic plant pot. The little apple tree in the pot had one small apple clinging from its droopy limb. The impact of Al's head into the pot shook the apple free and it fell on his back. Al was out cold I was pretty sure.

Behind Al stepped a very large individual. I didn't have time to make out any details of his face before Jim had sunk the blade of a Kama into his throat and ripped out the guy's trachea. I rushed in behind Jim as he flew through the door never missing a beat from the Kama strike. There were Kamas swinging and then escrimas. Two more were dead before the gunfire ever started.

The first gunfire Jim was prepared for and he dropped and took out the assailant's kneecap with a low side kick. He pulled the man's wrist downward while kneeing his elbow upward until the man's arm was in two pieces. I managed to bust off a few rounds into the guy covering Jim's present attacker. Jim proceeded to break the guy's neck as I continued the cover fire.

The van parked out front squealed out of the driveway and laid down some suppressing fire from an automatic weapon. Jim and I dove behind the upstairs stairwell for cover. We waited for a few seconds listening for movement.

"Jim, are we clear?"

"Not sure. You ready to cover me."

I changed the clip since the slide on the Glock was open, depressed the lever with my thumb and it closed, chambering a new round. "Ready now. On three and you stay low. One, two, three!"

I rolled out into the open and fired two rounds. Jim came out behind me and zipped across the room behind the couch and took cover again. I rolled across the floor behind him. "Ow shit that hurts!" I held my chest.

"You all right, Doc!"

"Yeah. Just pulled some stitches I think."

"I think we're clear. Let's get Al and get the hell out of here."

Al was coming to by the time we got out the back door. He was concussed and a bit goofy-headed. If you have ever been concussed, you know that "goofy-headed" is a good way to describe it. We dragged him to Jim's car and hit the road fast.

I grabbed Jim's phone and tried Tabitha again.

"Jim, is that you!" Tabitha answered.

"Tab, it's Anson. Listen it is still going on. Jim and I were just in a firefight. You better get some back up and get out of sight fast," I told her.

"Anson, I know! Dr. Reese caught one in the neck before I realized what was going on. Don't worry. We have the situation contained and I think everyone will survive. Are you okay?"

"Jim and I are fine. Al is banged up pretty badly but he'll be okay. I think we need to hide everybody's families. Jim and I will pick up Sara and meet you. Where?"

"Listen Anson, we're already on the move. We'll track Jim's phone and pick you up. You keep moving and stay safe. See you soon." Tabitha disconnected.

We grabbed Sara in record time and before we knew it a helicopter was shadowing us. Then my phone rang.

"Hello?"

"Anson, pull over in the next parking lot," Tabitha told me.

I turned to Jim. "It's Tabitha, Jim. Pull over there!" I pointed to a parking lot by a strip mall where a military helicopter was setting down—Tabitha was waving to us from the open doorway. We loaded into the chopper and were gone. *Safe again*, I thought.

"Dr. Clemons, you're bleeding." Sara pointed at my back.

"Yeah, I figured I was. It's just a few loose stitches. Nothing to worry about, I think," I reassured her.

Jim spoke to Tabitha through a headset. "Where's Rebecca?"

"Don't worry. She's been moved in a different chopper. We'll rendezvous with her in a few minutes."

The helicopter pilot landed us at the airstrip on the Redstone Arsenal where we loaded into a C-141 Starlifter evac plane. The closest they are based is in Memphis, Tennessee and Jackson,

Mississippi but they fly patterns in Huntsville, often. This one must have been close by when Tabitha put in the call. Come to think of it, I never did figure out how she got us a helicopter so fast either—I didn't care. I just wanted to get out of sight fast. As we boarded, Tabitha explained to me that our families were being hidden and that her daughter would meet us at the rendezvous point. Neither of us were sure how far the—whoever they are—would go to get what they wanted. Whatever that was. Were they looking for something or did they just want us out of the picture? And, who were they? I still voted for Chinese.

➤ CHAPTER 15

We landed a few hours later. Where, I have no idea. When we debarked the plane we were inside a very large hangar. There were other aircraft and vehicles inside the hangar, so it was a big place—wherever it was. I tried to be useful, but I was beginning to feel very tired and sore.

Jim had never left 'Becca's side throughout the flight. She seemed to have had no changes, good or bad. We all had hopes that there was something, anything that we could do for her. I hoped that the crazy quacks had just not been smart enough to figure out what was wrong with her and it was still a straightforward medical issue. I hoped so, anyway.

As we debarked I followed the group in a daze. We entered an elevator, a large elevator, and descended for what seemed like a full minute or two. The elevator doors opened into a large bright room. The wall directly to the right had a large red "Floor 31" painted on it. I did later find out where we were, but the location was classified even higher up than I realized existed. I was beginning to learn that there were many more levels of "Top Secret" than just the ones I had experience with.

"Anson, are you okay?" Sara asked as she approached the group.

"I'm . . . just a little tired." I would live for now I told myself.

I was trying to focus on my breathing, but since I'd had the damage to one of my lungs, breathing was more labor intensive. Just sitting still seemed like work. It reminded me of a comic book character I used to read a lot of. This guy had some sort of "techno-organic virus" that there was no cure for, but fortunately he had superpowers. He used his superpowers constantly to hold the virus at bay, yet he was still one of the most powerful superheroes in his universe. His friends would always mention that he was so powerful while fighting the virus that they couldn't imagine his strength if he were cured.

Well, I don't have superpowers. I wish I did. And I'm definitely not one of the most powerful people in my universe. I was tired and in pain.

"You just look a little pale is all." Sara laid her hand on my shoulder.

"I agree with you, Sara. He could use some sun. And maybe a haircut. At the very least run a comb through that unruly mop," Anne Marie added as she approached.

"Annie! How are you? It's good to see you." Seeing my future stepdaughter bolstered my morale a bit. It felt as though I were given a jolt of caffeine and epinephrine all at once.

"From the looks of it," she said, "a helluva lot better than you."

"Have you seen Tabitha?" I asked.

"Just for a sec. She's really busy right now. You know, saving the world and everything." Anne Marie laughed and patted me on the back as she gave me a hug. "It's good to see you, Anson." She looked into my eyes and smiled. "Did you force her to pick a date yet?"

I was confused at first. "A date for wha— Oh, when did she tell you?" We had only been groundside a day or two before all hell broke loose again. It is hard to believe Tabitha had much time to chat with her daughter.

"Mom always calls me immediately, or as soon as possible, after each mission. You guys had me real worried on this one. She says you saved her life, twice."

"She's just modest. It was a team effort, both times. She is too much of a handful for one person to save." I laughed and felt a twinge of pain in my chest. I grimaced at it but it soon went away.

Several days had passed and we settled into the underground Air Force facility—wherever it was. Tabitha made sure that we all had the bare necessities available to us and the facility seemed nearly endless. I was feeling much better, although we still were no closer to helping 'Becca or finding the identity and purpose of our attackers. Jim and Sara had conducted several experiments on 'Becca's invader and had concluded that the attached dumbbells were indeed Casimir-effect type devices. Or at least they had been at one time in their lives. Why they hadn't gone chaotic yet was a mystery. Perhaps the attached influenza virus was responsible for that, or perhaps being suspended in a liquid matrix that allowed them to align themselves to each other had something to do with it. I don't know for sure. Could've been just plain dumb luck. Sara had suggested that we try the simple electric discharge method on a small sample of 'Becca's blood. Why not? It had worked on all previous configurations of the dumbbells that we'd seen.

So, we took a sample of Rebecca's blood and prepared to electrocute it in the same manner we had used on a macro level, before. Sara had run the show at the ECC manufacturing facility back in Huntsville, Alabama, so I let her run the show now. We carried out the process on a very small sample, via robotic remote, on the lowest abandoned level of the facility, which turned out to be an old abandoned mine shaft. For extra safety, we added a solid, steel reinforced concrete wall. Things went well for the first ninety-three nanoseconds. Then the mineshaft was fused together with a fireball explosion from the Casimir effect devices going hypercritical much faster than they had in any previous experiments with the original configurations. These new viruslike dumbbells were much more energetic than the standard Clemons Dumbbells. We obviously couldn't just electrocute 'Becca. We had to be sharper than that. Hard problems are never easy to solve.

Jim and I had the idea of flowing 'Becca's blood through a filter that was electrically polarized in just the right way to attract the dumbbells out of the blood and capture them. The inspiration came from an old Skylab experiment that astronaut Owen Garriot conducted. Dr. Garriot used some sort of filter, flowloop, and microgravity to remove tumor-causing things from blood. I didn't remember what the tumor-causing things were, but the concept was all I needed for the current inspiration.

We modeled the new "flubells," as Sara had started calling them, and developed a map of their electromagnetic signature. Once that was done, we designed the filter, during about three days of nonstop effort. We were all beginning to get a little edgy and very tired. The long hours and my labored breathing was keeping me from doing my most creative thinking. Jim was really carrying me mentally. We looked to Sara for fresh innovations. Youngsters are good at that.

The idea worked! Well, sort of. It worked well enough that we could keep the virus in check, but, the virus replicated far too fast for us to filter it completely. What this meant was that we could keep 'Becca alive through constant filtration as long as the virus didn't mutate again. It was a simple Malthusian Population differential equation, or a damped forced oscillator in engineering terms. Filtering out the virus as rapidly as we technically could would act as a predator to the virus population. The virus was reproducing at an even rate with its death rate now. Previously it had been unchecked. When I had the energy, which was rare those first few days, I would take Sara to the whiteboard and work through the math with her, making sure she understood it well. Occasionally, one of 'Becca's physicians would join us but he never really seemed to grasp the dynamical systems analogy. He sort of got the population models. Anne Marie also joined us often. She was as sharp as a tack and never got left behind. Then again she hoped to fill her mother's shoes one day, so she had better grow some big-ass feet. She was well on her way.

Testing of 'Becca's blood did reveal some useful information. We found that outside of the blood the virus could be destroyed via an electric discharge without catastrophic circumstances. This at least bought us some time. We could filter the blood and then remove the filters and destroy them with an electric discharge.

Eventually, Tabitha forced Jim and me to go to bed. After the first successful test of the electrostatic filter system, we were both spent anyway. I hoped to get a few hours sleep and get back at it.

During the time we were testing the filter system, Tabitha, Anne Marie (when she wasn't hanging out with me), and Al had been working on a plan for our new homestead. Wherever we were, we still needed creature comforts. It looked like we would have to live in this hole for some time to come. At least until we found out what was going on with these attacks upon us. Obviously, this underground facility was some sort of well-equipped Air Force base. There were research facilities, bunkrooms, office rooms, a lot of abandoned areas, and there was constant regular Air Force staff roaming the halls. It was a big facility. My guess was that it was an old Cold War era base. I was oblivious to the fact, since I was mostly concerned with solving 'Becca's dilemma. However, somebody was taking care of us and doing a tremendous amount of work preparing quarters and gathering supplies for us. We had all arrived with basically what we had on our backs. In the room that Tabitha and I shared was a complete complement of male and female paraphernalia and wardrobe. For the most part, the clothes were my size and my style, jeans, T-shirts, and sneakers—heck, even the same kind of toothpaste I like was in our cozy bathroom. Tabitha was taking care of us.

As cozy as our accommodations were, we all still would've rather been at home. We couldn't go home until we knew we were safe from our terrorist friends (or whatever they were). A lot of debate continued as to who our attackers had been and why, but, there were no forthcoming answers—even the guy we killed at Al's place had no telltale clues on him. Tabitha reassured all of us that various civilian and military entities were investigating the problem. Perhaps something on the guys we ran into at Al's house or that Tabitha tangled with at the hospital will offer some leads. We hoped that our black bag guys would solve the problem soon. I hoped somebody would take care of Friday. I mentioned this to Annie. She said that Tabitha took care of it. I later found out that all of our parents, extended families, and even our pets were being protected in different locations.

I slept for about twelve hours straight. When I finally stirred, I found that Jim had been back at work for several hours. I guess he just couldn't sleep and worry at the same time. Apparently, I could. Of course, my injuries and pain medication did help with that some. I made a note to myself to wake the hell up, get with it, and do something to help around here.

"How is she, Jim?" I asked him.

"The doctor says 'Becca's improved, whatever that means." Jim had spent the morning discussing possible treatments with the facility physicians. Tabitha and the doctor, Doctor Smith—if you believe that name—continued to talk as I patted Jim's shoulder. Tabitha nodded to me.

I had asked Tabitha the day before, "How can we keep these people at this facility with the possibility of a major explosion at any time? It isn't fair to them."

Tabitha assured me, "They all volunteered, Anson. And besides that, I couldn't force Anne Marie, Al, or Sara away with a thousand wild horses." Then she mumbled something about national security. "Besides, there are most likely other things at this facility that are just as explosive. Erh, well, explosive enough anyway."

"Jim and I were thinking that instead of attacking the dumbbells, perhaps we should go after the flu part," Tabitha changed subjects. Dr. Smith, John Smith, (I get a kick out of that) joined the conversation.

"We could try creating antibodies in a large creature like a horse or perhaps use something like Acyclovir for suppression therapy," he said.

"Acyclovir? Isn't that an old Herpes treatment?" I asked.

"Yes," Dr. Smith explained. "The drug was designed to be the opposite of the viral receptor. It basically attaches to the virus's receptors before it can attach to a cell. Thus it becomes inert and is eventually filtered out by the body's waste disposal system. Let me explain it the way I do to kids. The virus is like the bottom of a Lego block and a cell is like the top of a block. Viruses stick to the cell kinda like the Leggos stick together. Well, Acyclovir was designed to look like the virus end of the block. The hopes with this type of therapy is that if you throw enough of the antiviral blocks into the mix, the virus will stick to them instead of the body's cells. Then your body's own filtration system will take care of it from there."

"Yeah. I remember seeing a television special on it one time. We would have to tailor a drug to the virus's electromagnetic field," Jim said.

"That might work," I thought aloud. "We have the field of the virus mapped."

"But I don't see how we're going to create a pharmaceutical. It took years for the development of most suppression therapy drugs available today." Dr. Smith frowned and shook his head. "A chemical or biological process has to be discovered that will grow just the right shaped drug molecule. That takes years of effort."

I looked at Jim and smiled. "We'll build one from the atom up."

"What?" Dr. Smith looked surprised.

"Of course." Tabitha perked up. She subconsciously pulled the hair down over the scratches on her forehead and added, "We will build the drug molecule just like we built the Clemons Dumbbells. Genius!"

"Exactly," I nodded. "Jim, do you think you could build up a 3D computer model of the apparatus needed to grow the prototypes in a deposition chamber?" I asked.

"Sure Anson. But there're two problems there. One, we have no deposition chamber and two we could only build a few at a time," Jim replied.

"Good point." I turned to Dr. Smith, "How many virus cells are in her now?"

"Are you serious? I have no idea. There must be millions. There's no way to know exactly. At least none that I can think of. And remember, they continue to replicate," Dr. Smith said.

"Yes, yes. But the filtering has stopped further deterioration in her condition, which would lead one to suspect a steady state. This is simple rate equation stuff. Besides, how many grams of antibiotics does one usually take before getting well? Much much less than a kilogram. So let's assume that we need ten kilograms worth of these virus huggers. That amount should be overkill. We just need a facility to grow them."

"Dr. Smith, we made tons of the dumbbells from the atom

up in about a year. We just need a manufacturing facility like Anson said." Jim had the gears turning in his head. I could see the look in his eyes. He wandered off into his mind and was designing something brilliant. He did that often. Jim's ability to solve problems on the spot had always amazed me. That was one of the things that interested me in being his advisor. I have to have a whiteboard or I can't think straight.

"Jim. Jim!" I got his attention. "Get to work designing the thing and Tab and I will get the equipment we need here like yesterday. Doc, you make sure she stays alive." He not only kept Rebecca alive, but he also convinced us that we probably only needed a few hundred grams of the virus huggers. I decided we should shoot for a kilogram.

Tabitha and I went back to our makeshift conference area, which was actually a conference area, and began listing materials and components. After a couple of hours, I realized that Anne Marie and Sara were bringing us sandwiches and soft drinks occasionally. About nine hours later, we had a complete list of the parts required to replicate the Huntsville nanotech factory. It's always easier to redo something better than it is to invent it in the first place. I intended that this nanotech lab would have updated gadgets and fixes to the things that we didn't necessarily like in the Huntsville lab. "Well that should do it. Now we just need somebody to acquire all of this stuff," I said.

"Leave it to me, Anson." Tabitha kissed me on the cheek, then she stood up and stretched.

"Some of this equipment is hard to find, Tabitha." I finished off another sandwich and stretched.

"Don't worry about that. I'll put a team of acquisition experts on it. We'll have it if we need it," she stated in a rather matter-of-fact manner that I was learning to be characteristic of Colonel Ames. If Tabitha said she would get something done, then by God it got done. I bet she was a bear to deal with in her teenage hormone years.

A few minutes later, she returned and promised me that we would have all of the components on our list by morning after next at the latest, plus a few more techs to help assemble them. Then she kissed me again.

This time I pulled her to me and kissed her long and deep and slow. I brushed a lock of her red hair out of her face revealing the pink new skin of the healing scratches from the plane crash. I had never thought of her as vulnerable to anything until now. I realized that she must be a little self-conscious of the scratches and bruises. I hoped they wouldn't leave a scar, for her sake; she was beautiful to me no matter what. "Tabitha, have you thought about a date yet?"

"Anson, sweetie, I haven't had time to think of anything personal. In fact, this is one of the first minutes I have taken for myself since we left the hospital. I will get around to it."

"Yeah yeah, Annie said you would be hard-pressed to pick a date. She suggested that I hog tie you and drive you off to the justice of the peace and get it over with." I goosed her ribs. She winced slightly in pain. Her ribs weren't quite well yet, either.

"She did, did she?" Tabitha looked as though she were already plotting vengeance against her daughter. "That little traitor. I'll have to fix her wagon." Tabitha laughed and goosed me back. I winced a bit, as my bullet wounds were just now healing. I swallowed back the pain and smiled. Then we kissed again and again. We decided that we should take a little while for ourselves and covertly made it to our room.

Most of the equipment arrived as planned. The rest arrived the next day, but that's another story. I overheard Colonel Ames dressing down an acquisition sergeant. He was at least a foot taller than her and more than a hundred pounds bigger, and she was scaring the living hell out of him. Me too!

"Ma'am," he said, "that piece of equipment will have to be manufactured. It's a onesy." He told the colonel.

"Did I ask for an excuse?"

"Uh, no, ma'am!"

"Well then. I don't care if you have to find a goddamned rainbow, trek to the end of it, capture a leprechaun, whup his ass and steal his pot of gold, take that pot of gold and buy a magic lamp, and use all three wishes to get that equipment here now. I don't care how, just get it here! I won't take no for an answer. Got it? Get it *here*!" The latter part was screamed at the top of her lungs into the man's face while she poked a finger in his chest. Although he was a giant of a man, he was shaking like a leaf on a tree in a thunderstorm.

"Ma'am, yes ma'am!"

The rest of the equipment arrived the next day. It took about four more days for us to assemble and test the nanotech factory and then another week and a half for Jim and me to build the first "flubell hugger." Once we adjusted the prototype to map directly opposite to the electromagnetic signature of the sialic acid receptors of the flubell virus, we then began tweaking of the automated manufacturing process. The process went fast. Our new facility was more efficient than the one that had evolved in our old Huntsville lab. It took some getting used to.

The flubell huggers were much easier to make than the Clemons Dumbbells because there were no moving parts. We were able to manufacture about twenty-three point eight grams per day. That added up to about forty-two days until we had one kilogram. I laughed at that. Perhaps this was the "ultimate question" to Douglas Adams's "ultimate answer." How many days does it take to produce enough flubell huggers to cure 'Becca's disease? The answer: forty-two. I just hoped that 'Becca would hold out that long. Of course, the doctor pointed out that we could start the suppression therapy with the flubell huggers as soon as we had a few tens of grams. So, we gave her the first dose of them at the end of the second day of automated manufacturing. For the first couple of weeks no dramatic changes in her condition were noticed. In fact, I was beginning to lose faith.

"Maybe it's not working," I told Tabitha one night while we were getting ready for bed.

"Don't give up, Anson. And don't you dare say that to anybody else, especially Jim. Everyone is sitting on pins and needles as it is."

"I would never do that. I just feel like there is something else I should be doing," I told her.

"We all feel that way," she said as she turned out the light and crawled into bed next to me.

"Tabitha."

"Yes Anson?"

"I . . . I was thinking about the wedding. Have you considered a date yet?"

"Yeah. How about as soon as 'Becca is well enough to be one of my bridesmaids?"

"Good idea."

➢ CHAPTER 16

Three weeks into the therapy, Rebecca regained consciousness. I spent some time sitting with her. We all did. I explained to her what had happened to her. She was as amazed as all of us, and got a real kick out of the flubell huggers.

"I bet no physicians ever thought of *building* a cure from the atom up. Or if they did they had no idea how to do it," she said.

"Pretty cool, huh?" We both felt pretty sure of ourselves.

After the fourth week of the therapy she was up and walking around. Oh, by the way, throughout the treatment process we had to capture all of her excreted body materials and dispose of them safely. That included mucus, urine, feces, sweat, body hair, sloughed skin, and even her toenails. We didn't want to take chances. We placed all of these in the destroyed lower floor and electrocuted the hell out of them. Then we incinerated them.

The thirty-eighth day of the therapy I was chatting with Jim and 'Becca about the wedding plans for me and Tabitha.

"I don't know if I prefer an indoor or outdoor wedding. What do you think?" I asked them.

"What does Tabitha want?" 'Becca said diplomatically.

"I think she wants a big church thing, but she won't come out and say it."

"I've always been fond of those. Of course, the cruise idea was pretty cool also." Jim smiled as 'Becca elbowed him in the ribs.

Tabitha always seemed to have a knack of entering a room when you were talking about her. She looked troubled.

"What is it, Colonel?" I poked at her. She didn't snap back with her usual wit and repartee. Something wasn't right.

"It . . . it's terrible," she said. "Colorado has been destroyed."

"*What?*" resounded uniformly from the three of us.

"Which part?" I asked.

"All of it! Turn on the TV," Tabitha said.

We turned on the idiot box and on all the channels was the catastrophe. Some of the talking heads were calling it an extinction level event like the one that had caused the demise of the dinosaurs. Eyewitnesses had claimed that—there were no eyewitnesses. They were all dead. Roughly fifty million people were estimated dead. The President was to make a statement soon. In the meantime, various astronomers were suggesting that the recent meteor strike in Florida was a precursor to the Colorado Catastrophe.

Tabitha, Jim, 'Becca, and I all knew that this theory must be right on the money, but not at all what the astronomers had in mind.

Obviously it was a warp weapon. The warp weapon struck somewhere near Boulder, Colorado. The total destruct radius was several hundred miles. The satellite photos could only look at the dust and smoke plume, it was too thick for even infrared to see through. Centroiding on the plume put the center of impact at Boulder. Strategically this was a well-placed hit. Multiple military and civilian infrastructures were eradicated, literally wiped from the face of the Earth. Cheyenne, Wyoming, just north of the Colorado-Wyoming border was well within the total destruct zone. Military bases further south of Denver were also taken out. Strategic Space Command had taken a deadly blow. Even further out than the total destruction zone there was still tremendous damage. The plume would wreak havoc on communications with the Midwest for weeks to come. Who knew what it would do to the global weather patterns? And on top of that, how do you mourn for so *many* people. You can't initially—all you can do is watch and be in shock for a while. Unless, you can do something about it—then you focus and act! There might be other states out there in great danger and we had to think about *them*, instead of Colorado.

"If the President's going to make a statement, then he probably doesn't know that this could be some sort of preemptive strike," I said.

"I've put in a call and someone is trying to get a message through to him, Anson. Right now that isn't easy," Tabitha replied still in a sad tone of voice.

"Doc, you can't think that they have already built a warp missile, do you?" Jim asked. From his tone of voice I could tell that he had "turtled-up" and was ready to take whatever punches he had to until we figured out a strategy to fight back with. Good boy.

"It adds up," I remarked. "They could have been working on this thing from the beginning. Johnny Cache must have been giving them data and blueprints and reports from the first day. We've got to find out if there were any ships up at the time of the incident."

"Already ahead of you, Anson," Tabitha laid some large printouts on the table. "A friend of mine that I roomed with in undergraduate flight training works for an agency on the Beltway. He just secure-faxed me these documents and satellite photos. An unannounced launch of a manned Chinese spacecraft took place yesterday. The location of the spacecraft at the time of the impact in Colorado was almost three hundred kilometers directly over Boulder."

"Damnit Jim. It looks like they did better on the guidance calculations than we did. Unless it was a mistake?" I glanced around the room and got the impression that nobody believed the accident theory. "Then are we all in agreement that we think this was deliberate?

"Anson, I can't see it any other way." Jim pulled at his lower lip.

"Uh . . . what is the lift capacity of the Chinese rocket?" Rebecca asked.

"Why?" I wanted to know just where was she headed with that?

"Well," she began, "could it carry two of them?" You could have heard a pin drop for about three seconds. Then Colonel Tabitha Ames marched to the door. She stuck her head out and began barking orders to several of the noncoms. Then she turned to our crew.

"Anne Marie, Sara, Al, I need to see you three now!" They came running up to her.

"What's up, Mom?"

"You three go find the lift capacity of the recent Chinese manned launch vehicles. Al, determine how many ECC's and warp generators could be put in one. Sara, work with Al. Annie, find out how many of these rockets the Chinese have and how long it takes to prep one for flight. I need that info yesterday."

"Yes, Colonel." Anne Marie snapped a salute and bugged out. Al and Sara followed.

Tabitha turned back to us, "Anson, you and Jim find us a way to detect those damn things before they get off the ground. 'Becca, you up to earning your keep?"

"I feel strong enough to wrestle a Gundark!" She smiled but none of us laughed.

"Good. Let's you and me figure out how soon before we could get another Zephram built."

"Okay!" 'Becca responded.

"Hey hold on a minute," Jim said. "We don't have to build another Zephram. A missile that weighs one kilogram moving near the speed of light would do just about as much damage. Remember that the kinetic energy transferred is one half mass times velocity squared. In this case velocity is orders of magnitude more than mass. So, the mass isn't a big factor."

I butted in. "We could build basketball sized missiles perhaps. We just have to reconfigure the geometry of the warp coils. God, I hope the Chinese haven't thought of that. Someone tell the girls to plan to that design. Jim and I will work it out later. First, we need to build a detector. Come on, Jim." We made a break for the door and were off to find a whiteboard somewhere.

Three hours later, Jim and I had discovered why our system wasn't as accurate as our counterpart's missile. During our tests of the warp fields, we could never get the mathematical models to converge to a solution that would match the experimental data. This was because there was another source somewhere else being operated at the same times that we operated our tests. Johnny must have been slipping our schedule to his contacts all along. The effects of the other warp field on the other side of the planet, although a couple orders of magnitude smaller due to distance, put a gravitational pole out at infinity (mathematically speaking) and our feedback calculations never could account for it. I never thought that there should be a pole there because it didn't fit the physical model I understood for the world. But it was experimental data and if something is there, it is there. The theory is just not right. I had always attributed our problem with some frame dragging effect or some other General Relativity phenomena that wasn't well understood. Incomplete theory was the problem, or so I thought. As soon as Jim and I thought to add a second warped field to our model and ran the calculation in the computer, the model converged to a solution! We had precise navigation licked. We also knew how to find other warp generators being tested. The field coils for any missile would have to be experimentally aligned. It's during that procedure that we would detect them as poles in our system and measure precisely where they were to within a few meters.

Anne Marie poked her head in the conference room. "Anson, Mom would like to see you and Jim. How's it going?" she asked.

"Great! Jim deserves a Nobel Prize," I said.

"Mom always said that he was the real brains of this outfit." Anne Marie laughed.

Annie led us to a hallway and handed us off to two armed guards. "See ya in a bit."

At the end of the hallway one of the guards handed me a clipboard and said, "Gentlemen if you will please sign in."

Jim and I signed the paperwork as the other guard worked a combination on the door. Jim handed the first guard the clipboard back and he handed us each a visitor's badge that said "Escort Not Required." Jim and I entered the room to find Colonel Ames in full dress uniform and talking to a large flat-panel screen. I felt a little underdressed. I'm not sure Jim cared.

"Mr. President, we're fairly certain that this was the only system in orbit at this time. The electromagnetic pulse created just before impact was detected by our early warning and nuclear detonation satellite system, which accurately measured it. The early detection satellite measurements allowed us data enough to determine the size of the warp missile. It was basically a carbon copy of the unit known as Zephram—the brief you have already seen." Tabitha stopped for air and turned to introduce us.

"Mr. President, you already have met Dr. Anson Clemons and this is his associate Dr. Jim Daniels." She paused.

"Hello Mr. President," I said. Jim just nodded.

The President began speaking, "This is a fine damn mess you've caused, fellows! There are over fifty million people that are estimated dead and what am I to tell the public?"

Tabitha started to speak but I stepped in.

"Tell them it was another meteor, a bigger one. Only a handful of people know otherwise, unless the Chinese have made some ultimatum we're unaware of. We have figured out how to detect them. It's just a matter of time before we can counter them."

"Counter them! Are you suggesting we get into some sort of all-out secret war? Congress would never go for that. Besides, in this day and age war would be hard to cover up, especially given large numbers of casualties."

"Mr. President, these missiles are undetectable by anybody on the planet except for the people in this room and the people in a room similar to this in China. Looking at what has happened thus far, I would venture to guess that our opponents plan to play this one out to the end. We can gather intelligence on them. Determine how far along they are with more of these weapons and slow them down until we can catch up and take them out. And when we do take them out, we will take out their entire government and infrastructure. We will remove their capability to make war at all, in one complete and precise strike. Then we can offer to go in and help them rebuild their government and infrastructure, but this time it will be a capitalist system that is completely allied with us, or else."

"Jesus, son. I'm glad you are on our side," the President said.

"Thank you, Mr. President. I have no sympathy for a people that will let their government kill millions of people in an unprovoked attack. They should get what they deserve." I grinded my teeth a bit and I guess I should've tried to hide my anger better.

"Okay, what if they have one of these things ready to go now?" he asked.

"Can't we just shoot it down? I mean rockets blow up all the time," Jim interjected.

"Good idea, Jim. Wouldn't the National Missile Defense System be able to shoot down something as slow and big as a manned rocket?" I asked.

"Of course it could. We simply need to modify some trajectory calculations and adjust the Kalman filtering sequence," Tabitha assured us. "Mr. President. We need resources and we need people. And until we know exactly what is going on I think you're in danger."

"Son," he pointed at me, "you started this mess. You better by God get us through it. We're counting on you. *General* Ames," he smiled as he emphasized "General," "you have whatever you need."

"Yes sir. Thank you Mr. President." Tabitha squirmed a bit uncharacteristically.

Jim and I nodded and then were asked to leave. So we did.

A few hours later the President was on television issuing a statement to the public. "Hello America. I speak to you tonight with a grave heart. We have experienced the greatest disaster in human history," he began. "Scientists have assured me that indeed Colorado was struck by a meteor of a scale only slightly smaller than the one that destroyed the dinosaurs. It is likely our national and maybe even global weather patterns will be erratic and cooler than normal in the near future. Unlike the dinosaurs however, we're intelligent and will overcome this obstacle.

"As of now, we have no way of discerning the total amount of damage that has occurred, but we will not stop until we have combed all of Colorado for survivors. We're keeping a vigil watch on the climate surrounding the impact. As soon as the strong weather patterns and the firestorms have subsided, we will begin rescue effort deployment. FEMA and other volunteer emergency professionals are standing by until that time.

"There have been questions as to the possibility of further meteor strikes. I have asked both NASA and the remaining Strategic Space Command officials to concert all efforts on searching the skies for further possible impact meteors. I have also implemented an executive order to enable development of some sort of protection system from events of this type.

"Please, do not panic. Astronomers assure us that these impacts are very rare. It is likely that the impact in Florida weeks ago was a fragment of this very meteor. Hopefully, this is the end of these meteor impacts. I ask that you go about your normal lives as well as you can. And finally, pray for our fellow citizens in Colorado and for better weather. God bless America. Goodnight."

Five days later, there were more than two hundred people in our corridors at the bottom of wherever we were (I still didn't know exactly where we were hiding). Tabitha assured me that there were even more at other locations attempting to reproduce our efforts. They would be given designs and instructions and told to manufacture equipment without ever knowing that equipment's final application. The floor above us had been completely converted to a Mini ECC manufacturing facility. 'Becca and Sara were overseeing that operation while Jim and I had our floor turned into a copy of the warp coil development lab we had back in Huntsville, but again with newer and more expensive equipment. Al and Tabitha (General Ames to you) took the preliminary sketches of a Mini Warp Missile (MWM) and were designing it up via computer simulation and analysis design software. A lot of models have to be conducted on any new system and they were trying to get us ready to cut metal by the time the Mini ECCs were ready. Al is a wizard at finite element analysis and engineering design, so we expected his part to be ready long before the manufacturing facility was running full speed.

Jim and I had completed our warp system detector. We tested it against a small prototype set of coils that we had rigged on the fly and it worked great. In fact it worked so great, that the first time we tested it we detected four other systems being tested. I can't tell you where they were being tested—that's classified. This meant that they had at least four missiles getting close to launch ready! I immediately ran down the hall and found Tabitha.

"Where are they?" she asked.

"Here. I wrote down the GPS coordinates for you. They're in four separate locations. Smart. That means it would take four missiles to take them out. Let's hope they can't find us like we can find them."

A few minutes later, she brought satellite photos of the area and pointed out the buildings that were the entrances to the Chinese warp missile manufacturing centers.

"Measures are being taken," is all that she said.

"What does that mean?" I asked.

"Just meet me down the hall in about three hours," she said as she turned and walked away. Everybody was busy and she had taken on the role as boss. I guess that made her even busier.

A bit later Tabitha returned and asked, "When you said I hope they can't find us, were you serious? Do you think they can detect us this far under ground?"

"Ground doesn't have that much to do with it. The gravity waves, for the most part, will only be attenuated by Beer's Law due to the ground. Distance helps on a much greater scale."

"Well, how far then? I mean, how far away do you need to be to hide from your detector?"

"Uh . . . haven't really thought of that. Give me a bit to turn the old crank on that one." It was a good question. I needed a whiteboard. After a few hours at the whiteboard, I had figured out that the *Dark Side of the Moon* was not only a good album but it was the place we needed to hide. Well, Farside, anyway.

Al found me staring at the whiteboard in the makeshift lab conference area. "Doc, you all right? You seem a bit upset."

"I was just trying to figure out where we could safely hide from the bad guys. We're in trouble I guess. We would have to hide—at the minimum—on the far side of the moon. I guess we'll just have to work in fear and from a defensive posture."

I was a bit frustrated, not to mention tired and sore. I hadn't had a good night's sleep in five weeks. Although my wounds were mostly healed up, I still had occasional aches with them. Tabitha was in the same boat. Her ribs still hurt her some.

"The far side of the moon, huh?" Al looked thoughtful. "What about—nah skip it. The general sent me to get you. You're supposed to meet her in ten minutes."

"I've been in here for three hours?" I must have completely zoned out on this problem. I do that sometimes. Most engineers do. I remember hearing a story about when Wernher von Braun first got to Huntsville. One day some cops found him at a stop light in what seemed to be a trance. He had apparently come up with an idea and just stopped where he was driving and started working out the concept in his head. It was after that incident that he was given a driver to chauffeur him anywhere he went.

Al laughed. "Well almost three hours. Hey Doc, I'm through with the missile design. Is it all right if I think about this moon thing for a little while?"

"Hell, Al, take a break or something. You've been working hard."

"Right," Al said and drifted off into the engineer's stare. I knew I couldn't stop him from thinking about it now. If you aren't a problem solver it is hard to explain the feeling. It's sort of like looking at a picture on a wall and realizing that the picture isn't hanging level. If it nags the hell out of you that the picture isn't hanging level, well that's the beginning of the feeling.

I left Al to think about whatever it was he was thinking. It was an exercise in futility though. There was no way we had time to develop a spacecraft that could get us to the moon. Maybe it would give him a break to do something fun. Who was I kidding? We were all scared shitless and at the same time still thrilled to be doing what we were doing.

I signed in and picked up my badge. As the guard let me into the secure area I noticed that Tabitha was sitting in the room with the lights dimmed and it was very quiet.

"The general is getting very tired, sir," Steve the guard whispered to me. I nodded that I understood. He pulled the door to, locking Tabitha and me in the room.

I slipped in behind Tabitha and was planning to rub her shoulders.

"Have a seat, Anson," she said, startling me.

"That's okay, gorgeous," I told her and started massaging her gently. "You're overworking yourself, General. When was the last time we had a good night's sleep?"

She rolled her head and stretched her neck. "Don't get me wrong, Anson, this feels great. But right now we don't have time. Sit down for second."

"Okay, what's up?"

She slid a panel open on the table and pressed a couple of buttons. "I wanted you to see this. In about three minutes two of the enemy warp development facilities will be in view of a couple of our spybirds in LEO. About four minutes later, we will pick up the other two facilities. Operations have been planned to take out those facilities. We're going to watch."

"Wait a minute. That would tip the world off. If they captured an American soldier, our meteor story is screwed." Images of a Chinese television broadcast of a beaten American soldier popped in my head.

"Don't worry, Anson. No ground troops will be involved. In fact, special black bag teams have taken over Chinese airfreight planes. These aircraft are going to fly into each of these locations. As far as anyone can tell, these were terrorist acts, accidents, who gives a damn what. We will have deniability."

"Who is going to fly those things? Will they be able to bail out in time? Then how do they get home?" I was upset. I hope these soldiers weren't asked to volunteer for a suicide mission.

"That isn't your concern, Anson." I could tell that this weighed heavy on her as well.

I hoped that if this was a suicide mission that there was a way to use soldiers that have been diagnosed with something terminal, who were going to die soon anyway, to conduct these types of missions. I guess generals have been ordering men to their deaths for thousands of years. That's something I'm not sure I could do. It takes some real balls to be a general. I'm glad Tabitha has the biggest set I've ever seen. Don't get me wrong. Tabitha is all hot-blooded American woman. She just must keep her balls somewhere besides a scrotum.

"Tabitha, are you sure that a plane crash will do enough damage?"

"These will. Our guys have made sure that there are some extra parcels on board." She nodded and sort of smiled, although she seemed too serious for it to be a real smile. There was a sadness and a no-nonsense down-to-brass-tacks air about her.

I reached over and held her hand as the view panel went from a blue screen with "unusable signal" bouncing around on it to four split panels of static. Then the static cleared into two separate images in grayscale. The images were of very normal-looking manufacturing type districts.

After a few seconds, an area that looked to be the size of a city block in the lower left quadrant of the screen turned bright and saturated the camera. Some software took over and adjusted the image somewhat.

I didn't see the aircraft but obviously, it hit. Then I saw a streak across the top left quadrant and a second explosion. I couldn't take my eyes off the screen. I remembered how I felt back in '01 watching a similar incident live on television. It is an eerie feeling. But for these soldiers on these planes my heart swelled. I felt a sense of sorrow and pride for them.

"Godspeed boys," Tabitha whispered. I noticed tears running down her face. I swallowed hard to keep from crying myself. Just because she has big balls doesn't mean she doesn't have a big heart also.

Tabitha squeezed my hand. I squeezed back and nodded to her. The American people would never know what had happened during the last six weeks. It would all be covered up to the point that even the people who were part of it would be confused as to what really happened. I just hoped that the families of these poor soldiers were well compensated and were told that their sons or daughters, whichever the case may be, died as great American heroes.

"Three minutes or so more to the next target," Tabitha informed me.

We sat in silence for the next three minutes. The two quadrants on the right side of the panel went to static and then an image of similar industrial areas. We watched for a few seconds in silence. Then on the upper right corner of the view screen a streak appeared and the center of the screen lit into a great bright spot. The attenuation program adjusted the scene and we could see that there had been another direct hit.

Almost immediately following the third crash, the center of the lower right quadrant exploded. All four targets had been hit. I assumed that not only were there extra parcels on board these aircraft, but that they were also full of fuel. It was my guess that these facilities would be on fire for hours if not days. There would be no more warp experiments conducted there. Tabitha watched until the screens faded to static, then automatically switched to the "unusable signal" blue screen.

"This is hard, Anson." She pulled me to her and I hugged her with all my heart.

"I know." I tried not to cry either.

We both had been accepting things too quickly and then being forced to move on to the next obstacle. We had had zero time for reflection, contemplation, or mourning. First there was the Shuttle explosion, the narrow escape from dying in space, fighting terrorists, the tornados and ECC explosion in northern Florida, escaping Huntsville by the skin of our teeth, 'Becca's flubell virus, an entire state with over fifty million American citizens destroyed, and now ordering at least four people to their deaths. We both needed to cry for a while. We hadn't even been able to attend the memorial service for our fellow astronauts on the Shuttle and now there were millions to mourn.

I held Tabitha for several minutes, both of us crying. I wiped the tears from my face and then hers. "We will make it through this, the United States of America will prevail. Besides, you still owe me a honeymoon." I smiled at her—*turtle-up and focus, this fight ain't over yet.*

She slugged me on my shoulder right were I had been shot. "Oww!" I laughed and rubbed my mostly-healed shoulder.

"Okay hotshot, we just bought us some time. Now get me some warp missiles before the Chinese get back on their feet," she ordered.

"Yes ma'am, General ma'am!" I saluted.

➤ CHAPTER 17

I checked with 'Becca and Sara on the progress of the miniature energy collection cubes or Mini ECCs. We were still two
months away from the first one being produced and about
three months away from the next four. The second and larger
automated Clemons Dumbbell deposition systems (on a higher
floor) were just now coming online and would be a couple of
months behind the system put in place in our basement. After
the first one was generated by the basement facility, production
starts over. So, in four months there would be enough Mini ECCs
to power six mini warp missiles or MWMs.

Jim and I had completed the design for the MWM's warp
coils and apparently, Al had completed the design for the MWM
airframes and internal hardware. Jim and I passed along notes
and design information to the manufacturing guys a few floors
up and they began to cut, roll, and weld metal. As soon as the
mini ECCs were ready we could plug them into the missiles and
integrate them into a Shuttle or an expendable launch vehicle
(ELV). I started looking through Al's notes and design data for the
blueprints for the mating hardware for the launch vehicle. When
I realized that no hardware had been designed for integrating the
MWMs into a launch vehicle, ELV or otherwise, I was a tad bit
heated to say the least.

I found Al in the lab conference room doing simulations and analyses of what looked like several of the Shuttle's External Tanks stuck together along with several other older mothballed spacecraft fuselages. "Al, I thought you said you had finished the MWM hardware design?" I blurted at him. He seemed surprised by my obvious anger.

"I . . . uh . . . did," he replied reluctantly.

"Well why then—" I paused, "—have you not designed the attachment hardpoints for the MWMs to interface with a launch vehicle?"

"Why do we need them?" He looked confused.

"'Why do we need them?' he asks. Well, how do you propose we get them to orbit?"

"The same way you get them down from orbit I guess." Al looked smug.

"What the hell are you talking abou— Well, son of a bitch dog in heat." It hit me like an uppercut to the chin. "Of course we don't need a launch system. We raise them to orbit with the warp drive. Hell, I can't believe I didn't think of that. Al hold on a minute—" I ran to the door and poked my head out. "Tabitha!" I yelled. "Tabitha I need you for a second." A moment passed and Tabitha didn't show. Anne Marie bounced up instead, looking as perky and young as ever. God, was I ever that young?

"Mom heard your, uh, page. She couldn't leave what she was doing just yet. She sent me to find out what the hubbub was all about."

I looked at her and smiled. She always makes me smile. I took her by the hand and said, "Come with me." I led her back to the conference table where Al still sat. He was looking at me as though I were nuts.

"Annie, do me a favor and kiss him." Annie just shrugged her shoulders and planted a wet one right on Al's lips. "Thanks." I said.

"Uh, yeah, thanks." Al said shyly, as he turned four shades of taupe, maroon, red, and pale all at once.

"Okay," Annie said. "Now you might want to tell Al and me why you just had me give him mono." Al looked startled. "Just kidding Al."

"Well, I wanted your mother to do it, but you worked out better. Al here has just given us a rapid strike capability and no need for launch vehicles." I explained the idea of not having to use rockets to launch and that we could use the warp system for main propulsion for any application. Just because space is warped by the device doesn't mean that the thing has to travel faster than light. Heck, Tabitha and I probably didn't do that on our first warp ride. But, we did go very, very, very, very fast. The warp drive could be used for slower speeds and even just for offsetting other forces, like gravity, for levitation. The speed is proportional to the amplitude of the poles and zeroes of the Alcubierre warp. The amplitudes of the warp are also proportional to the energy required to make the poles and zeroes. The slower speed would mean less amplitude on the warp, which in turn means less energy. In fact, the ECCs running at only a couple of percent capacity could gain the amount of energy to counter the Earth's gravitational well.

The concept of designing the warp drive as the main propulsion system had immediate useful applications. Imagine using the devices as a crane or safe transportation. The road to the Moon and the planets within our solar system was now at least graveled. With a little bit of systems engineering, testing, and manufacturing, we would have the road paved. And for the immediate problem, our *Secret War* with China, I was beginning to roll some ideas around.

I called an all hands meeting of our crew. That meant the general, the Doctors Daniel (Jim and Rebecca), Al, Sara, Anne Marie, and myself. We sat down over sandwiches and "cocolas" in the conference room and had an old fashioned brainstorming session. Some people might call it a "think tank."

"Al here has kluged together some concepts as to get us to the far side of the Moon near term," I said kicking off the meeting. "What I want to do today is for us to figure out just *how* we could get there, get enough stuff there to support at least fifty people and to live comfortably, and sustain a research, development and engineering laboratory plus a manufacturing facility. I want to emphasize that we would want to be taking low-gee strolls on the lunar surface in less than four months. Is it not just possible, but also doable?"

Al turned the projector on and clicked on his presentation file on his laptop. "My idea is to take as many space-rated pieces of hardware as we can get our hands on and just warp them to the moon. We could live in a Shuttle Orbiter with the old Spacelab module in the payload bay while we integrated the pieces via EVAs. My list shows some possible hardware. There are several External Tanks we could grab, we could appropriate at least one Shuttle and the Spacelab module, there are several commercial airframes we could use. Jim and I think it could be done with a warp drive powered by three of the ECCs. Jim."

Jim nodded. "That's right, Al. I've run the simulations a couple of times. The mass requirements that we're talking about and the size of the warp field that we'd need to maintain would require three of the mini ECCs that we're currently building. One modified warp coil will suffice though."

"What about lifting these things? How do we attach to them?" Sara asked.

I explained, "Well Sara, as Tabitha and I found, you don't have to be attached to the warp drive to make travel possible. You just need to be within the bubble. Anything in the flat spacetime region of the bubble will travel with it. So we just put these things near the warp drive and away we go," I explained.

"Anson," Tabitha interrupted. "What about the construction on the moon? There could be a lot of EVA time there. All of this hardware would need to be mated with airlocks and tubes to connect them. We would need to weld and God knows what else. These are things that haven't been done in space before."

"I understand that Tab—but can we do it? You are the expert astronaut here." I put the ball back in her court.

"Well, I suppose we would have to live like cosmonauts. We better bring a shitload of duct tape." She laughed.

I felt in my pocket and found the small flattened roll that I've kept with me since the incident in Florida. I vowed then that I would never leave home without duct tape. I pulled it out and grinned, "Never leave home without it." She laughed.

"Why do we need all of these extra airframes and things?" Sara asked. "Why don't we just use the warp bubble to make a big underground dome or something?"

I did a double-take on that one. Again, an application with the warp technology that I had missed. I must be getting old and slow. From the look on Jim's face as he slapped his own forehead, I wasn't alone.

"Of course," Jim said. "We slowly poke a small hole down about fifty meters or so by having the warp bubble force its way downward. The Moon couldn't resist that. Then we slowly expand the bubble to a size we decide we need and then oscillate the diameter of the outer Van den Broeck bubble by millimeters back and forth and very fast. The oscillations would turn the lunar rocks or dirt or whatever it is to a molten material. When we turn off the field we have a huge ball-shaped cave with hardened magma walls."

"Excellent, Jim!" I was thrilled by these new concepts. "How about we do some quick analyses to decide the volume that we would need and the most stable diameter for such a cave. If we need to, we will build multiple caves and tie them together. These caves could be built in a matter of minutes or hours I think."

Anne Marie added, "I think we should carry as much of the hardware on Al's list as we can. We will need safe places in case the caves leak our atmosphere and we will need entrance airlocks. And what about living quarters? I don't know about you guys, but I'm feeling a little stir crazy here and we have plenty of room."

"Actually, Annie," 'Becca replied, "we could keep a warp field on inside the caves to maintain atmospheric and structural integrity. Once we get there we might as well put these three ECCs and the warp coil to further use. The ECCs would give us more than enough power to maintain the warp field and to power our entire Moon base. Annie, I do agree though that we should carry everything we can get our hands on, including several kitchen sinks."

"That gives me an idea," Tabitha laughed. "What if we made one of these balls higher than the rest and then warped a large part of some freshwater lake to the cave. We could then set up a gravity-fed plumbing system."

"Brilliant Tabitha! I love it. Then we warp a ball of atmosphere right out of the sky into the domes, and some fruit trees to go with them, and we also abduct some livestock. This place could be self-sufficient in a matter of days! This is great stuff." I was exhilarated with the possibilities. It was cool to take my mind off of the war for a few moments. I think it helped the rest of the crew also.

"Something else, Anson," Tabitha got my attention. "Gravity is much less on the moon, about one-sixth gee. If I understand the warp theory correctly, and I'm sure I don't, couldn't we alter the gravity in the habitat dome to equal one gee?"

"Well, General, it appears to me that you do understand the warp theory," Jim said.

"Right." I laughed. "Jim, calculate a slightly slanted flat space region for me that will add to the lunar gravity to equal one gee."

We spent the next several hours batting ideas around and revising our concepts. By the end of the afternoon we had developed a complete concept plan and a drawing of the underground lunar facility. The facility consisted of the habitat sphere and "green" sphere, a manufacturing cylinder, a research and development cylinder, and there were multiple tunnels connecting them. Of course, there was also a spaceport pad on the lunar surface. The pad would be adjacent to a long wide cylinder that connected to the side of the habitat sphere. Pushing the lunar rock around with a warp field would create the pad. Jim and I were planning to work out a bulldozer scoop-shaped warp-field geometry. Creating cylinders would be easy. Pushing a ball along a straight path would create a cylindrical shaft with spherical ends. Who cared if they had spherical ends?

Anne Marie had the idea of just building a small town with all the infrastructure, power grid that would connect to ECCs, water purification pump and tower, stocked fish pond, living quarters, and anything else we could think of and then just warping that to the main habit sphere. I liked that idea a lot. Since time was a factor, we decided to go with manufactured homes. We would have the first trailer park in space.

Al realized that we couldn't use Jim's approach, which was to make a tiny hole and then expand the bubble. How would we get the town through the tiny hole? So we modified the approach. Instead, we would make a large diameter cylinder with a spherical bottom. The warp sphere used to make this cylinder would contain the trailer park and all of its infrastructure. Leaving that warp field on, we would then use the bulldozer warp field to push lunar material on top of the bubble to fill the hole. When the hole was filled, we would then oscillate the bubbles' outer Van Den Broeck bubble to turn the lunar rock to magma and then harden the cave. The outer bubble wouldn't allow heat and shock waves into the inner static non-Alcubierre bubble. We would then construct the outer cylinders and tunnels and place the equipment in the right locations. The tunnels and cylinders should be airtight at this point. So, we pressurize them with the liquid air that we brought with us in the External Tanks. We would seal off the airlocks to the outside and then open the tanks and let the air boil off into the caves. When all of the complex excavation and construction is completed, we then would simply turn off the field in the habitat sphere for a nanosecond and then turn it back on immediately but with a diameter large enough to encompass the entire Moon base. Sara had called this the "lights-off lights-on" method. There would be some strange weather for a few moments while the atmosphere reached equilibrium, but if we calculated the pressures right we should be fine. We would bring a butt load of plants and fluorescent lights. The lake would be large enough to support twice the people planned for the facility for at least a year. We would recycle the water and everything else, but we could eventually go back to Earth with new warp ships and pick up more supplies.

But how would we get the water back into the habitat cave? This led us to a solution for heating the caves and choosing a location also. First, the complex would be placed on the far side of the moon and near one of the lunar poles where it's always in the sunlight. Six open shafts would be dug running from directly over the half-acre stand of trees to the lunar surface. Each of these shafts would be roughly ten meters in diameter and would be stoppered by large windows. The windows would be in two layers ten centimeters thick, separated by one meter, and each windowpane would be constructed of spaceframe window materials. The top window would be reinforced by a central hub airlock window one meter in diameter, the hub made of steel I-beams with steel I-beams attached radially to an outer steel I-beam rim. It would look like a bicycle wheel sort of, whereas the hub opened downward. The bottom layer would be supported with steel I-beams the same way but there would be no door. Instead, the window would be uniformly perforated with one centimeter diameter holes over the entire surface.

The windows would allow sunlight to enter the habitat sphere over the half-acre stand of trees. When we needed to bring in new water we would warp the water into the shaft above the window, then extend the main field out past the water holding warp bubble via the lights-off lights-on method. The window central hub door would be opened. Then we would turn off the bubble holding the water and it would become supported by the window. As the water drained through the door onto the bottom perforated window, voila, it would be raining onto the trees below. When the water was completely drained, the airlock would be cycled and the warp fields turned off.

Installing the windows wouldn't prove too difficult. We could countersink the shafts so that they would sit onto a magmified lunar rock windowsill. Then we would seal them off. We might even place a couple windows over the lake, which we planned to be beside the tree grove anyway.

This all seems like a lot of work to accomplish short notice whilst a war is on that we were actively helping to fight. However, the warp field technology really changed the construction paradigm. We estimated it would take less than a day to make the holes and then only a month or so to install most of the hardware. We could use parallel crews to begin manufacturing while the final construction continues.

Of course, there were also some minor details and calculations to be made like what maximum mass could be lifted at what velocities, and how we do that without tipping off our enemy as to what we were doing, how much food, what about the effect of the big heat sink at minus 33 degrees Celsius (the Moon) below us, should we put some high R value insulation under the town, and how the hell would we do that anyway, how many windows are enough to heat and light a two-hundred-meter-diameter hemisphere. Sheesh! You get the idea.

Jim figured out that we could alter the warp bubble for the main habitat construction to the shape of a spheroid. The upper half would be a perfect hemisphere two hundred meters in diameter. The lower half would be a section of a much larger sphere only a few tens of meters deep at the bottom. We would go make the hole first. Come back and pick up a suitable surface area of dirt layered with several feet of insulation then covered with several feet of sand. Place it in the hole and hope the sand kept the nonspace qualified insulation from outgassing while we came back to get the town. Then we planned to pick up topsoil, fill dirt, trees, lake, fish, air, bees, birds, squirrels, and probably a lot more with the town.

After a few hours of Moon base design we decided to assign individual action items and go do them. We mutually decided that the move to the lunar surface would be priority second only to the development of the MWMs. Tabitha instilled in each of us the reality of the situation and that the Lunar Base would be a great idea and we needed to be there to hide from the Chinese if they have warp field detectors like ours. We all realized that six MWMs wouldn't be enough to keep the Chinese from developing further warp weapons. Actually, one of the bright analysts about eighteen floors above us had completed a study showing that we needed at least twelve well-placed simultaneous strikes to completely remove the Chinese infrastructure. One really big one would do, but we would risk the onset of greenhouse phenomena and God only knows what other types of global ecological nightmares. Carefully planned "surgical" strikes would be better. So, we needed to be out of reach of their missiles, and detection, soon. It would take us at least another year and a half to build that many MWMs. In the meantime, we would be sitting ducks at the mercy of our modified National Missile Defense system, unless our Chinese counterparts have a smart guy like Al to realize that they don't need launch vehicles. Then there would be no defense. This war was only going to be won by completely removing our enemy's ability to make war or by some miraculous diplomacy. Since neither side was admitting that there was a war to begin with, diplomacy seemed like a very big stretch.

Sara had asked me earlier why I thought the Chinese were

attacking us. I told her a story that a friend of mine is so fond of telling about the Chinese business world. The story goes like this.

Back in the early nineteen nineties the Chinese government announced that they were going to open their borders to American businesses with hopes of moving China into the world market place. Once China had opened their doors, American business-men rushed to the airports and headed off to China hoping to be the first to get a foothold on a billion new consumers. Well, these businessmen spent the first few days meeting their Chinese counterparts while being wined and dined and wining and dining some themselves. After a few weeks of this continued and none of these businessmen had even talked business yet, they began to start pressuring their hosts to discuss business opportunities. The response they got was that they were welcome to stay and enjoy themselves as long as they wanted. However, China hadn't needed to do business with the Western world or anybody else for that matter for thousands of years. So why should they be in a hurry to conduct business now? Needless to say most of these businessmen came home with their tails dragging and nothing to show for their huge trip expenses. That was more than twenty years ago and there are still no large western businesses based in China.

The Chinese falsely believe that they don't need the world and that they are a "chosen people." Well they sure needed the Rus-sians to upgrade their current military. And it was real nice of former President Clinton to give them the American guidance, navigation, and control technologies required to steer the rocket that launched the warp bomb into orbit that killed fifty mil-lion American citizens. Oh wait; Clinton didn't give the missile technology away. He got a big campaign contribution in return didn't he? That's okay. I'm sure he is "feeling the pain" of those poor souls in Colorado just as he did for the boys that had to run the "Mogadishu Mile" back in the early nineties.

Oh well, I digressed and Sara was four at the time and had no idea what the "Mogadishu Mile" was. Well, I'm sure that Tabitha and I won't forget it, fellows. That is one of the reasons we aren't going to back down now. If the Chinese wanted to be diplomatic, they wouldn't have destroyed fifty million people without saying, "Give up or else!" The ironic part here is that they did need the rest of the world just as they needed the Russians before. They needed the Americans to develop warp drive for them to steal.

"Now I don't want it misunderstood," I told Sara. And by this time the whole gang had gathered around my soapbox. "I have many Chinese friends. There are no quarrels I have with any people. That is, until they let their government do something as hideous as this. You can argue that it's likely that most of the Chinese people have no idea that these events are even occurring. Hell, most of them are living peasants' lives. But, does that make them innocent? Should the people be held accountable for the actions of their government? At least on some level, yes. Perhaps the outcome of this war will change China, America, the World, and our views on how things should be. We'll see. One of the biggest problems we had back in Gulf War II is that we would never hold the people accountable for their hideous government and the crazy factions that arose during the war. That is why that war dragged on and didn't seem to have a decisive end. This war must, it *will*, have a decisive end. We had better make sure we are on the winning side when it's over. The only thing that bothers me is why now? For thousands of years China was enough for China. Why did they feel they needed to take over the world, now, so aggressively at this very moment? Doesn't make sense to me. But we'll stop them anyway!"

➤ CHAPTER 18

Tabitha had put in the requisition to construct the "town" in a small lake area in a very large state park in Georgia. When the time came a forest fire would overtake the region. That is, after we yanked the town, trees, lake, bees, and all right out of the Earth. Tabitha hired a few ecologists and biologists to develop a closed system of plant and animal life. As far as these university types knew, this was just another "white collar welfare program." Pork, as it is referred to in political circles.

Jim and I went about designing a real-time modifiable warp field generator. This took several different sets of misshapen coils. The final product design reminded me of the old stellarator systems I worked on back in undergraduate school. The stellarators were really weird arrangements of electromagnets that were used to create tight fields. Plasmas would be captured in these fields. We would then pinch the fields even tighter with hopes that we could spark the fusion process. We were never very successful at creating a fusion generator back then. My understanding is that we're not much closer now, but I have to admit that I haven't really paid attention to that field (ha! pardon the pun) of physics in many years.

At any rate, we did create a modifiable warp field. Our new generator would allow us to modify the outer or Van den Broeck bubble simply by adjusting parameters on a three-dimensional graphic display. We soon realized that we could also modify the flat space region between the warp pole and zero. Flat space would mean no gravity or free fall. Jim and I figured out a way to create a slight curve in the so-called flat region so that we could have a one-gee environment inside the vessel, building, or whatever it was, that we planned to warp. In other words, we could build a spacecraft that had artificial gravity. That would be damned convenient. Since we could modify the gravity anywhere, we could ensure that there would be one gee environment on Moon Base 1. That way long mission duration to the base wouldn't be physically detrimental to the, uh I guess, astronauts.

Upon completion of the new warp field generator design, we sent blueprints to manufacturing a few floors up. The word we got back from them was that they would have it finished in a few days. I had yet to visit the machine shop upstairs, but those guys were on the ball. I hoped that some of them would volunteer to go to the Moon with us.

Most of my crew, besides the general, were through with their war tasks and were developing ideas of their own for the Moon base or overseeing (micromanaging is more like it) some of the manufacturing. Sara and 'Becca had been spending most of their time together. Jim and I figured that they were just collaborating on how to improve the manufacturing process for the mini ECCs. The process was slow—perhaps they could make it more efficient—thus shaving off a few days of the wait.

Al and Anne Marie and a couple of regular military girls that they had befriended focused on integration issues of the Moon base. They seemed very excited and enamored by the idea. I've said it before and I'll say it again; if I had the power, I would grant Al a doctorate in Aerospace Engineering and predate it by a year or two. I felt the same way about Jim and 'Becca as they were going through the doctoral inquisition. We used to have a saying: "You will never graduate until you can convince your committee that you know that you will never be as smart and enlightened as they are and that you will forever be in their debt and can never imagine a way to repay such a deep debt." Such is the way of American higher education.

Did I forget to mention the fact that Al and Anne Marie were spending an inordinate amount of time together? As Tabitha has always told me, I'm dense about these things. Hell, I didn't even realize Jim and 'Becca were a thing until they decided to get hitched! I think I'll just keep my nose out of that one. Or as we say in the South, "Damn, I ain't gittin' my dawg in that fight."

Several weeks had passed and I was getting a little bored. Most of my work was complete. The field coils were finished, but with no ECCs to power them, they were just a lot of scrap superconductor. I spent some of my time helping Tabitha analyze intelligence data "down the hall." When I was being a fifth wheel to Tabitha I would give her time off by just hanging out in the break room and watching television.

I got caught up in the Senate hearings deposing the NASA administrator as to why we hadn't detected the meteors before they struck Florida and Colorado. Why had NASA not done its job, the Senate wanted to know? As I listened to the hearings, the current administrator of our nation's civilian space agency held his ground.

"Well, Senator," he began, "for years we have begged for a budget to watch for Near Earth Objects, or NEOs. And we have received one. The budget has been roughly three million dollars per year. That is enough money to run one telescope, for about an hour a day, about three hundred days a year. If we got lucky and the meteor just happened to be in the minuscule percentage of the sky that we were able to cover with that one telescope during that hour during one of those days, well yes Senator we should have detected it."

Even though the problem facing the world right now wasn't due to a meteor threat, the NASA administrator was right. We're, in the first place, not seriously looking for threats from space. In the second place, we have no developed way to defend against them. I remembered seeing some movies back near the end of the last century—or near the beginning of this one, I forget which—about asteroids hurtling toward Earth and brave astronauts flying up on modified Shuttles or some such nonsense and destroying them with one nuclear weapon. That was silly then; it's still silly. Asteroids and meteors are bad enough—*they* aren't intelligent.

What if the threat from space *was* intelligent? Well, if they got here, then they must be far superior to us. We wouldn't stand a chance. If they showed up and said, "We are the Borg. Your uniqueness will be added to our own. Prepare to be assimilated. Resistance is futile." If that happened, *we would absolutely be fucked.* No polite way to say it. No amount of nuclear weapons could help. Hell, I'm not sure that warp weapons would help.

And a race as advanced as *Star Trek:TNG's* Borg might not even be the worst case scenario. What if a race showed up in our past and tricked us into worshiping them? Say, perhaps the race had wings and wore a shiny bubble around their heads since they didn't breathe our atmosphere. They could use their technology to perform so-called miracles that would convince us that they were deities. By every version of the word we would be screwed even worse than with the Borg. At least with the Borg it would be over quickly and we'd go down fighting. With these deities they could trick us into fighting among ourselves for thousands of years. Then they could, for some reason, leave our planet, leaving behind no evidence that they were ever here. We would continue to fight about them amongst ourselves for millennia and we would never know what really happened. If they showed up now claiming to be angels of the lord, at least some of us would stand up and flip them off. But you better believe that many more would jump on the fiery chariots of these creatures and help them slaughter us in the name of the very vain, loathsome, and petty Almighty.

Presently, there are no Department of Defense or Civil Defense measures in place to defend against such an attack, or at least none that I know of. Hell, people know for a fact that there are asteroids and meteors and we have no contingency plans for them. Why develop plans against aliens? After all, the SETI folks have everybody convinced that aliens are far advanced dope-smoking Utopians who will one day email us the cure for cancer.

Yeah, they might do that. And as my great aunt Meg is so fond of saying, "And if a frog had wings it wouldn't bump its ass on the ground when it hopped either."

I believe in statistics. The universe is a damn big place. Statistically there should be just as many aliens out there that want to eat us as there are who want to feed us. A lot of the Pasadena and Boston intellectual crowds would have you believe that intelligent aliens would have evolved beyond war. Then, I guess, *we* ain't intelligent.

Politics and the battle for resources will exist no matter how evolved a society gets. I always find these Hollywood science fiction shows humorous when they say things like "we don't have money in the future." If one guy wanted to build a new football stadium at the bottom of the sea and one guy wanted to build a new hospital downtown, which do you think would get priority and who gets to make that decision? Unless there are infinite resources, sooner or later a similar decision must be made in any resource-limited society. So, of course, the football stadium would get built. There may not be paper money in that society but the decision itself becomes the money and is just as valuable. If the aliens have infinite resources then they must live outside our universe since it is finite in size. Ha, so take that Utopians!

Sorry; I digressed. We should have contingency plans just as we do for earthquakes and floods. At any rate I was thinking these things as I watched the hearings. I knew we *now* had a contingency for meteors and asteroids though nobody would ever know it. I watched and thought, "Just convince Congress to let you look Mr. Administrator. We'll knock 'em out of the sky if you find them."

Warp missiles could easily be used for defense against meteors, but we could never tell the public that. What could humans have done without warp technology? Nothing maybe. I have always been a big fan of building a mag-lev catapult on the Moon that could throw big rocks very fast. The amount of money that we spent on intercontinental ballistic missiles would almost pay for it. We could do as much damage to ourselves with it or more. We could also throw swarms of rocks at incoming NEOs until we have altered their courses or broken them up into small enough pieces as not to destroy the Earth. Needs more study, but could be viable. Now that we have warp the point is moot.

➤   ➤   ➤

A few times a week 'Becca, Jim, and I would meet downstairs in an abandoned area of the "facility" and practice some katas or takedowns or holds. 'Becca and I were both getting well enough to do some light sparring drills.

One evening while the three of us were practicing, a guard making his daily rounds found us. He stopped and watched for a bit. He asked us if he could join the next night. Anne Marie and Sara followed 'Becca down a few days later. Before long, we had a regular class schedule with students. Jim and I ran the class for a while until one of the regular military fellows watched me make a particular arm bar. It was the sergeant that Tabitha had dressed down weeks ago.

He watched and then politely said, "Uh, excuse me, sir."

"Hey, don't sir me. I'm a civilian. My name is Anson."

"Okay sir, uh Anson sir, uh Anson. I like that technique. But, have you thought about what would happen if you are countered this way?" He reversed the hold from me having him arm barred, to me lying face down with his foot on my neck.

"Uncle!" I cried. We hit it off real quick. Jim and I asked him to jump in any time he wanted to and take over.

After some conversation, we found that his name was Sergeant Calvin Perry. Calvin had been in the security detail for over nine years and had taken multiple martial arts over the years. He had only recently taken on acquisition as one of his duties. His style was more of a useful blend of everything, rather than a set traditional style. Jim and I both liked that. Without explaining the details of why the fight took place, I told Cal and Jim about my run-in with Johnny Cache. I told them how I felt like I should have defeated him earlier, because when I finally did beat him, I was so exhausted that I couldn't have countered anything else. I choreographed the fight as best as I could from memory using Jim as Johnny. Calvin, Jim, and I began shaving off useless techniques. Before long, the three of us were developing simpler more deadly techniques. Calvin had had the advantage of *not* fighting on the tournament circuit. Jim and I had trained ourselves with too many scoring techniques for tournament fighting instead of deadly ones. Calvin began teaching us to unlearn some of that.

The three of us held these training sessions on our own time outside of the regular class, while we took turns instructing the regular class. Then afterwards we would practice becoming more deadly. Soon, all of the students started staying for the whole affair. 'Becca and I were getting back into real serious fighting condition. I was proud to see her doing somersaults and flips and jump spinning tornado roundhouse kicks again.

"I wish I had a black belt to give her," I told Jim and Calvin.

"Yeah," Jim nodded.

"You want me to pick one up on my way in tomorrow?" Calvin asked.

Jim and I did a double take with a twist of confusion.

"What do you mean," I asked.

Calvin looked surprised, "I forget that you guys are bottled up down here, under protection and all. Heck, I get to go home every weekend if I want to. There's a martial arts supply not far from where I buy groceries. Besides, the general told us to get you folks anything you want or need no questions asked. I double as one of your acquisition officers, so, I'm authorized to get stuff for you. You guys want anything else?" He smiled and winked.

Jim and I hadn't really thought about it. Until now, somebody had always furnished us with anything we needed after we complained that we didn't have it. But, we had been in camping-out mode and not living mode. Tabitha had personal stuff in our room. I guess I just thought that it was stuff she was able to grab on her way here. Or perhaps she had a friend that picked it up for her. She has lots of friends and connections. I was beginning to realize that we hadn't been taking advantage of our situation. We should at least be comfortable, even if we didn't want to admit this was a long-term situation, right?

Calvin, Jim, and I made out a list of things that we needed to have for a fully equipped martial arts dojo, including kicking bags, judo mats, a well stocked store of uniforms, rebreakable boards, pads, and weapons. Calvin got all of it; it was justified as fitness training supplies. I also ordered stuff for a cookout, including an electric grill. I wanted a real charcoal one but we decided that we might set off some fire alarm system somewhere. And what is a cookout without beer and hunch punch I ask? Calvin laughed when I gave him the order. "Don't laugh, you have first duty on the keg tap," I told him.

I asked Tabitha about our material situation a few nights later when she finally made it to bed at the same time I did. She laughed, "Anson sweetie you are dense. This is a witness protection type program. You people could be the witnesses that save the country and our way of life. If you need to spend some money on R&R why didn't you ask before?"

"Too busy worrying about the country being taken over, I guess. Hey, I have never actually been at war before. Give me a break."

"I love you," is all she said. It's none of your business what we did next.

When we weren't training in the dojo or having cookouts we did tend to the war and Moon base efforts. Without my knowledge, 'Becca and Dr. Smith had squirreled away some of 'Becca's tainted blood and 'Becca and Sara had been studying the blood and the flubells extensively in their spare time. Jim had posed the question when we discovered them as to why hadn't they gone chaotic and exploded. We never got around to studying that. Apparently, 'Becca was plagued with the same question, but only more hauntingly so. The fact that she could have exploded and destroyed a county must have been a lot for her to deal with both emotionally and technically. So she and Sara had set out to solve the riddle.

Soon into their research effort, they coerced Jim into helping them. They kept all of their research a secret from both Tabitha and myself. I had later asked them why and the three of them said that they knew neither of us would let them do it. We both scolded them for violating safety protocols and risking their necks; had the outcome been different they could have killed us all. Since the outcome turned out for the good we let it go. Besides, both Jim and 'Becca are good responsible scientists and Sara is becoming one. One of these days Tabitha and I will have to quit looking at them as children, our children. I doubt that day will ever come. At any rate, their research was very successful. But I'm getting ahead of myself.

➤   ➤   ➤

It was one of those days where I was feeling useless so I spent it with Tabitha attempting to help her analyze intelligence on our enemy's war effort. I spent a lot of time squinting at satellite imagery ranging from visible to infrared to microwave to radio maps of the Asian continent. The most interesting imagery that we analyzed was one of the launch sites in south China. The site is just south of Canton and is called Hainan Island. The imagery showed a launch vehicle being moved out to the pad and integrated. From the data it appeared that we would be seeing a Chinese launch in a matter of days. There were images of other launch sites at Jiuquan, Taiyuan, and Xichang that showed identical launch preparations. We were still at least a month from the first working mini ECC. We were in big trouble!

More detailed analysis showed that there was massive naval buildup in the Taiwan Strait between south China and Taiwan. There was also major troop movement and buildup on the North Korean and South Korean border. Some bright analyst brought to Tabitha's attention that there was a launch preparation going on in Kazakhstan and near Svobodny, Russia. Was it possible that the two simultaneous Russian launches were a coincidence? The Chinese and the Russians had been allying themselves for years under the auspices of "the enemy of my enemy is my ally" philosophy. The Russians had publicly been our allies for years since the end of the Cold War, but, there had been, and will always be, factions of the old Red Party that will forever despise the United States. The other possibility is that the economically ravaged Russians had fallen into the survival-of-the-meanest mode and were overtaken by organized crime. These criminals would do or sell practically anything for the right price. Who knows the motives? The fact of the matter was simple. The Chinese and the Russians were going to launch at least six different rockets with warp missiles on them within the next day or so. They must have already tested them before we built our detector. They were probably waiting on ECCs like we were—but they apparently could make them faster. Chinese naval vessels were most likely going to mount an assault on Taiwan. And the North Koreans were going to take South Korea. World War III was about to begin.

"Oh God, Tabitha, what can we do?"

"Get everybody together, Anson. Five minutes!" she ordered.

Five minutes later we were in the conference room explaining the situation. "It's obvious that we don't and won't have enough warp missiles ready for launch for weeks. Our only chance is for our missile defense systems to save us, or to go into a preemptive first-strike posture. This will be my recommendation to the President unless we come up with better ideas," Tabitha explained.

"According to my estimates as to our progress," I continued when Tabitha stopped, "we have about seventy five percent of one mini ECC complete. Maybe we can rig something out of that. Maybe a very small more decisive missile."

"Uh, Anson, hold on." Jim interrupted. He looked at 'Becca and Sara and nodded.

'Becca continued, "Jim and Sara and I have been developing a new Casimir effect energy collection system. The system is based on the flubells and is three orders of magnitude more efficient than the original Clemons Dumbbells."

I was surprised and happy, but we didn't have time for a development program. We had at the most twenty-four hours. Maybe we could launch ICBMs at the launch sites. This would ensure that a global war would start but just maybe the U.S. would survive or even win. Boy it would be nice if we had actually developed those rapid-force deployment spaceplanes that NASA and the Air Force have been drawing pretty pictures of for fifty years.

"'Becca that's excellent work and we'll talk about it when or if we survive this upcoming war. We don't have time for a development effort," I scolded.

"Damnit Doc!" Sara cried. "You don't understand."

"Yeah Anson," Jim started, "we already built one of the damn things and it's big enough to generate more power than all three of Zephram's ECCs put together!"

"You mean you have a working prototype?" Tabitha was exhilarated.

"Yes!" was uniformly shouted by Sara, Rebecca, and Jim.

"Well why didn't you say so?" Al said.

"Okay, okay, let's calm down. So we have six complete warp coils installed in MWM bodies waiting for the mini ECCs, the modifiable warp field generator, a seventy-five percent mini ECC, and one fully operational large ECC. Not enough." I shook my head.

"How much time to make more of these new ECCs?" Anne Marie asked.

"A couple of weeks apiece," Sara replied.

"Too long," Tabitha noted. Then Calvin came in and interrupted us.

"General, ma'am! You are needed immediately." He saluted.

"At ease, Calvin. Anson keep at it. I'll be right back." Tabitha and Calvin departed down the hall.

Five minutes later she returned, pale as a ghost. "They launched!"

"What do you mean they launched? They weren't quite on the stands yet," was my response.

"It turns out that the imagery was right. But no integration was required. They just rolled out and launched. Never been done before. All six of them, launched!"

I couldn't believe it. How did they manage to integrate inside without us seeing it, roll out, and liftoff in a period of an hour or so? I have worked payload integration at the Cape before and it takes days. This was a systems engineering miracle. Now we were only half hour to an hour before they could deploy over a target and fire their warp missiles.

"Can we get real-time trajectories announced or mapped?" I wanted to know where they were.

"Yes, down the hall," Tabitha said.

"I want them announced every five miles. We're not out of this game yet. We have a modifiable warp field generator and a lot of damned power. And I ain't afeard to use it!" I put on my worst Southern.

"What are we going to do, Anson?" Anne Marie asked.

"We're about to pull a damned rabbit out of a hat sweetheart. Just hide and watch. Jim get that new ECC hooked up to the new modifiable field generator like five minutes ago. 'Becca you and Sara go get the almost completed mini ECC, divide it into two separate supplies, and get it connected to two of the completed MWMs. They may not go faster than light, but they should still pack a mean wallop and be controllable in space. Two missiles are better than none. Al you help them. Tabitha, I need a layout of this facility. I mean everything—power plant, plumbing, elevators, rats, you name it. As soon as you can get it, Annie get it to me in my office instantaneously." I didn't mean to take control and Tabitha never let on like I had, but I had things to do and I didn't have time to okay it all with the general. A good commander knows when to let her troops do what they need to do, and that is just what Tabitha did.

"Anson, I'm going to alert the President that we have an offensive weapon but most likely cannot stop the incoming weapons. Is this correct?" Tabitha wanted confirmation on what we were doing.

"That's the best we've got Tab. Sorry. I love you too," I told her. Then we each went about our separate tasks.

I went to my simulation system and I started mapping out warp fields containing large masses in the flat space of the warp bubble and stresses on the system due to slow impacts on the outer bubble. We could warp from point to point with these things but real-time steering was a bitch because you couldn't see out of the Van den Broeck bubble. Then I remembered my old *Star Trek: TNG*. Anytime the Borg would attack, you would modulate the *Enterprise*'s protective shields. That's it! Modulate the damn Van Den Broeck bubble. It was so simple a child could have done it! I laughed when I thought that. Isn't that what McCoy told Kirk when he learned how to put Spock's brain back in?

Sara's lights-off lights-on method would work. I would set up a function generator to drive the outer bubble on and off every few microseconds. I would add a half wave phase shift to that switching signal and use it to drive the sample frequency of the high-speed video cameras we had in the lab. So, the video cameras and the outer bubble would be completely out of phase with one another. When the bubble was on the camera would be between video frames. When the bubble was off the camera would take a frame. Now the big question would be where to put the camera and how to connect it. Oh, connect it to what you ask? Hold your horses, I'm getting to that.

Annie and Calvin rushed in pushing a roll-around cart loaded with notebooks full of blueprints and facilities drawings.

"Great guys, thanks. Annie, find me a top-level drawing of the entire facility, preferably, one with some dimensions on there also. Calvin, find out where there are outside video cameras with the best view of the outside world. Then have somebody take these three cameras here and swap them out. Mount them however you can, but get me that video signal down here, ASAP. Also, get me a global positioning system mounted up there and route that data to me here. Figure out how. We have about twenty minutes."

Calvin rushed off with the three high-speed cameras. Annie began flipping frantically through the books. "Annie, I'll be right back. I've got to see Jim a sec." I told her. I ran two doors down the hall to the main lab where I was just in time to overhear Jim shouting.

"Owwch! Goddamnit all to hell!" He let a crescent wrench slip and fall on his fingers.

"Jim, you all right?" I asked, any other time I would've chuckled.

"Yeah."

"How's progress here?"

"I'm ready to fire it up and test it. You got the control algorithm ready?"

"Yep! I just finished it. And I know how to see to steer it. You know the problem we were going to have on the Moon making one swipe then recalculating the next trajectory or swipe? Well, to hell with that. We're going to modulate the field so we can see through it. Since we will be nonrelativistic we can see through the Alcubierre warp and by modulating the outer Van Den Broeck bubble we can see right where we're going."

"Nonrelativistic?" Jim sounded shocked. "Doc, what are you planning?"

"If you can't take the mountain to Muhammad my ass. By God, we'll rip the fucking thing right out of the Earth!"

➤ CHAPTER 19

The next five or ten minutes were a flurry of, "Go hook that up over there. Try it now. NO! Wait a minute. Turn that on first, then connect this. Okay, I'm triggering the software. The coils are on. Do we get any readings from the detector?"

"Anson, I'm reading gravity modification as expected." Jim checked the detector twice. "It works. What now?"

"Shut it off for second. Let's get the general down here."

I ran back into my office. "Annie, check on the video system and the GPS. Have the signals sent down the hall instead. That big flat panel in there will be our window. And get me a shitload of walkie talkies will ya?"

"Jim!" I yelled down toward the lab. He stuck his head out of the door.

"What!?"

"This has now become the Engineering section of our spaceship. You're the chief engineer, got it?"

"Got it. Where will you be?" he asked.

"Somebody has to drive this thing. Do me a favor and see if your spousal unit needs help with that warp missile. We're going to need it soon."

I grabbed my computer setup and made it double time to the

secure room with Tabitha. I told Tabitha to open the door and let any of our crew in. "We're going to need them on call. Also, we have to have communication with the lab, uh, Engineering."

"Anson, what are you talking about?"

I held up the overview drawing of the facility that Anne Marie had found in the pile of blueprints Calvin had supplied us. "This is what I'm talking about." I thumbtacked the drawing to the wall and drew a big red circle around the facility with a whiteboard marker. If my calculations were right, and if 'Becca's claims of the energy available from the new flubell ECC were correct, we had more than enough power to warp the entire facility out of the ground and use *it* as a spaceship and weapon. "Where are the enemy?" *Okay, I've recovered. It's time to unturtle and come out swinging and kicking!*

Tabitha turned to the flat panel controls and punched in a world flat map. Six different trajectories traced out across the globe. "They got to high LEO before our missile defense systems could do anything. Now they're out of range. We're the last line of defense. The President has been scrambled to Air Force One and I'm sure Congress has been mobilized."

"Do we have any idea what their targets are? Where do they plan to hit?"

"Not exactly sure but the trajectories all track over plenty of U.S. critical targets."

A corner of the flat-panel screen sectioned off and the face of a blue-suit general appeared. "Tabitha we just got this image and we lost contact from Ramstein." The general on the other end seemed grim. A satellite image from space showed us a large dust plume where Germany used to be. The death toll must have been staggering. A second box separated on the flat panel and another satellite image popped up. "There was also an impact that looks centered on the Vandenberg Launch facility in California."

The second image showed a plume that covered all the way down to Los Angeles, California to the south and three quarters of the way up to San Jose to the north. Millions had to have been killed. I was getting to the point of being so emotionally devastated by the destruction and death, which I was mainly responsible for that I could barely function. Sheer will to see the

American way of life survive and years of martial arts training pressed me to focus. I focused on what needed to get done now and I could feel remorse, and mourn, later. What other choice did I have? *Keep fighting, Anson!*

Anne Marie burst into the room panting for air and wielding a walkie talkie. "Anson, here. Calvin said that the video hook-up is completed. He said just turn the flat panel to channels zero, one, and two. We also distributed the walkie talkies to everyone."

"Great," I took the radio from her. "Tabitha section us off part of the panel for those three channels." She did and three nice images of outside appeared on the screen. I touched the talk button. "Calvin are you out there?"

"Right here Doc! What you need?"

"Which direction is each of these cameras looking?"

"Okay let me see. Camera zero is looking due north, one is south, and two is a little west-northwest."

"Great, thanks Calvin. Where is my GPS?" I asked and wrote front, back, and left on three different sticky notes. Then I stuck the sticky notes on the three different images. I arbitrarily chose the north view as front.

"You're talking to him. I have a handheld GPS right here. Couldn't figure out how to get it to work down there."

"Okay, that'll have to do I guess. You hold on up there and whatever you do, don't panic. We're going for a little ride." I told him.

A third panel separated off showing an image of the eastern coast of Florida. Tabitha screamed, "They just hit Kennedy Space Center. They think we will need launch facilities."

I freaked out, "Tabitha your folks!?"

"Don't worry Anson, they were moved after the hospital fiasco. They are miles away from Titusville."

"I'm glad." I felt better. I liked her parents.

"Tabitha," the other general's face appeared back on screen. "Yes Mike."

"Track Four will be right over you in about five minutes. Track Six will be over Washington D.C. on its next orbit, we're still guessing as to Track Five's target."

I looked at the world map and zoomed in on Track Four. In

about five minutes it would be right over Roswell, New Mexico. "Well I'll be damned, that's where we've been hiding all this time." I pushed the talk button and flipped my laptop on at the same time. "Jim, you there?"

"Roger that, Anson."

"Okay, Jim. Start us up. We're about to go one thousand kilometers straight up." I opened the guidance program and started it. "Jim, are you picking up my computer signal okay in there?"

"Great, Anson. I'm getting about nine gigabits per second communication with you. More than enough." The wireless modem was working well through the walls of the facility.

"Okay, Jim, I'm starting the warp field. You tell me if there are any problems in there." I toggled the warp bubble on and the lights blinked on and off for a second.

"You must have cut the outside power line and the backup generators kicked in," Tabitha pointed out.

"Jim, did the power surge damage anything in there?"

"No, Anson. We are A-okay."

"Look at the view screen, Tabitha. We can still see out through the warp bubble. I'm going to create a hole in the bubble directly over Calvin that will oscillate at a much slower frequency. That way his GPS might still function. And our communication system might still function." The cameras worked great. But I had just thought about the sample frequency of the GPS system and our communications with the outside world. It probably worked at a much lower frequency than the high-speed cameras. The communications systems used both a satellite connection and an omnidirectional digital microwave transmitter. The satellite connection would be lost for now. But the omnidirectional signal would last as long as we could see a TDRSS satellite. The screen only flickered a few times but we maintained communications. Amazing!

"Calvin, you there?"

"Doc! It just got pitch black out here and the outside lights came on!"

"Don't panic, Calvin; that is a good thing. Listen, is your GPS still working?"

"Uh, yes. It looks fine."

"Great, just a minute." I turned to Annie, "Annie go help 'Becca get those missiles ready. Tell them that they have to carry them up to where Calvin is."

I punched the talk button again, "Calvin what are our GPS coordinates?" He responded with a set of numbers. I typed them into the program as zero point. Then I entered the command to increase the radial axis by one thousand kilometers. I pressed enter.

The images on the view panel were suddenly dark and then I could see star fields. Good thing the Sun would be to the east of us or we could have fried the cameras. I also started thinking about the amount of oxygen we had trapped in our warp bubble, but I quickly put that out of my mind—as big as our warp bubble was more than enough atmosphere would be trapped in it to keep us going for days or more.

"Tabitha, where is that oncoming traffic?"

Tabitha looked at the data a bit longer. "Anson, I think we're about a hundred kilometers too high and about eight hundred kilometers east of it."

I adjusted our location accordingly and pointed the left camera in that direction. Before long we could see a shiny spot in the view panel.

"There!" Tabitha pointed it out.

"Got it!" I put the software in joystick mode and guided the warp field with the tiny joystick on the laptop keyboard. I flew us to within a few thousand meters of the spacecraft. I called up to 'Becca, "Where are my missiles?"

"The first one is ready, Anson. I'm turning it on . . . now." Immediately following her reply an icon popped up on my desktop.

The RF link in the MWM was working! I grabbed the warp field oscillator program and dropped it into the MWM icon. This loaded the lights-off lights-on software into it. Then I opened the icon for the MWM, which looked identical to the control panel for the larger warp system of the facility spaceship. I clicked the pointer into the MWM control stick mode and activated it.

"Anson, the MWM just lifted a meter straight up and is hovering there. Nothing there but a faintly glimmering blue and red bubble," 'Becca called over the talkie.

"Great, that means it works." We hadn't had time to develop a nose camera for these things yet, so I was going to have to guide it from the facility cameras. Making sure the North camera had the enemy rocket in central view, I lifted the little warp missile straight up another twenty meters or so until it was in the north camera's field of view and then I toggled the main facility warp field.

"Lights off!" I said and pushed the stick full forward. The MWM shot straight about five hundred meters per second out of the realm of the facility, "Lights on!" The atmosphere outside never had a chance to realize it was in a vacuum.

"There it is," Tabitha pointed at the screen. I had over shot the rocket by several kilometers, which was apparent by the faint red plasma trail that shot out in front of the Chinese rocket.

"Just like Beggar's Canyon back home!" I told her and yanked the joystick left, right, forward, a little left, then forward full, and BANGO! The little warp missile zigged and zagged and left the light red plasma trail behind it where it ripped through and ionized the few atomic oxygen atoms per cubic meter in the upper atmosphere. A fireball filled the screen and the rocket was destroyed. Unfortunately, the MWM's power supply was dead too. "Take that you sons a bitches!" I shot a bird at the view panel.

"Tabitha, what's going on?" Mike the general asked. I didn't know his last name. It didn't dawn on me to read his nametag on the right chest of his uniform. Okay, okay, but I was busy.

"Mike, we just waxed track four's ass and we are headed for Track Six. Can you tell me where it is in GPS coordinates right now? I need lat, long, and altitude." Tabitha answered.

"Gives us a second, Tabitha."

"Anson this is 'Becca." My walkie buzzed.

"Go 'Becca." I depressed the talk switch.

"We have the second MWM ready and are sitting in the parking lot next to Calvin. Where are we?" I realized that since the human eye couldn't see fast enough, none of our crew upstairs could see through the bubble. They had no idea we were in space.

"You're asking me? Calvin is right there beside you with a GPS system. Ask him."

"Those damn numbers don't mean anything to me, other than the altitude. Are we in space?"

"Yeah. High LEO. I'm kind of busy right now. I'll call you back in a second."

The general was talking to Tabitha again. "Tabitha, what is left of Space Command is picking up a huge mass above you on radar."

"No, Mike. That's us. The mass is actually the facility we were using at Roswell. We turned it into a spacecraft. Hey get the radar guy at Space Command directly in contact with us here. We will have him guide us right to the other missiles." Tabitha took the time to smile at me.

"Great work gorgeous!" I smiled with hope we would win this thing, trying not to think about the fact that we only had one more missile left. I began steering toward the west coast of the U.S. If Track Six was one orbit away from the capitol, it would be somewhere over Asia about now. The voice of the radar operator came on the speaker of the view panel.

"Uh hello General. This is Lieutenant Phillip Black speaking."

"Hello Lieutenant Black. This is General Tabitha Ames speaking. The large mass in high LEO that you are detecting is me. I need you to guide us into the other inbound tracks. Assume we can travel instantly in straight lines. Do you understand?"

"Uh, yes ma'am. How do you want me to guide you? I mean GPS coordinated or what?"

Tabitha turned to me. "Anson?"

"Well, how about just north, south, east, west, up, and down?" I shrugged my shoulders.

"Can you do that Lieutenant Black?"

"Easy, ma'am. Which track first?" Lieutenant Black asked.

"The one closest to flying over the U.S.," Tabitha ordered.

"Roger that," Lieutenant Black said. "One of them is tracking into our west coastal waters airspace at this time. You're approximately the same altitude but are about nine hundred miles north and six hundred miles east of the target."

I adjusted by vectoring the joystick to the southwest. "How's that?"

"Uh, hold on." The max velocity Lieutenant Black was measuring for us was probably making his head spin. "Okay. Now you are about eighteen hundred miles north and about twelve hundred miles east of the target."

"Lieutenant, are you telling me I went the wrong way?" I asked a little embarrassed.

"Eh, yeah. Sorry," he said.

Tabitha seemed to frown but said nothing.

I cursed, almost laughed, and undid what I just did twice. Tabitha expressed to me later that a similar thing had happened to Jim Lovell on Apollo XIII, so I didn't feel as bad about it.

"How's that?" I rechecked my bearings. Somehow I had gotten turned around.

"Okay. Let's see. You should be within a few miles of the target. Perhaps you are a bit low. Hold one . . . yes. You need to go up by about fifty miles."

"We can't see up or down or right. Hold on," Tabitha announced.

I raised the facility up about fifty miles. It was weird for me to change from kilometers to miles all of the sudden but miles was still standard in American aviation. I had to do quick conversions in my head before I typed in the altitude increases or decreases. The joystick would've worked for vertical maneuvering, but typing in the exact distance was more accurate.

We still didn't see the spacecraft. "Hold on, Tabitha," I told her. I put a slow rotation about the center of the warp bubble. We started rotating and the star field in the camera view began to transit the screen. "There it is!" I pointed it out to Tabitha.

"Lieutenant Black. We have a visual on the target. Please stand by to confirm target destruction." Tabitha nodded to me. "Kick his ass, Anson!"

I adjusted our altitude until we were in the same angular plane with the spacecraft, making sure it was in the center of the field of view.

"Stand clear of MWM two!" I yelled over the talkie.

"All clear, Anson!"

I translated the warp missile up twenty or so meters and pointed it straight at the enemy rocket.

"Lights off!" I pushed the joystick right through where the target used to be. "Lights on!" Again the red plasma trail followed the missile and again the big red fireball. "Scratch two!"

Unfortunately, we were out of missiles now; this one died on impact also. One half of seventy-five percent finished of a mini ECC just couldn't generate enough power to take the stress of the impact.

"Lieutenant, locate the remaining target and give us a heading." Tabitha ordered crisply.

"Roger General Ames. The final target is currently over Irkutsk, Russia."

"Hold on a minute," I said. "I can travel in spherical coordinates also. Tell me how many miles along a curve from my present location to the target. I will adjust altitude and north and south when we get there."

"Sure. I can do that. You need to travel about sixty-five hundred miles westward then three hundred to the north." Lieutenant Black was on top of his game.

"Okay, now what?" I said after adjusting our location. It took a second for the communications to catch back up. That was a big jump and it took the TDRSS satellite nearest us a second to realize that it was getting a signal from us. Then it had to determine where to route it.

Tabitha looked perplexed for a split second, "Lieutenant, this is General Ames are you still there?" Nothing but static. The flat panel was all blue except for the three windows marked front, back, and left.

"Well Tabitha, looks like we lost their signal for now," I told her. I started rotating the facility looking around for the last missile. "Do you see it?" I asked.

"No. Keep looking."

" . . . General Am . . . Lieutenant . . . Bla . . . do you copy?" The blue screens popped back on displaying imagery, missile tracks, and video of Mike the general's counterpart facility. "I repeat. General Ames this is Lieutenant Black, do you copy?"

"Roger that Lieutenant. Mike are you still receiving us also?" Tabitha adjusted the volume slightly.

"We copy you, Tabitha." Mike replied.

"Lieutenant, where is the target?" I asked.

"It just passed under you, sir. You are due west of it and about thirty-four miles high."

I adjusted the altitude and—bingo! A bright shiny spot appeared in the screen labeled back. "I got it!"

"Anson, we have no choice." Tabitha knew what I had in mind. She took my hand without taking her eyes from the screen. "Do it!"

"Don't worry gorgeous, we were gonna dig up the Moon with it. The bubble will hold . . . I hope!" I increased the velocity of the facility and slammed into it. The last enemy warp missile disappeared into a million points of light. The cameras saturated solid white then readjusted themselves.

"Bite me!" I let out a sigh of relief; the warp bubble of the facility had enough power to go faster than light, which was more than nineteen orders of magnitude more energy than needed to destroy that piece of crap foreign rocket. "Tabitha what do you say we take out their ability to ever launch an attack on us again? Lieutenant, get me a vector to Beijing."

"Hold it, Anson. General Tapscott, we're now in an offensive posture. Do we have a go ahead to take out the target's ability to make war?" Tabitha interrupted.

"Hold that General Ames. We're awaiting orders from the President. Tabitha, good job."

"Thanks Mike." She explained to me later that she had known Mike Tapscott for over twenty years and that they were good friends. I had asked her about protocols and how she got away with calling him by his first name, even though they knew each other. She said that she or Mike were never big on them except in public. Kind of like how I prefer to be called Anson, not Dr. Clemons. I guess.

"Tabitha do we have a mute button?" I said under my breath.

She picked up the remote and pressed a button, "Okay we're muted. What's on your mind?"

"We have to take out the enemy's ability to ever build another warp missile now, or we will have another arms race—but this one will destroy the world. Look at the damage already. Few people know about this technology or few could rebuild it. I will guarantee that the scientists that built these missiles are near those launch sites."

"Anson, millions might die."

"As opposed to billions living as Communist Chinese? Besides, millions of Americans have already died. We will do unto others . . ."

"We will do unto nothing until the President gives us the order."

"Then we have to give him deniability. The meteor strikes will still work as a cover. Nobody will ever believe this story. Even if they claim they detected us on radar we'll just laugh and say they're nuts. Remember, nobody can see us with their own eyes."

"Anson, what do you propose?"

"Just like we planned with the Moon, I'm going to bulldoze China into one huge-ass parking lot. Then I plan to move on to Kazakhstan, then Moscow and Svobodny and any other Russian launch site and then North Korea. They joined the wrong team. Screw 'em!"

"You mean all of China?"

"No, no. Just Beijing and every one of their military and space facilities. We will completely remove their army. And their government. We will land on every Chinese government official. Then all that will be left is the people. And the troops massing in North Korea and the navy ships on the Taiwan Strait are history also. Sure, there will be some collateral damage and many civilians killed—but this is war not lasertag for God's sake. And look how many of *us* they've killed. We'll show them that you absolutely under no circumstances ever, and I mean *ever*, fuck with the United States of America!"

"I'm with you, Anson. But not without presidential approval," she said.

"Tabitha we just got word that if you can give the President deniability then we will go with any offensive plan you have. The President said to hit them and hit them hard." General Tapscott snarled triumphantly.

Tabitha unmuted the room, "Roger that, General. First priority is to remove the enemy's ability to launch weapons." Tabitha nodded to me.

"Lieutenant Black, guide me to Hainan Island," I said.

"Roger, sir." He vectored me into the South China launch site. I brought the Roswell Air Force Underground Facility down right on top of the launch platform. I lowered the warp field until the warp bubble was half way underground. Now I had a huge five hundred meter diameter bulldozer blade at my disposal. Several times the cameras saturated.

"What is that?" I asked.

"General Ames. This is Lieutenant Black. You are being fired upon by antiaircraft and surface to air missiles. Are you okay?"

"Hold on. Anson?"

I pressed the talkie button. "Jim, are you there?"

"Yeah, Anson, what's up?"

"How are things with the warp system?"

"Everything is fine. We haven't taxed it more than a hundredth of a percent of the required field stress that would be caused from faster than light travel."

I had guessed that would be the case. But you never know. "Everything is fine here," I replied as I continued to level off Hainan Island.

Ten minutes had passed and I was sure that the island was completely leveled and devoid of life. Nothing was left standing on the island. I didn't want to take any chances that there would be witnesses. I pushed the top of the island right off into the Gulf of Tonkin. Then I raised up above the Island a few miles and slammed into it at a few hundred miles per hour. This would give the area a small impact-crater look. Just to help with the cover story. I only allowed the warp bubble to penetrate the island about a mile or so. When we retracted from the hole we had made, it filled with water and Hainan Island no longer existed on this Earth.

Lieutenant Black then vectored me to Xichang. I razed that Chinese launch site to the ground. This time I didn't bulldoze it; instead, I merely slammed into it at about two thousand miles per hour. Jim called me and warned me that we reached a full three percent stress on the warp system. We then moved on to Jiuquan and then Taiyuan. Then, Beijing. We also drug through the Taiwan Strait and sank a fleet of ships.

"Let's take out all military targets first," Tabitha said several times.

We hit several other targets in China and then moved on to the Baikinor Cosmodrome in Kazakhstan. I hated to destroy such a landmark of human space history, but hey, those bastards destroyed Kennedy Space Center. Tabitha and I both apologized to Yuri under our breath. Then we started peppering Russian launch sites. Svobodny went first, then Kapustin Yar, Plesetsk, Omsk, Yekaterinburg, Orenburg, Moscow, and Star City. We then traveled to North Korea and relieved them of all capabilities to make modern warfare.

At one point 'Becca had expressed her enthusiasm about getting to fire the warp missile but was disappointed that she couldn't see how it performed. Hell, I'm just glad it was ready and it worked. She and Calvin did tell me later that they had a rather boring ride otherwise. From where they stood, they never saw outside but for brief flashes and never knew what was going on.

Pretty much the same was discovered throughout the rest of the facility. Many people never even realized that we had left the ground. Alarms were sounded and people were told to stay where they were. The entirety of the final battle of World War III had pretty much taken place in a matter of a couple of hours and was now basically over. China, Russia, and North Korea were bleeding profusely. So was the United States, but we were still an unstoppable military might with the mastery of warp field technology. Not that that is what I had set out to do with my life. But we do what must be done in order for our way of life to go on. *Or, it will cease being our way of life.*

We discussed our next moves with General Tapscott who in turn discussed this with the President. He was still in hiding and only had direct links to certain facilities. Mike patched him through to all of us. We discussed the possibility that our secret was out. I assured the President that if any average people saw anything it was just a big blurry spot in the sky since the warp field would have forced light around it instead of reflecting it. Since we had modulated the outer field in order to communicate with our ground facilities and the TDRSS satellites, it is possible that the other military radar systems of the world detected us.

That might just be a good thing. They have seen what we can do. They had better keep their damn mouths shut and stay out of it. And of course we could always leak misinformation about a Secret War with aliens or some nonsense to the tabloids. The truth of World War III would never be public knowledge. To add even more fuel to the conspiracy fire, I landed the base right back in the hole in the Earth that it came out of. I sat the base down and compared the view from the cameras to the view I had seen a few hours before when we lifted off and presto! We were back on good old terra firma. I cycled the software off and Jim assured me that the warp field was down.

"Calvin, this is Anson. How are you guys up there?" I called over the walkie talkie.

"We're getting wet, Anson. It is raining cats and dogs out here."

"Can we come in yet?" Anne Marie asked.

"Get inside," Tabitha interjected.

"Is it over?" 'Becca asked.

"Did we win?" that was Al.

I nodded at Tabitha. She pressed her walkie talkie button.

"We won."

➢ CHAPTER 20

I relaxed in my chair and Tabitha finally sat down and joined me. We both had to let the day's events sink in. A few seconds of reflection was all the luxury that we were awarded. The flat screen had not yet faded out to blue and General Tapscott was still on the other end.

"Give us an update on your status General Ames, and realize that the President is listening," Mike ordered.

Tabitha sat up straight. "Yes, General. The Roswell facility is now grounded in Roswell as if it had never left New Mexico. There is most likely major damage along the periphery of the installation that will need repairing.

"As I'm sure that satellite imagery will verify, all launch facilities in China, Russia, and North Korea have been totally eradicated. The governments of each of these countries have been destroyed along with their abilities to make war. In fact, we would like to see global satellite imagery data here to see the extent of the damage. Perhaps we will learn more efficient methods for using this technology. And it's always good to see the havoc one has caused after a battle to maintain perspective of its horror. Hopefully, we won't need it for warfare again.

"It is possible that some of the knowledge of the warp technologies used in today's battles remains in the enemy locations since we didn't remove the entire populations of these countries. And it is always possible that they have sleeper contingencies. However, they have much larger problems now than building weapons to take over the world. Survival should be first and foremost on their minds. Most likely they won't be able to survive without aid from the rest of the world. My guess is that our economy will suffer greatly from our disaster relief also.

"I would suggest two efforts. One is to continue ahead with plans to place the warp research and development facility on the far side of the moon. This technology needs to be advanced and protected at the same time. We saw today that the masters of this technology were nearly unstoppable. We should maintain the only mastery of this awesome power. I should mention here, that it is also likely that we will find a way to use the technology as a defensive shield itself.

"Second, I also suggest to create an intensive intelligence gathering effort to determine if anybody on the planet has any knowledge of this technology and track them. What if terrorists got their hands on this thing also, or another group bent on global domination? In order to maintain the secrecy of this technology, this intelligence group should be placed under the same compartmentalization as the research and development facility. Perhaps the new intelligence group should even be located on the Moon. Travel to and from Earth will be simple and cheap. This way we will be able to know when and if someone is conducting an operation.

"Since the destruction of the Space Shuttle, this has been a global war of proportions great enough to remove the human race from existence. We can only now realize the devastating ability of warp weapons and of the sheer gall and lack of humanity of an enemy that would initiate a preemptive strike with such a weapon. I hope it will never happen again. However, in order to prevent it from recurring, a constant vigil must be kept." Tabitha remained straight in her chair and didn't move a muscle.

"I would like to add something." I interrupted the uncomfortable silence following Tabitha's speech, debrief, or whatever it was. "My original plans for this technology was simply to travel to the stars and see if there is other life and inhabitable planets out there. As it turns out, the power required for that goal can be twisted and used for more evil purposes. I for one never wanted to see that. As long as we maintain the possession of this capability, we can never let it fall into the wrong hands. We saw that today. However, I would hate to deny the world some of the awesome peaceful applications the warp drive can bring us. I can think of some applications useful right now in the disaster relief efforts.

"But, I guess I have to agree that Earth isn't ready for power like this yet. Perhaps after the effects of this war are tended to and the governments of the superpowers become more aligned, we can have a space-faring society, one with various civilian uses of warp field technology. I don't know. In the meantime, we can't let our guard down. And today is absolute proof as to why we can't." I slouched back into my chair again. I was tired and wanted to go home.

The President had little to say other than the fact that nobody would ever know that World War III ever took place. The events of today would be reported as impacts of meteors from space. He issued an executive order compartmentalizing all knowledge of the warp technologies and all data was to be moved to the far side of the Moon away from the Earth.

In essence, he had excommunicated all of us from the human race. Maybe it wouldn't be that bad. Once we got there and got settled, living on the Moon could be pretty cool. Maybe. Besides, we would have to be awarded near infinite resources to maintain such a facility and conspiracy. We had infinite power with the flubells. And if we ever needed anything, hell, we could just fly down to Earth at night and abduct it. I thought of some funny crop circle patterns that I was planning to make with a warp field on some of those trips also. Hey if there is a fire, you have to throw gas on it.

Well, we were going to live outside of the Earthly society and develop technologies years ahead of anything anybody had ever dreamed of. Living on the Moon would be cool. How about that?

➢   ➢   ➢

It took us several days to gather our thoughts, technologies, personal stuff, and implement a security plan. The entire facility was surrounded and protected by armed guards from various branches of the military. Any individuals who knew anything about what had happened were debriefed, sworn to far far above top secrecy, and then reassigned to Tabitha or to Alaska or they were discharged immediately. During the debrief all individuals were warned that if any of the details of the technology or events were leaked they would be publicly and actively ridiculed by expert sources. Debunking government conspiracy nuts is always easy. Who really believes in Roswell, alien abductions, and flying saucers? Nobody does in public, because it labels him or her as nuts. Well, there are some that are making money off of the alien folklore; they are either brave to put themselves out on such a limb, smart for raking in the money from the entertainment industry, or just don't care what happens to their reputation in quest for the truth.

But nobody really believes them, do they? Seeing how the really secret world works, I was beginning to wonder.

Oh well, the security plan was in place and it was working. About fifty personnel had to remain on the payroll. Tabitha and I discussed it and decided to take a month off. She ordered leave for the fifty personnel and told them to return in exactly one month. The facility was locked down and placed under armed guards. The rest of us went home.

By the time we got to Huntsville International Airport, our parents were already there waiting for us. My mom had been carrying Friday in a travel cage. I'm sure she didn't like that, Mom not Friday. Friday is a lazy cat. She was probably asleep, Mom on the other hand was tired of carrying her. Tabitha and Annie hugged and kissed their parents/grandparents and cried. It was a lot of fun. We rented a minivan and headed for my house.

My house had been trashed. Probably by the same team that got Al's house. We weren't really concerned about our personal safety any longer for two reasons. The first is that mercenaries usually only kill for money and their paying customers had been smashed into the Earth or pushed into the sea. The second reason is that we were always being shadowed by plain-clothes security. Tabitha had ordered my house to be a safe zone. So, there were guards waiting for us when we arrived. I guess this is how life would be for all of us from now on.

I took Friday out of the cage and nuzzled her to me as we entered the living room. I sat her down and she looked around, then up at me and said, "Raaooww?"

"I know it's a mess girl, but it's home. Go on." I said. I looked around at the mess and wasn't sure where to start.

Jim dragged in behind with his arms full of luggage, "Ah, home crap home." He laughed. "Nobody worry about the luggage, I've got it," he said sarcastically. Al and I turned to help him.

We spent a few hours cleaning up. It made us all feel normal again to do menial daily type tasks. Jim, Al, and I drove to town and picked up some steaks, hamburgers, hotdogs, buns, potatoes, charcoal, chips, dips, limes, lemons, margarita mix, and a lot of beer. We stopped by the package store on the way back and picked up some ice and tequila and triple sec and decided we better get more beer.

By the time the grill was ready for the steaks, burgers, and dogs, I had about three beers down. My fiancée stepped through the back door wielding two very large margaritas. The sunlight nowadays was redder than usual because of all of the dust thrown into the upper atmosphere from the Warp Weapons of the Secret War. The strange reddish summer sun illuminated the glitter in Tabitha's blue bikini top in a most unusual way. Her cutoff denim shorts brought out her, uh Southern charm. And the fifteen or twenty degrees cooler weather than usual for July brought out some of her other, uh perky, features. She sure didn't look like General Tabitha Ames the astronaut and warrior-leader of the super secret Warp Weapons Contingent of the United States Space Force. I chuckled inside.

"Hey Anson, brought you something." She said. I reached for one of the margaritas and she pulled it back. "Not that. These are for me. I brought you this." She leaned forward and kissed me deeply. "August fifteenth." She said, "And happy birthday!" She kissed me again and then took a big draw from her left margarita and then her right one.

"Thanks," I replied. Then I thought about what she had said for a second longer. "Hey that is like three weeks from now."

"Uh huh." She said. "We're a fixin' to git hitched!" she said in her best Texan and then hit the margaritas in reverse order this time.

"Okay with me. Can we get it arranged that fast?"

"Our moms, 'Becca, and Anne Marie are in there just a plottin' and a schemin' as we speak."

I wiped my hands off on my *Kiss the Physicist Please* apron and then planted my hands on each side of her face. "I love you," I told her, then kissed her again. Then the hamburgers flared up and I had to attend to the grill. I never did get a margarita.

➤ CHAPTER 21

The wedding planning had gone off without a hitch. The girls had decided it would be best to have it in the big nondenominational church downtown. Tabitha somehow pulled some strings and managed to get us in on such short notice. She spread the rumor that the NASA Administrator, Secretary of Defense, and the Vice President were on the invitation list. Things started happening. Of course, I'm not sure that Tabitha hadn't really gotten an R.S.V.P. from any of their offices, but it was a good ploy one way or the other. Imagine my surprise when not only were they there, but they were seated next to the President himself.

Jim was my best man and Al and Calvin and my brother stood up with me. The bridesmaids were Sara, 'Becca, and an old flight school buddy of Tabitha's, Colonel Margie Finest. Anne Marie stood beside her as her maid of honor. The men were wearing charcoal tuxedos with tails except for my brother, who wore his dress blues. The ladies all wore long slender sky blue gowns, except for Anne Marie and Colonel Finest, of course, who were both in their Air Force dress blues. Tabitha, not being General Ames at the moment, of course was wearing white. She sported a long white form-fitting backless gown with lace trim covering the chest and open cleavage and a train that had to be carried by two flower girls. Fortunately, a cousin of mine had two twin youngsters who fit the bill perfectly.

I was a nervous disastrous mess! I fumbled over the words that the preacher had me follow and even put the ring on Tabitha's wrong hand. She changed it without anybody ever noticing. She was cool as a cucumber, her typical head-astronaut-what-be-in-charge self. I had never been more in love. Eewww God this is mushy. Sorry. Weddings are like that.

The President and his entourage stayed just long enough to let Tabitha salute him. He saluted her back smartly, then shook my hand and whispered to me, "Good luck son!" Not real sure if he was talking about with Tabitha and marriage or about protecting the world and living on the Moon. Either one was a daunting task. I couldn't wait to get started on both, but the Moon was just going to have to wait tonight.

"Thank you, Mr. President!" I should have swelled with pride but I didn't. But as he walked away and Tabitha hugged and kissed me, I sure enough did.

The reception was at Tim's place. He shut down the place and catered to Tabitha's every whim. There were shrimp cocktails, raw oysters on the half shell, and crawfish in a cajun remoulade sauce as appetizers. We had a choice of blackened trout or chicken as the entrée, each with appropriate sides. The wedding cake was typical in shape and three tiers high. The only unusual part was that somebody had the idea of putting two action figures in spacesuits on top of the cake instead of a bride and groom. Fortunately, they had the foresight to paint one of them the same color as my tuxedo. My guess was that they got the action figures from the Space and Rocket Center.

The groom's cake was the shape of a Space Shuttle. The first layer looked like the External Tank with the two Solid Rocket Boosters attached. The second layer was the Orbiter itself. There were miniature beer cans on a string tied behind the Orbiter and "Just Married" was iced on the wings of the Orbiter and on each Solid Rocket Booster. It looked cool. I hated to have to cut it. We got plenty of pictures.

Somehow, Tim or Tabitha or somebody, had managed to get my favorite local band to play the reception. We had a good crowd of forty or fifty people who partied on through until about two in the morning when the band finally quit. At one point, 'Becca, Sara, and Anne Marie got up and sang with the band. It was a hoot, an absolute hoot!

Nobody ever asked who the gentlemen in the suits standing in the corner were. Those of us who knew they were security didn't let on. Everybody else just thought they were part of the other family that they hadn't met. After having the President's entourage in town, seriously, nobody paid any further attention. Besides, everybody was real drunk.

A week later, we were back in Roswell planning our massive Exodus to the Moon. We weren't in a big hurry this time. So, we decided to take a little better detailed care in designing the facility now that we had time to do so. Along with the trailer park, we had permanent homes constructed. We now had more power with the modifiable warp field and the flubell ECCs. So, we planned a much larger facility. The central dome would be seven hundred meters now instead of three hundred. There would be two other domes three hundred meters in diameter for the manufacturing plant and the lab. We would have much more space.

The trailer park would be for temporary and short-term visitors as well as crew bunks for the noncommissioned military men and women. We decided to allow the main science and engineering core a twenty by twenty-five meter area for housing and yard. The houses could be as tall as desired up to three stories above the surface. Each of these residences were then allowed five meters on each side between houses and a ten meter by ten meter back yard and a five meter deep front yard. A small two-meter diameter window would be placed over each residence. Each of the windows would be tinted to act as the atmosphere on Earth does for filtering harmful sunlight. The windows would be cycled with the rest of the facility to allow night and day. Forty-eight, three story houses were built with privacy fences. Tabitha and I picked out our interior and house design and so did Jim and 'Becca. Our two houses were adjacent at the end of one of the cul-de-sacs. Those lots were twice as big. There were six cul-de-sacs off of Main Street. Main Street ran circumferentially about a hundred and twenty meters inside the dome. Each cul-de-sac had three houses on each side and two at the end or eight houses per street. Sara, Anne Marie, and Al were each given a house as well. They were on the same street. We named our street Warp Drive. Hey, if we were all going to be living on the Moon for the rest of our lives, it had better be comfortable. I soon found out that Colonel Finest would be living on our street also. Somebody had managed to get her transferred to the Special Group WW as we were now being called. The WW stood for Warp Weapons and I just wondered who got Margie transferred. There was a saying filtering around us that if you think that Group W was crazy, you ought to see Group W squared.

We all visited the town site in Georgia at least once a week to make sure things were going as planned. Things were going well. At the same time, we were constructing new flubell based ECCs and new modifiable warp field generator coils. We contracted out to a small aerospace company to build several aerodynamic spaceframes from lightweight composite materials. The frames looked like miniature Orbiters but a little sleeker and a little more aerodynamic. The little spacecraft were designed to accommodate about eight people very comfortably. They even had a space-qualified standard restroom and shower facility. We had five of the vehicles constructed. Tabitha and Margie flew the first one during its drop test out at Dryden. It performed beautifully. Tabitha said it flew a lot easier than the Shuttle Orbiter during its glide path. Margie said it handled like a cargo jet. But I guess that is about how the Shuttle Orbiter feels. You'll have to ask Tabitha. I told them that it would for sure fly easier when we retrofitted it with a warp core and she could vertically take off and land. And oh by the way, fly faster than the speed of light. "After all," I told them, "it's bound to fly better than the Roswell facility and it flew pretty damn good!"

Upon delivery of the last spaceframe, the first two warships were completely retrofitted and ready to fly. Tabitha, Jim, 'Becca, Anne Marie, Margie, and myself test drove one of them to the far side of the Moon. We picked out a nice spot for Moon Base 1 and marked it by using the spacecraft to dig a big X in the lunar surface.

Tabitha spent the trip back at a slower pace. It took a couple of hours. She used this pace to train each of us how to fly the little warpships. Then we each got a turn landing them at the Roswell facility. It turned out that Annie was a natural born pilot, go figure. That apple didn't fall far from the tree did it? By the end of the day we were all checked out and Tabitha gave each of us the go ahead to pilot the ships by ourselves. However, all flight plans had to be approved by her or Margie first. After all, they were the two most experienced pilots we had available. Tabitha had thousands of hours including in space and Margie was a test pilot instructor from the National Test Pilot School.

Jim, Al, and Margie spent the next couple of days digging holes and tunnels in the far side of the lunar surface. About six months later, the town was completed. All the construction was kept to simple slab and sticks with very comfortable interiors. The town had its own power plant of flubell ECCs, a power grid, and modifiable warp field generators. When it was complete, we simply ripped it out of the ground: houses, trailers, streets, trees, vegetable garden, lake and beach equipped with volleyball net, birds, bees, cats, post office, water tower and purification plant, waste recycling plant, air handlers and scrubbers, electric buggies, mountain bikes, food storage facility and country store (although Tabitha called it the PX), one beach bar and grill, and a shitload of other stuff. At the last minute we added a full court concrete slab with poured rubber surface basketball court. The court was flanked on each side with outdoor aluminum bleachers. We also added a martial arts school and fitness training center equipped with a full complement of machines and weights. There were picnic areas in the trees and near the beach. And we added a gazebo here and there for aesthetics. We also made certain that there was enough room for a school building and football field. Sara named it "Force Field." With about a hundred employees planned, it is possible that we would have enough for two or three intramural teams. All of these people might have kids or need to do distance training. We added a library to the school and filled it with books, periodicals, and technical journals. It was one of the best technical libraries ever assembled. We would definitely use that. The library also had a full print shop and electronic database. Our goal was to do most stuff electronically so we wouldn't need much paper. But, I still like to print documents out to read them, though.

We were thinking way into the future when one day we might have a complete society living there. Nobody questioned our budget line so we spent as much money as we could on anything we could think of.

Then we warped all of it to the Moon. I flew the town while Jim and Al came in over the top and covered it up with lunar soil. I then oscillated the Town's outer warp field and hardened the dome around it. It took several more weeks to install all of the windows. We had to run flame pots and heaters and oscillate the warp field some to maintain temperature until the windows were in place. The next week or two involved moving the manufacturing facility and lab that had been constructed at other secret locations. They took a week or two to completely install at Moon Base 1 also. Then we installed the landing strip and docking facility. With all construction complete we did a lights-off lights-on maneuver to encompass the complete Moon Base in one warp bubble. Then we turned the periphery bubbles off.

Everything was finally complete and people began moving in. Jim and I had the idea of building a mountain bike trail around the Town, Lab, and Plant. We cut trails inside the domes on the outer circumference and then used a small warp bubble to cut switch back trails alongside and up and over (or down and under in some cases) the tunnels that connected the various domes. We added a couple of whoops and a few doos. We even stuck in a "hellacious up hill" and a "screaming elevator shaft down to hell." We put up historical markers explaining that this was "the first mountain bike trail in space don't ride when raining." The trail was wide enough to ride two-up and was roughly two and three-quarter miles long. We put fluorescent lighting all through the trails that were in tunnels and we planted grass, weeds, and flowers. Since the trails were within the Moon Base warp field they were at one gee everywhere. We worked on the trail during our spare time and it only took us about a month to complete it.

We spent a month or two moving in and slowly developed a routine. Occasionally we would slip back to Earth to pick up more supplies and beer. But for the most part, we lived and worked at Moon Base 1 and seemed to always have to send someone back to Earth for beer and pretzels.

Our first technical priorities were to improve detection capabilities, invent new warp technologies that would enable new methods of warfare, develop new intelligence gathering abilities, and to develop transportation capabilities. It was a lot of fun. We spent a lot of time brainstorming and testing these new ideas. One of the ideas that I had was a bulletproof force field. If we could design an ECC and Van Den Broeck bubble generator that was light enough, foot soldiers could wear them as armor. Tabitha suggested that they could replace spacesuits also. We just needed to figure out how to replenish oxygen.

After brainstorming the personal warp field concept a while, I began to see many possibilities for it. A personal warp field could be used to enhance strength if the control system for the bubble was designed to react to movements inside the field. The personal warp system would also enable the individual to warp himself around or fly. This could be the first possible design for a Supersuit. We put this concept on the to-do list, even if it was five or more years off.

We had already developed warp cranes and float tables to enable us to move heavy stuff around. These would have been useful for the disaster relief if the public could have been told about them.

I was also thinking about a technique of using the warp field to create a giant gravitational lens that could be used as the primary objective for a telescope. If we could warp spacetime hard enough to create a short focal length lens that was kilometers in aperture diameter, we could see freckles on an ant's ass from the moon. Or we could image planets around other stars. This gave me an idea about the Solar Focus, but we can talk about it later.

And of course, there was always the original reason for my designing the warp drive. Interstellar space travel! I indeed planned to do this soon. In fact, Tabitha and I were planning a trip to Mars real soon to test out the speed of our little warpships. We had yet to prove that we could go superluminal. But there was no doubt in my mind it would soon be done.

By the way, I never really talked about the effect our Secret War had on Earth. With the wedding, our one-week honeymoon that we spent on my couch in Huntsville, and building and moving into Moon Base 1, I tried not to dwell on it. The last estimate of dead was somewhere around sixty-five million Americans, one hundred million Chinese, forty-seven million Russians, and two hundred thousand North Koreans. There were countless acres of forests and wildlife destroyed. Last count was three hundred or more species of animals and insects were now extinct. It was estimated that the damage was in the trillions of U.S. dollars. The three hypercanes caused by the Warp Weapon impacts pumped a tremendous amount of dust and moisture into the upper atmosphere. And there was talk of the subsequent moderate greenhouse effect causing higher coastal waters and much larger tropical regions for the next hundred or more years. Like Huntsville wasn't hot and humid enough already. Now it would be like beach weather without the beach. Oh, there was some talk about "nuclear winter" kinds of nonsense and ice ages and other things, but none of that really panned out scientifically. Just our weather was a little more erratic is all.

But don't worry. Humans are quite resourceful. We will survive this and in fact thrive again in no time. I feel bad about all the damage and especially about the lost lives. However, and I'm not just trying to justify myself here, the Earth is becoming a better place now. China finally had to really open its borders to Western business or it was going to starve to death. The destruction of most of the Russian government destroyed a lot of their organized crime problem since most of the crime bosses were government officials. The Russian people asked us for help. So we moved in and helped them prop themselves up and clean up their act a little. Europe joined in to help since they were least affected. Although there was no longer a Germany, the rest of Europe was trying to help. Interestingly enough, no governments tried to take advantage of the situation. Also, the stock exchange was unfrozen a few weeks ago. World trade is back to normal or much better. Again there was some initial concern about global climate changes causing mass crop failures and global starvation. And once again this was mostly junk scientists making noise to get themselves on television. All of that original Carl Sagan nuclear winter nonsense continued to rear its ugly head—idiots. I wanted to strangle some of the fools I saw on TV bitching about the coming ice age and the end of the world. Tabitha eventually convinced me that I just had to let it go.

One thing that really bites me in the butt is that not long after the Secret War a damned group of Islamic Jihad fools car-bombed the American Embassy in Kuwait. Then they claimed that the meteors were due to us being the infidel and some other nonsense. About fifteen Americans were killed and a few from other countries. And we didn't do a damned thing! For now the world still depended on oil so we had to let those fools act as they had for thousands of years. Like fools.

I vowed that day that I was going to design a less efficient and less explosive energy collection dumbbell that we could leak into mainstream technology. If these weaker dumbbells generated only a millionth of the energy that the flubells do, the Middle East would be out of business in no time. Then we wouldn't have to put up with the bastards. I put Sara to work on the new dumbbell design. Jim was more than happy to volunteer to help her. Tabitha and I went to work on a plan to leak the technology.

The American way of life barely made it through the Secret War. We got lucky in a lot of respects. Tabitha and I talk about it every now and then. We both agree that neither of us would have thought of another way to defend against the final Chinese/ Russian assault in time. If 'Becca hadn't been infected by that damn flubell virus, the outcome could have been a lot different. We might could have escaped with the partial Clemons Dumbbell ECC we had but who knows? I don't like thinking about how lucky we really were. Tabitha tells me that I think about "what-ifs?" way too much. I think she is right. We survived, America prevailed, the human race will continue.

➤ CHAPTER 22

It was going to take a while to figure out the tricks of inter-stellar navigation. We decided to start small and take baby steps out of the solar system. We warped to Mars in about two and a half minutes. We had christened our little warpship the *U.S.S. Einstein.* Tabitha and Margie were at the controls. Jim and I were in charge of celestial navigation. Rebecca and Sara were watching the power plant and warp core. Al and Anne Marie were in charge of general mission logistics. We entered into an orbit around Mars and started looking for interesting things. We landed in Cydonia. There were no pyramids to be found anywhere. We found no face either. I was always hoping there would be something.

We traversed several canals and headed to the Martian North Pole. Near where the ice caps met the desert, we took a few core samples. I never noticed any living creatures crawling around. It's possible that there might be some microbes in the core samples. When we had completed checkout of our exploration capabilities, we would come back to Mars and hang out a while. This time was more of a shakedown flight. We did hit the list of experiments and observations that a lot of planetary scientists had been writing about for decades.

We started near the equator then flew southwest to Ophir

Chasma and back around east to Juventae Chasma. We saw all sorts of slope and bedrock material, cratered plateaus, and degraded craters. Then we turned northward toward the northern plains, Kasei Vallis, and the Viking I landing site. We finally sat down on the peak of Olympus Mons.

We hadn't developed individual warp fields yet. In fact, we were several years from that if at all, so we had to steal about ten new SAFER EMUs from NASA. We had our Earthside black bag connection take care of the paper work. NASA never knew that they had the spacesuits to begin with. We sat up a group in the Research and Development Dome back on Moon Base 1 to reverse-engineer the EMUs, redesign them, and make them more mobile and useful. That would take a year or so also.

At any rate, we suited up, cycled through the airlock with a lights-off lights-on maneuver, and descended the loading ramp of the *Einstein*. Once we had set foot on the Martian surface, Tabitha and Margie set up an American flag. The view from Olympus Mons was incredible. Sara scratched into a rock with a screwdriver "Sara Tibbs was here." Then she passed it around and we each took turns. Jim signed it last and dated it.

This wasn't a science mission. This was a technology demonstration mission. We had proven we could fly about four times the speed of light and navigate to a specific point. We had proven we could determine where we were once we dropped out of warp. We then demonstrated that we could locate and land on a planet and conduct EVAs. It was time to head back home. Tabitha corralled us back into the *Einstein* and we began the liftoff checklists.

"Ramp up?" Tabitha asked.

"Check." Margie replied.

"Everybody on board?"

"Check."

"Okay, liftoff."

"Check."

Not much of a checklist. The warpships made spacetravel almost as easy as a Sunday drive, as long as there were no technical difficulties. This time we stressed the ECCs up to three percent and shaved another minute and thirty-seven seconds off the trip. It took about twenty-three seconds in warp to travel back to the

Moon. The average speed was about twenty-four times the speed of light.

Tabitha brought us into the spaceport's waiting zone, which was just outside the spaceport warp field. The spaceport's field is always set to oscillate on and off at a kilohertz or so. She simply flew *Einstein* through it when it was in the off position—of course, that was done in fractions of a second via a flight control computer and was transparent to her. We debarked and transferred the samples and EVA suits to a quarantined lab for analysis and cleanup, respectively.

Analysis of *Einstein* showed that it was in tip-top condition. The space travel at twenty-four times the speed of light had had no ill effect on it. It was a good ship. We prepared it for our next flight. This time we planned to visit every planet in the outer solar system and a few Kuiper Belt objects to boot.

Our flight trajectory was designed as multiple warps. The first warp would be straight to Jupiter space. We clocked out at about thirty times the speed of light. I'm here to tell you that Jupiter is beautiful! We did a very fast orbit around it so we could look at the giant red spot. Absolutely amazing. A few times, we actually turned off the warp field so we could see it with our own eyes for a few seconds. Then we clicked the field back on and looked through the viewscreen. We wanted closer looks at the moons, and the radiation from Jupiter was a bit more than we wanted to deal with. After all, both Tabitha and 'Becca were about five weeks or so pregnant. Oh, I guess I forgot to mention that. It would appear that they are having a race to see who can have the first baby in space. We wanted to attempt our first interstellar jump before they got too uncomfortable and big for space travel. The EMUs aren't designed to accommodate a woman in her third trimester. And both Tabitha and 'Becca said that we're not setting foot on an alien world without them.

We mostly wanted to see Europa. It supposedly had a very deep ice coating along with a water ocean underneath the ice. We pushed *Einstein* through the thick layer of ice on Europa's surface. The ECCs operated at only two percent to do this. At about ninety-four kilometers, the stresses on the warp field stopped and we could tell that we had broken through to a water ocean.

The hole that we had just made through the ice immediately froze shut above us. We slowly panned around and illuminated the dark ocean with the outside lights, which were set to oscillate opposite the outer warp field. Near what seemed to be the bottom of the Europan ocean we found a lava flow. There was a lot of particle debris floating and drifting in the water but we couldn't tell if it was alive or not. A larger piece of the floating material seemed to alter its path and then it darted toward a smaller chunk. The smaller chunk took off like a bat out of hell. We focused the cameras in on the region a little tighter and realized that the debris floating in the water were actually schools of some type of fish.

"I want one of those!" Al said.

"Not sure how we could catch it, Al," Margie responded. "We can come back and get one some other time."

We sat still for a while and watched the fish swim and eat each other. These weren't ordinary fish. Upon closer inspection, we could see that they had no eyes. I also wasn't sure if I saw any gills or not. We would have to catch some of these things and have the right folks study them. Some other time. We'd watched the fish for about twenty minutes when Tabitha decided we should continue with our mission. Again, we were on a technology demonstration mission, not a science exhibition.

We tunneled back up through the ice and out to a very high orbit around the Jupiter system. Jim and I did a little celestial navigation and then on to Saturn.

Okay maybe I'm an old softy when it comes to the beauty of our solar system, but Saturn is an incredible sight. It is hard to say which I like better, Jupiter or Saturn. The big ticket item at the Saturn system was Titan. Ever since I read *The Puppet Masters* I wanted to know if there really were Titans. Titan's dense atmosphere has kept its surface a secret from astronomers. We learned its secrets. In fact, the planetary scientist had hit it pretty damn close. At about a hundred and eighty kilometers from the surface we hit a layer of nitrogen that was at one Earth atmospheric pressure. At about twenty kilometers from the surface, we hit a cloud of methane vapor. Just below the clouds it was raining methane and the stresses on the warp field suggested atmospheric pressures on the order of a thousand or more times greater than that of Earth. Visibility was very poor and we couldn't see well enough to navigate. Infrared didn't help, because there was none. The cloudy moon was cold. We had to switch to radar navigation and if we came back, we would bring a sonar system or something also. We did feel our way around with the radar for a while until we found a lake. The lake was at about minus one hundred seventy-seven degrees Celsius. The lake was liquid methane.

There were no Titans. I wasn't disappointed. In fact, I expected not to find anything. But childhood aspirations and fantasies should be entertained every now and then.

We oohed and ahhed as we stopped at Uranus and then Neptune. They weren't necessarily close to each other, but with warpdrive at thirty times the speed of light, no place in the solar system was that far away. Even the Pluto-Charon system, which is about thirty astronomical units from Earth, is pretty close at those speeds. The total trip to the three outer planets including the ooh and ah time of about thirty minutes was only an hour or so. It was obvious that things were going to be a lot different for the human race, at least for those "with the need to know."

We spent some time at the Pluto-Charon system looking around. We actually landed but didn't get out. There wasn't much to see. Pluto is an ice ball. The humorous part of the trip was the fact that we had beaten the NASA Pluto-Kuiper mission by several years. I thought about trying to track down the approaching spacecraft to just take a look at it. Maybe some other time. Our mission was to develop warp capabilities that would enable inter-stellar travel. We had to continue with learning how to navigate over large distances. So far, we had only been as far out as about thirty times the distance from the Earth to the Sun. The distance to the nearest star is about a hundred thousand times that. We still had quite a ways to go. At thirty times the speed of light, the trip to the nearest star would take about two months.

We wandered around in the Kuiper-Belt a bit and then decided to travel through the Oort Cloud and then the Heliopause. The Heliopause where the solar system meets the rest of the galaxy is considered the edge of the solar system at about a hundred astronomical units. There were some really neat plasma light shows there. Our spectrum analyzer systems picked up radio noise centered around the two to three kilohertz range and at awesome power levels. We pushed through the Heliopause out to about three hundred AUs. I checked our navigation and suggested to Tabitha that we bounce back to the Moon just to make sure. The nonstop trip took about an hour and a half. We docked at the moon for a few hours and had lunch at home.

By three o'clock that afternoon, we were ready to try for the solar gravitational focus. According to General Relativity any large massive body like the sun actually bends spacetime enough in its near vicinity that the paths of light rays traveling near that massive body are bent. In other words, the big object acts like a very large lens. This fact has been verified experimentally in many different ways since 1919. However, nobody has yet travelled to the focus of the large solar lens.

I had more reasons than just curiosity for traveling to the solar focus. Lets digress for a second.

The largest telescope built by mankind so far is on the order of about a hundred meters. It is a multiple mirror interferometer in Hawaii. The idea of making large telescopes is to increase the resolution. This means that the better the resolution the smaller the objects you can see, farther away. The way to determine the smallest object seeable by a telescope is to use the Rayleigh Criteria equation. The formula states that the minimum resolvable object diameter is found as 2.44 times the wavelength of the light (assume 550 nanometers for yellowish green light) times the distance to the object (five light years or 4.55×10^{16} meters) divided by the diameter of the telescope's primary optic. Assuming that you want to image an Earth-like planet that has a diameter of about 12,000 kilometers, Rayleigh's Criteria says that we need a telescope at least two kilometers or more in diameter! The Hubble Space Telescope is 2.4 meters in diameter and the James Webb Space Telescope is only a few times bigger than that. So we're a long way from imaging planets even around the nearest star even if you consider the ground-based interferometer in Hawaii.

Now consider the solar focus. The diameter of the Sun is on the order of a million kilometers. Using that as the diameter of the telescope primary in the Rayleigh formula shows that we could see a hair up an ant's ass on planets around stars out to a few tens of light years away. We could image planets much much further out than that. Talk about the ultimate telescope. I had what is known in amateur telescope making circles as "Big Aperture Fever" or BAF. Even worse, my case was acute, chronic, and was a special strain called BMFAF. You can guess what the MF stands for.

According to General Relativity, the solar focus should be somewhere between five hundred and eight hundred AUs depending on the wavelength you wish to view. The lensing effect works for all electromagnetic radiation not just visible light. Anyway, imagine a telescope that large. All that would be needed to use old Sol as the primary optic would be to place a detector at the focus. I planned to add other optics to do some image correction and cleaning up but the complete system is simple commercial adaptive optics and software. The hard part is getting to the solar focus. The other hard part is lining the star you wish to view up with the Sun and with the detector. The three objects must form a straight line: the star, then the Sun, then the detector. Assuming the solar focus is six hundred AUs from the Moon Base, then that means a trip time of about three hours to view one star. Of course there would be multiple stars in the field of view of the telescope depending on which eyepiece you use, but we were most immediately interested in stars close to Earth. Now we're talking about maybe fifty stars sparsely spaced whose light paths were rays passing through the surface of a sphere six hundred AUs in radius. It would take some time hopping around the solar focus to get images of all of these star systems. Three hours one way, there then a day or so of observation, then three hours back. Let's assume two days per star system. That means that it would take about a hundred days to look at each of our local stellar neighbors. I decided to start with the closest and move outward. That is once we got the telescope system working properly.

So, we zipped out to the solar focus in line with Alpha Centauri, which is the closest star to Earth. Tabitha popped open the hatch that enclosed our telescope secondary system. It took Jim and me another five or six hours before we had the system functioning the way we wanted it to perform.

There were several planets in the Alpha Centauri system but there was no hint of any planets that could support life as we know it. Using a visible spectrometer, we could analyze exactly what elements were in the atmospheres of these planets. None supported our kind of life. No water, chlorophyll, or oxygen.

Slightly disappointed, we warped back to the Moon. This time we decided to tax the ECC's to ninety-nine percent. Using most of the energy we had available enabled us to deepen the Alcubierre warp. We only shaved off about half of the trip time. In other words, it took about thirty-three times more power to increase our warp speed by a factor of two. Obviously there was some nonlinear function involved here that I hadn't counted on. My solutions to the Einstein equations were only accurate at low warp speeds. Between twenty and fifty times the speed of light, something else was going on. I'm still thinking about that. Jim suggested that spacetime might be quantized like the excitation levels of an atom and that there is some Moor's potential well that we have to overcome. Interesting idea. Like I have said before, Jim deserves a Nobel Prize.

We had proven that there was no life around Alpha Centauri. The next step was to look at Barnard's Star, which is only slightly further out. Barnard's Star is about six light years from Earth and is a faint red giant or M class star on the Hertzsprung-Russel diagram.

Using the solar focus telescope system, Jim brought the star system into view at low magnification and stopped out the bright spot caused by Sol, and by Barnard's Star. An array of planets came into view. Two were fairly large gas giants, one of which was twice the size of Jupiter, and three were planets in the realm of Earth-like in size. The spectrometer computer dinged at us and said that oxygen and chlorophyll had been detected. The light from Barnard's Star had illuminated the planet's atmosphere and the wavelength bands that get absorbed by oxygen and chlorophyll had been absorbed and not reflected off one of the planets—the spectrometer instrument enabled us to measure which bands of light were received by the telescope and which ones weren't. But which planet?

We zoomed in on the inner three planets one at a time. The

first planet was a barren rock much like Mercury. The second planet closest to Banard's Star was blue and green and looked like a Mars-sized Earth. We spent hours zooming in on the planet. There were oceans, mountains, trees, and even grass. We saw no artificial structures of any sort. There was life there, but most likely not intelligent life.

The third planet was mostly like Venus.

We bounced back to Moon Base 1 and began discussing who was going to visit Barnard's Star. We decided that we were all going. We were too valuable to America to risk getting lost in space, but we didn't care. Was that selfish? We knew we could get back.

We had one problem. At fifty times the speed of light, the trip would take at least fifty days there and fifty days back. That's a little more than three months. Tabitha and 'Becca were pushing two months pregnant. The *Einstein* was very comfortable for few hours, just like a minivan is comfortable for a ten-hour drive to the beach. But you can't live in a minivan for three months. We had to build a real starship. We would just have to be patient.

The crew split up into three groups. Tabitha and Sara and I made up one group, Annie, Al, and Margie made up the second, and Jim and 'Becca made the third group. We took turns. One week you got to bounce out to the solar focus and continue planet hunting. One week you got to work the starship construction project. The third week you watched over the military research and development aspects of our Moon Base 1 operations. Each team alternated through the three jobs. There were over a hundred and fifty personnel on the Moon Base now but we were the original brain trust. We felt an obligation to making sure it functioned and continued all of its missions, not just the really fun ones.

Tabitha, Sara, and I took the first watch designing the starship. We took blueprints from the International Space Station habitat modules and began redesigning them. Our idea was to build three habitat size modules, just a little larger, and connect them side by side, then lay two on top of those three, and then one on top of the two. So we would have a pyramid of six cylinder-shaped modules. We would then attach the *U.S.S. Einstein* to the middle cylinder module in the bottom line of three. Remember that the *Einstein* doesn't have rocket engines in the back of it where the Shuttle does. In fact, this is where the loading ramp is located. We could retrofit *Einstein* fairly easily to the new configuration. There were two side doors also so loading and unloading wouldn't be a problem.

Tabitha and Sara went about setting up the contracts Earthside to get construction of the modules under way. It would take about a year to complete the modules. We contracted the same aerospace firm that built *Einstein*. We decided to have them go ahead and build the retrofit faring that would connect the little warship to the habitat cylinders.

A few days later, Annie had the idea to put a retrofit faring on both ends of the cylinders so that we could dock one of the other warships to the other side. This way, we could land and then split up into two teams to cover more ground more quickly. She had the contracts modified to allow the new designs.

Occasionally, Jim and I would compare notes on the warp field and energy anomalies. We still hadn't quite put our finger on a solution to the nonlinear energy requirements for fast warp speeds. But we were new to warp theory. We had only been doing it for a year or so. We also compared notes on pregnancy. Tabitha hadn't had a lot of trouble with morning sickness. 'Becca on the other hand, was miserable. I told Jim that Tabitha had been an astronaut for so long that probably nothing made her sick anymore.

A couple of months later we compared notes on the so-called "honeymoon trimester." We both decided that it would be a lot more fun without having to deal with a three to six month pregnant woman. Both of them exercised every day but their mobility was beginning to suffer. So, Jim and I had a clever idea. We redesigned the curvature in the flat space portion of the protective warp bubble of the habitat dome. The area around our respective bedrooms we designed a curvature that would be modifiable to zero gee and would be centered about the bedroom. The low gravity field would slowly taper back to one gee at the edge of the room. We each rigged us a transmitter to trigger the new software via the push of a button. We could also modify the amount of gravity in our bedrooms from zero to one gee. That gave me another idea about a high gee training facility, but that is another story. In fact, I remember seeing that idea on a cartoon I used to watch years ago.

I told Tabitha that I had a surprise for her. "I have remodeled the bedroom," I told her.

"What did you do?" she said nervously.

I led her into the room and said, "Tada!"

"I don't see any difference," she remarked.

"Look here." I pointed to the slidebar switch by the headboard of the bed. The switch had a zero at the bottom and a one at the top. "Stand here by the bed and lower the switch slowly," I said.

She reached up and slid the bar downward about halfway. My stomach lurched and tickled. I'm sure hers did. The baby kicked also. "Whoa!" she grabbed the headboard and steadied herself.

I leaned over and picked up the bed with one hand. "See, I rigged it so we could modify the gravity in here. You can probably get more comfortable to sleep at lower gee."

Tabitha slid the panel to zero and did a slow spin backwards above the bed.

"You don't think this will hurt the baby do you? The baby is suspended in water anyway. If anything, it might get motion sick with no gravity, right? Perhaps we shouldn't go all the way down to zero?" I asked.

"Oh, phooey. We and the Russians did long-term studies on pregnant mammals in both ISS and on Mir. We tested pregnant rats, rabbits, and a few others and never observed any differences between the spaceborn animals and Earthborn ones." She balanced herself and slid the bar upward to about one tenth gee. "We *will* have to be careful at this gravity not to get up too fast or you will get a bump on the head from the ceiling or the doorframe or whatever." She did another back flip.

"Yeah, okay, just be careful. Also, the gravity is only modified in this room and the bathroom—there's another slidebar in there. I thought the low gee bathroom might make it easier on you for getting up and down. Although, I'd leave some gravity on when I used the toilet or took a shower." I smiled at her.

"This is great Anson. 'Becca has got to have one of these!" she said.

"She does. Jim and I worked this out together. He is showing her theirs about now also."

Tabitha smiled and replied, "Good. Would you like for me to show you mine?" She laughed as she undid her maternity top. Praise the Lord for the honeymoon trimester and low gravity bedrooms!

The effort to maintain military superiority Earthside was continuing as planned. No further skirmishes had popped up anyway. The Earth was battered and tired. World War III had done a lot of damage. It takes a while to mourn millions of deaths. It takes even longer to clean up. We kept an eye on the news and our favorite television broadcasts and the Internet. Nothing dangerous was going on. We continued at a steady and careful pace. No need to take undue risk during peacetime.

The status of the individual warp system or Supersuit wasn't great. A closed bubble that small with a hundred Watt heater (a person) inside it will need a good deal of air conditioning.

Also, the warp core and the ECCs required would take up a certain amount of volume. That couldn't be helped; things take up space. I pushed the group of engineers and scientists working the Supersuit to lead toward an armored suit, sort of like that suggested in *Starship Troopers*. The warp core and ECCs could be distributed throughout the suit. This would be the simplest and most likely first doable Supersuit design. We continued to work on it. And I began to create some new friendships in that group. Of course, we had handpicked everybody on the base and they were all our friends. However, none of them were really in our immediate family. Time changes that. We were becoming a lunar community.

Over the next three months we continued popping out to the solar focus and cataloged many other star systems. We looked closely at a red planet very similar to Mars around Wolf 359. Luyten 726-8 A and B supported a myriad of planets and asteroids, a few gas giants and one planet about twice the size of Earth that had liquid water and green vegetation.

Lalande 21185 had a set of twin medium sized gas giants similar to Uranus and Neptune. Sirius A and B had two different planets that could support life. One was more of a desert planet with very small oceans, while the other was in an ice age. Most of it was covered with ice except for the equatorial regions. There was liquid water there.

We continued looking and found planets around nearly every star we tried. Ross 154, 248, and 128. 61 Cygni and Luyten 789-6. Epsilon Eridani had a world that looked just like Earth but with two moons. I couldn't wait to get out there and look at these places. I was hoping that we would've found a civilization by this time though. We had looked at about twenty planets closely. I decided that we should take a couple of days per star system. Wouldn't want to miss anything. Out of all the planets we studied thus far, no intelligent life. The odds were at least worse than one in twenty for intelligent life. Although, it had been about one in three for plant life. The universe is a damn big place. We just had to keep looking.

A month or so later, Jim and I had plenty to do other than warp technology. I was constantly getting up in the middle of the night to change little Ariel Eridani Clemons. And I'm sure Jim was having a time with the twins, Mindy Sue and Michael Ash Daniels. Of course, we had no shortage of people volunteering to baby sit. Oh, who was the first baby born on the Moon you want to know? It was Mindy Sue, then Michael Ash was born a few minutes later. Ariel was born a week later. Fortunately, Ariel looks just like her mom and her older sister.

Tabitha and Annie had little Ariel in the bedroom in zero gee before she was two months old. She never seemed to get sick from the microgravity. Tabitha must have some super inner-ear gene that Ariel and Anne Marie inherited.

In our spare time, Jim and I dug out a small fifteen-meter diameter dome and put a gravity modification switch in it. We designed the gravity meter to enable gravity from zero to fifteen gee. We then padded the floor and walls and ceiling and started using that room to exercise in. I could do all sorts of flips and multiple spin kicks at a quarter gee. I could even stand and balance on one hand. We all spent time in the "gravity room" as it came to be known. After balance work, we would then do strength training. I was hoping to slowly work up to withstanding fifteen gee, but that is damned heavy. I was at least hoping to build my strength until I could do multiple flips and very high aerial kicks in standard one gee. I also spent time with Ariel and Tabitha in the room at low gee trying to get Ariel to walk early.

Life on the moon was swell. A few times we visited my and Tabitha's parents and let them play with the baby. How many kids do you know that got to fly back and forth between the Earth and the Moon on a regular basis? Our little Ariel was an astronaut at one month if you don't count being born on the Moon. Over the period of Ariel's first year she grew about twenty percent taller than the average, according to the Internet. Tabitha and I wondered if it was due to the low gee we often had her in. We soon decided that anytime we exposed her to low gee, we would then slowly expose her to higher gee. Say two and a half gee for a few minutes. However, more than ninety-five percent of her time was in normal gee.

Ariel, Mindy, and Mike became a handful. They were crawling all over the place and in the low gee rooms were walking. They were also beginning to jabber something fierce.

Finally, on Mindy and Mike's second birthday the starship was complete and parked on the surface of the Moon just outside Moon Base 1. We boarded *Einstein* and flew up to the surface and out of the warp barrier of the Moon base. Anne Marie docked us to the main section of the starship and we were ready for liftoff. The crew consisted of Tabitha, Margie, Anne Marie, Rebecca, Jim, Al, Sara, and myself. Our mission was to fly to the second planet from Barnard's Star, look around for a couple of days, and safely return to the Moon. We planned to bring the ECCs of both the *Einstein*, which was docked in front, and the *Starbuck*, which was docked, in the rear. The two ECCs would enable us to use much more energy and perhaps push our warp velocity even further than the fifty times that of light we had maxed out at previously. Jim and I calculated that we should be able to reach seventy times the speed of light. That meant a month out and a month back.

We had shaken hands with most of the lunar community in a

prelaunch ceremony we had the previous day. We had said our goodbyes and left the base in the charge of a new colonel Tabitha was grooming, Lieutenant Colonel James Duvall. He was a good man as far as I could tell. Besides, he had the aid of the head NCO on base, Sergeant Major Calvin Perry. He would be fine.

We had also dropped all of the kids off with my parents. The Clemons and the Ames grandparents had adopted Mindy and Mike as their own grandchildren. So, we left all three of them. They would stay with my parents for the first month and then my folks were going to take them down to Gulf Shores where Tabitha's parents had moved to after the Secret War. We would pick them up on our way back. We all cried when we left them. The kids didn't seem to care that much. My dad said they started crying that night when they realized we weren't coming back for a while. Why didn't we take them? I just couldn't see taking toddlers into such a dangerous situation. What if something went wrong? Our kids should still get to grow up and have full lives. Besides, we didn't need toddlers bumping into spacecraft controls and warping us into a black hole or something. That sounds like stuff out of a bad science fiction novel.

So, we left the Sol system like a scalded dog headed for the creek. At warp speed seventy as we were beginning to call it, we just had a month to kill.

We talked several times about the search for extraterrestrial intelligence and why we hadn't found it yet. Using three of the little warpships, we had hopped out to the solar focus and observed most of the stars out to ninety light years. We had yet to find any signs of E.T.s. None of us were about to give up though. They were out there somewhere. Statistics just ensures that. It was just a matter of time before we found them. The problem was that everyday the trip to visit the E.T. kept getting longer and longer. At a minimum, E.T. lived somewhere out past ninety light years. At warp seventy that had to be at least a two and a half year round trip. We needed much bigger ECCs or a much bigger ship, or both. The problem is that Jim and I had found a curve to fit the power requirements to the warp speed. We were approaching an asymptote and we didn't know if the thing went up to infinity or if it was just a potential well that we had to jump over. Either way it was going to take a buttload of energy to overtake even warp speed ninety. The ECC factory back on the Moon was pumping out flubell ECCs as fast as they could make them, but it would be another five or more years before they had enough of them to create the type of energy that I feared we would require for journeys any further out than a hundred and twenty light years away. We would get there eventually though. I just had to be patient. That's hard to do when you are pushing fifty.

A month went by rather like a turtle crossing the street in the midst of rush hour. I missed the kids terribly. So did everybody else. We popped out of warp about a thousand astronomical units from Barnard's Star, then made a couple of short warps into the interior of the star's system of planets. We approached the second blue green planet and entered into a LEO type orbit. Well it wasn't Low Earth Orbit, but what were we supposed to call it?

"Why don't we call it 'Anson'?" 'Becca asked.

"Yeah, Low Anson Orbit! Ha, that's great." Al laughed.

"What do you think, Anson?" Tabitha asked me.

"Okay. But I get to name the next one." I smirked.

Tabitha took the controls and led us around the planet multiple times. We spotted a location that looked like a lush tropical area and decided to give it a try. She brought us down in a field of something that looked like sea oats that grow along the beaches in the Gulf of Mexico. A few hundred meters to our south was a beautiful white sandy beach and an ocean frothing against it. The red sunlight gave the planet a dim appearance. There was plenty of light but nothing seemed very bright. Not like on Earth the way you have to squint your eyes or wear sunglasses at the beach.

We spent a few minutes checking the air for anything that would be harmful to us. We could see no microbes or deadly gasses. It was a mixture of oxygen, nitrogen, argon, and other gasses. The oxygen was a little richer than on Earth, but that was no problem. We sat still in the ship and waited a while and watched for signs of indigenous lifeforms that could be harmful: snakes, bees, bugs, crocodiles, and three headed humanoid-eating E.T.s. Nothing other than an occasional alien sea oat reared its head.

An hour passed. We had made every measurement we could think of. Jim finally said, "To hell with this, let's go outside."

Tabitha reminded him that the protocol that he helped write required two hours of tests, analyses, and observation before running out into an alien world to be eaten by monsters or alien bacteria. So, we waited a little while longer.

The air was fine. I never even saw an insect. Perhaps they just didn't evolve here. We took a lot of vegetation samples. None of us could figure out how they pollinated without bugs. The ecosystem was completely different here. I guess the wind was good enough.

A couple of days later we split up. Tabitha, 'Becca, Jim, and I flew *Einstein* further inland while Margie, Anne Marie, Sara, and Al hopped continents in the *Starbuck*. We were to meet back on the beach in two days where we would leave the habitat cylinders.

We finally found insects and 'Becca swore that she saw a rodent of some sort. It would take years and teams of scientists to catalog all of the species of life there. We were physicists and engineers, not botanists, entomologists, and exobiologists. We would have to bring some next time. Two days passed quickly, and no creatures tried to eat us, not even the insects.

Margie and Annie were docking the ships back to the habitat cylinders. Tabitha and I stood on the beach with the crystal clear water frothing at our feet. Even our treks to the bottom of the oceans of this world didn't reveal any underwater cities, although we had seen some big fish.

I was watching the alien red sunset. Tabitha, of course, was watching the docking procedures and muttering to herself about "teaching Annie how to fly better than that." I laughed at her and nudged her.

"Hey General, you got time to look at this really cool alien sunset?"

Tabitha turned away from the spacecraft and looked out over the ocean. "Yeah. It is pretty. You seem sort of solemn tonight. What's bothering you?"

"Nothing really. I just wanted to find more, you know?" I held my hands out as if to encompass the planet. Then I shrugged my shoulders.

"Yeah, I know. You wanted to find aliens. You did, just not the kind you can talk to."

"Maybe someday we . . ." I shook my head. "There are just so many stars out there. And it appears the potential alien home-worlds are farther away than we might have imagined. I keep telling myself that it is statistics. They are out there and we're bound to find somebody somewhere someday. One of the things that burns me up is that the people of Earth will never know we have been here. They'll never know what we, the human race, have accomplished."

"We will find aliens, one day, Anson. And some people on Earth know what you did. You saved the world from itself and have ushered in a new era of technology."

"Yeah a technology that they will never know exists. And I had a lot of help, Tabitha. And the world isn't out of the woods yet. Eternal vigilance and all."

"I know you had help, sweetheart. But you did it nonetheless. You, did it. And I have come to know you enough that I think you'll continue to do it. As long as it takes."

"I guess," I said.

"We *will* find intelligent aliens out there and we *will* get to tell the Earth, some day. But in the meantime, I miss my little girl and I'm sure she misses her mommy and daddy. What do you say we go home?" Tabitha held my hand and pulled me to her.

"Sounds great to me." I kissed her. "You know this is what I always dreamed of. I've always fantasized about inventing the warp drive and flying off to new and alien worlds with my beautiful wife and having wonderful adventures and saving the world. It's a childhood dream come true; I guess I can't think of anything that could make me happier."

She held me a little while longer and looked into my eyes. "I'm pregnant again," she said.

"Well, except for that." I laughed.

We went home.

➤ APPENDIX

THE CURRENT STATUS OF WARP DRIVE

In 1994 a scientific paper was written by Miguel Alcubierre entitled "The warp drive: hyper-fast travel within general relativity." It was a short "Letter to the Editor" and was published in the scientific journal Classical and Quantum Gravity. In that paper Alcubierre showed that within the confines of the currently understood theory of General Relativity that:

> ... without the introduction of wormholes, it is possible to modify a spacetime in a way that allows a spaceship to travel with an arbitrarily large speed. By a purely local expansion of spacetime behind the spaceship and an opposite contraction in front of it, motion faster than the speed of light as seen by observers outside the disturbed region is possible. The resulting distortion is reminiscent of the "warp drive" of science fiction.

Alcubierre went on to show that there was no reason to believe that such a warp drive would be impossible. That point has been the topic of debate at many conferences since then. The contraction of space required in front of the spaceship is nothing more than a gravity well. On the other hand, the expansion of spacetime behind the spaceship is an inverted gravity well, which to date has not been observed anywhere in the universe as far as we understand it. The problem with the expansion in spacetime can be explained simply. What causes a contraction in spacetime or in other words what causes a gravity well? The answer is matter. Massive objects cause gravity wells. Okay, we understand how that part works. Then what could cause an inverted gravity well? The answer could be negative matter? What the hell is negative matter? There in lies the rub! Then is it over with for warp drive?

No. Matter is also energy and vice versa. Energy can be portrayed in many forms: matter, electricity, magnetism, and possibly other more strange quantum phenomena. The equation Anson talks about in this story that I like to call the Warp Equation describes this very well. That equation in laymen's terms is written as:

Curvature or Warp of Spacetime = Energy per Volume

This equation is actually known as the Einstein equation and each side of it represents a God-awful set of matrices (tensors) and some things to account or discount for the expansion of spacetime, but this is basically how to think of it. The point here is that it might be possible to create some form of energy per volume that would cause an expansion in spacetime rather than a contraction. Many of the world's theoretical physicists are trying to figure this out. Oh and by the way, the amount of energy per volume required on the right hand side of the equation is enormous with a very big E, much larger than all of the energy the human race has ever generated. This brings us to the Casimir Effect.

The Casimir Effect is a phenomenon that has been shown theoretically to exist in which two very closely spaced parallel plane conductors are actually pushed toward each other by the vacuum energy of spacetime itself! It turns out that the spacetime between these two very closely spaced plates should theoretically expand!! The theory predicts that the speed of light between the plates is slightly higher than that in a vacuum due to the expansion, in other words light travels faster than light due to the Casimir Effect.

Also, the Casimir Effect expansion between the plates will cause the plates to attract toward each other or be pushed together by the spacetime outside them depending on your point of view. If a clever scientist were to arrange several of these parallel plates in the right configuration and connect them with springs of some sort it might be possible that as one set of plates pull together another set gets pulled apart. Then the set that gets pulled apart would get pushed together thus pulling the others back apart. This motion could be set up to generate electricity in a generator and therefore allow us to extract power right out of spacetime itself damn near perpetually and for free. Imagine that!

Interestingly enough, the Defense Advanced Research Projects Agency or DARPA has been looking for novel new ways to power small sensors and unmanned vehicles for various defense applications. NASA also has a similar requirement for small space probes. In late May 2003, I went to DARPA headquarters in Arlington, Virginia and presented an idea much like the Clemons Dumbbells to them. The possibility of extracting energy right out of spacetime intrigued them. It is quite possible that one day in the not too distant future we will be developing and maybe even testing a Casimir Effect energy supply. That would be cool. And a little further down the road from that, say ten to fifty years, we might have solved the Warp Equation correctly, developed a big enough power supply, and be testing a Warp Drive. Now that would be real cool!

—Travis S. Taylor